Praise for

CHRISTINE FEEHAN AND HER GHOSTWALKER SERIES

"The queen of paranormal romance. . . . I love everything [Feehan] does."
—J. R. Ward

"Romance, suspense, danger, action-packed excitement, hot hot men, and on top of all that, a couple that sizzles all throughout the book. . . . Sexy as hell." —The Reading Cafe

"I cannot wait to see where Ms. Feehan takes us next."
—Fresh Fiction

"Packed with adventure. . . . Not only is this a thriller, the sensual scenes rival the steaming bayou. A perfect 10."
—Romance Reviews Today

"One of the best storytellers around!"
—RT Book Reviews

"Sultry and suspenseful . . . swift-moving and sexually charged." —*Publishers Weekly*

Titles by Christine Feehan

TOXIC GAME	MURDER GAME
COVERT GAME	PREDATORY GAME
POWER GAME	DEADLY GAME
SPIDER GAME	CONSPIRACY GAME
VIPER GAME	NIGHT GAME
SAMURAI GAME	MIND GAME
RUTHLESS GAME	SHADOW GAME
STREET GAME	

HIDDEN CURRENTS	DANGEROUS TIDES
TURBULENT SEA	OCEANS OF FIRE
SAFE HARBOR	

LEOPARD'S RUN	LEOPARD'S PREY
LEOPARD'S BLOOD	SAVAGE NATURE
LEOPARD'S FURY	WILD FIRE
WILD CAT	BURNING WILD
CAT'S LAIR	WILD RAIN

BOUND TOGETHER	AIR BOUND
FIRE BOUND	SPIRIT BOUND
EARTH BOUND	WATER BOUND

SHADOW WARRIOR	SHADOW REAPER
SHADOW KEEPER	SHADOW RIDER

VENGEANCE ROAD
JUDGMENT ROAD

DARK ILLUSION	DARK POSSESSION
DARK SENTINEL	DARK CELEBRATION
DARK LEGACY	DARK DEMON
DARK CAROUSEL	DARK SECRET
DARK PROMISES	DARK DESTINY
DARK GHOST	DARK MELODY
DARK BLOOD	DARK SYMPHONY
DARK WOLF	DARK GUARDIAN
DARK LYCAN	DARK LEGEND
DARK STORM	DARK FIRE
DARK PREDATOR	DARK CHALLENGE
DARK PERIL	DARK MAGIC
DARK SLAYER	DARK GOLD
DARK CURSE	DARK DESIRE
DARK HUNGER	DARK PRINCE

SHADOW GAME

CHRISTINE FEEHAN

JOVE
New York

A JOVE BOOK
Published by Berkley
An imprint of Penguin Random House LLC
penguinrandomhouse.com

ISBN: 9780515135961

Jove mass-market edition / September 2003

Printed in the United States of America
25 27 29 31 33 32 30 28 26 24

Cover image: Woman © BenAkiba / Getty Images
Cover design and image composition by Judith Lagerman
Book design by Kristin del Rosario

For my brother, Matthew King, many thanks for all the help with the research necessary for this book. And for McKenzie King, for her dynamite smile and her help in turning those book covers in the proper direction!

Special thanks to Cheryl Wilson. I have no idea what I'd do without you.

ONE

CAPTAIN Ryland Miller leaned his head against the wall and closed his eyes in utter weariness. He could ignore the pain in his head, the knives shredding his skull. He could ignore the cage he was in. He could even ignore the fact that sooner or later, he was going to slip up and his enemies would kill him. But he could not ignore the guilt and anger and frustration rising like a tidal wave in him as his men suffered the consequences of his decisions.

Kaden, I can't reach Russell Cowlings. Can you?

He had talked his men into the experiment that had landed them all in the laboratory cages in which they now resided. Good men. Loyal men. Men who had wanted to serve their country and people.

We all made the decision. Kaden responded to his emotions, the words buzzing inside Ryland's mind. *No one has managed to raise Russell.*

Ryland swore softly aloud as he swept a hand over his face, trying to wipe away the pain speaking telepathically with his men cost him. The telepathic link between them had grown stronger as they all worked to build it, but only a few of them could sustain it for any length of time. Ryland had to supply the bridge, and his brain, over time, balked at the enormity of such a burden.

Don't touch the sleeping pills they gave you. Suspect any medication. He glanced at the small white pill lying in plain sight on his end table. He'd like a lab analysis of the contents. Why hadn't Cowlings listened to him? Had Cowlings accepted the sleeping pill in the hopes of a brief respite? He had to get the men out. *We have no choice, we must treat this situation as if we were behind enemy lines.* Ryland took a deep breath, let it out slowly. He no longer felt he had a choice. He had already lost too many men. His decision would brand them as traitors, deserters, but it was the only way to save their lives. He had to find a way for his men to break out of the laboratory.

The colonel has betrayed us. We have no other choice but to escape. Gather information and support one another as best you can. Wait for my word.

He became aware of the disturbance around him, the dark waves of intense dislike bordering on hatred preceding the group nearing the cage where he was kept.

Someone is approaching. . . . Ryland abruptly cut off telepathic communication to those of his men he could reach. He remained motionless in the center of his cell, his every sense flaring out to identify the approaching individuals.

It was a small group this time: Dr. Peter Whitney, Colonel Higgens, and a security guard. It amused Ryland that Whitney and Higgens insisted on an armed guard accompanying them despite the fact that he was locked behind both bars and a thick glass barrier. He was careful to keep his features expressionless as they neared his cage.

Ryland lifted his head, his steel gray eyes as cold as ice. Menacing. He didn't try to hide the danger he represented. They had created him, they had betrayed him, and he wanted them to be afraid. There was tremendous satisfaction in knowing they were . . . and that they had reason to be.

Dr. Peter Whitney led the small group. Whitney, liar, deceiver, monster maker. He was the creator of the GhostWalkers. Creator of what Captain Ryland Miller and his men had become. Ryland stood up slowly, a deliberate ripple of muscle— a lethal jungle cat stretching lazily, unsheathing claws as he waited inside his cage.

His icy gaze touched on their faces, lingered, made them uncomfortable. Graveyard eyes. Eyes of death. He projected the image deliberately, wanting, even needing them to fear for their lives. Colonel Higgens looked away, studied the cameras, the security, watched with evident apprehension as the thick barrier of glass slid away. Although Ryland remained caged behind heavy bars, Higgens was obviously uneasy without the barrier, uncertain just how powerful Ryland had become.

Ryland steeled himself for the assault on his hearing, his emotions. The flood of unwanted information he couldn't control. The bombardment of thoughts and emotions. The disgusting depravity and avarice that lay behind the masks of those facing him. He kept his features carefully blank, giving nothing away, not wanting them to know what it cost him to shield his wide-open mind.

"Good morning, Captain Miller," Peter Whitney said pleasantly. "How are things this morning with you? Did you sleep at all?"

Ryland watched him without blinking, tempted to try to push through Whitney's barriers to discover the true character guarded behind the wall Whitney had in his mind. What secrets were hidden there? The one person Ryland needed to understand, to read, was protected by some natural or man-made barrier. None of the other men, not even Kaden, had managed to penetrate the scientist's mind. They couldn't get any pertinent data, shielded as Whitney was, but the heavy swamping waves of guilt were always broadcast loudly.

"No, I didn't sleep but I suspect you already know that."

Dr. Whitney nodded. "None of your men are taking their sleeping meds. I noticed you didn't either. Is there a reason for that, Captain Miller?"

The chaotic emotions of the group hit Ryland hard, as it always did. In the beginning, it used to drive him to his knees, the noise in his head so loud and aggravating his brain would rebel, punishing him for his unnatural abilities. Now he was much more disciplined. Oh, the pain was still there, like a thousand knives driving into his head at the first breach of his brain, but he hid the agony behind the façade of icy, menacing calm. And he was, after all, well trained. His people never revealed weakness to the enemy.

"Self-preservation is always a good reason," he answered, fighting down the waves of weakness and pain from the battering of emotions. He kept his features totally expressionless, refusing to allow them to see the cost.

"What the hell does that mean?" Higgens demanded. "What are you accusing us of now, Miller?"

The door to the laboratory had been left standing open, unusual for the security-conscious company, and a woman hurried through. "I'm sorry I'm late; the meeting went longer than expected!"

At once the painful assault of thoughts and emotions lessened, muted, leaving Ryland able to breathe normally. To think without pain. The relief was instant and unexpected. Ryland focused on her immediately, realizing she was somehow trapping the more acute emotions and holding them at bay, almost as if she were a magnet for them. And she wasn't just any woman. She was so beautiful, she took his breath away. Ryland could have sworn, when he looked at her, the ground shifted and moved under his feet. He glanced at Peter Whitney, caught the man observing his reactions to the woman's presence very closely.

At first Ryland was embarrassed that he had been caught staring at her. Then he realized Whitney knew the woman had some kind of psychic ability. She enhanced Ryland's abilities and cleared out the garbage of stray thoughts and emotions. Did Whitney know exactly what she did? The doctor was waiting for a reaction so Ryland refused to give him the satisfaction, keeping his expression totally blank.

"Captain Miller, I'd like to present my daughter, Lily Whitney. Dr. Lily Whitney." Peter's gaze never left Ryland's face. "I've asked her to join us; I hope you don't mind."

The shock couldn't have been more complete. Peter Whitney's daughter? Ryland let out his breath slowly, shrugged his broad shoulders casually, another ripple of menace. He didn't feel casual. Everything inside of him stilled. Calmed. Reached. He studied the woman. Her eyes were incredible, but wary. Intelligent. Knowledgeable. As if she recognized him, too, in some elemental way. Her eyes were a deep startling blue, like the middle of a clear, fresh pool. A man could lose his mind, his freedom in eyes like hers. She was average height—not tall, but not exceedingly short. She had a woman's figure encased in a gray-green suit of some kind that managed to draw attention to every lush curve. She had walked with a decided limp, but when he looked her over for damage, he could see nothing to indicate injury. More than all of that, the moment he saw her face, the moment she entered the room, his soul seemed to reach for hers. To recognize hers. His breath stilled in his body and he could only stare at her.

She was looking back at him and he knew the sight wasn't very reassuring. At his best, he looked a warrior—at his worst, he looked a savage fighter. There was no way to soften his expression or lessen the scars on his face or shave off the dark stubble marring his stubborn jawline. He was stocky with a fighter's compact build, carrying most of his weight in his upper body, his chest and arms, his broad shoulders. His hair was thick and black, and it curled when it wasn't kept tight against his skull.

"Captain Miller." Her voice was soothing, gentle, pleasant. Sexy. A blend of smoke and heat that seared him right through his belly. "How nice to meet you. My father thought I might be of some use in the research. I haven't had much time to go over the data, but I'll be happy to try to help."

He had never reacted so forcefully to a voice before. The sound seemed to wrap him up in satin sheets, rubbing and caressing his skin until he felt himself break out in a sweat. The image was so vivid that for a moment he could only stare at her, imagining her naked body writhing with pleasure beneath his. In the midst of his struggle to survive, his physical reaction to her was shocking.

Color crept up her neck, delicately tinged her cheeks. Her long lashes fluttered, drifted down, and she looked away from him to her father. "This room is very exposed. Who came up with the design? I would think it would be a difficult way to live, even for a short period."

"You mean like a lab rat?" Ryland asked softly, deliberately, not wanting any of them to think they were fooling him by bringing in the woman. "Because that's what I am. Dr. Whitney has his own human rats to play with."

Lily's dark gaze jumped to his face. One eyebrow shot up. "I'm sorry, Captain Miller, was I misinformed, or did you agree to volunteer for this assignment?" There was a small challenge in her voice.

"Captain Miller volunteered, Lily," Peter Whitney said. "He was unprepared for the brutal results, as was I. I've been searching for a way to reverse the process but so far, everything I've tried has failed."

"I don't believe that's the proper way to handle this," Colonel Higgens snapped. He glared at Peter Whitney, his bushy brows drawing together in a frown of disapproval. "Captain Miller is a soldier. He volunteered for this mission and I must insist he carry it out to its conclusion. We don't need the process reversed, we need it perfected."

Ryland had no trouble reading the colonel's emotions. The man didn't want Lily Whitney anywhere near Ryland or his men. He wanted Ryland taken out behind the laboratories and shot. Better yet, dissected so they could all see what was going on in his brain. Colonel Higgens was afraid of Ryland Miller and the other men in the paranormal unit. Anything he feared, Higgens destroyed.

"Colonel Higgens, I don't think you fully understand what these men are going through, what is happening to their brains." Dr. Whitney was pursuing what was obviously a long-standing argument between them. "We've already lost several men. . . ."

"They knew the risks," Higgens retorted, glowering at Miller. "This is an important experiment. We need these men to perform. The loss of a few men, while tragic, is an acceptable loss considering the importance of what these men can do."

Ryland didn't look at Higgens. He kept his glittering gaze fixed on Lily Whitney. But his entire mind reached out. Took hold. Closed like a vise.

Lily's head snapped up. She gasped out a soft protest. Her gaze dropped to Ryland's hands. She watched his fingers slowly begin to curl as if around a thick throat. She shook her head, a slight protest.

Higgens coughed. A barking grunt. His mouth hung open as he gasped for air. Peter Whitney and the young guard both reached for the colonel, trying to open his stiff shirt collar, trying to help him breathe. The colonel staggered, was caught and lowered to the floor by the scientist.

Stop it. The voice in Ryland's mind was soft.

Ryland's dark brow shot up and his gleaming gaze met Lily's. The doctor's daughter was definitely telepathic. She was calm about it, her gaze steady on his, not in the least intimidated by the danger emanating from him. She appeared as cool as ice.

He's willing to sacrifice every one of my men. They aren't expendable. He was just as calm, not for a moment relenting.

He's a moron. No one is willing to sacrifice the men; no one considers them expendable; and he isn't worth branding yourself a murderer.

Ryland allowed his breath to escape in a soft, controlled stream, clearing his lungs, clearing his mind. Deliberately he turned his back on the writhing man and paced across the cell, his fingers slowly uncurling.

Higgens went into a fit of coughing, tears swimming in his eyes. He pointed a shaky finger toward Ryland. "He tried to kill me, you all saw it."

Peter Whitney sighed and walked with heavy footsteps across the room to stare at the computer. "I'm tired of the melodrama, Colonel. There is always a jump on the sensors in the computers when there is a surge of power. There's nothing here at all. Miller is safely locked in a cage; he didn't do anything at all. Either you're trying to sabotage my project or you have a personal vendetta against Captain Miller. In any case, I'm going to write to the general and insist they send another liaison."

Colonel Higgens swore again. "I'll have no more talk about reversing the process, Whitney, and you know what I think about bringing your daughter on board. We don't need another damn bleeding heart on this project—we need results."

"My security clearance, Colonel Higgens, is of the highest level and so is my commitment to this project. I don't have the necessary data at this time, but I can assure you I'll put in whatever time is necessary to find the answers needed." Even as she spoke, Lily was looking at the computer screen.

Ryland could read her thoughts. Whatever was on the screen puzzled her as much as what her father was saying, but she was willing to cover for him. She was making it up as she went along. As calm and as cool as ever. He couldn't remember the last time he had smiled, but the impulse was there. He kept his back to the group, not certain he could keep a straight face while she lied to the colonel. Lily Whitney had no idea what was going on; her father had given her very little information and she was simply winging it. Her dislike of Higgens, compounded by her father's unusual behavior, had put her firmly in Ryland's camp for the moment.

He had no idea what Peter Whitney's game was, but the man was buried deep in the mire. The experiment to enhance psychic ability and bring together a fighting unit had been his project, his brainchild. Peter Whitney had been the man who'd persuaded Ryland the experiment had merit. That his men would be safe and that they would better serve their country. Ryland couldn't read the doctor as he now could most men, but whatever Whitney was up to, Ryland had become convinced it wasn't anything that would benefit him or his men. Donovans Corporation had a stench about it. If there was one thing Ryland knew for certain, Donovans was about money and personal profit, not national security.

"Can you read that code your father uses for his notes?" Higgens asked Lily Whitney, suddenly losing interest in Ryland. "Gibberish if you ask me. Why the hell don't you just put your work in English like a normal human being?" He snapped the question at Peter Whitney irritably.

At once Ryland swung around, his gray gaze thoughtful as it rested on the colonel. There was something there, something he couldn't get hold of. It was shifting, moving, ideas formulating and growing. Higgens's mind seemed a black ravine, twisted and curved and suddenly cunning.

Lily shrugged. "I grew up reading his codes; of course I can read it."

Ryland sensed her growing puzzlement as she stared at the combination of numbers, symbols, and letters across the computer screen.

"What the hell are you doing getting into my private computer files, Frank?" Peter Whitney demanded, glaring at the colonel. "When I want you to read a report, I'll have the data organized and the report will be finished and up-to-date, neatly typed in English. You have no business in my computer either here or at my office. My research on many projects is on my computer and you have no right to invade my privacy. If your people go anywhere near my work, I'll have you locked out of Donovans so fast you won't know what hit you."

"This isn't your personal project, Peter." Higgens glowered at all of them. "This is my project too and as the head of it, you don't keep secrets from me. You don't make any sense in your reports."

Ryland watched Lily Whitney. She remained very quiet, listening, absorbing information, gathering impressions, and soaking it all up like a sponge. She seemed relaxed, but he was very aware she had glanced toward her father, waiting for some sign, for a hint of how to handle the situation. Whitney gave her nothing, didn't even look at her. Lily hid her frustration very well. She shifted her gaze back to the computer screen, leaving the others to their argument, clearly another long-standing one.

"I want something done about Miller," Higgens said, acting as if Ryland couldn't hear him.

I'm already dead to him. Ryland whispered the words in Lily Whitney's mind.

All the better for you and your men. He's pressing my father hard about pushing this project forward, not terminating it. He isn't satisfied with the findings and doesn't agree it is dangerous to all of you. Lily didn't look away from the computer or give away in any manner that she was communicating with him.

He doesn't know about you. Higgens has no idea you're telepathic. The knowledge burst over him like a light from a prism. Brilliant and colorful and full of possibilities. Dr. Whitney was hiding his daughter's abilities from the colonel. From the Donovans Corporation. Ryland knew he had ammunition. Information he could use to bargain with Dr. Whitney. Something that might be used to save his men. His flare of excitement must have been in his mind because Lily turned and regarded him with a cool, thoughtful gaze.

Peter Whitney scowled at Colonel Higgens, clearly exasperated. "You want something done? What does that mean, Frank? What do you have in mind? A lobotomy? Captain Miller has performed every test we've asked of him. Do you have personal reasons for disliking the captain?" Dr. Whitney's voice was a whip of contempt. "Captain Miller, if you were having an affair with Colonel Higgens's wife, you should have disclosed that information to me immediately."

Lily's dark eyebrows shot up. Ryland could feel the sudden amusement in her mind. Her laughter was soft and inviting, but her features gave nothing of her inner thoughts away. *Well? Are you a Romeo?*

There was something peaceful and serene about Lily, something that spilled over into the air around them. His second-in-command, Kaden, was like that, calming the terrible static and tuning the frequencies so that they were clear and sharp and able to be used by all the men regardless of talent. Surely her father hadn't experimented on his own daughter. The idea sickened him.

"Laugh all you want, Peter," the colonel sneered, "but you won't be laughing when lawsuits are filed against Donovans Corporation and the United States government is after you for botching the job."

Ryland ignored the arguing men. He had never been so drawn to a woman, to any individual, but he wanted Lily to remain in the room. He *needed* her to remain in the room. And he didn't want her to be a part of the conspiracy that was threatening his life. She seemed unaware of it, but her father was certainly one of the puppet masters.

My father is no puppet master. Her voice was indignant and faintly haughty, a princess to an inferior being.

You don't even know what the hell is going on so how do you know what he is or isn't? He was rougher than he intended but Lily took it well, not responding to him but frowning at the computer monitor.

She didn't speak to her father, but he sensed her movement toward him, a slight exchange between them. It was more felt than seen, and Ryland sensed her puzzlement deepen. Her father gave her no clue; instead, he led Colonel Higgens toward the door.

"Are you coming, Lily?" Dr. Whitney asked, pausing just inside the hall.

"I want to look things over here, sir," she said, indicating the computer, "and it will give Captain Miller a chance to fill me in on where he is in this."

Higgens swung around. "I don't think it's a good idea for you to stay alone with him. He's a dangerous man."

She looked as cool as ever, her dark brow a perfect arch. Lily stared down her aristocratic nose at the colonel. "You didn't ensure the premises were secure, Colonel?"

Colonel Higgens swore again and stomped out of the room. As Lily's father started out of the room, she cleared her throat softly. "I think it best we discuss this project in a more thorough way if you want my input, sir."

Dr. Whitney glanced at her, his features impassive. "I'll meet you at Antonio's for dinner, and we can go over everything after we eat. I want your own impressions."

"Based on . . ."

Ryland didn't hear a hint of sarcasm, but it was there in her mind. She was angry with her father but Ryland couldn't read why. That part of her mind was closed off to him, hidden behind a thick, high wall she had erected to keep him out.

"Go over my notes, Lily, and see what you make of the process. Maybe you'll see something I didn't. I want a fresh perspective. Colonel Higgens might be right. There may be a way to continue without reversing what we've done." Peter Whitney refused to meet his daughter's direct gaze, but turned to Ryland and asked, "Do I need to leave an armed guard in this room with my daughter, Captain?"

Ryland studied the face of the man who had opened the floodgates of his brain to receive far too much stimuli. He could detect no evil, only a genuine concern. "I'm no threat to the innocent, Dr. Whitney."

"That's good enough for me." Still without looking at his daughter, the doctor left the room, closing the door to the laboratory firmly.

Ryland was so aware of Lily, he actually felt the breath leave her lungs in a slow exhale as the door to the laboratory closed and the lock snicked quietly into place. He waited a heartbeat. Two. "Aren't you afraid of me?" Ryland asked, testing his voice with her. It came out more husky than he would have liked. He had never had much luck with women and Lily Whitney was out of his class.

She didn't look at him, but continued to stare at the symbols on the screen. "Why should I be? I'm not Colonel Higgens."

"Even the lab techs are afraid of me."

"Because you want them to be and you're projecting, deliberately enhancing their own fears." Her voice indicated a mild interest in their conversation, her mind mulling over the data on the screen. "How long have you been here?"

He swung around, stalked to the bars, and gripped them. "They're bringing you onboard and you don't even know how long my men and I have been locked up in this hellhole?"

She turned her head abruptly. Tendrils of hair, fallen loose from the tight twist at the back of her head, swung around her face. Even in the muted blue light of the room, her hair was shiny and it gleamed at him. "I don't know anything at all about this experiment, Captain. Not one small fact. This is the highest-security compound this corporation has and, while I have clearance, this is not my field of expertise. Dr. Whitney, my father, asked me to consult and I was cleared to do so. Do you have a problem with that?"

He studied the classic beauty of her face. High cheekbones, long lashes, a lush mouth—they didn't come like this unless they were born rich and privileged. "You probably have an underpaid maid whose name you can't even remember, who picks up your clothes when you throw them on your bedroom floor."

That bought him her entire attention. She crossed the distance from the computer to his cage in a slow, unhurried walk that drew his attention to her limp. Even with her limp she had a flowing grace. She made every cell in his body instantly aware he was male and she was female.

Lily tilted her chin at him. "I guess you were brought up without manners, Captain Miller. I don't actually throw my clothes on the bedroom floor. I hang them in the closet." Her gaze flicked past him to rest briefly on the clothes strewn on the floor.

For the first time that he could remember, Ryland was embarrassed by a woman. He was making an ass out of himself. Even her damn high heels were classy. Sexy, but classy.

A small smile curved her mouth. "You're making a *total* ass out of yourself," she pointed out, "but fortunately for you, I'm in a forgiving mood. We elitists learn that at an early age when they put that silver spoon in our mouths."

Ryland was ashamed. He might have grown up on the wrong

side of the tracks in the proverbial trailer trash park, but his mother would have boxed his ears for being so rude. "I'm sorry, there's no excuse."

"No, there isn't. There's never an excuse for rudeness." Lily paced across the distance of his cage, an unhurried examination of the length of his prison. "Who designed your quarters?"

"They constructed several cages quickly when they decided we were too powerful and posed too much danger as a group." His men had been separated and scattered throughout the facility. He knew the isolation was telling on them. Continual poking and prodding was wearing and he worried that he could not keep them together. He had lost men already; he was not about to lose any of the others.

The cell had been specially designed out of fear of reprisal. He knew his time was limited—the fear had been growing for weeks now. They had erected the thick bulletproof barrier of glass around his cell believing that it would keep him from communicating with his men.

He had volunteered for the assignment and he had talked the other men into it. Now they were imprisoned, studied and probed and used for everything but the original premise. Several of the men were dead and had been dissected like insects to "study and understand." Ryland had to get the others out before anything else happened to them. He knew Higgens had termination in mind for the stronger ones. Ryland was certain it would come in the form of "accidents," but it would definitely come eventually if he didn't find a way to free his men. Higgens had his own agenda, wanting to use the men for personal gain that had nothing whatsoever to do with the military and the country he was supposed to serve. But Higgens was afraid of what he couldn't control. Ryland wasn't about to lose his men to a traitor. His men were his responsibility.

He was more careful, speaking matter-of-factly this time, trying to keep the accusations, the blame he put squarely on her father's shoulders from spilling over into his thoughts, in case she was reading him. Her eyelashes were ridiculously long, a heavy fringe he found fascinating. He caught himself staring, unable to be anything but a crass idiot. In the midst of being caught like a rat in a trap, with his men in danger, he was making a fool of himself over a woman. A woman who very well might be his enemy.

"Your men are all in similar cages? I wasn't given that information." Her voice was strictly neutral, but she didn't like it. He could feel the outrage she was striving to suppress.

"I haven't seen them in weeks. They don't allow us to communicate." He indicated the computer screen. "That's a constant source of irritation to Higgens. I bet his people have tried to break your father's code, even used the computer, but they must not have been able to do it. Can you really read it?"

She hesitated briefly. It was almost unnoticeable, but he sensed the sudden stillness in her and his hawklike gaze didn't leave her face. "My father has always written in codes. I see in mathematical patterns and it was a kind of game when I was a little girl. He changed the code often to give me something to work on. My mind . . ." she hesitated, as if weighing her options carefully. She was deciding how honest to be with him. He wanted the truth and silently willed her to give it to him.

Lily was quiet for a moment more, her large eyes fixed steadily on his, then her soft mouth firmed. Her chin went up a miniscule notch but he was watching her every expression, every nuance, and he was aware of it, aware of what it cost her to tell him. "My mind requires continual stimulation. I don't know how else to explain it. Without having something complex to work on, I run into problems."

He caught the flash of pain in her eyes, fleeting but there. Dr. Peter Whitney was one of the richest men in the world. All the money might have given his daughter every confidence, but it didn't take away the fact that she was a freak . . . a freak like he was. Like his men were. What her father had made them into. GhostWalkers, waiting for death to strike them down, when they should have been an elite team defending their country.

"So tell me this, Lily Whitney, if that code is real, why can't the computer crack it?" Ryland lowered his voice so that anyone listening wouldn't hear his question, but he kept his glittering gaze fixed on hers, refusing to allow her to look away from him.

Lily's expression didn't change. She looked as serene as always. She looked impossibly elegant even there in the laboratory. She looked so far out of his reach his heart hurt. "I said he always wrote in code, I didn't say this one made any sense to me. I haven't had a chance to work with it yet."

Her mind was closed so completely to him that he knew she was lying. He arched a dark brow at her. "Really. Well, you'll have to put in for overtime because no one seems to be able to read how your father managed to enhance our psychic abilities. And they sure can't figure out how to make it go away."

She reached out, gracefully, naturally, almost casually, to grip the edge of a desk. The knuckles on her hand turned white. "He enhanced your natural abilities?" Her mind immediately began to turn that bit of information over and over as if it were a piece of a jigsaw puzzle and she was finding the proper fit.

"He really let you walk in here blind, didn't he?" Ryland challenged. "We were asked to take special tests. . . ."

She held up her hand. "Who was asked and who asked you?"

"Most of my men are Special Forces. The men in the various branches were asked to be tested for psychic ability. There were certain criteria to be met along with the abilities. Age, amount and type of combat training, ability to work under pressure conditions, ability to function for long periods of time cut off from the chain of command, loyalty factors. The list was endless but surprisingly enough, we had quite a few takers. The military issued a special invite for volunteers. From what I understand law enforcement branches did the same. They were looking for an elite group."

"And this was how long ago?"

"The first I heard of the idea was nearly four years ago. I've been here at the Donovans laboratory for a year now, but all the recruits that made it into the unit, including me, trained together at another facility. As far as I know we were always kept together. They wanted us to form a tight unit. We trained in techniques using psychic abilities in combat. The idea was a strike force that could get in and out unseen. We could be used against the drug cartels, terrorists, even an enemy army. We've been at it for over three years."

"A wild idea. And this is whose baby?"

"Your father's. He thought it up, convinced the powers that be that it could be done, and convinced me and the rest of the men that it would make the world a better place." There was a wealth of bitterness in Ryland Miller's voice.

"Obviously something went wrong."

"Greed went wrong. Donovans has the government contract. Peter Whitney practically owns this company. I guess he just doesn't have enough money with the million or two in his bank account."

She waited a long moment before responding. "I doubt my father needs any more money, Captain Miller. The amount he gives to charities each year would feed a state. You don't know anything about him so I suggest you reserve your opinion until all the facts are in. And for the record, it's a billion or two or more. This corporation could disappear tomorrow and it wouldn't change his lifestyle one bit." Her voice didn't rise in the least, but it smoldered with heat and intensity.

Ryland sighed. Her vivid gaze hadn't wavered an inch. "We have no contact with our people. All communication to the outside must go through your father or the colonel. We have no say in what is happening to us at all. One of my men died a couple of months ago and they lied about how he died. He died of a direct result from this experiment and the enhancement of his abilities—his brain couldn't handle the overload, the constant battering. They claimed it was an accident in the field. That's when we were cut off from all command and separated. We've been in isolation since that time." Ryland regarded her with dark, angry eyes, daring her to call him a liar. "And it wasn't the first death, but by God, it's going to be the last."

Lily pushed a hand through her perfectly smooth hair, the first real sign of agitation. The action scattered pins and left long strands falling in a cloud around her face. She was silent, allowing her brain to process the information, even as she was rejecting the accusations and implications about her father.

"Do you know precisely what killed the man in your unit? And is there the same danger to the rest of you?" She asked the question very quietly, her voice so low it was almost in his mind.

Ryland answered in the same soft voice, taking no chances the unseen guards would overhear their conversation. "His brain was wide open, assaulted by everyone and everything he came into contact with. He couldn't shut it off anymore. We can function together as a group because a couple of the men are like you. They draw the noise and raw emotion away from the rest of us. Then we're powerful and we work. But without that magnet . . ." He broke off and shrugged. "It's like pieces of glass or razor blades slashing at the brain. He snapped— seizures, brain bleeds, you name it. It wasn't a pretty sight and I sure didn't like the glimpse of our future. Neither did any of the other men in the unit."

Lily pressed her fingers to her temple and for just a moment, Ryland caught the impression of throbbing pain. His face darkened, gray eyes narrowing. "Come here." He had an actual physical reaction to her being in pain. The muscles in his belly knotted, hard and aching. Everything protective and male in him rose up and flooded him with an overwhelming need to ease her discomfort.

Her enormous blue eyes instantly became wary. "I don't touch people."

"Because you don't want to know what they're really like inside, do you? You feel it too." He was horrified to think her father may have experimented on her too. *How long have you been telepathic?* More than that, he didn't want to think about never touching her. Never feeling her skin beneath his fingers, her mouth crushed to his. The image was so vivid he could almost taste her. Even her hair begged to be touched, a thick mass of shiny silk just asking for his fingers to toss away the rest of the pins and free it for his inspection.

Lily shrugged easily, but a faint blush stole along her high cheekbones. *All of my life. And yes, it can be uncomfortable knowing other people's darkest secrets. I've learned to live within certain boundaries. Maybe my father became interested in psychic phenomena because he wished to help me. For whatever reason, I can assure you, it had nothing to do with personal financial gain.* She let out a slow breath. "How terrible for you, to lose *any* of your men. You must be very close. I hope I can find a way to help all of you."

Ryland sensed her sincerity. He was suspicious of her father in spite of her protests. *Is Dr. Whitney psychic?* He knew he'd been broadcasting his sexual fantasies a little too strongly but she was unshaken, handling the intensity of the chemistry between them easily. And he knew the chemistry was on both sides. He had a sudden desire to really shake her up, get past her cool demeanor just once and see if fire burned beneath the ice. It was a hell of a thing in the middle of the mess he was in.

Lily shook her head as she answered him. *We've conducted many experiments and have connected telepathically a few times under extreme conditions, but it was sustained completely on my side. I must have inherited the talent through my mother.*

"When you touch him, can you read him?" Ryland asked curiously in a low voice. He decided men were not all that far from the caves. His attraction to her was raw and hot and beyond any experience he'd ever had. He was unable to control his body's reaction to her. And she knew it. Unlike Ryland, she appeared to be cool and unaffected, while he was shaken to his very core. She carried on their conversation as if he weren't a firestorm burning out of control. As if his blood weren't boiling and his body hard as rock and in desperate need. As if she didn't even notice.

"Rarely. He is one of those people who has natural barriers. I think it's because he believes so strongly in psychic talent, whereas most people don't. Being aware of it all the time, he's probably built up a natural wall. I've found many people have barriers to varying degrees. Some seem impossible to get past and others are flimsy. What about you? Have you found the same thing? You're a very strong telepath."

"Come here to me."

Her cool blue gaze drifted over him. Dismissed him. "I don't think so, Captain Miller, I have far too much work to do."

"You're being a coward." He said it softly, his hungry gaze on her face.

She lifted her chin at him and gave him her haughty princess look. "I don't have time for your little games, Captain Miller. Whatever you think is going on here, is not."

His gaze dropped to her mouth. She had a perfect mouth. "Yes it is."

"It was interesting meeting you," Lily said and turned from him, walking without haste away from him. As cool as ever.

Ryland didn't protest, instead watched her leave him without a single backward glance. He willed her to look back, but she didn't. And she didn't replace the glass barrier around his cage, leaving it for the guards.

Two

THE sea was angry. Waves rose up, cresting high, a boiling cauldron of dark rage. White foam was left behind on the cliffs as the water receded, only to return, reaching ever higher. Reaching with hunger and fury, with deadly intent. The dark, fathomless waters spread, a dark eye seeking. Hunting. Turning toward her.

Lily wrenched herself awake, fighting for air. Her lungs burned. She pressed the button to bring the window down. Slightly disoriented, she told herself it was a dream, nothing but a dream. Cool air rushed in and she inhaled deeply. She noticed with relief that they were nearly to the house, already on the estate property. "John, would you mind stopping the car? I feel like walking." She managed to keep her voice steady, in spite of the way her heart pounded in alarm. She detested the nightmares that so often plagued her sleep.

Lily had wanted to dream of Captain Ryland Miller, but she'd dreamt of death and violence. Of voices calling to her, of death beckoning with a bony finger.

The chauffeur glanced at her in the rearview mirror. "You're wearing high heels, Miss Lily," he pointed out. "Are you ill?"

She could see her reflected image. Pale, eyes too big for her face, dark circles. She looked like hell. Her chin lifted. "I don't mind the heels, John. I need the exercise." She needed to get the remnants of the nightmare out of her mind. The oppressive feeling of danger, of being hunted, was still accelerating her heart rate. Lily tried to appear normal, avoiding John's gaze in the mirror. He had known her all of her life, and he was already concerned with the shadows in her eyes.

Why did she have to look so pale and uninteresting just when she finally met a man she connected with? He was so gorgeous. So intelligent. So . . . everything. She had walked into the meeting without one iota of information and had come off looking a complete fool rather than a woman of extraordinary intelligence. Miller probably dated model-thin blonds with big breasts, women who hung on his every word. Lily brushed a hand over her face, hoping to wipe away the nightmares that refused to allow her rest. Hoping to rid herself of the image of Ryland Miller embedded in her brain. He had somehow branded himself deep into her flesh and bones.

Come here to me.

His voice had whispered through her body, heated her blood, melted her insides. Lily hadn't wanted to look at him. She had been all too aware of the cameras. All too aware she knew nothing of men. She was bewildered by her father's behavior, bewildered by the sheer weight of her attraction to Ryland Miller. And she had run like a rabbit, wanting to find her father and learn what was happening.

The limousine slowed to a stop on the long, well-paved road winding through the enormous estate up to the main house. Lily hastily climbed out, not wanting to risk further conversation. John leaned out his window and studied her for a long moment. "You aren't sleeping again, Miss Lily."

Lily smiled at him as she pushed a hand through her thick mass of dark hair. The chauffeur claimed he was still in his early sixties, but she suspected he was probably in his seventies. He acted more like a relative than a driver and she could never see him in any other light than as beloved family. "You're right," she said. "I'm having those strange dreams I get once in a while. I'm trying to catnap during the day. Don't you worry about me, it's happened before." She shrugged her shoulders in a dismissing little gesture.

"Have you told your father?"

"As a matter of fact, I had planned to tell him over dinner, but he stood me up again. I thought he might be in his lab, but he didn't answer the phone or his page. Do you know if he's home yet?" If he were home, she would have a few words to say to him. It had been unforgivable to drop her into the situation with Miller without giving her the least indication of what was happening.

She was furious with her father this time. Miller didn't belong locked up in a cage like an animal. He was a man, a strong, intelligent man, loyal to his country, and whatever was going on at the Donovans laboratories had better be stopped immediately. And what was the nonsense with the computers and her father's codes? He had written reams of gibberish and acted as if the mess were legitimate notes on his work. She couldn't consult with nothing to work with. Dr. Peter Whitney, father or not, had a lot to answer for and he'd ducked out on their appointed meeting like a coward in retreat.

Impatience crossed the chauffeur's face. "That man. He needs an assistant to walk along behind him and kick him every now and then so he notices he's actually living in the real world." The renowned doctor had a long history of ignoring or forgetting his daughter's important moments and it annoyed John. The event never mattered—birthdays, planned outings, graduation ceremonies, Dr. Whitney just never remembered. The chauffeur had attended each and every event, watching Lily earn honor after honor without a family member present. It was a sore point with John Brimslow that his boss would treat his daughter with so little care.

Lily burst out laughing. "Is that what you say about me when I'm researching and I forget to come home?" She kept her gaze centered on the top button of John's coat, hoping she had become an expert at hiding emotion. She was used to her father's absentminded ways concerning her. Their dinner date would never have been important enough to him to try to remember it and normally she would have been understanding. She often was caught up in a research project and forgot to eat or sleep or talk with others. She could hardly condemn her father for being the same way. But this time, he was going to get a well-deserved earful, and he was going to sit down and tell her everything she wanted to know about Captain Miller and his men, with no excuses.

Her chauffeur grinned unrepentantly. "Of course."

"I'll be up to the house in a few minutes. Tell Rosa, will you please, otherwise she'll worry." Lily stepped away from the car with a small wave, turning away so John couldn't continue to look at her face. She knew her face had thinned, making her cheekbones stick out, and not in the complimentary way of a model. The nightmares had put dark smudges under her eyes and a droop in her shoulders. She had never been all that much to look at, with her too large eyes and her limp, and she had never been fashionably thin. Her body was curvy at a young age and insisted, no matter how much exercise she did, on being truly feminine. She had never minded much before about her looks, but now . . .

Lily closed her eyes. Ryland Miller. Why couldn't she have looked stunningly attractive just once? He was so unbelievably sexy. She had never been attracted to classic handsomeness. Miller wasn't handsome, he was too earthy, had too much raw power. Her entire body felt hot just thinking about him. And the way he looked at her . . . No one had ever looked at her like that before. He looked hungry for her.

She slipped off her heels and stared up at the house. She loved San Francisco, and living in the hills overlooking the beautiful city was a treasure she never tired of. Theirs was an Old World country estate, several stories high and sprawled out with balconies and terraces, giving it an elegant, romantic charm. The house had more rooms than she and her father could ever possibly use, but she loved every inch of it. The walls were thick and the spaces wide. Her refuge. Her sanctuary. God knew she needed one.

The wind blew softly, ruffling her hair and touching her face gently. The breeze brought her a sense of comfort. After a nightmare, the impression of danger usually dissipated a few minutes after waking, but this time it lingered, an alarm that was becoming frightening. Night was beginning to fall. She stared up at the skies, watching the gray threads spinning into darkening clouds overhead and floating across the moon. Dusk was a soft blanket enfolding her. Wisps of fog began to drift

across the terraced lawns, white lace in ribbons curling around
the trees and bushes.

Lily turned in a circle, taking in the rolling manicured
lawns, the shrubbery and trees, the fountains and gardens art-
fully placed to please the eye. The sprawling acreage to the
front was always perfectly immaculate without so much as a
leaf or blade of grass out of place, but behind the house, the
woods were left wild. There always seemed to her a balance in
nature, a quiet and a sense of peace. Her home gave her a freedom she couldn't find anywhere else.

Lily had always been different. She had a gift—a talent, her
father called it. She called it a curse. She could touch people
and know their private thoughts. Things not meant to be out in
the open. Dark secrets and forbidden desires. She had other
gifts as well. Her home was her one refuge, a sanctuary with
walls thick enough to protect her from the assault of intense
emotions bombarding her night and day.

Fortunately, Peter Whitney seemed to have natural barriers
so that she couldn't read him when he had tucked her into bed
at night as a child. Still, he had been careful of physical contact,
careful the barriers in his mind held firm when she was around.
And he had taken great care in finding others with natural barriers so that her home was always a sanctuary for her. The people who had cared for her became her family and were all
people she could safely touch. It had never occurred to her until
that moment to ask how Peter Whitney had known the people
he hired were people his unusual daughter would be unable to
read.

Ryland Miller had been totally unexpected. She could have
sworn the earth moved when she first set eyes on him. He had
gifts and talents of his own. Lily knew her father considered
him dangerous. She sensed Ryland was dangerous but she
wasn't certain in what way. A small smile curved her mouth. He
was probably dangerous to all women. He certainly had an effect on her body. She had to corner her father and make him listen to her for once. She needed a few answers that only he
could give her.

Anxiety settled in the pit of her stomach and Lily pressed a
hand to her midsection, wondering at the persistence of the
threatening omen. She knew better than to ignore a continual

disquiet so deeply imbedded in her bones. With a soft sigh, Lily headed determinedly for the house. The path she took was a narrow one, made of blue-gray slate, leading around the maze, through the tea garden toward a side entrance.

Lily stepped on the smooth slate stair and the earth rocked. She caught at the ornate banister, her shoes falling to the ground as she used both hands to steady herself, it took her a moment to register that there was no earthquake, but the motion was very much as if she were standing on a boat as it was riding over the waves in the ocean. She heard the lapping of the water against wood, a hollow sound that echoed through her mind. The vision was so strong, Lily could smell the sea air, feel the spray of salt water misting her face.

Her stomach clenched in reaction. Lily's fingers tightened until her knuckles turned white. Again she felt the rocking of the waves. She lifted her face to the darkening sky and saw the ominous clouds whirling faster over her head, spinning wildly until only the center was clear and dark and moving relentlessly, searching, searching. Lily jerked her hands from the banister and wrenched open the kitchen door. Staggering inside, she slammed the door and leaned against the wall, her breath coming in hard gasps. She closed her eyes and drew the air of her home, her sanctuary, into her lungs. She was safe inside the thick walls. Safe, as long as she didn't fall asleep.

The kitchen smelled of fresh-baked bread. Everywhere she looked there were gleaming tiles and wide-open spaces. Home. Lily patted the door with her palm. "Rosa, it smells wonderful in here. Did you cook dinner?"

The short, buxom woman spun around, a large chopping knife in one hand, a carrot in the other. Her dark eyes widened in surprise. "Miss Lily! You nearly gave me a heart attack. Why didn't you come through the front door like you're supposed to?"

Lily laughed because it was normal for Rosa to scold her and she needed normalcy. "Why am I supposed to come through the front door?"

"What good is a front door if no one ever uses it?" Rosa complained. Her gaze took in Lily's pale face, her haunted eyes, and then traveled down to Lily's bare feet and shredded nylons. "What in the world have you done now? And where are your shoes?"

Lily gestured vaguely toward the door. "Has my father called yet? He was supposed to meet me for dinner at Antonio's but he didn't show up. I waited an hour and a half but he must have forgotten."

Rosa frowned. As always there was only acceptance in Lily's voice, a gentle amusement that her father had once more forgotten an appointment with his daughter. Rosa wanted to box Dr. Whitney's ears for him. "That man. No, he didn't call. Did you eat? You're getting skinny, Lily, like a boy."

"I'm only skinny in places, Rosa," Lily contradicted. When Rosa glared she shrugged hastily. "I ate all their bread—it was fresh-baked, but not nearly as good as yours."

"I'm fixing you a plate of fresh vegetables and insist you eat it!"

Lily smiled at her. "Sounds good to me." She hoisted herself onto the countertop, ignoring Rosa's frown. "Rosa?" She tapped out a small nervous rhythm with her fingernail. "I found out the most disturbing thing about myself today."

Rosa turned quickly back to her. "Disturbing?"

"All this time I've been around men dressed in suits and ties, good-looking, intelligent men with a portfolio my father would admire, but I've never once been attracted to them. I don't think I even noticed them."

Rosa broke out into a smile. "Ah . . . you met someone. I've always hoped you'd get your nose out of your books long enough to meet someone."

"I didn't exactly meet him," Lily hedged. The last thing she needed was for the housekeeper to repeat her foolish confidences to her father. He'd pull her off the project immediately if he thought she was attracted to his subject. "I just saw him. He's got these shoulders on him and he looked . . ." She couldn't say "hot" to Rosa. She fanned herself instead of coming up with words.

"Oooh, he's sexy. A real man then."

Lily burst out laughing. Rosa always helped to rid her of demons. "My father wouldn't be too happy hearing you say that."

"Your father wouldn't see a woman if she had a perfect figure and stood naked in front of him. He'd only notice if she could speak in seven languages at the same time." Rosa pushed a plate of vegetables and dip into Lily's hands.

"The picture is too awful to contemplate," Lily said as she slipped to the floor. "I've got to spend some time tonight studying." Lily blew Rosa a kiss as she skirted around her toward the door. "This new project I'm working on is giving me a few problems. Dad just dumped it in my lap with hardly any data and it isn't making sense." She sighed. "I really needed to talk to him tonight."

"Tell me about it, Lily, maybe I can help you."

Lily snagged an apple as she passed the fruit bowl and added it to her plate. "You know I can't do that, Rosa, and you'd just roll your eyes and tell me it's all so silly anyway. This is a project for the Donovans Corporation."

Rosa did roll her eyes. "All that secrecy. Your father is like a little boy playing secret agent games and now he has you doing it, too."

Lily couldn't help smiling. "I wish it was secret agent stuff. It's all paper and lab work, nothing exciting at all." With a little wave she went on down the wide spacious hall, not looking at the huge open rooms. The library was her favorite sanctuary and she headed right for it. She preferred working there to her own office. John Brimslow would have left her briefcase on the desk for her, knowing right where she would go.

"Because I'm so darned predictable," she muttered aloud. "Just once I'd like to shake everybody up."

The fireplace was already lit, thanks to John, and the room was warm and comforting. Lily flung herself into the deep-cushioned armchair, ignoring her briefcase containing her laptop and the work she'd brought home with her. If she had the energy she would have turned on music, but she was bone weary. She couldn't remember the last time she had willingly, without apprehension, gone to sleep at night. In her sleep, all her natural protections came tumbling down, leaving her vulnerable and open to attack. Normally, because the house had such thick walls, she felt safe in her home. Lately, though . . .

Lily sighed and allowed her lashes to drift down. She was so tired. Little catnaps during the day and during work hours weren't cutting it. She felt as if she could sleep for weeks.

Lily! Almost at once she heard the water, the sound loud and persistent. Lily jerked upright and looked around, blinking to bring the room into focus.

She had no anchor, nothing to hold her to her world, but the safety of her home. She was in familiar territory and she hoped that would help. Whatever was lurking outside, riding the waves of energy to find her, was insisting she reach for it. Lily took a deep breath and resolutely opened her mind, allowing all her protective walls to come down so she could embrace the flow of information.

Waves rolling and pounding. It was loud. So loud she pressed her hands over her ears while she forcibly turned down the volume. She smelled the salt water. There were warehouses, unfocused, as if her vision were blurry. The stench of fish was strong. She had no idea where she was. But the warehouses were growing smaller as if she were moving away from them.

Her stomach rolled. Lily caught at the edge of her chair for support, her legs rubbery. There was movement. They were moving out away from shore. She smelled blood. And something else. Something familiar. Her heart nearly stopped beating, then began to pound in alarm. *Daddy?* It couldn't be. What would he be doing on a boat on the ocean? He didn't go on boats.

Peter Whitney had no real telepathic powers, but he had experimented with Lily for years and they sometimes had managed a faint connection. Lily frantically caught up her father's back pillow, clutching it between her hands to better focus on him. *Daddy, where are you?* He was in danger. She felt the vibrations of it all around him, she felt the violence lingering in the air. He was hurt.

Her head, his head, was hammering from the terrible wound. She could feel pain ripping through her body, through his body. Lily breathed deeply, trying to reach past pain and shock, trying to reach for him. *Where are you? I need to find you so I can send help. Can you hear me?*

Lily? Her father's voice, so weak, almost tinny, as if he were fading away. *It's too late for that. They've killed me. I've already lost too much blood. Listen to me, Lily, it's up to you now. You have to make it right. I'm counting on you to make it right.*

She could feel his fear, his great determination in spite of his weakness. Whatever he was trying to convey to her was of the utmost urgency to him. She fought down panic and her need to scream for aid. She fought down a daughter's reaction and reached out with all the power of her mind to stay connected. *Tell me what you want, I'll do it.*

There's a room, a laboratory no one knows about. The information is there, everything you need. Make it right, Lily.

Daddy, where? Donovans or here? Where should I look?

You have to find it. You have to get rid of everything, the disks, the hard drive, all my research, don't let them find it. They must never repeat that experiment. It's all there, Lily. It's my fault, but you have to set it right for me. Don't trust anyone, not even our people. Someone at the house discovered what I was doing. They betrayed me.

In our house? Lily was horrified. Their people had all been with them from the time she was a little girl. *There's a traitor in our house?* She took another deep breath, dragging air into her lungs to center herself. *Daddy, tell me where you are, I can't see anything of value. Let me send help.*

The men are prisoners. You'll have to free them. Captain Miller and the others, get them out of there, Lily. I'm sorry, baby. I'm sorry. I should have told you what I did right from the beginning but I was too ashamed. I thought the end results always justified the experiment, but I didn't have you, Lily. Remember that, don't hate me. Remember I never had a family before you came along. I love you, Lily. Find the others and make it right. Help them.

Lily's body jerked as she felt her father being dragged across the deck. She realized whoever was dragging him thought he was unconscious. She caught a brief glimpse of a shoe, of wrists and a watch, then nothing at all. *Daddy! Who is it? Who is hurting you?* She flung out her hand as if she could hold him there, hold him to her. Stop the inevitable.

There was silence. She was connected: she rocked when the boat rocked, she smelled the sea air and felt the pain wracking her father's body. But his blood had drained out on the deck of the boat and with it, most of his strength. Only a small flicker of life remained. He had to reach for the words, images in his mind, to communicate with her. *Donovans. Lily, let go now. You can't stay with me.*

He was fading fast. Lily couldn't bear to let him go. *No!* She wouldn't leave him to die alone. She couldn't. She felt the burn of the ropes on his wrists, on hers. He had closed his eyes. She never saw the face of the killer. But she felt the bump of the rail, the free fall, the plunge into icy water.

Break off! The command was a roar. A strong directive issued by a powerful male. The masculine voice was so strong, so authoritative, it actually drove her away from the scene of her father's murder and left her floundering alone in the library of her house, rocking back and forth, a low keening wail of grief coming from her raw throat.

Lily forced her mind back under control, driving out all panic while she reached for her father. There was . . . complete emptiness. A black void. She stumbled to the hearth, knelt, and was sick in the brass kindling bucket. Her father was dead. Thrown, like so much garbage, into the ocean, still alive, to drown in the icy waters. What had he meant saying Donovans was responsible? Donovans wasn't a person, it was a corporation.

She rocked back and forth, hugging herself, seeking some kind of comfort. She couldn't save her father, she knew in her heart he was already gone from her. She could hear herself weeping, the pain so deep she could hardly bear it. Her instinct was to rush to John Brimslow and Rosa for comfort. But she didn't move. She continued kneeling there by the fire, rocking back and forth, the tears running down her face.

Lily had never felt so alone in her life. She had a gift, yet she hadn't been able to save her own father. If only she had allowed the contact earlier. She had been too busy protecting herself. He had suffered such pain, yet he had held on and forced the connection. He had no real talent, yet he had managed the nearly impossible, wanting her to promise to set things right. She felt cold and empty and frightened. And alone.

The warmth stole into her mind first. A steady stream, pushing through her guilt and anguish. It moved through her body, wrapped around her heart.

It took minutes before she recognized she wasn't alone. Something, *someone,* had gotten through the thick protective walls of the house and, with her in her vulnerable state of grief, had entered her mind. The touch was powerful, stronger than she had ever encountered, and purely masculine. *And she knew who it was.* Captain Ryland Miller. She would have recognized his touch anywhere.

She wanted to be comforted by him, accept what he was offering, but he had hated her father. Blamed him for the incarceration and deaths of his men. He was a dangerous man. Did he have something to do with her father's murder?

Lily snapped to attention, swiping at the tears on her face, slamming her mind closed, shoring up her walls of resistance as quickly as she could. It hadn't been her father ordering her to break away from him in such a commanding tone. Someone else had shared their link. Someone else had heard every word her father had whispered in her mind. That someone had been strong enough to sever a connection she had been holding, probably saving her in the process, for she didn't have an anchor to hold her while her father was dying in the cold sea. Ryland Miller, the same man who had flooded her with warmth and comfort. The prisoner locked in a cage deep underground in the Donovans laboratories. She should have recognized his voice at once. His arrogant commanding voice. And she should have noticed the moment he had touched her connection with her father.

Until she learned more about what was going on, she couldn't afford telepathic contact with anyone. Not even someone who saved her life. Especially not Ryland Miller, who would have his own agenda and who blamed her father for his present circumstances. Lily shivered and pressed a hand to her aching heart. She had to use her brain and figure out what was happening and who was responsible for murdering her father. Her grief was so strong she could barely think with the pain, but it wouldn't help her. The raw, ugly wound must be pushed aside to allow her brain room to maneuver.

She didn't want to remember the last heated exchange between her father and Ryland Miller but it was impossible to ignore. It hadn't been pleasant. Captain Miller hadn't exactly threatened Peter Whitney, but he didn't have to put it in words. He exuded power and his very demeanor was a threat. It was obvious her father wanted Miller freed, but she simply didn't have enough information to be able to judge who was her enemy. The colonel had obviously disagreed with her father on whatever experiment was being secretly conducted in the Donovans laboratory.

Resolutely Lily sank back and stared into the flames. She couldn't trust anyone in the house or at work, which meant she couldn't admit to knowledge of her father's death. She had never been much of an actress, yet she would be forced to play a part while she kept her promise to her father. She had no evidence that anyone at Donovans was guilty. The police wouldn't believe she had a psychic experience that had connected her to her father as he was dying. What were her options?

Standing up was difficult. She felt as if a great weight was pressing her down and her legs were shaky. She had to clean out the brass kindling bucket. There could be no evidence that anything unusual had happened. She made her way to the nearest bathroom, grateful there were so few people in her huge home. Who could be the traitor her father had warned her of?

Rosa? Beloved Rosa? She couldn't remember a time when Rosa Cabreros wasn't in her life. Always there to comfort, converse, talk about all the things young girls want to talk about. Lily had never missed having a mother because Rosa was always there with her. Rosa lived and worked in the house, was completely devoted to Peter and Lily Whitney. It couldn't be Rosa. Lily dismissed the possibility at once.

John Brimslow? He had been with Peter Whitney even longer than Rosa. His official job was chauffeur, but only because he had insisted on the jaunty cap and wanted to be able to order the cars and care for them as he cared for the estate. He lived and worked his life there on the Whitney estate and had been the closest thing to family and friend that Peter had aside from Lily.

The only other permanent resident living inside the house was Arly Baker. Arly was in his fifties, a tall thin man with a domed head and thick glasses. A true geek, or nerd, as he proudly referred to himself. He kept the estate up-to-date in every type of gadget and gizmo known to man. He was responsible for the security and electronics. He had been Lily's best friend and confidant growing up, the one with whom she chose to discuss every important idea she had. He had taught her to take things apart and put them back together and helped her build her first computer. Arly was more like her uncle, or brother. Family. It couldn't possibly be Arly.

Lily ran her hands through her thick mass of sable-colored hair, sending the last of her hairpins scattering in all directions. They tumbled to the bright, gleaming tiles to lie all around her. Lily choked back another sob. There was old Heath, seventy if he was a day, still in charge of the grounds, living in his own little cottage in the interior of the forest behind the main house. He had lived on the property his entire life, born and raised and staying on to carry on his father's duties. He was entirely loyal to the family and the estate.

"I hate this, Dad," she whispered. "I hate everything about this. Now I have to suspect people I love of treachery. It makes no sense." For the first time she wished she could read the people in her household. She would try, but in all their years together, she had never done so. Her father had been very careful in his choices for her safety, for her benefit. So that she could live as normal a life as possible.

She returned the kindling bucket to the hearth, positioning it several times to make certain she had it just right. She knew she was being paranoid about it. Who would care if she moved the bucket three inches one way or the other? She was doing trivial things to keep her mind focused and occupied so she wouldn't scream and cry in her sorrow.

What had her father said? He wanted her to promise that she would set it right. What in the world was *it?* It had been so important to him, but she had no idea what he meant. What was she supposed to set right? And what had he been doing in his private laboratory? And Peter's last wish was for her to set Ryland Miller and his men free. What in the world had he meant about finding the others? What others?

"Lily?" John Brimslow pushed open the door and stuck his head in. "I've paged your father several times but there's no answer. Rosa checked Donovans. He signed out late in the afternoon." There was a worried note in his voice. "Was there a fundraiser or somewhere your father was giving a speech?"

Lily forced a thoughtful frown, though she wanted to burst into tears again and fling herself into his arms for comfort. She dared not look him fully in the eye. He knew her so well. Even with the poor lighting, he would notice her tear-streaked face.

She shook her head. "He was supposed to meet me for dinner at Antonio's. I waited over an hour but he didn't show up. I left the standard message with Antonio should he wander in, that I had given up and come home, but there was nothing else. Did they say if he left with anyone? Maybe he went to dinner with someone from the lab."

"I don't think Rosa asked that."

"Did you look at the planner on his desk?" Her throat ached, raw and painful.

John snorted. "Please, Lily, no one can find anything on your father's desk and if we did, it wouldn't make sense. He has that weird shorthand code he writes in. You're the only one who's going to make sense out of anything on his calendar."

"I'll go look, John. He probably went back to the labs and just isn't picking up. Call the desk and ask if he signed back in." She was proud of herself for sounding so practical. So in control. Not really worried yet, but slightly amused at her father's continual absentmindedness. "And if not, ask if he left with anyone. And you might have them check on that ridiculous car he insists on driving."

Deep inside, she heard weeping and she knew it was her own voice. The sound was frightening in its intensity and she had no idea how she was making it when she was talking with John so naturally.

For one moment she felt the warmth pouring into her again. Surrounding her, caressing her. There were no words, but the feeling was strong. Unity. Comfort. Her emotions were too strong and they were spilling out in spite of her protections.

As she neared the doorway and the chauffeur, Lily deliberately twisted her foot on the priceless Oriental rug on the floor and stumbled. She caught at John Brimslow's jacket to save herself, falling hard enough against him to shake them both.

John steadied her, helping her back to her feet. Lily longed for a flood of information so she could be absolutely certain John was innocent and she would have an ally, but there was nothing whatsoever. John's mind was, as always, even with her trying to read him, protected from the intrusion of hers.

"Are you all right, Lily?"

"I'm just tired. You know how clumsy I can be when I'm tired. Either that or Dad's Oriental rug will have to go." Hard as she tried, she couldn't pull off a smile. She didn't want to think that John could have betrayed her father. She didn't want to think of her father lying at the bottom of the ocean.

The only thing enabling her to walk toward her father's office was that warmth spreading inside of her. Aid from the very stranger who might wish her father dead. She sat at her father's desk and stared at the multitude of papers and the stacks of books without really seeing them. She was holding on to the warmth and courage pouring into her body from that unexpected and unwanted source. Ryland Miller. Was he her enemy? If she hadn't been so carefully protecting herself, she might have learned earlier that her father was in danger. Whoever had planned to kill him may have been in the very room. Whoever had betrayed him lived in her home.

RYLAND Miller sat down heavily in the one decent chair provided for him. Lily Whitney's grief swamped him, weighed him down like a heavy stone sitting in the middle of his chest so he could barely breathe, her pain a knife through his heart. He felt sweat beading on his skin. Like him, Lily was an enhancer, amplifying emotions already powerful enough to ride the waves of energy between them. Between the two of them, the emotions were nearly uncontrollable.

Peter Whitney had been his one hope. He hadn't trusted the man, but Ryland had worked on the scientist, pushing at his mind to sway him into helping Ryland plan the escape. It had taken tremendous concentration and a great deal of overload to connect all the men telepathically so they could talk in the dead of night. They were waiting for him now, waiting for him to be able to shake off Lily's terrible grief and sorrow. He admired her for the way she was trying to handle her father's death. How could he not? She didn't know whom to turn to, whom to trust, yet he sensed her deep resolve.

Lily. Ryland shook his head. He needed to get to her more than he needed anything else. He wanted to comfort her, find a way to lessen the pain in her, but he was locked up in a cage with a team waiting for his plan. With a sigh, he closed his eyes, centered himself, and sent out the first message.

Kaden, you will go out with the first group. We'll all have to make it out the first time or they'll double the security. All of you will have to be ready. I've worked on the computers and electric locks. I can handle those. . . .

THREE

LILY normally smiled absently at the guards as she walked through the space between the metal detectors. She had gone through the routine so many times she had long ago ceased thinking about it. Now everything was changed. The enormous enclosure with its high electric fences and coils of barbed wire, the multitude of guards and dogs, the rows of ugly concrete buildings with their underground maze of rooms—this had been her second home most of her life. She had never given the security measures much thought—they just seemed routine. Now she was aware every moment that someone had murdered her father. Someone she probably talked with every day.

Lily walked down the narrow corridor, lifted a hand in greeting, inwardly flinching as the armed guards hurried toward her. She half expected them to grab her and drag her off to the underground cages. She let out her breath as they moved past her, hardly glancing her way. At the second elevator she punched in her ten-digit code. The doors slid open and she stepped in.

The elevator glided silently to the lower floors hidden deep beneath the earth. This was her world, the labs and computers, the white coats and endless equations. The tight security, cameras and codes and keys. Her life. Her world, the only one she had ever known. Where always before the rigid routines had comforted her, now she was all too aware of being watched. The Donovans laboratories had been built just south of San

Francisco. The sprawling complex was deceptively innocent-looking with so many buildings inside the high fence. Most of the laboratories were actually located deep beneath the earth and heavily guarded. Even when going from one department to the other, security was always present.

In spite of her desire to remain calm, her heart was pounding alarmingly. She was entering fully into a cat-and-mouse game with her father's killer. And she was seeing Ryland Miller again. The idea was nearly as unsettling as returning to the laboratories. There was no way to ignore the attraction between them—it was magnified by every thought, every movement.

She leaned over the retinal scan, fitting her eye to the lens at the heavy door leading to her father's domain. As she moved into the lab, she snagged a white coat from a peg on the wall, buttoning it over her clothes without missing a stride. Someone called her name and she waved the obligatory hand, still moving quickly.

"Dr. Whitney?" One of the techs halted her determined progress. Lily looked at him, keeping her expression carefully blank. The waves of sympathy nearly swamped her. "I'm so sorry, *we're* so sorry about your father. We all hope he's found very soon. Has there been any word at all on his disappearance?"

Lily shook her head. "Nothing at all. If someone took him for money, they haven't asked for a ransom. The FBI thinks they would have already demanded money. There's been nothing at all, just silence." She was reaching for every emotion pouring out of the technician. The man couldn't possibly have been involved in her father's murder. He was genuinely upset at the way his boss had simply vanished. He had liked and respected Peter Whitney. Lily smiled at him. "Thank you so much for your concern. I know everyone feels his loss."

Right now Lily couldn't think about her father and how much she would miss him. She wouldn't think about being alone and frightened. She couldn't talk, she didn't dare. Her emotions were raw, far too close to the surface. She had waited all week, torn between impatience and a terrible dread, to be officially asked by the president of the corporation to take over her father's work. She hadn't dared appear too eager and had stayed locked up in her home, mourning her loss, grieving privately, away from even those whom she called family, all the while planning carefully her every move to find her father's murderer.

She had searched for a hidden laboratory in her enormous home, but there were so many rooms, hidden and not, that it seemed an impossible task. There were secret passageways leading belowground and up to the attics. She had meticulously gone over the blueprints and the floor plans, but to no avail. So far she had not found her father's secret world, and she hoped he'd left her a clue to its whereabouts in his office at Donovans.

Lily moved quickly through the rows of bottles and burners, through two rooms filled with computers to halt at another door. Firmly she pressed her palm and fingertips into the print scanner and leaned close to speak her coded phrase, waiting as an unseen computer analyzed the combination of her speech patterns and hand scan to verify her identity. The heavy door slid aside and she went into another, much larger complex.

The laboratory had muted lighting, turning the world into a bluish, tranquil setting. It was filled with plants and trickling waterfalls. The sound of water added to the calm atmosphere kept at all times in the lab. In the background was the continual sound of the ocean playing on a tape, waves rushing the shore and retreating, adding to the soothing ambiance of the laboratory.

"How was he last night?" Lily asked after greeting the dark-haired lab tech, who had snapped to attention in his chair when she entered. She had known Roger Talbot, her father's assistant, for five years. She had always liked and respected him.

"Not good, Dr. Whitney; he didn't sleep again. He's pacing back and forth like a wild animal. The level of aggression and agitation has risen daily this last week. He's asked for you repeatedly and has ceased all cooperation with testing. His pacing is driving me crazy."

Lily pinned him with a sharp gaze. "From what I read in the reports, his hearing is extremely acute, Roger—I doubt if he cares much for your admission. You're not the one locked up, now, are you?" Her voice was low but it carried a lash of reprimand.

"I'm sorry," Roger apologized immediately. "You're right. I don't have an excuse for being so unprofessional. I'm letting the colonel get to me. Colonel Higgens has been extremely difficult. Without your father around to provide some kind of a buffer, we're all . . ."

"I'll see what I can do to keep him out of here for a while," she soothed.

"About your father . . ." Roger trailed off as she continued to look at him. "It must be difficult for you," he tried again.

Lily was monitoring his emotions as she had with the other technician. Roger had no idea how her father could have disappeared and he was desperate for his boss to return. She tilted her chin. "Yes, it is difficult not knowing what happened to him. Take a break, Roger, you've earned it. I'll be here for some time. I'll beep you when I leave."

Roger glanced around the room as if they might not be alone. He lowered his voice. "He's getting stronger, Dr. Whitney."

She followed his gaze toward the other side of the lab, waited a heartbeat, her mind assimilating the information. "What gives you the impression he's growing stronger?"

Roger rubbed at his temples. "I just know. He becomes very quiet when he's not pacing; he sits there, perfectly still, concentrating. The computers go crazy, alarms start going off, everyone scrambles, but it's a bogey. I know it's him. And I think he might be able to talk to the others." He leaned closer still. "Not only has he stopped with testing, but so have all the others. They aren't supposed to be able to communicate with the heavy glass and all, yet it's like they have a collective brain or something. No one is cooperating."

"They're all isolated from one another." Her hand went to her throat, her only sign of agitation. "You've been in here cooped up with him too long. My father chose you because you're always so calm, but you're letting the talk spook you."

"Maybe, but he's changing, and I don't like the way it feels. Your father's been gone over a week, Dr. Whitney, and Captain Miller is different. You'll see what I mean when you see him. When I'm with him, he feels invincible to me. I'm afraid to leave you alone with him. Maybe the guards should be here inside the lab with you."

"That would only agitate him more, and you know he needs it quiet. The more people around him, the worse it is for him. He's been trained in the Special Forces, Roger, I'd say he's always had confidence in himself." Lily rubbed the pad of her thumb over her lower lip. "I'm perfectly safe with him." Even as she said it, a shiver of fear crept down her spine. She wasn't certain it was the truth, but she managed to look serene, unconcerned.

Roger nodded, recognizing defeat. He scooped up his coat, hesitated at the door for one more warning. "You call for help if you need it, Dr. Whitney."

She nodded. "I will, Roger, thanks." Lily stared at the closed door for a full minute, allowing the breath to move slowly through her lungs, to allow the peace of the room to seep into her pores. The entire lab was soundproofed, free from all outside noises. She rubbed her hand over her face and took another deep breath before turning resolutely toward the partitioned room on the far side of the lab.

Captain Ryland Miller was waiting for her, pacing back and forth like a caged tiger. She knew he would be. He would have known the moment she entered the complex. His gray eyes were turbulent, angry, storm clouds betraying the violent emotion swirling beneath his expressionless mask. The force of his gaze penetrated straight through her body to her heart. They regarded one another through the thick glass of his cage. His dark hair was wild from his hands raking through it, but he took her breath away. He knew how to get to her, and he used the knowledge shamelessly.

Open it. The words shimmered in her mind, his ability to use telepathy growing stronger with each use.

Her heart began to pound. Obediently she pressed the required sequence of buttons to activate the mechanism. The heavy glass partition slid aside so he was left staring at her through the thick bars.

He moved with lightning speed. That surprised her, how fast he was. She had thought herself safe, out of his striking distance, but he caught her wrist and jerked her against the bars. "You left me alone in here like some rat in a cage," he snarled, his mouth pressed close to her ear.

Lily didn't struggle. "Hardly a rat, more like a Bengal tiger."

But her heart melted at the word "alone." The thought of him alone in his glass cage was heartbreaking.

When he continued to glare at her she sighed softly. "You know I couldn't come back here without an official invitation. I received it this morning. If I had tried before that, they would have been suspicious. They *had* to ask me. I made certain I showed no interest at all, and don't pretend you don't know why." She raised her voice just enough to reach the recorders. "I'm sure you must have heard my father has disappeared. The FBI suspect foul play. I have all of his projects and my own to take care of and with all the work here and at home too, I'm afraid my time is at a premium." Deliberately she glanced up at the camera to remind him they were not alone.

"You think I don't know it's there?" He hissed the words, anger seething in the deep timbre of his voice. "You think I don't know they watch me eat and sleep and piss? You should have come here immediately."

Her eyebrow shot up. It was a struggle to keep her face without expression. Her gaze began to smolder. "You're lucky I came at all, Captain Miller." She made a supreme effort to keep her voice soft even when she really wanted to lash out at him. "You know my father disappeared." She lowered her voice even more. "You were there with us, weren't you? How dare you be angry with me!" For one awful moment tears threatened and she fought them back.

His voice changed completely, dropping an octave so that it whispered in her mind, weaving them together as if they were bound in some way. *You can't think I had anything to do with his death.*

The intimacy in his tone robbed her of air. Worse, he was flooding her with warmth and comfort. His thumb was stroking small caresses along her sensitive inner wrist. She attempted again to jerk her arm away from him, the movement reflex, one of self-preservation. His fingers settled around her wrist like a shackle. His fingers were warm, enormously strong, yet he was very gentle.

"Don't fight, Lily, you'll have every guard in the compound running to save you." There was an edge to his voice as if he couldn't quite make up his mind whether to laugh at the thought or be angry for the accusation in her mind.

Can you command from a distance, one human being to kill another? She refused to look away from him, staring directly into his eyes, speaking back to him in the same way, mind to mind. *Can you do that?*

Ryland couldn't look away from the deep blue of her eyes, a mirror reflecting his soul. He wasn't certain he wanted to see what she saw. And he wasn't certain he could afford for her to see him as he had become. There was so much raw anger seething in him.

The disembodied voice of the guard crackled over the speaker. "Dr. Whitney, do you require assistance?"

"No, thank you, I'm perfectly fine." Lily continued to stare into Ryland Miller's eyes. Challenging him. Accusing him. Seeing him.

His fingers still circled her wrist like a vise, yet his thumb feathered over her rapidly beating pulse, to soothe her. He said nothing, only continued to look at her.

Tell me. Can you do that?

What do you think?

She studied him for a long while, her gaze penetrating beyond his mask, seeing the predator prowling just below the surface. *I think you can.*

Maybe. Maybe it's possible if the person was already filled with malice and capable of killing, wanted to kill, it's possible I could manipulate them to do so.

I felt your dislike of him. You believed he put you here, that he was responsible for killing the men in your unit.

I'm not going to deny that, it would be a lie. But you're touching me. Read me, Lily. Did I have anything to do with your father's death?

Her blue eyes drifted over his face, returned to his glittering gray ones. *Am I supposed to believe you can't hide your true nature from me? I see only what you want me to see.*

I'm not shedding tears over his death, I'll give you that, but I did not order anyone to kill him.

"Peter Whitney was my father and I loved him. *I'm* crying over him." And she was, deep inside where no one could see. She felt alone. Bereft. Vulnerable.

His thumb stroked again, sent heat curling through her, sent her pulse skittering. *I would be a fool to kill the one man who might save our lives.* Aloud he murmured to her softly, "I'm sorry he's missing, Lily, sorry for your loss." His other hand moved up to slide over her hair, lingering just long enough to steal the breath from her lungs. *You left me alone. I couldn't comfort you. I felt you, Lily, your sorrow, but I couldn't comfort you. You knew I was there when it happened, I knew the truth. There was never a need to cut off contact with me. You needed me, and damn it, Lily, I needed you. You should have talked to me. I understand the need to stay away, but you should have talked to me.*

She didn't want to acknowledge that, the implication of his words. She didn't need any more complications in her life. She didn't need or want Ryland Miller. She concentrated on gathering information. *How were you there with us? My father had no telepathic ability, how could you connect with him? How could you break my connection with him?*

I connected through you, of course. Your distress was so strong you touched me, even here in this prison designed to keep me from touching other minds.

Her heart jumped. His answer suggested a connection between them. A strong connection. She struggled to understand. Lily stared at him for a long moment, feeling her way, trying to see beyond his mask to the man beneath it. She studied him critically. He wasn't particularly tall, but he had wide shoulders and a muscular build. His hair was thick and so black it was nearly blue. His eyes were ice cold, the color of steel. Merciless. Slashing. Eyes so cold they burned. His jaw was strong, his sculpted mouth tempting. He moved with fluid grace, power and coordination, a hint of danger. He was pure magic to her, he had been from the moment she had laid eyes on him. And she didn't trust something so instant and so strong.

When Colonel Higgens was here before with my father, could you read him? Was he involved in my father's death?

Every muscle in Ryland's body went taut under her inspection. Her gaze was direct, assessing, speculative. It was so Lily. Being in her head gave him the advantage of knowing her far more intimately. Her brain processed information at rapid rates of speed, but when it came to something personal, she was much more cautious, taking her time before deciding on a course of action. He wanted to crush the silk of her sable hair in his large hands, to bury his face in the fragrant strands and inhale her. She smelled fresh, like a bed of roses. Her hair glinted with lights—glossy, so shiny, even with the blue lights, he was captivated.

Higgens made no secret of his dislike of your father. They didn't agree on anything. I can pick up his emotions when he's broadcasting anger but he never gets close enough for me to touch. And he's careful to keep his possessions out of my reach. I didn't detect any plots against your father.

Her eyes were almost too large for her face, thick-lashed and incredibly blue, unexpected with her dark hair. And her mouth . . . He had spent far too much time fantasizing over her mouth.

Lily took a deep breath and let it out slowly. His gaze was unexpectedly hot. Hungry. Devouring her. And his thoughts had suddenly turned to erotic fantasies. She tried to ignore it, tried not to let it affect her. Her gaze shifted momentarily to the surveillance cameras. "I'm taking over his research. You have to be patient. I'm not my father and I have to backtrack to catch up." She said it for the benefit of the cameras, and the ever-present watching eyes. "I'm coming into this cold." Her wrist was hot where his thumb had caressed it. "Stop looking at me that way, it isn't helping." She paced away from the cage and then turned back to face him almost resolutely.

Ryland watched with interest as she looked at him coolly. She had been rattled for a moment, but just that fast she recovered, turning into a cool, haughty ice princess. He wanted very much to shake her up again. "I can't help what I feel when I'm around you." He pitched his voice low, a husky invitation to hot sex and wild times.

Lily blinked. Color tinted her cheeks but she met his gaze steadily. He had to give her that. She was courageous.

She stepped to the bars, gripped them with her fingers. "Have you even bothered to wonder why we're so connected? It isn't natural."

Ryland studied her face for a long moment then covered her hands with his own. "It feels natural."

His voice had a way of whispering over her skin like the brush of fingers. Lily's stomach flipped, her heart doing a curious meltdown she couldn't control. "Well, no one feels this much physical attraction without some kind of enhancement."

"How do you know?"

She tilted her chin at him, her eyes beginning to smolder a warning. "Well? Have you? Do you feel this sort of connection with every woman who walks into a room with you?"

That look in her eyes made him want to pull her right through the bars. The urge to kiss her was so strong he leaned toward her.

Lily shifted away from him in sudden alarm. "Don't!" She glanced again toward the camera. "You know this isn't real. Think with your brain, not other parts of your anatomy. We have to know everything that's going on, not just the pieces of the puzzle."

She was right. The attraction went far beyond anything he had ever experienced. It bordered on obsession. His body was hard and hurting and he knew better. It didn't seem to make much difference though. From the first moment she'd entered the room, he had been wrapped up in her. "What do you think it is?"

"I don't know but I'm going to find out. My father was acting strange that last day, do you remember? He asked me to come here. I was busy and said I had to make it another afternoon, but he insisted, practically ordered me to come." She lifted her fingers, signaling to let her go.

Their voices were pitched too low to be overheard, and both were careful to keep their faces turned away from the cameras so no one could read their lips, but body language could just as easily betray them. Ryland complied with her request very slowly.

Lily took one step back in an attempt to allow both of them to breathe. Skin-to-skin contact served to deepen the physical attraction, the chemistry between them arcing with electricity, sizzling so it seemed alive to her. "He didn't tell me anything about you or what they were doing. I walked into the room and saw you and . . ."

There was a small silence as they stared at one another. In a rare display of agitation she pushed her hand through her hair. Her hand was shaking and he instantly wanted, *needed,* to pull her into his arms and comfort her. "The earth moved," he finished quietly. "Son of a bitch. Lily, he was watching us together. That damned cold-blooded scientist was watching us like two insects under his microscope."

She shook her head in denial, but he could see she was computing. She couldn't have it both ways. Either her father had expected something to happen between them when she walked into the room, or he hadn't. Ryland closed his eyes momentarily against the glimpse of her raw pain. It was bone deep and overwhelming. What had possessed him to make such an accusation? She'd lost her father, she didn't need to learn what an all-out bastard the man was. He had crushed her with his careless comment.

"Lily." He said her name very softly, a whisper of a caress. An apology. He breathed it, so that it sounded sensual. So that it connected them intimately.

"Stop it!" she snapped in a low voice. "If this isn't real, if we're being manipulated in some way for an experiment, we need to know."

"Maybe it isn't that," Ryland suggested, wanting it to be real.

"I anchor you, that's all. That's probably all it is. We're different and I have some kind of emotional magnet in me and it enhances . . ." She trailed off, her mind obviously attempting to fit more pieces of the puzzle together for a logical explanation. "That's got to be it, Captain Miller. . . ."

"Ryland," he interrupted. "Say my name."

She had to take a breath. He managed to turn the mere speaking of his name into something intimate. "Ryland," she agreed. How could she not? She felt as if she'd known him forever. As if they belonged. "We're attracted and somehow our special gifts enhance what we're feeling. That's got to be it. It's the way you smell."

He burst out laughing. The sound was so foreign to him he was as startled as she was. "You're trying to explain away our rather explosive chemistry by calling it enhanced pheromones? That's priceless, Lily." She could even make him laugh in the midst of everything. Lily Whitney was an extraordinary woman and quite unexpected.

"Well," she pointed out, "pheromones can be nasty little traps for the unwary."

He shook his head. "I think we're just attracted to each other, but we'll leave it there if it makes you feel better."

"Whatever the reason, Captain"—a brief smile lit up her eyes as she corrected herself—"Ryland, I think we have enough on our plates without that." She raised her voice to a normal level. "I've read all the reports my father generated for the colonel—I was given copies—but there's no data at all stating *how* my father accomplished what he did." She looked at him very steadily. *You heard what he said to me. He believes you're a prisoner here. I can't find the laboratory he spoke of before they murdered him.* . . . She faltered for a moment, and he felt the wrench in the vicinity of his heart. *I need the information in that room if I'm going to help you.*

"You don't actually think you can find a way to reverse the process when your father couldn't do it?" *You have to find it, Lily. Whatever is there is important to us. I don't know if my men can survive on the outside. And if Higgens has his way, some of us will be terminated. I have a feeling I'm number one on his list.*

Lily turned away from him, afraid the shock would show on her face. "I don't know if I can reverse it, or even if it's necessary, but consider this: You and the others have had terrible side effects. Is it possible one of the side effects is paranoia?" Lily willed him to act out a part for the camera. If she couldn't convince Higgens she was impartial and willing to go along with whatever the colonel wanted, the possibility of her being excluded was very real. *I'll find the room, Ryland, but we have to buy ourselves some time. You have to appear somewhat cooperative or Higgens might move before we're ready. Surely you have a contact in the military I can go to.* She had a feeling Ryland might be right, that Higgens wanted to go forward with the experiment and Ryland Miller stood in his way.

I don't have a clue who I can trust. I trusted Higgens. Ryland paced the length of his cage, as if contemplating the question. He raked both hands through his hair, playing to the camera. "I hadn't considered that. Colonel Higgens was always behind us, but when he locked us up and separated us, I felt as if . . ." Deliberately he trailed off.

"As if he had deserted you. Left you alone. Cut you off from your command."

Ryland nodded. "All of those things." He sat down heavily in a chair and regarded her with glittering eyes and the beginnings of a smile in his mind as he teased her. *You rich types can act with the best of them, can't you?* He admired the cool way she played her part, the cool way she handed him cues and lines. With her brains and quick thinking, she would fit right into their team.

Do you have a prejudice against money? She actually teased him.

Only because you have too much. It puts you out of my league.

Lily ignored his response, the only sane thing to do. "I think the possibility of paranoia induced by the experiment is a possibility we have to consider."

He nodded. "I want to see my men. I want to know they're all right."

"That's not an unreasonable request. I'll see what I can do." *Now you're trying to get to me.*

I'm trying to make you laugh. Your sorrow is weighing on me like a stone. Ryland pressed a hand to his temples.

Lily was instantly contrite. She'd felt the shards of glass on more than one occasion from strong emotions she couldn't block out. Telepathic communication was difficult and prolonged use was downright painful. She went to his cage and once more gripped the bars. "I'm sorry, Ryland, I can't help grieving over my father's disappearance. I'm hurting you, aren't I? Would it be easier if I put the glass barricade up to protect you?"

"No." He rubbed his throbbing temples one last time as he came out of the chair, stretching as he did so, a lazy ripple of muscle she couldn't help but notice. "I'm fine. It will pass." He crossed unhurriedly to her, took her hand in his.

The jolt hit them both like a lightning bolt. Lily half expected to see sparks flying. "It isn't going to go away, is it? We just . . ." She trailed off, unable to think clearly with him so completely focused on her.

For the briefest of moments his white teeth flashed at her. "Fit." He supplied the word for her. "We fit."

She tugged to free her hand. Ryland retained possession, a glint of male amusement in his eyes. Deliberately he raised her knuckles to the warmth of his mouth, swirled his tongue over and between each separate bone.

She shivered at the sensuous contact. Fire sparked and raced over her bare skin each time his tongue tasted. He lifted his head, his gaze meeting hers. Everything in her went still; even her heart seemed to cease beating. The amusement in the depths of his eyes was gone, replaced by stark possession. It glittered there in plain view for her to see. A challenge. A promise. Her breath caught in her throat.

The camera. She reminded him, struggling to pull her hand away. He held on to her. "What's your relationship with Roger?"

The question threw her, completely taking her by surprise it was so unexpected. There was an edge to his voice, his eyes gleaming with icy menace. She blinked at him. "Roger? Roger who?"

"Roger, the tech I make so nervous he wants the guards in here with their guns." There was the merest whip of contempt in his voice. "As if that would help him in time."

"What does Roger have to do with anything?"

"That's what I'm asking you."

Are you completely crazy? I'm trying to help you. There's a major conspiracy going on and a murderer running around loose. Roger is completely beside the point.

"Dr. Whitney?" The voice floated over the intercom. "Do you need assistance?"

"If she needed assistance, pal, it would be apparent," Ryland snapped, glaring up at the camera, daring the unseen observer to reveal himself. *Roger is the point. He was drooling over you.*

"I don't require assistance, thank you." Lily smiled for the camera as she yanked her hand away from Ryland. *I think being in that cage has finally gotten to you. Will you focus on what's important here?*

This is important to me.

"Ryland." Couldn't he see the chemistry between them had to be artificial? Enhanced in some way, the way his psychic abilities had been enhanced? He could tune in with much more clarity around her. She was obviously an amplifier.

I'm sorry, I know I'm distressing you, but it's getting worse.

I feel like some caveman, wanting to drag you off by your hair or something. Honest to God, Lily, I hurt like hell. Just answer the damn question and give me a little reassurance.

Lily studied his face. He had suffered. He was suffering. "Why doesn't any of this make sense to me?" She asked it softly, afraid of the answer. Her world had always been balanced, necessarily so. Her father was a man who'd protected her from the outside world, yet at the same time, gave her every opportunity to expand her mind and gather knowledge. He'd opened so many doors for her. He'd been kind and considerate and loving.

She knew that Ryland Miller believed her father had betrayed him and his men. Her father had conducted an experiment on human beings and something had gone terribly wrong. She had to find out exactly what it was and how it had been done. The attraction between Ryland and her was threatening good sense on both sides. She was a practical person, logical and serious. She easily put aside emotion when it was called for.

"It doesn't make sense to me either." *God damn it, Lily, I'm being eaten alive with jealousy. It's ugly and uncomfortable and I don't like myself very much.*

Roger is a good man, a friend, but I've never laid eyes on him outside this building. Nor do I intend to do so.

Ryland pressed his forehead against the bars of the cage, taking in a deep breath to steady his roiling gut. There were tiny beads of sweat on his skin. "What the hell is happening to me? Do you know?"

Lily shook her head, her fingers itching to stray to the unruly spirals falling across his forehead. "I'll find out, Ryland. This has never happened to you or to any of the men?"

He lifted his head and looked at her and there was a mixture of turbulence, anger, and despair. "Kaden is able to draw the angriest and most violent emotions away from the rest of us so we can cope better. I think he's like you in some way. When we're out in the field together and he's with us, things run smoothly and all the signals come in clearer. We have more power to project. At least three others are like him in varying degrees. We try to keep one of them with the others at all times in the field when we're working."

"And the man who died recently in training?"

Ryland shook his head. "He was alone and he ran into the wrong people. By the time we got to him it was too late, his mind was gone. He couldn't handle the overload of noise. We can't turn it off, Lily." *Can you turn it off?*

She knew he wasn't asking for himself. She knew his concern was for his men and she admired him for it. She could feel the weight of his heavy responsibility nearly crushing him. *I've learned over the years to build up barriers. I live in an environment that is very controlled. It allows me to rest my brain and prepare for the bombardment the next day. I believe you and the others can be taught to build barriers.*

Who taught you?

Lily shrugged. She couldn't remember a time when she didn't have to protect herself. She had learned at an early age. *I think because I was born with it, my mind began to find ways to cope. You haven't had it that long. Your brain is exposed to too much too fast. It can't catch up and give you the barriers you need.*

"Unless the barriers are gone for good." He said it grimly, uncaring of the cameras. He had a sudden desire to tear down the bars, rip something apart. He had to find a way to save his men. They were good men, every one of them, dedicated and loyal, men who had sacrificed for their country. Men who had trusted and followed him. "Damn it, Lily."

Raw sorrow shimmered through the storm in his eyes and nearly broke her heart. "I'm viewing the training tapes tonight. I'll figure this out, Ryland," she assured him. "I'll find the information we need to help the others. You just have to give me a little time."

"I don't honestly know how much time my men have, Lily. Any of them could break down. If I lose any of them . . . Don't you see? They believed in me and they followed me. They put their faith and trust in me and I led them into a trap."

She could feel the shards of glass now, cutting and grinding in her head. He was a man of action and they had locked him up in a cage. His frustration and sorrow were wearing him down.

"Ryland, look at me." She touched him, slipping her hand through the bars to curl her fingers around his. "I'll find the answers. Trust me. No matter what, I'll find a way to help you and your men."

For one brief moment he stared into her eyes, searching, reading her mind, knowing what it cost her to open herself up even more to him. He nodded, believing her. "Thank you, Lily."

FOUR

THE murmur of voices went on and on, an invasion buzzing in her head, driving her mad. Each time she drifted into sleep, the voices were there, filling her mind, yet she couldn't catch the words. She knew there was more than one voice, more than one person, and yet she had no idea what was being said, only that it was the whisper of conspiracy. Only that there was great danger and an edge of violence in those voices.

Lily lay in her huge bed, staring up at the ceiling, listening to the sound of her own heartbeat. The soft music she normally played to help mask sounds she couldn't quite block out had been turned off long ago in frustration. She wasn't going to be able to sleep again. She didn't even want to sleep. It wasn't safe. The voices claimed her, soft and persuasive, voices whispering of danger and tactics.

She sat up amid the thick pillows scattered along the intricately carved headboard of her bed. Where had that come from? Tactics implied training, perhaps even military. Was she hearing Ryland and his men as they used their telepathic abilities to plot an escape? Was it possible? They were miles from her home, deep beneath the earth, with glass barriers guarding their cages. Her walls were thick. Were they so connected that she was in some way tuned to their frequency? Like a radio wave, a band of sound, the *exact* one? "What did you do, Dad?" she asked aloud.

She could only sit there in the comfort of her familiar bed-room while her mind played back the facts of the training tapes she had viewed and the confidential reports she had read. How her father had gotten away with writing reports with such in-complete descriptions of what he had done was beyond her. Why in the world had he gone to all the trouble of filling his data bank in the computers at Donovans Corporation with utter gibberish? The file was marked confidential and only his pass-word and security codes supposedly could access such a thing, yet Higgens had obviously done so.

Her head was pounding, little white dots floating around in a black void that was pain. The aftermath of using telepathy. She wondered about Ryland. Did he still suffer the painful repercussions of prolonged use? He certainly had in earlier years. She had read the confidential reports on the training the men had endured. All of them had suffered terrible migraines, the backlash of using psychic talents.

Lily threw back her comforter in resignation and dragged on her robe, tying the sash loosely around her waist. She opened the double doors to her balcony and wandered out into the cool night air. The wind immediately whipped the thick mass of her hair into a cloud that tumbled around her face and down her back. "I miss you, Dad," she whispered softly. "I could use your advice."

Her hair was annoying her, blowing across her eyes, and she caught at the heavy mass, twisting it quickly and expertly into a loose braid. Her gaze followed the white tendrils of fog swirling through the trees a foot or two above the rolling lawns. Movement caught her eye on the far edge of the flower beds, a shadow sliding into deeper shadow.

Startled, Lily drew back from the railing, shrinking into the safety and darkness of the interior of her room. The grounds were protected, yet the shadow had been no animal—it was creeping about on two legs. She stood perfectly still, straining to see through the dark and fog to the grounds below. Her senses were shrieking a warning at her, but she was on sensory overload and afraid her fears had more to do with the continual whispering of voices than an actual threat to her home. It was possible Arly had hired extra security and not told her. He might have done so after her father's disappearance. He had wanted her to have a full-time bodyguard, but Lily had adamantly declined.

Lily lifted the phone and pressed the button to reach Arly automatically. He answered at once, on the first ring, but his voice was sleepy. "Did you hire extra guards to sneak around my property, Arly?" she demanded without preamble.

"Do you ever sleep, Lily?" Arly yawned heavily into the phone. "What's wrong?"

"I saw someone on the lawn. On the property. Did you hire extra guards, Arly?" There was accusation in her voice.

"Of course I did. Your father disappeared, Lily, and your safety is my primary concern, not your squirrelly ideas about privacy. You have an eighty-room house, for God's sake, and enough property for your own state. I think we can hire a few extra men without danger of bumping into them. Now go away and let me get some sleep."

"Not without authorization you can't hire extra guards."

"Yes, I can, you little snip. I've been given absolute authority to guard your butt in any way I see fit and I'm going to do it. Stop bitching at me."

"There's something to be said for 'Miss Lily' or 'Dr. Whitney,'" she groused. "Who was stupid enough to put you in a position of power?"

"Why, you were, Miss Lily," Arly said. "You made it part of my job description and signed it and everything."

Lily sighed. "You sneaky geeky nerd. You stuck that paper in with all the other stuff I had to sign, didn't you?"

"Absolutely. That should teach you about signing things without looking at the contents. Now go back to bed and let me get some sleep."

"Don't call me Miss Lily again, Arly, or I'm going to practice my karate on your shins."

"I was being respectful."

"You were being sarcastic. And when you're lying in bed, right before you go to sleep and you're feeling all proud of yourself for pulling one over on me, gloating at how smart you are, just remember who has the higher IQ." With that pathetic parting shot, Lily hung up the phone. She sat on the edge of her bed and burst out laughing, partly from the exchange and partly from sheer relief. She had been far more frightened than she had acknowledged even to herself.

She *loved* Arly. She loved everything about him. She even loved his atrocious manners and the way he growled at her like an old bear. A *skinny* bear, she amended with a little grin. He hated to be called skinny almost as much as he hated the reminder that she had the higher IQ. She used it only on rare occasions when he had totally bested her at something and was feeling particularly smug.

She padded down the hall on bare feet, down the winding staircase, without turning on lights. She knew the way to her father's office and she hoped his familiar scent, still lingering there, would bring her a measure of comfort. She had instructed everyone to stay out of the office, including the cleaning staff, because she needed to be able to find his papers, but, truthfully, she didn't want to part with the scent of his pipe that permeated the furniture and his jacket.

She closed the heavy oak door, shutting out the rest of the world, and settled into his favorite armchair. Tears welled up, clogging her throat and burning her eyes, but Lily blinked them determinedly away. She leaned her head into the cushions where her father had leaned so many times while he talked with her. Her gaze drifted around his office. Her night vision was acute and she knew every inch of his office so it was easy to make out the details.

His floor-to-ceiling bookshelves were symmetrical, the books perfectly aligned and arranged in order. His desk was at a precise angle to the window, his chair pushed in two inches from his desk. Everything was in order, so like her father. Lily stood up and wandered around the room, touching his things. His beloved collection of maps, neatly laid out to be easily accessed. His atlas. To her knowledge he had never touched it, but it was displayed prominently.

An ancient sundial sat to the left of the window. A tall glass Galileo barometer stood on a shelf closest to the enormous grandfather clock with its swinging pendulum. Next to the barometer was a thick hourglass wrapped in lead spirals. Lily lifted it, turned it over to watch the grains of sand slip to the bottom. His most prized possession was the large world globe on the mahogany stand. Made of crystals and abalone shell, the perfect sphere had often been examined as he talked with her late at night.

She touched the smooth surface, sliding her fingers over the highly polished shell. Sorrow washed over her. She sank into the armchair closest to the globe and slumped down, pressing her fingers against her temples.

The ticking of the grandfather clock was overly loud in the silence of the office. The sound beat in her head, disturbing her solitude. She sighed, got restlessly to her feet, and wandered over to the clock, brushing the intricately carved wood with loving fingers. It was magnificent, fully seven feet tall and nearly two feet deep. Behind the beveled glass the mechanism worked with precision and the giant golden pendulum swung. On each hour, beside a distinctive gold Roman numeral, a different planet emerged from behind double doors of shooting stars, beautiful glittering gems spinning through a darkened sky, complete with moons revolving. Only at noon and midnight did all the planets emerge together in a spectacular display of the solar system. Three o'clock had the emergence of a brilliant spinning sun. And the nine o'clock position held the moon, filling the entire clock with wondrous delights.

She had always loved the clock, but it belonged in a different room, where the loud ticking didn't drive a person crazy while they tried to think. Lily turned away from the unique masterpiece and threw herself into a chair, stretching out her legs and glaring at her feet without seeing them. There were nine planets, the sun and moon and solar system display, but during the night, the moon display was empty. It came out faithfully at nine in the morning, but steadfastly refused to make an appearance at nine in the evening. Lily has always been vaguely irritated by the inconsistency of the moon's appearance. A flaw in something so precise. It bothered her enough that she'd begged her father to have it fixed. It was the one thing he didn't keep in perfect condition.

Her head came up slowly, her eyes locking on the Roman numeral nine formed in gold. Images crept into her brain; the pattern lined up and she could see it so perfectly, just the way it always worked. She sat up straight, staring at the grandfather clock. A surge of adrenaline burst through her, carrying sudden elation. And sudden fear.

Lily knew she had found the way to her father's secret laboratory. She carefully locked the door to her father's office, then went back to the clock, moving around it, studying it from every angle. Carefully, Lily opened the glass door. Very gently, she spun the hour hand in a complete rotation, nine times, ending on the gold Roman numeral nine. A soft snick told her she found something.

The entire front of the clock moved aside, revealing the entrance into the wall. Her breath catching in her throat, she found and opened the door without much trouble, entering the narrow space to stand there staring at the walls. It didn't really go anywhere. Lily frowned at the walls, ran her hands up and down the panels, feeling for something hidden. Nothing. "Of course not. The clock. It's in the clock." She turned back to look at the door of the clock. The solar system etched into the mirrored background. The golden sun, so radiant and in plain sight. She pressed the sun hard with her thumb.

The floor in between the walls slid away to reveal the steep narrow stairway below the floor. Lily stared down into the utter darkness, her mouth suddenly dry, her heart pounding in alarm. "Don't be a coward, Lily," she whispered aloud. Peter Whitney was her beloved father and she was suddenly terrified of what hidden secrets lay in his secret laboratory.

Taking a deep breath, she started down the stairs. To her horror, as she stepped on the fourth stair, the floor slid into place above her head with an eerie silence she found frightening. At once a faint light glowed along the edges of the stairs, illuminating the descent. She was instantly claustrophobic, the feeling of being buried alive overwhelming. The staircase was extremely steep and narrow, obviously to make it more difficult to find sandwiched between the basement walls.

Lily? The voice swirled in her mind. *Lily, talk to me. You're afraid. I can feel it and I'm trapped in this damn cage. Are you in danger?*

She remained at the top of the stairs, startled at the clarity of Ryland Miller's voice in her head. He was so strong. Lily could see why he would terrify Colonel Higgens. Ryland Miller just might be able to influence someone to kill. He might be able to influence someone to commit suicide.

Ryland swore, a harsh, brutal string of words, venting his frustration. *Damn it, Lily, I swear if you don't answer me, I'm going to rip this cage apart. You're killing me. Do you know that? You're taking a knife and driving it through my heart. I need to get to you, to protect you. I don't have any control over the feeling.*

The desperation in him penetrated her fear. She could feel the strength and wildness of his emotions. Captain Ryland Miller, so in control with everyone else, cool under pressure, so out of control with her, burning like a wildfire neither could hope to contain. Lily let her breath out slowly, made every effort to conquer her aversion to tight quarters.

She stood on the stairs, awareness creeping in. The murmuring voices were gone abruptly, disappearing with the strength of Ryland's voice. She gripped the banister, wondering what she was more afraid of, finding out what her father had been involved in, or the fact that the tie between Ryland and her was growing stronger with each passing hour. She couldn't resist the hoarse plea in his voice. He sounded raw with tension, edgy with the need to know she was unharmed.

Most people sleep in the middle of the night. Have you and your friends been playing together on the Ouija board? You're coming in loud and clear. I wonder who else is hearing you?

She sensed him letting out his breath. Felt the tension leave his knotted muscles. *What frightened you?*

Voices. Your voices. They . . . She searched for some way to explain. *It's like a thousand bees . . .*

Stinging your brain, he finished for her.

His voice gave her an added confidence. She looked up at the trapdoor and saw the same characters etched into the door. She wasn't imprisoned. Unlike Ryland and his men, she had a way out. Lily started down the stairs. *I know you're planning an escape, Ryland. That's what you're doing at night. You've found a way to communicate with the others and somehow I'm in on the loop.*

I'm sorry, Lily, I had no idea we were hurting you. I'll do my best to shield and ask the others to do so also.

She hesitated only a moment. *I think I've found it. My fa-*

ther's secret laboratory. Don't do anything crazy until I see what's in there.

We can't take the chance of staying here, Lily. Higgens has some plan to get rid of us. I need to get to General Ranier. I'm not certain he'll believe you, because Higgens has to be lying to our people about what's going on here. The colonel is a decorated officer and respected. It won't be easy to convince anyone that he's a traitor.

She could believe that. Higgens had stayed away from her, preferring to have Phillip Thornton, president of the Donovans Corporation, ask her to take over her father's work. But Colonel Higgens had been pushing for her father's computer password and the codes to override his failsafe so his work would not self-destruct should they access it carelessly. She knew everything on the computer in her father's office at Donovans was carefully planted gibberish. Codes and formulas that had nothing to do with a psychic experiment. *I think my father became suspicious that Higgens was up to something and that someone at Donovans was helping Higgens. There is nothing in the computers at Donovans and Thornton sent over men to pick up Dad's private office computer. I'd already checked it and there was nothing usable there either.*

Did you view the training tapes? There was pain in his voice.

Her heart ached for him. She had viewed the earlier tapes and she had seen two of the original members of the team in the second year of training become increasingly unstable and violent. Ryland Miller had paid the high price right along with his two friends. It had been heartbreaking to watch; it must have been a terrible thing to have to endure.

The experiment should have been stopped right then.

The stairs continued downward, deep beneath the earth, sometimes squeezed so tightly between other rooms she felt she could barely breathe. But the air moved and the light glowed, guiding her beneath the basement level.

I told Dr. Whitney all of us were in jeopardy, but Higgens convinced him to continue. He pointed out all the things we could do. There is no other team like us in the world, we can enter an enemy camp completely undetected. We function in total silence. We're GhostWalkers, Lily, and Higgens wants to succeed at any cost. Even if we short-circuit and have to be terminated. I had to kill one of my friends and watch another one stroke out. I lost another, Morrison, a couple months ago to brain bleeds, a good man who deserved better than what he suffered. I'm going to save the rest of them somehow, Lily. I have to get them to safety.

She was at the bottom of the stairs at last, staring at the closed door to her father's laboratory. She knew his every security code and password. But the door had a scanner for prints. *I'm sorry Ryland. I'm hoping to find out much more. You can't just take the men out of a protected environment with no real plan. Their potential for great violence has already been proven and there's the danger of losing the others the way you did your friend Morrison. You don't want that. I'll come in tomorrow and let you know what I've found.* She tried not to feel guilty. Her father should have insisted on calling a halt to the project, yet he had agreed to incarcerate the men, rather than find a way to return them to the world. She was ashamed of Peter Whitney and it didn't sit well with her.

Damn it, Lily, I can't bear it when you're feeling so much grief. You didn't do this. You didn't know about this and it isn't on your shoulders. It tears me up inside when I feel your pain.

Lily was aware the connection between them was growing stronger, the physical, emotional, and mental attraction enhanced and amplified by something deep within both of them they couldn't control. She shook her head, wishing for the logic that always enabled her to solve every problem. Her bond with Ryland Miller was uncomfortable and unexpected and something she didn't need in the midst of an increasingly dangerous and complex situation.

I'll let you know what I find, she reiterated, wanting him to know she wouldn't abandon him.

Are you certain you're safe? Whitney implied someone in your home betrayed him.

She had the impression of him gritting his teeth, distressed that he couldn't be with her when she was in need of comfort and perhaps even protection. Her heart reacted to his need, the way he wanted to be with her, the way he reached out to her. He was twisting his way into her soul. No matter how many times she shored up her defenses, he said or did something that touched her.

No one knows where I am, Ryland. I'll be fine. She broke the link between them, carefully placing her hand in the scanner, trusting that her father would have coded her prints into the door.

The door slid smoothly and quietly aside. She entered the laboratory without hesitation. The lights blinked once when she flipped the switch, then surged brightly. A bank of computers ran along the left wall. A small desk sat in the middle of an area surrounded by shelves of books. The laboratory was as fully equipped as the labs at the Donovans Corporation. Her father had spared no expense in putting together his private sanctuary. Lily looked around, feeling a mixture of disbelief and betrayal. It was obvious he had used the room for years.

She walked around, discovered the rows of videos and disks, the small bathroom off to the right, and the other door leading to another room. This one had an observation wall made entirely of one-way glass. She looked into the room and saw what looked like a child's dormitory.

Her stomach lurched. She pressed her hand tightly to her middle, staring through the glass while faint memories swirled in her head. She'd seen the room before, she was certain of it. She knew if she entered the room, there would be another bathroom and a larger playroom through the two doors she could see.

Lily didn't go in. Instead, she remained quietly outside the room staring at the twelve small beds, children's beds, blinking back tears. Her father had told her he'd contracted tremendous renovations to the already enormous house to be built because he loved English castles and estates, but Lily knew she was looking at the real reason. She knew the stairs leading to the laboratory were sandwiched between the basement rooms. The laboratory itself was below that, completely hidden, and she already knew that there was no evidence in blueprints anywhere showing the location of the laboratory. These rooms were what the house was protecting, not her.

She pressed a hand to her trembling mouth. She had stayed in that room. She even knew which bed had been hers. Lily turned away from the sight and looked carefully around the laboratory. "What did you do here?" She asked it aloud, afraid of the answer, afraid the knowledge was already blossoming in her logical brain.

That room with its little beds sickened her. Her head buzzed worse than ever, a swarm of angry bees, stinging, hurting, so painful she pressed both hands to her temple in an attempt to alleviate the throbbing. "It's only memories," she whispered to give herself courage. She had no choice but to face her past.

Lily walked reluctantly to her father's desk and turned on the laptop sitting in the precise middle of the desktop. As the notebook was powering up, she noticed her name on his day planner. Below it was a long handwritten letter scribbled in haste. It was written in one of his strange codes, but one she was familiar with, one she recognized from early childhood.

She picked it up, her fingers smoothing the ink over his handwriting. She read his words aloud, wanting to bring him back to life again. "'My beloved daughter. I know the errors of my past are catching up with me. I should have done something about it long ago. I should have told you the truth, but I was afraid to see all the love shining in your eyes gone forever when you looked at me.'"

There were several blots, places he had scribbled over, not liking the words he had chosen. "'Your childhood is completely documented. Please remember you're an extraordinary woman as you were an extraordinary child. Forgive me for not being able to find a way to tell you face-to-face. I didn't have the courage.'"

There were more scribbles, one so deep the pen had torn the paper. "'You are my daughter in every sense of the word. Although, biologically you are not.'"

Lily read the sentence over and over. *Biologically you are not.* She sat down slowly in the chair, staring at the words. Her father had told her over and over of her mother giving birth to her and dying hours later. "'I've never been married, never knew your mother. I found you in an orphanage overseas. There was no record of your birth parents, only of your extraordinary abilities. Lily, I love you with all my heart. You will always be my daughter. The adoption is completely legal and you inherit everything. Cyrus Bishop has all the papers.'"

Cyrus Bishop was one of Peter Whitney's attorneys, his

most trusted and the one he used for all personal business. Lily slumped back against the backrest. "This isn't the worst, is it, Dad? You could have easily told me I was adopted instead of making up such an elaborate story." She let her breath out slowly and glanced toward the long room to her left. The dormitory. The one with all the little beds.

She remembered voices. Young voices. Singing. Laughing. Crying. She remembered those voices crying.

"'I told you that you had no grandparents. I wasn't lying. My family is dead. They were lifeless people, Lily, without emotions. They had money and brains on both sides, but they didn't know how to love. I hardly saw them as a child, only when they wanted to reprimand me for not doing as well as they thought I should. It's my only excuse. No one taught me how to love, until you came into my life. I don't even know when or how it started, only that I looked forward to waking up in the morning and seeing you. My parents and grandparents left me more money than was good for anyone, and I inherited their brilliance, but they gave me no legacy of love. You did that for me.'"

Lily turned the page to find more. "'I had an idea. It was a good one, Lily. I was certain I could take people who already had the beginnings of psychic talents and enhance those abilities, allow them free rein. You'll find all my notes in the laptop. The results are in the videos and disks I've recorded along with my detailed observations.'"

Lily closed her eyes against the sudden tears burning so strongly. She knew what the rest of the letter was going to reveal and she didn't want to face it.

Lily? The voice was faint this time, far away, as if Ryland were very tired. *What's wrong?*

She didn't want him to know. She didn't want anyone to know. Lily forced air into her burning lungs. She didn't know if she were protecting herself, or her father, only that in that moment, she couldn't reveal the truth. *Nothing. Don't worry, I'm just working my way through dry notes.*

There was the smallest of hesitations, almost as if he didn't believe her, but then his presence was gone.

Lily turned her attention back to the letter. "'I brought back twelve girls from overseas. I chose third-world countries, places getting rid of their children. I found the girls in orphanages, where no one wanted them, where most would have died, or worse. All were under the age of three. I chose the females because there were so many more unwanted girls to choose from. Parents rarely abandoned their sons in those countries. I was looking for very specific criteria and you, along with the other girls, met them. I brought all of you here and worked with you to enhance your abilities. I took excellent care of you all, had trained nurses for each of you and I'll admit, I convinced myself I had given you all a much better life than you could ever have had in the orphanages.'"

Lily tossed the letter down and paced across the floor, adrenaline pumping through her body. "I hope I'm getting this straight, Dad. I'm an unwanted orphan from a third-world country you brought home along with eleven other lucky girls to conduct experiments on. We had nurses and probably toys so that makes it all right." She was furious. Furious! And she wanted to weep. Instead she retraced her steps and sat at her father's desk.

How could he have possibly found traces of psychic adepts in children younger than three? What had he looked for? It shamed Lily that her mind wanted the answer to that question almost as much as she was outraged by the idea of what her father had done.

"'At first everything went well, but then I began to notice none of you could stand noise, and you didn't like most of the nurses near you. I realized all of you were taking in too much information and that there was no way to shut it off. I did my best to provide a soothing, calming atmosphere and I worked at getting employees none of you could read. I had to enhance barriers at times, but it did help.'"

There were more scratches indicating extreme agitation. "'Blue lights helped, as did the sound of water. It's all in the reports I've laid out for you. But the problems didn't stop there. Some of the girls couldn't be alone without you or two or three of the others. You seemed to help them function, drawing the overload of noise and emotions away from them. Without you, they could become almost catatonic. Seizures were common, along with a multitude of other problems. I realized I couldn't cope with so many children with such enormous problems. I found the other girls homes; it wasn't that difficult with the amount of money I offered prospective parents. And I kept you'"

Lily pressed the heel of her hand to her throbbing forehead. "Not because you loved me, Dad, but because I was the least problematic." She saw it so clearly, her father as a young man, logically choosing the one child who would give him the least amount of trouble. He knew he should give up his experiment, but he couldn't bring himself to do so after all the time, effort, and money he had poured into it. So he had kept her. "And what of those other little girls, trying to cope without help, not knowing what was wrong with them? You abandoned them. Half of them could be dead by now or in institutions." Tears were burning and she struggled against them. How could he have done such a hideous thing? It was so wrong, so against nature.

"'I know you so well, Lily. I know I'm hurting you, but I have to tell the truth or you won't believe any of it. I grew to love you over the years, and I realized what I really owed those other children. That's no excuse for my neglect of them. I'm responsible for the problems I know they must be having in their lives even now. I've hired a private detective to track them down. Some I've found, and those files are included for you to read. You won't like the results of my meddling any more than I have. I know you'll be angry and ashamed of me.'"

Lily lifted her head. "I'm already angry and ashamed," she said. "How could you do this? Experimenting on people, on children, Dad, how could you do this?"

She tried to remember the other children, but all she could hear was the sound of little voices mingling together in laughter and tears. She felt an affinity for the other girls. Women now, out there in the world without a clue as to what had happened to them. Where were they all now? She wanted to drop her father's letter and find the private investigator's reports. Instead she forced herself to continue.

"'I can only say in those early days, I didn't have much of a heart or conscience. You're the one who provided those two important elements in my life. I learned from you. From watching you grow up and seeing the love in your eyes when you looked at me. Those years of you following me around asking so many questions and arguing with me, I cherish every single day. Unfortunately, Lily, you know how my mind is. I watched over you for years, protected you as best as I could, but I saw your potential and in seeing it, I realized how a tight team would benefit our country.' "

Lily shook her head. "Ryland." She whispered his name as if to protect him.

" 'I thought I'd gone wrong by choosing such young subjects. In the beginning it made sense because their brains weren't developed; I could use that, teach them to use the parts that were just dormant, waiting for someone to awaken them. But children were too young. I determined that if I chose men with superior training and discipline, I wouldn't run into the same problems. I could depend on them to do all their practices, build shields, erect the necessary barriers when they needed respite. You were able to do it, so a fully grown man would be stronger, a military man more apt to obey and make use of all the training.' "

Lily sighed softly and turned the page. " 'Everything has gone wrong again. You'll see the problems in the disks and the reports. There is no way to reverse this process, Lily. I've tried to figure a way, but once it's done, it can't be undone and these men, the women, and you all have to live with what I've done. I have no answers for Ryland Miller. I can hardly look him in the eye anymore. I think Colonel Higgens and someone at Donovans is conspiring to get the reports and sell the information to other countries. I've been followed, and my offices at home and at work have been broken into. I believe Miller and his team are in danger. You must get a message to General Ranier (he is Colonel Higgens's direct superior) and let him know what's going on. I can't get through to him. You know him well and I can't imagine him not responding to you. I've left him countless messages to call me or to come to Donovans but I've heard nothing back.' "

Lily stared at the familiar symbols, aching to hear her father's voice. She could be hurt and she could be angry, but she couldn't change anything that he had done. " 'I've set up bank accounts for Miller's team just in case. If I fail, you'll have to help them all for me. You'll have to tell them the truth. Without someone like you, with your talent to draw sound and emotion away from them, they will need to work continually to find private quiet places or they will eventually overload. Watch the tapes, read the reports, and then you must find a way to lessen the damage and teach these men and the others to live as you have lived. In a protected environment, useful to society, but living. Please think of me with all the love and compassion I know you have in your heart. I'm afraid, Lily, afraid for both of us and afraid for all of those men.' "

Lily sat for a long time with her head bowed and her shoulders shaking. Tears burned but didn't fall. She had been so unprepared for this, yet somehow she wasn't as shocked as she should have been. She knew her father, knew his belief that the laws were too stringent and only hindered medical and defense research. His name was revered in so many circles. His name had always been above reproach, yet he had conducted secret experiments on children. It was unforgivable.

Lily pushed herself up from the desk and made her way to the videos. She looked at the shelves of tape. Her life. Right there. All numbered neatly in her father's hand. It wasn't going to be of her first steps, as many parents recorded, or graduating with honors from a university, it was going to be a cold-blooded documentary of a psychic adept whose abilities were enhanced in some way by a man who claimed to love her.

She didn't think she could bear to sit through it. She couldn't even run to her father for reassurance. He was at the bottom of the cold sea. Murdered. A chill went through her. Peter Whitney had most likely been murdered in an attempt to gain the very information she possessed. Someone wanted to know how he had enhanced a psychic adept's abilities. Her father hadn't shared his actual process with anyone, not at Donovans Corporation and not with Colonel Higgens or the general above him.

Lily pulled the first video off the shelf with shaking fingers. Ryland Miller and his entire team were alive because her father *hadn't* provided the information. Why would they kill the only man who could give it to them? If they couldn't get the information one way, they would certainly go at it from another angle.

An accident would provide a dead subject, one they could dissect. One they could take apart and study in the hopes that they would gain the secret. They would have such power if they utilized the talents her father's work had unleashed. Had Morrison's death really been unintentional? Had he suffered the seizures from what Whitney had done to him or had someone given him a drug to cause seizures so they could study him?

Knowing she had a great deal of information to go through in a very short time, Lily inserted the videotape in the player and began to watch.

LILY felt absolutely numb as she watched the little girl with enormous eyes "play" games for hours. Her father's voice was without inflection as he gave data and recited her growing abilities. She tried desperately to detach herself from emotion the way her father was so obviously able to do as he watched and filmed the little girl vomiting repeatedly from the migraines. Light hurt her eyes, sound hurt her ears, she cried and rocked and pleaded, and, through it all, Peter Whitney filmed and documented and spoke in his impersonal monotone.

Lily stared at the video, sickened that the man she called her father, the man she loved as her father could do such things to a child. He stood there filming all the while the nurse worked to comfort and help her. He even ordered the nurse aside as he went in for close-ups as Lily pressed her hands to her ears. Several times when she had disconnected, withdrawing from the world, into herself, rocking back and forth, he had become annoyed and had instructed the nurse to isolate her from the others so she wouldn't "infect them with her methods of retreat."

Lily turned off the video, tears tracking down her face. She hadn't even known they were there. Her hand shook as she pushed open the door to the room where she had spent so many months being trained. Being watched and documented. Her breath caught in her throat. Like Ryland and his men. No matter what, they couldn't stay at the Donovans laboratories. She had to find a safe, protected place until she could sort out the information and find a way to help them.

Lily lay down on the third bed from the left. Her bed. She curled up in the fetal position and pressed both hands over her ears to drown out the sound of her own sobbing.

FIVE

RUSSELL Cowlings was still missing. Ryland counted his one-hundredth push-up and continued thinking his way step by step through the planned escape. He had managed to bring the men together telepathically, with the exception of one. Russell had not answered or been felt by any of the team for several days.

Ryland felt helpless, cursing as he raised his body up and down, working his muscles to stay fit. He had to convince Lily that every one of his men was in danger. There was no concrete evidence, but he *felt* it. In his heart and soul he *knew* it. If they remained much longer in the cages of the Donovans laboratories, they would all disappear, one by one. Like Russell.

In sheer frustration. Ryland leapt to his feet and paced restlessly across the length of his prison. His head was throbbing from holding the telepathic link for so long for all the team members while they discussed how to survive on the outside if their escape succeeded. It had been a longer conversation than usual, and they had continued to test and disrupt the alarms and security system often, using even more energy. He rubbed his temples, feeling slightly sick.

Pain hit him hard. Drove him to his knees. *Lily.* It was a knife in his gut, doubling him over. A stone in his chest crushing him. Sorrow such as he had never known and never wanted to experience. At that moment nothing else mattered but to get to her. Find her and comfort her. Protect her. The need was alive and crawling through his body and mind.

He began to build the bridge between them. A bridge strong and sure so he could cross the boundaries of time and space.

Lily dreamt of a river of tears. Tears filling up the sea and splashing onto land. She dreamt of blood and pain and monstrous men lurking in shadows. She dreamt of a man kneeling beside her, gathering her into his arms and holding her tightly to him, rocking her back and forth in an attempt to comfort her. When he couldn't stop her tears, he began to kiss her face, following the wet trail from her eyes to her mouth. Kissing her over and over. Long, drugging kisses that robbed her of her ability to think or breathe or even grieve.

Ryland. She knew him. Dream lover. He had stolen into her nightmare to carry her away. "I feel so empty and lost." Even in her dream, she sounded forlorn.

"You're not lost, Lily," he replied gently.

"I am nothing. I belong nowhere. With nobody. None of this is real, don't you see? He robbed us of our life, of our free will."

"You belong in my world where there are no boundaries. You're a GhostWalker. It doesn't matter how it came to be, Lily, it simply is. We belong together. Be with me." Ryland stood up, held out his hand to her.

"What are we doing?" she murmured, reaching to take his offered hand, shocked that they were outside a cage, outside the thick walls of her home. Away from the secrets kept beneath the earth. "Where are we going?" His fingers closed around hers, strong and reassuring. Her heart gave a peculiar lurch in recognition of him.

"Where would you like to go?"

"Anywhere, anywhere away from here." She wanted to be far from that laboratory and the truth buried beneath the stories of her house. The weight of her knowledge crushed her until she could barely breathe.

He wanted her to trust him enough to tell him what had distressed her, but he simply tucked her hand into his and took her out into the night.

"How can you be here, Ryland? How can you be here with me?"

"I can walk in dreams. Raoul, we call him Gator, can control animals. Sam can move objects. There's a lot of talent among us, but there's only a few who are dreamwalkers."

"Thank you for coming to me." Lily said it simply. She meant it. She had no idea why he made her feel whole when she had been so shattered, but walking beside him, tucked beneath the protection of his shoulder, gave her a semblance of peace.

They wandered through the darkened streets together, not really paying attention to where they were going, simply being together. "Tell me about it, Lily." Ryland walked very close to her, his larger body brushing against hers protectively.

She shook her head. "I can't think about it, not even here."

"You're safe here with me. I'll keep you safe. Tell me what he did to you."

"He didn't love me. That's what he did, Ryland. He didn't love me." She wouldn't look at him. She stared off into the night, her face averted, her expression so sad it threatened to break his heart.

Ryland gathered her into his arms protectively, holding her close, transporting them across time and space. Far away from laboratories and cages. Away from reality so that the wind blew on their faces and they could simply be together. A respite her brain grabbed at and held on to. Their bodies soared free and they could go where their minds took them, but her sorrow walked with them in their dreamworld. And so did his worries. "One of my men is missing, Lily. I can't reach him."

She knew what he wanted. "I'll find him. I'll ask to speak with all the men tomorrow. I've supposedly been given access to everyone. Which man?" She ducked her head, guilt weighing heavily.

"Russell Cowling. And I don't blame you, Lily. I know that's what you're thinking. Your father . . ."

"I don't want to talk about him." Her dreamworld was beginning to dissolve around the edges as the harshness of reality intruded.

Ryland framed her face with his hands. "I saw his eyes when he looked at you. He loved you very much. Whatever sins he committed, Lily, he did love you."

She looked up at him, her long lashes wet with tears. "Did he? I thought he did, but there's an entire room filled with tapes neatly labeled 'Lily' to prove otherwise."

Ryland bent his head, taking her mouth, needing to take away her sorrow. His mouth was exquisitely gentle on hers, tender and coaxing. A kiss meant to be innocent. Healing. It was his intention to comfort her. But fire raced through him. He felt it in his veins. In his belly. In the heavy fullness of his groin. It burned along his skin and took him by surprise.

Lily melted into him, pliant and yielding. Her mouth opened to his, her arms creeping around his neck so that he could feel her generous breasts pressed tightly against the wall of muscles along his chest. Energy arced between them, snapping and sizzling as if alive. His skin to hers and back again. Small bolts of lightning whipped in his bloodstream. His arms tightened possessively.

Lily lifted her head to look at him, searching his face for answers. Nothing could prepare her for the instant and overwhelming physical attraction. She didn't trust anything so strong. She shook her head silently in denial.

Ryland could see it in her face. A groan escaped. "Lily, can't you see there's more than just something physical between us? I ache for you, I won't deny it, but I feel sad when you're sad. I want more than anything to make you happy, to know you're safe. I think about you every minute of the day. You refuse to see what's between us. I look at you and see clouds in your eyes when you're looking back. Does it matter so much to you the why of it?"

"This isn't real, Ryland. You're here with me, talking to me because you felt my need, but it still isn't real. It's a dream we're both sharing."

"I felt your need, across time and space, I still felt your need of me. Doesn't that tell you something, Lily?"

"It's still a dream, Ryland."

"It's real enough that we could be caught in it. Dreamwalking isn't easy, Lily." He allowed his arms to drop to his sides, unable to bear her body touching his when she didn't want him.

Lily caught his hand, weaving her fingers through his because she couldn't stand to be without physical contact with him. "What do you mean, we could be caught in it? Caught in the dream itself?"

He shrugged his broad shoulders. "No one knows for sure how it works. Your father was the one who warned me to be careful. He said it was too difficult holding the bridge in this state and that anyone riding the same wave might enter and be able to harm me if I wasn't expecting it. And if I were caught in the dream, living in this world, I might not return to the other. I'd be in a dream state, appearing much like I'm in a coma to the outside world." Ryland glanced down at her and found himself smiling. Lily reacted as he expected she would, assimilating the information with great interest.

"I had no idea it was possible. Can any of the others walk in dreams?"

"One or two. We found it was very rare and it does take a tremendous concentration and focus. Even more than sustaining the telepathic link for an extended period of time." He brought her hand to his chest, trapping her palm over his heart. His thumb stroked along the back of her hand, small caresses she felt all the way to her toes.

"I'd like to see the recorded data on it and read my father's notes to see what he thought. It doesn't make sense that it seems so real. I can feel you." She ran her free hand over his chest. "I can taste you." He was still in her mouth, on her tongue, deep inside her where she would never get him out.

"And yet we can be anywhere. Anywhere at all." He tugged at her and Lily found they were in a park, surrounded by trees. Leaves glittered silver in the moonlight above her head. "I can't see trees in that cage I'm in so sometimes I come here."

Lily laughed with delight and looked up at Ryland. At once the smile faded from her face and her heart began to pound. It was the way he looked at her. The intensity of his hunger for her alone. The stark desire he never tried to hide from her. His hot gaze burned over her possessively, marked her for his.

Her entire body went hot. Deep inside, molten heat swirled and pooled low, leaving her aching and bereft. Her fingers splayed wide across his chest. For one moment she thought of removing his shirt, to feel the warmth of his skin. She wanted to be melded to him, skin against skin. Bodies tangled together. Sweat mingling.

"Stop it," Ryland said quietly. He tipped her chin up to claim her mouth. There was nothing innocent or comforting in his kiss. His hand moved over the silk of her shirt to capture her breast. "What you feel, I feel. You broadcast loudly and I can't think straight." His thumb stroked her nipple right through the material, even as he bent his head once more to hers. "Are you wearing anything under this blouse?"

His kiss rocked her. Flames danced in her blood and colors burst behind her eyelids. He robbed her of breath, yet fed her air. With the weight of her breast resting in the warmth of his palm, every muscle in her body tightened and ached for fulfillment. For just one moment, Lily allowed her body to rule her brain. She kissed him back just as possessively, just as wantonly. Without thought or inhibition.

She *wanted* him. She had dreams often of the right man, what it should be, what it would be. In every dream she had cast aside her inhibitions. Here he was, the perfect man. Her man. Standing right in front of her and anything she did wouldn't count.

Her hands moved instinctively over his body, claiming him as intimately as he was claiming her. She was bold and sure, unable to control the wildfire burning out of control. There was a roaring in her head, a dizzy kaleidoscope of pure feeling, fire and color. Silks and satins. Candlelight. Everything she'd ever dreamt of and more. She simply gave herself up to him, willing to be in a dream. Willing to feel nothing but obsession and belonging.

Lily stiffened. Jerked back to stare up at Ryland's face. At the passion stamped there, the dark possession. The naked love. She pushed hard at the wall of his chest, shaking her head. "No, this is going too far, change it. Change the dream."

His hands framed her face. "This is our dream together. It isn't just me, Lily."

"I was afraid of that," she murmured. Lily rested her forehead against his chest, trying to breathe air into her lungs and clear her mind. "I've never once in my life been like this around anyone."

Ryland's palm curved around the nape of her neck. His lips brushed the top of her head. "Is that supposed to make me feel bad? I would rather you didn't want every man you saw, Lily." There was a hint of laughter in his voice.

She lifted her head to glare at him. "You know exactly what I meant. I can't keep my hands off you." Even in her dream she blushed a vivid red at the admission.

"Close your eyes." He ordered it softly.

Lily felt his kiss, featherlight on her eyelids. When he lifted his head, she opened her eyes in puzzlement. She was standing in her favorite museum. Her comfort spot. She roamed the museum often, sitting sometimes on the benches to look at the beauty of the paintings. The artwork never failed to bring her peace. For some reason, while she was in the building surrounded by such priceless treasures, she could fend off the emotions of those around her and simply soak up the atmosphere.

"How did you know?"

"That you love it here?" He took her hand, drew her to stand in front of a fantasy depicting dragons and warlords. "You thought of it several times. It mattered to you so it mattered to me."

Lily smiled up at him, her heart in her eyes. She couldn't help it. It touched her that he would trade his outdoor dream for her museum. "I'm not exactly certain what I am wearing under these clothes, Ryland." She laughed softly, invitingly, knowing she shouldn't but unable to stop herself.

Ryland kissed her again because he couldn't help it. She was looking at him with her eyes too big for her face and her tempting mouth and she shook him all the way to his soul. He lifted his head to look at her clothes. The thin silk of her blouse. The long skirt that covered her legs all the way to her ankles. He raised an eyebrow. "Very nice."

"I thought so. But you have to guess what I have on underneath."

Every muscle in his body contracted, tightened. Every cell went on alert. His gaze immediately swept her figure, searching for clues to the mystery. Lily laughed softly and led him around the room, pointing out her favorite paintings.

As they stood in front of a large crystalline sculpture of a winged dragon, Ryland reached out casually and slipped his fingers inside the neckline of her blouse. Loosely. The pad of his fingers feathered over her bare skin. "Are you wearing underwear, Lily? I have to know." And he did have to know. It seemed the most important thing in the world.

She skimmed her hand down his chest, knowing she was being provocative, but no longer caring. She was in a dream and she meant to take full advantage. In a dream she could do anything, have anything, and she wanted Ryland Miller. "And you think I should be talking about such things here in this very public place."

Ryland laughed softly. "Not so public tonight. I had them shut it down for us. A private showing. And I can't stop thinking about the underwear, Lily, whether you're completely naked beneath that outfit, or whether you're covered." His fingers dipped lower, over the swell of her breast. "I have to know."

"What are you doing?" Lily asked breathlessly. His hand skimmed down the front of her blouse, as if brushing crumbs from her silken top, yet lingering on the dark nipples hidden beneath the thin material. He brought her body to instant life, her nipples taut, her breasts full and aching.

His fingers brushed over her breasts a second time. Slow. Unhurried. This time sliding a button open. Her blouse gaped slightly, giving him a better view of her cleavage. She was beautiful, her breasts full and firm, swaying gently beneath the silk as she walked beside him. And she wasn't wearing a bra, just as he had suspected. His body instantly reacted, hard and thick and full with heat.

"I don't know, honey, something about this place just turns me on." He grinned at her, outrageously uninhibited, sinfully wicked. His eyes were hot with desire. His fingers tangled with hers and he tugged her off balance so that she fell against him. Her body molded to his, fit perfectly.

Right there, in the room filled with hundred-year-old paintings, he lowered his mouth to hers. She tasted his desire, a hot, masculine passion that instantly ignited an answering flame in the pit of her stomach. She lost herself in his strength and hunger. His hands slid down her back, shaped her body, feeling his way through the material of her skirt.

At once his heart began to thud in reaction to the knowledge. His groin tightened to the point of pain and a fire spread in his belly. There wasn't a single pantie line. His mouth grew hotter and he pressed her tightly into him. Whips of lightning streaked through him with the contact against his throbbing arousal. "We need a bed, Lily," he breathed into her mouth. "Right now. The bench is looking darned good."

She kissed him, deliberately rubbed her body along his, her breasts pushing hungrily into his chest, her hands exploring the muscles of his back. "We don't need a bed, we don't have time for a bed. I don't have a single stitch on underneath this skirt." It didn't matter, it was a dream. She could go with erotic, she could be totally without inhibitions. She didn't want reality, she wanted Ryland.

His breath slammed out of his lungs. "Are you wet, Lily, hot and wet waiting for me? Because I'm as hard as a rock."

"I never would have guessed."

She was laughing at him, teasing him. The world would be bleak and cold without Ryland. It would be empty and the knowledge of betrayal would come creeping in to push a knife through her heart. "They have security cameras," she reminded, determined to stay with him within the framework they had set.

He dragged her to the relative privacy of a small enclosure housing three rare paintings by some artist he couldn't name. "We're in a dream so it doesn't matter, now does it?"

His mouth was hot and wild, deliberately dominating, demanding her response. She opened for him like a blossom, heat for heat, her tongue as demanding as his own. Breathing hard, he sat on the small bench, stretching out his legs to ease the bulge in his jeans as much to pull her between his thighs.

"What are you doing now?" Her breath caught in her throat, her entire body shivering in anticipation as his fingers circled her ankle and he began to slowly raise her skirt. Instantly she was hot and moist, her muscles clenching and throbbing. Hungry for him, hungry for him to fill her emptiness. The temperature of the room seemed to go up a hundred degrees. She waited, her body still, every nerve ending aware of his hand circling her bare ankle like an anklet.

Slowly he began to slide his palm up the contour of her leg, caressing the back of her knee, stroking her thighs. His legs urged her to a wider stance, exposing her more fully to him.

The slow revealing of her expanse of skin nearly caused an

explosion in his gut. It was like unveiling a masterpiece. Exquisite. Beautiful. For him alone. Moisture glistened in the dark curls of her triangle. He bent his head to taste her unique flavor. His tongue caressed her lightly, just a taste. Her body clenched, jumped. He took his time, his fingers stroking, memorizing every secret place. When she caught his shoulder in a tight grip, in a silent plea, he pushed two fingers into her tight sheath, in a long stroke that had her crying out.

He knew what they were doing was dangerous. They could be caught in a dream, lost forever together, but he couldn't have stopped if his life depended upon it and maybe it did. Ryland didn't know all that much about walking in dreams. The excitement, the sheer pleasure washed over him in such intense waves it was difficult to remember it wasn't wholly real. She was so beautiful wanting him. He loved the cloudy, sultry look on her face, the heat of her body as her muscles clenched tightly around his fingers. He loved the way she trusted him so completely even if she thought it only an erotic dream.

He pushed deep, insistently, long strokes so that she moved with him. Her body tightened, a hot, moist sheath for his fingers. He felt it coming, the beginnings of hard release, and he pulled his fingers away, dragged her to him and buried his tongue deep. Her climax was wild and he shared it, the rippling explosion, the hot liquid, the intensity of pleasure exploding in her body, in her mind.

Lily's legs were rubbery, shaking, fine tremors seizing her. She opened her eyes to look at him. His face was so perfect to her she brushed a caress over his scarred jaw. She could see the lines of strain. It wasn't difficult to see why. The bulge in his jeans was huge, as hard as a rock. She simply reached down and unzipped him so that he sprang free, erect, thick, engorged with need.

"Lily." It was a protest. A plea for mercy. "It's too risky. We can't, baby, not here." But it was already too late, she simply lifted her skirt and straddled him, right there on the bench while the eyes from the portraits stared at them with shock. Or maybe indulgence. "I'll never hold the bridge, never, not when you're distracting me," he told her, his hands at her waist to lift her away.

She settled over him slowly. It was torture. She was so hot, so wet, so tight he had to push his way into her velvet folds. A growl escaped him, a throaty note of pleasure/pain he couldn't stifle. Her muscles, still rippling from her orgasm, gripped and milked him as she began to move.

"Let them come, Ryland," she whispered wickedly, her blue eyes staring straight into his. "I don't care if they find us locked together. Do you know what it feels like to have you so deep inside me?"

Her words nearly shattered him. He knew what it was like to fill her, to stretch her. He knew what it was like to have her ride him, slick with hot heat, and he knew what it was like to thrust almost helplessly, violently into her, spearing her deeply. Over and over, hard and fast, uncaring that they might be locked forever in this dream. Nothing mattered at that moment except the sheer indulgence of each other's hunger.

The roaring started in his head. The fire flamed in his belly. Her muscles spiraled around him, her sheath so tight she milked him into an explosion so intense he couldn't muffle the yell torn from his throat. For a moment colors seemed to burst around him. He clung to her, breathing deeply, trying to regain some semblance of control. They clung together tightly, holding each other while their hearts tried to slow down, while their lungs tried to find air.

The low murmur of voices drifted to them. Late-night visitors to the museum. Intruders into their dreamworld. Lily reluctantly slipped off of him, felt his seed trickle down the inside of her thigh. How had visitors managed to invade their dream? She looked around, saw the sudden flashing light of the alarms. Blazing lights spilling around them, pointing an accusing finger at them. Two freaks of nature who no longer belonged in the world with others.

Ryland wanted to cling to her, hold her to him, sensing her grief rising as she began to slip away from him. His mouth was hard on hers, demanding. His hands moved over her body with loving caresses, with greedy eagerness, with trembling need. At the melding of their mouths, fireworks erupted around them, orange and red and white.

Lily could feel his muscles beneath her fingers, hear his heart slamming hard against her breast. The fireworks burst once more around her, into her, flashing red and white. The light was distracting, pulling her away from her erotic world of lovers and comfort and back to reality where the sand had shifted out from under her feet for all time. No matter how hard she clung to her dream, the light buzzed a warning insistently in her head, determinedly pulling her out of Ryland's arms and into the cold reality of the dormitory.

Lily looked around, slightly disoriented, with unfocused sight, blinking repeatedly to clear her vision. Red light was strobing into the room. Bursts of it coming and going as if shouting an alarm. She pushed herself up off the bed, shocked that her body was throbbing and burning, fully aroused, craving Ryland's possession. She did crave him, needed him. There was no point in lying to herself, but the intensity was shattering. She had felt his touch on her bare skin, felt his hand on her body, caressing her. She heard his soft cry of protest fading as she stumbled away from the bed. Away from the dream.

The red light was hurting her eyes and pushing needles into the walls of her mind. Bold red stripes of pain like the lash of a whip. She pushed into the outer room and hurried to find the controls for the cameras she knew would have been installed. Pressing a button instantly turned on the screen over her head. She saw her father's darkened office, saw the door was ajar despite the fact that she'd locked it. A shadowy figure moved through the room, opened and rifled through drawers at her father's desk.

The intruder was dressed in black and wore a mask over his face, hiding everything but his eyes which she couldn't see clearly in the darkness. Her heart in her throat, she watched as he examined the grandfather clock, then turned away from it to run his penlight over the titles of the books on the shelves. She watched the way he moved, no wasted motion, clearly a professional. He had entirely ignored the computer, as if he knew already it was useless to him. He completely ignored her father's day planner, still sitting neatly beside the computer.

He pulled a few books at random, rifling through the pages, then neatly returning each to the exact spot where he had pulled it. It made no sense to her that he would go through her father's office without really searching. What was he doing?

The intruder glanced at his watch and left the room, looking back once to make certain everything was in place. He closed the door softly and the empty room was all that was on the screen.

Lily felt her wrist, realized her communicator, the one Arly insisted she wear for emergencies, was on the nightstand by her bed where she'd dropped it in utter annoyance. For obvious reasons, there was no phone in her father's hidden laboratory so she hurried back up the stairs, wound the hand of the clock etched into the ceiling around nine times, leaving it pointing toward the Roman numeral IX and watched the trapdoor swing open.

The intruder had to have planted surveillance equipment and she had to find it before he got it online. She would need entry to the lab to study the documents. She couldn't have anyone looking over her shoulder all the time. Picking up the phone, she stabbed the button to ring Arly's room.

"I'm already on it, sweetie pie. He triggered a silent alarm when he went through the door of your father's office," Arly said without preamble. "Stay in your room while we round him up."

"I'm in my father's office and he's planted little bugs everywhere. So much for your extra men, Arly," Lily pointed out.

"Don't you move, Lily," he snapped, fear for her creeping into his voice. "Why the hell aren't you hiding under your bed like a normal woman would be?"

"Ask yourself how he got in when you have this place locked down, you chauvinistic smart aleck. And how did he manage to get through my father's locked office door? He would need prints, Arly. My father's prints. He got through three security systems and didn't know about the safeguard, but he knew about the others."

"You listen to me, Lily, lock that door and don't open it for anyone but me. I'll come for you when I know you're safe."

"I'm not exactly worried, Arly. You and Dad made certain I could protect myself. They may have gotten my father, but they won't find me such an easy target."

Arly swore at her before slamming down the phone. Lily didn't care. He was the security expert. He had access to enough money to install all the latest toys to stay ahead of everyone else, but still, someone had gained entrance to the

house and had bypassed the security to the office she had acti-
vated when she'd locked the door.

She was shaking with fury. She absolutely refused to be intimidated by an intruder to her home. She would not let them
shake her up or hide under her bed. She didn't know who was
the enemy or who was a friend, but she was going to find out
and make her home safe again.

Lily began searching for the bugs she knew the intruder had
dropped casually in her father's office. The drawers, the coffee
table. She retraced his steps, finding the books easily. Her brain
had recorded the pattern, random to him, but seen as a precise
configuration to her. There was an order to randomness she
could see clearly where others could not. She destroyed every
bug as she found it. Arly could make a sweep of the room later,
but she was certain she had found all of them.

She wanted the intruder caught and questioned. She wanted
the name of the traitor in her home. She wanted the name of the
conspirators in the Donovans Corporation and the military.
Lily's soft mouth firmed as she lined the remains of the expensive surveillance bugs across her father's desk.

Tell me, Lily. Talk to me. Open your mind to me.

You're too distracting. She didn't want to talk to him. She
couldn't talk to him. She was trying to cope with too many
things. When Ryland was in her mind or near her body, guilt
and white-hot heat were predominant, not cool logic. *My mind
is open enough for you to contact me whether I want it or not.*
She was shocked at how far away Ryland seemed, as if his
powers had faded.

*I find you crying, swamping me with grief, now something
else is very wrong. Damn it, I'm locked up like an animal in a
cage and I can't get to you. I used too much holding the bridge
between us. My head . . .*

Her heart jumped at the pain in his voice. She could hear the
note of sheer frustration. There was a raw edge to his voice, a
harsh implacable note that warned her he was becoming dangerous. She weighed her options. The last thing she wanted was
for Ryland Miller to try to reach her and overload. Their shared
erotic dream had drained him and pushing beyond his limit was
dangerous. Lily sat heavily in her father's chair.

It's nothing. An intruder. This place has security measures to rival Donovans yet a man got into the house.

There was a small silence while she felt some of the tension drain out of him. *You should have contacted me immediately.*

The reprimand irritated her as much as it frightened her. She did not want him getting the wrong idea about her, thinking she needed protection. Most of all she knew he needed rest. If he continued pushing their communication, he could easily overload. *I realize I've been broadcasting extreme emotion, but I hope you realize with my father's murder and the knowledge of the experiments he conducted and the sudden distressing and very uncomfortable physical attraction to you, I've been under duress. You are broadcasting anger and on the edge of control yet I know from being in your head you're a man with extreme control. Make certain you know that I'm a capable woman and very much able to take care of myself. I would hope you don't have the wrong idea about me.*

There was a long silence. Lily absently played with the small electronic pieces on the desk, turning them over and over, creating patterns while she waited. She found she was holding her breath waiting for his answer. Waiting for something she needed from him. The silence stretched for an eternity.

Distressing and uncomfortable physical attraction? Damn you for saying that, Lily. I am very aware you're way out of my class. You're smart and beautiful and so damn sexy I can't breathe when you're in the same room with me. I'm sorry if my needing to protect you bothers you in some way, but that's part of my personality. I'm rough around the edges, and I'm nothing to look at, but damn it all, I have a brain. I can see exactly what you are.

The knock on the door had Lily jumping out of the chair, her heart accelerating before she could prevent it. *I like the way you look, Ryland. I like just about everything about you.* Unfortunately that was the truth. She admired him and his need to protect those around him. She sighed. They didn't have time for a heart-to-heart. *Arly's here.*

Lily shouldn't have admitted it to him, but she loved the way he looked. Everything about him appealed to her and she didn't trust it. She didn't want the intensity of their chemistry, so explosive they could barely control themselves. It was utterly foreign to her nature. Had her father done something besides the despicable experiments he had conducted on young children and then on grown men? Had he decided to meddle with her life even more? Had he found a way to enhance physical attraction between two people?

No! Lily, I don't know what you found that was so devastating but whatever is between us is real.

You weren't born adept. You were enhanced.

The knock was louder this time, accompanied by muffled shouting. Lily sighed and moved toward the door. She was tired. Bone weary. She wanted to close her eyes and sleep forever. Dream forever but even that was lost to her if what she suspected was true.

But it's real now, Lily, I can't turn it off. I'll never be able to turn it off. If your father made you part of an experiment and it involves us both, we aren't going to be able to turn it off any more than I can stop the information flooding my brain.

I have to be sure, Ryland. My world has turned upside down. She coded the door and opened it for Arly. He was looking frantic, but recovered quickly, even scowling at her when she stood arching her eyebrow coolly at him in inquiry.

"We didn't get him." He held up his hand to prevent her protest. "He was good, Lily, I'm talking a major professional. I'd like to know how he knew the codes and what kind of systems we have. He was busy planting bugs and a camera or two in your private office."

She let her breath out slowly. "He knew the way to my office in a house with eighty rooms in it? Nobody knows where all the rooms are, not even me. How would a complete stranger have that information, Arly? He came straight to my father's office, planted bugs, and he does the same to my office. What does that tell us?" She tilted her head at him in challenge.

"That I'm not on top of the security and that you're in more danger than I suspected." Arly balled his fist and smacked his palm. "Damn it, Lily, someone has to be feeding them information. He knew the layout of the house and he was out of here like a damned ghost."

Lily stiffened. Could Ryland break through the security of her home? He was trained to walk in enemy camps unseen. Were there other GhostWalkers? Men she didn't know about, men working with her enemy? *Is that possible? Are there others?*

"I'm sorry, Lily, I thought the house was impenetrable."

"We have to look closely at the day staff, go over their backgrounds with a fine-tooth comb." *Is it possible, Ryland? Are there others?*

Arly shook his head. "Day staff wouldn't have the information on our security systems. They might be able to give the location of your office or Dr. Whitney's office, but they would never have the codes. And they wouldn't have Dr. Whitney's prints. That's a pro all the way, Lily, with big money behind him."

There could have been others. There were a few men they said they phased out, men who didn't meet the exact criteria. They could have been taken somewhere else.

Do you think they were?

God only knows. Ryland sounded utterly weary.

Lily silently cursed her father. She looked around for a chair to sit down. How could one man have done so much damage to so many people's lives? And how could she not have ever suspected?

"Lily?" Arly caught her arm and guided her to a chair. "You've gone pale. You're not going to faint on me or anything stupidly female like that, are you?"

Lily laughed softly, the sound bitter and distant. "Stupidly female, Arly? Where did Dad ever find a woman basher like you?"

"I don't bash women, I just don't understand them," he countered, hunkering down beside her chair, his fingers loosely circling her wrist, taking her pulse. "I'm brilliant and handsome and can talk circles around most guys and women shudder when they see me coming. Why is that?"

"Could be the way you curl your lip every time you say the word 'woman.'" Lily pulled her wrist away from him. "You've worked with Dad for years. I grew up with you, following you around . . ."

"Asking questions. Nobody asked as many questions as you." He grinned suddenly. She caught a brief glimpse of pride in his eyes. "I never had to tell you the same thing twice."

"Did you ever help with his experiments?"

At once Arly's face closed down, the smile fading. "You know I don't discuss any of your father's business, Lily."

"He's dead, Arly." She kept her gaze fixed steadily on his, watching for a reaction. "He's dead and you can't protect the things he's done."

"He's missing, Lily."

"You know he's dead and I think one of his projects got him killed." She leaned toward him. "You think it too."

Arly drew back. "Maybe, Lily, but what difference does it make? Your father knew people most of us hope we never meet in a lifetime. His mind was always working on ways to make the world a better place and in thinking that way, he managed to find the dregs of society. He thought it would help him understand how people worked."

"Did you like my father?" She asked it directly.

Arly sighed. "Lily, I've known your father for forty years."

"I know you have. Did you like him? As a person? As a man? Was he your friend?"

"I respected Peter. I respected him a great deal and I admired his mind. He had a great mind. He was a true genius. But no one was his friend, expect perhaps you. He didn't talk to people, he used them for sounding boards, but he couldn't be bothered knowing anyone. He used people to further his own interests—oh, not for monetary gain, he didn't need that, he already had enough money for a small country, but for his endless ideas. In all the years I knew him, I doubt he ever once asked me a personal question."

She lifted her chin. "Did you know he adopted me?"

Arly shrugged his thin shoulders. "Since I never saw him with a woman, I figured he had to have adopted you, but we never discussed it. If you weren't his biologically, he would have made damn sure you were his legally. The only thing he loved in his life was you, Lily."

"Did you know he had other children here?"

Arly looked uncomfortable. "That was years ago, Lily."

"And the men?" She took a stab in the dark, watched his reactions closely.

Arly held up his hand. "Anything to do with the military I don't see or hear. That's just the way it is, Lily."

"This is important, Arly, or I wouldn't ask. I think whatever this project he was working on at Donovans, something for the military, got out of hand and someone killed him for information he wouldn't turn over. I'm being asked to take over that project and find the missing information. I need to have all the pieces of the puzzle. Were there men here recently? Men he may have been working with?"

Arly stood up, paced across the room. "I've kept this job and my home here for over thirty years because I knew how to keep my mouth shut."

"Arly," Lily said softly, "my father's dead. Either your loyalty swings to me and you're working for me and you're a part of my family and my household or you're not. This is information I need in order to stay alive. You'll have to make up your mind which it's going to be."

"My loyalty swung to you the moment I laid eyes on you." He said it stiffly.

"Help me then. I intend to find out what's going on and who murdered my father."

"Let the police handle it, Lily. They'll find a lead eventually."

"Did he bring men to this place? Military men? And did they stay here for any length of time?" Lily's gaze was steady on her security man's face, not allowing him to look away from her.

Arly took a deep breath. "I was certain he brought three gentlemen in and I know they didn't leave that same day. I never saw them again, and I never saw them leave. He didn't take them to his office, but up to the second-story rooms in the west wing."

"Are you in my employ or that of the United States government?"

"Damn it, Lily, how can you ask me that?"

"I am asking you, Arly." Deliberately Lily reached out to take his hand, settling her fingers around his wrist. Lightly. Yet her fingers found his lifeline, searched for his emotions. Searched for the truth in him.

Arly instinctively attempted to pull away from her but she tightened her fingers.

She reached for Ryland. *Can you read him?*

No. I have no ability to do that, not even with you enhancing his emotions for me. He would have to be in the room, touching me, or me touching something of his to tune him in so clearly. Be careful, Lily, he's going to know you're acting out of character.

"I don't work for the government." There was heat in Arly's voice.

"Do you work for the Donovans Corporation?" Lily pursued.

Arly did jerk his arm away and stumbled backward, nearly tipping over. "What the hell's wrong with you? Do you blame me for this? Maybe it is my fault, maybe your father's disappearance is my fault too. I let him drive that old beat-up car he loved so much when I knew he could be a target of any number of whackos."

Lily dropped her head in her hands. "I'm sorry, Arly, I really am. Everything in my life is off-kilter right now. I don't blame you for Dad. No one could have made him stop driving his car. He loved that old thing. He just didn't see himself as rich or famous or working for something others might take exception to. You know that. It wasn't your fault any more than it was mine. But someone in this house is leaking information and we have to find out who it is."

Arly sat on the floor and regarded her with steady eyes. "It isn't me, Lily. You're the only family I have. You're it. Without you, I'm completely alone in the world."

"Do you know why my father brought me here?"

"I imagine he wanted an heir." He waved his hand at the huge house. "He needed to leave it all to someone."

She forced a smile. "I guess he did."

"You look tired, Lily, go to bed. I've reported the break-in and I'll handle the police. There's no need for you to talk with them."

"Arly, I want complete control of the east wing of the house. All the rooms on every story of that wing. I want security on the outside but not a single camera or motion detector on the inside. I want complete privacy. One place I can go where I have absolute privacy after I lock it down. And I don't want anyone else to know. You handle the work yourself."

He nodded slowly. "Will you at least consider a bodyguard?"

"I'll think about it," she promised.

"And wear the transmitter. I went to the trouble of putting it into your watch, the least you can do is wear it." Arly hesitated then took a deep breath. "There's an underground tunnel below the basement levels. It runs beneath the estate and leads to two separate entrances. Your father used the tunnels to bring in people he didn't want you or the staff to see."

"I should have suspected something like that. Thank you, Arly. Will you show me the tunnels?"

He nodded reluctantly. "I'll take you there after the police leave."

SIX

RYLAND was waiting, his mercury-colored eyes hot with emotion. The moment her gaze clashed with his, the memory of his mouth crushing hers rose up to taunt her. Her body instantly grew hot and uncomfortable. Became soft and responsive. Her breath caught in her lungs and she tasted him. Felt him. She felt him deep inside her, filling her, a part of her.

Stop it, Ryland.

He was angry with her. She had cut herself off from him. He had been unable to reach her even in her sleep. Ryland had resolved to let her know just what he thought of her behavior, but the moment he saw her he changed his mind. He detested seeing the dark circles under her eyes, shadows that hadn't been there before. She was suffering and he wasn't about to add to it. Forcing down the tidal wave of emotion he spoke softly. *It isn't me. I swear to you, I don't do this.*

Yes, you do. You have a . . . vivid imagination and you broadcast very loudly.

He saw it then, her need to push him away from her. He had thought it would be the erotic dream they shared, embarrassment or shyness with him. He could get around that. Persuade her. Tempt her. But Lily couldn't believe in him because she couldn't believe in anyone. Whitney had done that to her. Damn the man for leaving her with nothing. "Lily." He said her name gently. Enticing her. Coaxing her. "Thank you for coming when I know it's so difficult for you right now."

Her blue eyes widened. It was nice to see shock instead of wariness. Ryland tried a smile. "Come here, talk to me."

Lily stared up into his face, studied his feathery lashes, his strong jaw, the black hair spilling across his forehead. His strict military cut was long gone, replaced with shaggy unruly waves that left him immensely attractive. *I do need to talk to you, but not like this. I need to arrange it so we can go someplace where the recorders and cameras won't pick us up.*

His cool gray eyes rested thoughtfully on her face. Lily looked away from him, faint color stealing into her cheeks in spite of her determination to appear serene. She had dreamt of this man. Hot, steamy dreams of sinful sex and passionate responses. She hadn't been alone in that dream. Ryland had somehow been with her, sharing her every fantasy, touching her, kissing her. She closed her eyes, remembering how she had straddled him wildly, without inhibition. It had been a dream. She had needed to escape and she threw herself into it with everything she was. And he knew it.

"Lily, it was beautiful."

"I'm not discussing it."

Ryland let it go because she didn't need to be uncomfortable. The moment he'd laid eyes on her, he knew she was the woman born for him. She might not know it, but it didn't matter. He did, and he was relentless once set on a path. *I can shut down the cameras and recorders. I've been doing it for a while, on and off, at first for the practice, now to get them complacent about it. They're used to it enough now they don't come by right away to check on me. You don't want to talk with me this way.*

She didn't. It was too intimate and she didn't trust the intensity of what they shared. She feared every time they spoke telepathically, it strengthened the bond. But more than that, she feared for his health. She could feel his constant pain, felt the drain on his strength. And she had no idea of the consequences of prolonged use of a telepathic connection. If he could remove the threat of the cameras, it was better for them. Better for him. The desire to keep him from harm bordered on obsession. And she couldn't trust that someone else might not be listening.

Lily looked up at Ryland, drowning in the stark need in his eyes. No one had told her it would be like this, a wild craving that crawled over her skin, heated her blood, and created hunger so deep, so elemental she could hardly bear being separated from him.

She turned away from him, unable to continue looking at his face. He would know, he could read her easily. The chemistry between them was storming out of control. Sometimes she was afraid if he were out from behind the bars, she would do anything with him, right there, cameras or not.

"Stop it," his voice was husky, a raw ache in it. "I can't move, not a step. Now you're the one projecting. You're messing me up until I can't think straight."

"I'm sorry," she whispered the words, knew he could hear her. She didn't turn around, keeping her face averted. "You haven't slept in days, would you like something to help you?"

"You know why I can't sleep. You can't sleep either. Damn it, you're afraid to sleep." His tone was pitched so low it smoldered. It played over her skin, seeped into her pores, stroked her body so that every cell was alive with a hunger that was edgy and needful. *When I sleep I dream of you. Of your body beneath mine. Of my body deep inside yours.*

She knew he dreamt of her, of their bodies tangled together. She shared his erotic dream, his wild fantasies she couldn't hope to match in reality. "It's a complication we didn't expect." She cleared her voice, it was hoarse and unfamiliar. "That's all it is, Ryland. We can get past it if we're disciplined enough."

"Look at me."

Lily lifted her gaze to his. She couldn't stop herself from crossing the distance to his side. His hands found hers through the bars even as she felt the heightened awareness of energy, his outpouring to interfere with the equipment.

"What is it, baby?" He moved beside her, silent, calm, his larger, heavily muscled body brushing against hers protectively right through the iron bars. "Talk to me. Tell me what you found."

Lily listened to the sound of the ocean, in the background, the water soothing, even though the waves sounded angry. She imagined them rushing toward the shore, crashing against the rocks. Foam gushing into the air, spraying white water high.

She wished she could roar like the waves, escape out onto the wide raging sea with her wild emotions, not just listen to a tape being played.

"I was an experiment, Ryland." She said the words so low he had to strain to catch them. "That's what I was to him. An experiment, not his daughter." She tasted the bitterness of betrayal as she spoke the words out loud, her world crashing around her.

He remained silent, holding her through the bars, feeling the pain in her like a living, breathing entity. Ryland didn't want to say or do the wrong thing. Lily was close to shattering like glass, so he stayed silent.

Lily took a deep, calming breath, let it out slowly. "I found his secret laboratory. Everything was there. Videotapes of me, of other children. A room where he kept us, where we ate and slept and did his tests. I had a very regimented diet, all the best nutrition, watched only educational tapes. I was given only educational material to read. Every game was designed to strengthen my psychic abilities and further my education." She pushed an unsteady hand through her hair. "I didn't know any of it, he never let on, not once. I never suspected, I really didn't."

Ryland desperately wanted to take her into his arms and shield her from every hurt. He silently cursed the bars between them. This was the biggest blow Lily could have suffered. Peter Whitney had been her father, best friend, and mentor. Ryland leaned closer, rubbed his jaw along the top of her head so that her hair caught in the stubble of his shadow. It was a small caress, a gesture of affection, or tenderness.

Lily was grateful he remained silent. She wasn't certain she could have told him everything if he had protested or sympathized. Her faith and trust were shaken. The foundation that had been her world was cracked. "He said . . ." Her voice wobbled, trembled and broke.

Ryland's heart broke right along with her voice. He found he was gripping her hand far too tightly and made an effort to ease his strength. She didn't seem to notice. She cleared her throat and tried again.

"He tried the enhancement of psychic ability first on orphans. He tested young female children from countries where orphans were plentiful and neglected. He had the money and the connections and he brought the ones into the country he thought would suit his needs. I was one of them. No last name, just Lily. The female subjects"—she cleared her throat—"that's me, Ryland, a female subject. We were taken directly to his underground laboratory. We were tested and trained every day much like the regimen you were put through."

She did look at him then. Her eyes swam with tears. Before she could blink them away, Ryland bent his head to hers and took them with his mouth. Tasting her tears. Kissing her eyelids gently. Tenderly. Lily blinked up at him, confusion in her gaze.

"Tell me the rest of it, get it out, Lily."

She lifted her head to study his face, her blue eyes so grief-stricken he felt sick. But something in his steady gaze must have reassured her. Lily took a breath and continued. "He felt the other girls and I were unwanted anyway and he was providing a decent home, medical care, and food. It was more than we had where he found us, that's how he excused his behavior. He couldn't be bothered with our names, so he called us flowers and seasons and things like Rain and Storm." She tore her hand from Ryland's, knotting her fist against her trembling mouth. "We were nothing at all to him. No more than rats in a lab."

There was a small silence while they stared at one another. "Like me. Like my men. He repeated the experiment on us."

Lily nodded slowly, paced away from the cage and back to him, a restless anger growing. Ryland watched the shadows chasing across her pale face as she paced back and forth, unable to remain still, and his heart went out to her. She was fighting back in the only way she knew how, with her brain, thinking things through logically.

"And the worst of it is, all the same problems he had here, with you, he already knew about with us. My God, Ryland, he just sent those little girls out there, unprotected, unwanted, when they became too much trouble."

Her voice was so low he could barely hear her. She was too ashamed, as if she were to blame for what her father had done.

Ryland reached through the bars of his cage, tried to catch her arm, to pull her to him, but she was already pacing away, withdrawn, pulling her emotions in close.

"I never saw his data, Ryland, I never had a chance to really know how he did it. What he did was pure genius—wrong, but nevertheless genius. He noticed the older antidepressants like amitriptyline decreased psychic ability, while the newer serotonin reuptake inhibitors were either neutral or they enhanced it. Dad was able to do a postmortem study on a clairvoyant. The subject demonstrated a sevenfold increase in serotonin receptors in hippocampal and amygdala tissue, compared to controls."

"You're losing me."

She waved a dismissing hand, not looking at him, still pacing. "Parts of the brain. Never mind, just listen. Moreover, it was a receptor subtype with completely new binding characteristics. He sequenced the protein, found the associated gene, cloned it, and inserted the gene and expanded it in a cultured cell line. He elucidated the protein structure with computer modeling and then modified an existing serotonin reuptake inhibitor to have high specificity for the newly discovered ligand. The tricky part was to keep the molecule lipid soluble, so it would cross the blood-brain barrier. Presto! Suddenly the radio was tuned to the right station."

"Baby, I'm not understanding a word you're saying." Lily didn't realize it, but she had shifted from hurt daughter to interested scientist. "Can you speak English for me?"

Lily continued to pace, quick, agitated movements betraying her inner turmoil; she was speaking more to herself than to him. "Not all subjects had the same abilities. Like a poorly performing weight lifter, the answer was more drugs. Using a threefold program of training was a stroke of brilliance. Each separate avenue provided a way to enhance the natural abilities. And he used pulses of electricity, much like they've tried with Parkinson's disease in the hopes that it would stimulate more activity. But the little girls all began to fall apart, on sensory overload. He found there were a few anchors in the mix and all the other girls gravitated toward them. He thought it was their young ages. They began to have severe emotional and physical problems. Seizures causing brain bleeds, hysteria, night terrors, symptoms associated with severe trauma. I think the pulsing electricity probably caused the brain bleeds, but I'll have to study it further. They were just children. *We* were just children."

She turned away from Ryland, crossing her arms across her breasts. "He turned off the natural filters and then abandoned them all. I was a subject. He called me that. Subject Lily."

Staring away from him toward the computer, she looked desolate. "He realized the girls were going to overload, burn out, so he hastily found them families, came up with some plausible explanation for their problems, and turned his back on them. He kept me because I was an anchor and he hoped to use me again." She turned her head then, her blue eyes cloudy with pain. "And he did."

"Lily." Her name was an ache between them. Her beautiful name, so much like her, pure and perfect and elegant. He wanted to strangle her father with his bare hands. Ryland knew there was much more to it. Peter Whitney was a scientist driven to achieve. He wasn't a man who would deliberately hurt another human being, but he was ruthless in his methods. Ryland could see him "purchasing" the little orphan children from a country that didn't want them anyway. He had the money and the connections.

"When he decided to try again, he used grown men, already well disciplined." She looked at him. "I don't even know my real name."

Ryland managed to catch her shirtsleeve and reel her in. He pulled her against the bars, close to him, slipping his arms around her, unable to stop himself. She was stiff and resistant, but he tucked her beneath the shelter of his shoulder, close to his heart where she belonged. "Your name is Lily Whitney. You are the woman I want at my side night and day. I want you to be the mother of my children someday. I want you for my lover. I want you for the person I turn to when the world gets to be too much."

She made a soft sound of protest, a cry deep in her throat, and tried to turn away from him, but he caught her face with his hands, bent over her protectively, instinctively shielding her from the camera, even though it was not functioning. "I know you can't hear me when I say this right now, but you were Peter's world. He was a man without laughter or love, driven by his brain's need to learn more. I saw the way he looked at you. He loved you; he may not have started out that way, but he grew to love you. He may not have brought you into his life for the right reasons, but he kept you because he loved you. He couldn't bear to part with you. You made him know what love was." Ryland would have said anything to take away her pain, but as he uttered the words, he felt they were true.

She shook her head in denial, not daring to believe him because if he were wrong it would be another knife through her heart. "You can't know that."

His gray eyes glittered with truth. "I do know. Remember what he said to you? He wanted you to find the others and make it right. He was talking about those other girls. He knew what he did was wrong and he attempted to make up for it, finding the children homes, setting up trust funds for them. It was wrong, Lily, but he didn't operate on the same kind of wavelength as the rest of us." He had caught the rest of her father's intentions in her mind and used the knowledge shamelessly.

She waved her hand toward the surface. "They're out there somewhere. He poked in their brains, turned something on they can't turn off, stripped away every natural filter they had; he left us all to fend for ourselves." She looked up at him. "Higgens and the people here can never know about the girls. If they find them, they'll use them—then kill them."

"You have to destroy the tapes," Ryland said. "There's no other way to protect everybody, Lily, to protect others in the future. Your father knew that or he wouldn't have asked you to destroy his data. They couldn't pull any information off his hard drives. He made certain he never recorded anything of use where they could get to it."

"Those tapes are the only things I have that might give me a clue as to how to reverse the process, Ryland. If I get rid of them, there's no going back."

"We already knew that, honey. Peter knew it too. He repeated his experiment, a little more refined, with older, much more disciplined subjects, but the end result was still the same. Breakdowns, seizures, trauma. Sensory overload."

"I have to view them all. I can't take a chance on missing any of the details. I have a photographic memory. What I read or view, I'll remember. It's going to take time. My father was suspicious over at least two deaths, Ryland, and I'm worried about you and the men. He wanted you out of here, enough to ask me to help. After reading his report, I think he might have had reason to worry. I agree with him that you and the others aren't safe here. There are records of phone calls from my father to several military officials, yet no one pulled the plug on Higgens. I have no idea how far up the chain of command the stink goes. That's your department. You have to figure out who you can trust. I'll try to feel out General Ranier, but I haven't been able to reach him. He's been a family friend since I was a child."

He nodded, his gray eyes intent on her face. "Lily, we have to talk about last night. We can't pretend it didn't happen."

Lily shook her head. He wanted her to believe he could fall in love with her when he didn't even know her. They didn't know anything about one another. He thought it would reassure her that in some way she was lovable, but it only reinforced her belief that her father had enhanced the chemistry between them.

Ryland Miller and his men needed sanctuary. She could not distance herself from him when he needed her so much. "Arly, who's head of my security, showed me two entrances to tunnels that lead through the property to my home. My father used them when he didn't want anyone in the house to see people he brought in."

"Are you certain you can trust this man?"

Lily shrugged. "I gave up being certain of anything, Ryland. I can only hope he's on my side. The entire east wing of my house will be set up to keep you and the men hidden. There's something like fifteen rooms along with my suite of rooms and the wing is entirely self-contained. Arly is filtering in supplies and you can use the house as a base, but there are patrols and security cameras inside and out. I'll give you the codes you need to get in."

"Thank you, Lily." His heart swelled with pride in her. Damn, but she was courageous and willing to put herself on the line for his men. For him.

"I believe Higgens is going to arrange for more accidents and I think he has a GhostWalker or two of his own, unless one of your men is working with him. In which case, your escape isn't going to work."

"My men are not traitors." He made it a statement.

"I would never have believed someone in my household would betray my father but someone did. I would never have thought someone here at Donovans would help murder my father, but they have. And I would never have thought my father would have taken a child from an orphanage and experimented on her, but he did. Don't count too heavily on loyalty, Ryland, you'll get your heart handed to you."

He was silent, feeling the waves of sorrow and shame wash over her.

"I've already visited your other men on the pretense of asking their cooperation in further testing. I couldn't find Russell Cowlings. According to the log he had a seizure over a week ago and was rushed to the medical unit. I checked with the hospital and they signed him out to transport by medical helicopter within twenty minutes of receiving him. That doesn't wash. If he were that unstable they would have needed time before they sent him off. I'm trying to track him down, but I'm afraid he's lost. Nobody seems to have the paperwork on him. I put in a call to Higgens but he hasn't returned it."

"Damn it, Lily." Ryland hung his head, his fists clenched at his sides. "Russell's a good man. This isn't right."

"No, it's not," she agreed. "None of it is right."

"Lily . . ." Her blue eyes drifted over his face, stopping his words before he could say them.

She shook her head. "I don't want whatever happened between us to go any further. It's not right and I'll never trust it. You don't know me, how could you possibly think you could love me? I don't know myself. We haven't even talked."

"I've walked in your mind. I know what kind of woman you are. I know exactly who you are, Lily, even if you think I don't. I see what you've done, what you are doing for us. That's extraordinary, whether you want to think so or not." He had her wrist again, his thumb sliding back and forth in small caresses over her sensitive inner wrist. His eyes on hers, he brought her hand to his mouth, his tongue tasting her skin.

"You don't play fair at all, Ryland."

His smile actually climbed to his eyes, a brief flash that fanned an ember deep inside her into sizzling fire. "It isn't a game to me, Lily. I saw you. I knew you were meant to be mine the moment I laid eyes on you. It doesn't matter that we're in the middle of all this bullshit. You're forever. You're real." As he reluctantly released her wrist, she backed away from the bars, cradling her hand close to her body. Her knuckles throbbed and burned, branded for all time by the brief, searing contact with his mouth.

"And if you think you're perfectly safe," he continued, "remember, the cameras aren't working."

"I'm sorry," she whispered the words, knew he could hear her. She didn't turn around, keeping her face averted. It was humiliating to know she couldn't control the wild flares of desire she felt each time she was near him. Lily had always been in control, now she felt confused and off-center.

"Look at me."

Lily shook her head silently.

"You're a little coward, aren't you?" he taunted.

She did turn then, her eyes flashing sparks at him, her shoulders straight. "You'd better pray I'm not a coward or you don't have a chance, now do you?"

He swore, his hands curling into fists at his sides. He forced air through his lungs, tamped down his frustration, and focused on her. She was always so professional, and it annoyed the hell out of him. He wanted her in the worst way, *craved* her. And the shared dreams hadn't helped. It only left him wanting more.

Needing her had eaten at him day and night since he'd first met her, crawled through his body until he knew the meaning of the word "obsession." Every fantasy he had ever had, he wanted to share with her. "I'm sorry, Lily. You're not the one in this cage. My body's one hard pain and my mind is roaring at me. Jackhammers are ripping at my head."

Lily heard the stark truth in his voice and hurried over to the cage to look at him closely. "My God! Ryland!"

It was too late to protect her. He had kept up the barriers as best he could in his weakened condition. But he couldn't help trying to protect her. She was an enhancer, an amplifier, as was he. She felt his pain and echoed it back tenfold. He gripped the bars of his prison so hard his knuckles turned white.

"Why didn't you let me see this?" She stilled in sudden comprehension. "Last night. Holding the bridge between us, you were doing that alone." Her hand slid through the bars, trailed fingers over his face in a gentle caress. "Ryland, you can't put yourself in jeopardy for me. The voices I was hearing, that was you checking on the men. You're using your talents too much. You have to rest, think about yourself."

He trapped her hand against his mouth. "I'll rest when they're safe. I talked most of them into this experiment. I could always do things, things other people couldn't. I wanted to do more. I'd like to blame Dr. Whitney, your father. But I thought it was a brilliant idea. I liked being able to walk into the camp of an enemy and 'suggest' the guard look the other way and have him do it. The team, we were invincible together."

The pain was real, shards of glass stabbing deep into his brain. His pulse was too fast and small beads of sweat stood out on his brow. "Ryland, I would order you medication to sleep but I'm afraid of what they're doing. I can get you something myself but it will take a little time. You need to rest and let your brain relax."

He shook his head. "I won't take medication. Just get me the hell out of here, Lily. I can rest when I'm safe with you."

He made it sound so intimate. Lily couldn't force a protest. Ryland had given so much energy to her. To his men. He thought of everybody but himself.

He smiled at her, a brief flash of his cocky confidence. "I was thinking of myself last night, Lily, not just you."

The color rose in spite of her determination to ignore his every reference to their night. "The guards are probably worried about me since it's been a while. You should conserve your energy and stop disrupting the security. Where is your family, Ryland?" She could only distract him.

He allowed her hands to slip off of him only because he needed to sit down. Ryland made his way to the bed and stretched out, closing his eyes so the dim light couldn't pierce his brain. "My mother raised me alone, Lily. You know the story. Unwed teenage mother without prospects." There was a smile in his voice that told her he adored his mother. "She didn't believe in living by other people's rules, though. She had me in spite of everyone telling her to get rid of me, and finished high school at night. She worked and took one class at a time until she got through junior college."

"She sounds impressive." Lily sat in a chair near his cage as the computer blinked and the monitors came to life, signaling Ryland had given up shutting them down.

"You would have liked her," he confirmed. "We lived in this old beat-up trailer, in the middle of a cruddy park. Our house was the cleanest trailer on the lot. There were all these flowers and bushes around our place. She knew the name of every flower in the garden and she made me pull all the weeds." Ryland rubbed his forehead with the heel of his hand. "Well, she pulled weeds with me. She believed in talking things out."

A small, reluctant smile tugged at the corners of Lily's mouth. "Is there a lesson in this I'm about to hear?"

"Probably. I was getting to it."

"I'll just bet you were." Lily lifted an eyebrow at the guard as he rushed in. "Is there some reason you're disturbing us while we're talking?"

Her voice was ultracool. Ryland couldn't help but admire how confident she appeared, dismissing the guard with her haughty tone. Her face was completely expressionless as her disinterested gaze drifted over the intruder. Ryland was pleased that she appeared an ice princess to everyone else but burned like fire for him.

The guard cleared his throat, visibly squirming. "I'm sorry, Dr. Whitney, the microphones are fried, the security cameras weren't working, and—"

"They often don't work," she interrupted. "I see no reason to break a cardinal rule and enter a laboratory while I'm conducting a private interview, do you?"

"No, ma'am" The guard hurried from the room.

"You're supposed to be resting," Lily reprimanded Ryland.

"I am resting," he said piously.

"You're broadcasting blatant sexual interest."

"Am I?" He turned his head to grin at her. "I've been thinking about that. I don't think it's me at all."

"Really?"

He started to shake his head and thought better of it. "Yes, I've been giving it quite a bit of thought. Kaden's an enhancer, but when he walks into the room I certainly don't have this obsessive sexual attraction toward him."

Lily choked back a laugh. Ryland felt the sound all the way to his toes. Her voice alone could touch him. He smiled in spite of his pounding head. "Think about it, Lily. You're the one generating all the sexual feelings toward me and, you being an enhancer, the feelings are especially strong." He did his best to sound innocent.

"You have burst a few brain cells, haven't you? You aren't a very good liar, Ryland. I'll bet you never got away with a single thing when you were a little boy." For some reason the thought of him as a curly-headed boy melted her heart.

Ryland laughed softly at the memories. "It had nothing to do with my ability to lie. My mother had eyes in the back of her head. She knew everything. I don't know how, she just did. She knew I was going to do something before I did it."

Lily laughed aloud, the sound playing along his body like the touch of caressing fingers. "You probably confessed all and didn't even know you were doing it."

"Probably. She had a real thing about education. I didn't dare slack off in school. I could get away with the messy room occasionally and forgetting to do my chores to play sports with my friends, but I didn't ever miss a single homework assignment. She checked every one and insisted I read books every evening with her."

"What kind of books?"

"We read all the classics. She had a voice that brought the story alive. I loved to listen to her read. It was better than television any day. Of course, I didn't let on, I groused a lot so she'd think I was doing her favors by reading with her." There was a shadow of regret in his voice.

"She knew," Lily said firmly.

"Yeah, I guess she did. She always knew."

Lily blinked back tears. "What happened to her?"

There was a small silence. "I surprised her with a visit and she decided she had to make me one of her famous dinners. We drove to the grocery store. A drunk driver ran a red light and hit us. I survived but she didn't."

"I'm so sorry, Ryland. She sounds like she must have been extraordinary. I would love to have met her."

"I miss her. She always had a way of saying the right thing at exactly the moment it needed to be said." Like Lily. He was beginning to think Lily shared that same trait.

"Do you think she was a natural adept?"

"A psychic? Maybe. She knew things. But mostly she was just a wonderful mother. She told me she took classes and read books to find out how to raise a kid." Amusement tinged his voice. "Apparently I didn't react like the kids in the books."

"I'll bet you didn't." Lily wanted to hold and comfort him. She could feel his aching loneliness and it ate at her. She smothered a groan. It didn't seem to matter how reasonable her arguments were, the attraction to Ryland only grew in his company. The need to see him happy and healthy was fast becoming essential to her own happiness.

"I gave her a lot of trouble," he admitted. "I was always fighting."

"Why does that not surprise me?" She lifted an eyebrow at him, but it was the small smile hovering along the curve of her mouth that caught his attention.

He sat on the edge of his bed, raked both hands through his hair. "Living where we did, we were fair game for comments. Both Mom and me. I was kid enough to think I had to defend us, to take care of us."

"You still are like that," she pointed out. "It's a rather charming trait." She sighed with regret, knowing time was slipping away from her. She enjoyed his company, enjoyed talking with him. "I have to go, Ryland. I have so much work to do on other things. I'll be back before I leave for the night to check on you."

"No, Lily, just take off." His gray gaze was steady on hers. He stood up, fatigue in every muscle of his body. He walked over to the bars, even though each step seemed to drive spikes through his head.

She sucked in her breath audibly. "Maybe you should wait."

"I can't afford to take the chance, Lily. Clear out and stay clear."

She nodded, a small frown touching her mouth. Her profile was to him, she was deep in thought, and Ryland took the opportunity to allow himself the luxury of drinking in her voluptuous figure. There were no hard angles on Lily, she was all feminine curves. Her white coat was thrown over her clothes carelessly, moving when she moved, giving intriguing glances of generous breasts. When she walked, the material of her slacks stretched across her round bottom, drawing his attention. Her body was a blatant temptation he couldn't think about too much, without going up in flames. He would have her. She would walk beside him, lie beneath him, come alive, come apart in his arms. She was his match in every way, she just hadn't accepted it yet.

"You're doing it again, Captain," she reminded, a gentle reprimand, the color flaring under her pale skin.

His hands curled around the bars of his cage, his palms itching to see if her skin was as soft as it looked. "Not yet, I'm not, Lily." He said the words beneath his breath, uncaring if she heard or not.

She stood there looking helpless for a moment, completely out of character. "Don't let anything happen to you," she whispered before she turned and left him there alone with his pain and his guilt and the cage holding him prisoner.

SEVEN

THE night was unexpectedly cold. Lily shivered as she looked up at the thin crescent shape of the moon. Dark clouds swirled across the sky, dulling the sparkling stars scattered above her. The wind tugged at her clothes and whipped strands of hair into her face and eyes. Threads of white fog whirled in small eddies, curling through the heavy wire of the fences, reaching toward her like ragged claws. She could smell the storm coming in off the sea.

"Dr. Whitney! I thought you'd gone home for the night." A tall guard emerged out of the shadows. He was one of the older, much more experienced men. Looking at him closely, she wondered if he were military.

She feigned fright, jumping as if startled. "You scared me, I didn't hear you."

"What are you doing out here?" There was a trace of worry in his voice. She wasn't wearing a jacket.

Lily shivered in the icy wind. "Breathing," she answered simply. "Wondering whether to go home and get some sleep or go back and work so I don't have to face my father not being there." She raked her fingers through her thick hair.

"It's cold out here, Dr. Whitney. I'll walk you to your car." The note of concern caused tears to burn behind her eyes, to clog her throat. Grief welled up, sharp and clear and strong. She had shoved sorrow and the knowledge of her father's death aside all day, held it at bay with work, all the while meticulously planning the aftermath of the escape. Guilt fed her stormy emotions. If anyone should be harmed in the escape it would fall directly on her shoulders. Peter Whitney had told her what he wanted, what his last wishes were, but ultimately, it was her responsibility.

There had already been enough mistakes made by the Whitneys, and she was uncertain whether she was doing more harm than good. What if the men couldn't survive outside the conditions of the laboratory? Their escape would give Higgens the excuse needed to carry out any plan he had to terminate any who opposed him. It would brand any in the military as a deserter.

"Dr. Whitney?" The guard took her arm.

"I'm sorry, I'm all right, thank you." Lily was uncertain whether she would ever be all right again. "My car is in the parking lot over by the first guard tower. You don't have to walk me, I'm fine, really."

"I was heading that way myself," he told her, urging her in the direction she'd indicated, his larger body between her and the wind.

As they walked, something inside of her went very still. Knowledge blossomed, flared into full life. She felt the movements, the presence of the others in the night. Chameleons—GhostWalkers, they called themselves—phantoms moving, blending with any terrain, at home in the dark, in the water, in the jungle and trees. They were shadows within the shadows, able to control their heart and lungs, able to walk among the enemy unseen. Lily felt them, the vibration of power they wielded, as they moved through the high-security compound, keeping the guards looking the other way with the sheer force of their minds.

The plan had been for Lily to be far away from the area, her alibi indisputable, but she had lingered, drawn by guilt and fear. It was difficult to break *into* the facility, but much easier to break out. Ryland Miller and each of his men had psychic abilities to varying degrees. She knew Ryland had planned to lure Colonel Higgens to his cell so suspicion would fall directly on the colonel as the last man to be with him just before Ryland was able to escape. Ryland would free the others. The men would find safety in numbers at first, allowing their various skills to benefit everyone, but once out of the compound, it was far safer to scatter, going in twos or singly to their ultimate destination—her home.

She allowed her gaze to slide casually along the deeper edges of the buildings, the towers and equipment in the compound. Her chest was unexpectedly tight. She couldn't spot them, but she *felt* them. They were moving through the high-security compound like the phantoms they called themselves. A dog barked somewhere to her left, set her heart pounding. The animal stopped abruptly as if silenced by a command. Her guard tightened his hold on her arm, suddenly uneasy.

He swung his head in the direction of the dog. Lily stumbled, distracting him. "I'm sorry," she sounded more breathless than she intended as he caught her, preventing her from falling. "It's dark out tonight. The storm is coming in faster than anticipated."

"It's supposed to be a bad one. You should get home before it hits," he advised. "The gusts could reach a hundred miles an hour and your car is small."

She had purposely refused the limousine, knowing every car would eventually come under suspicion and a limousine could easily transport several escapees outside the compound.

The guard's concern was nearly her undoing. She was wound much tighter than she realized, grief for her father swirling close to the surface, threatening to spill over. Distress for the knowledge she had been part of her father's scientific experiments. Guilt for the escape battering her conscience. Fear that someone would be hurt or killed gnawed at her until she was afraid she might scream. Tears shimmered in her eyes, blurred her vision. Were the lives of the men going to be any better on the outside where no one protected them? She had to tell herself at least they were safe from deliberate harm.

"You're shaking, Dr. Whitney," the guard observed. "Maybe you should go back inside and spend the night here." He stopped in the middle of the yard, bringing her to a halt beside him.

Lily forced a bright note into her voice. "I'm fine, just a little shaken up. I've had weeks to get used to my father's disappearance, but the thought of facing an empty house in the middle of a storm is daunting. We always talked together. Now there's just silence."

Without warning, lightning burst across the sky. The flare instantly lit the compound and surrounding area with a white-hot spotlight. To Lily's horror, the flash illuminated the dark shape of a man only feet away from them. His eyes were fixed on them. Focused. Steady. The eyes of a predator. His hand moved and she caught the glint of a knife. *Kaden.* She recognized him instantly. He was one of the stronger talents.

Lily threw her body between the phantom and the guard, knocking into the guard so that they both went down in a tangle of arms and legs. The flash of light was gone, leaving them trapped and vulnerable in the darkness. They both hit the ground hard, Lily bumping her head hard enough that a soft cry escaped. The guard swore, rolling to his feet, reaching to bring her up with him just as thunder clapped loudly, splitting the sky apart so that rain poured down in long drenching sheets.

"You shouldn't even be contemplating driving a car if you're this afraid of lightning," the guard warned, his hands holding her still for his inspection.

She realized he had been looking in the opposite direction. He hadn't seen the nearly invisible threat so close to them. For all she knew they could be surrounded by the phantoms. The idea sent a surge of adrenaline racing through her bloodstream. The rain ran down her face and soaked her clothes. Would it be better to go back to the building or go to her car? Where would the guard be the safest?

Lightning veined in the clouds, sizzling and crackling, zigzagged from ground to sky, shaking the earth beneath their feet and once again illuminating the compound. Kaden had melted into the night, but in the flash, she saw another face. A pair of merciless silver eyes raked her face, fixed on the guard still holding her arms. Ryland was close, so close she could almost reach out and touch him over the guard's shoulder. The brief flare was gone in the clap of thunder, leaving inevitable darkness behind.

Lily sagged against the guard, terrified by the striped, menacing mask on Ryland's face. He was highly skilled in hand-to-hand combat, in martial arts. He carried death in his large hands. She didn't know what to do, whom to protect. Whether to keep the guard's attention centered on her, or whether to warn him of the very real danger.

Relax, sweetheart. The voice drawled lazily in her head, played over her senses like a velvet glove. *I'm not going to hurt your hero. And get out of the damned rain before you catch pneumonia.*

Relief rushed through her. She raised her rain-wet face to the sky and smiled for no reason at all. *You can't catch pneumonia from rain.*

"We need to get out of this right now," the guard said, tugging at her arm to get her moving. "I'm taking you back to the building. It's dangerous out here."

"I agree," she answered wholeheartedly.

I have two more men who haven't made it out. Keep him away from the labs.

"But I can't face going to the labs again tonight. Let's head for the general cafeteria," she improvised swiftly.

The guard flung his arm around Lily in an attempt to keep the rain from her and together they sprinted across the long expanse of pavement toward the largest row of buildings. Lily was looking at the ground, her eyes straining to see where she was going, when the next bolt of lightning hit. This was much closer and it rattled windows and shook the towers, causing one of the guards to yelp in fear.

"Those men should get off of there," she yelled, just as the thunder exploded. The noise was astonishing, so loud it nearly knocked them down. Her ears hurt from the impact.

"The towers have lightning rods, they'll be okay," the guard assured her. But he sped up, dragging her with him.

On the heel of his words was a loud explosion as the tower took a direct hit. Sparks rained down, fire in the sky, bursting like gems in the air. Lily was looking around her frantically, shielding her face, wanting one last glimpse, one last look, but the shadow figures were gone and she was left alone in the raging storm.

She felt bereft. The emotion drained her as nothing else could.

The guard's arm propelled her into the main building just as the alarm sounded. "It's probably nothing," he said. "The siren's been going off regularly with no explanation—a glitch, or maybe it's the storm, but I have to go. You stay here out of the rain." He patted her arm in reassurance and took off.

Lily stared out the window, oblivious to her rain-drenched body and soaked clothes, praying she had done the right thing. Ryland was gone, slipping away with his men. It was up to her to find a way to help them live in the world again. She had no idea how she was going to do such a thing. She had no idea if the water on her face was rain or tears.

She leaned her forehead onto the glass pane, staring sightlessly. How would the men survive in a world filled with raw emotion, with violence and pain? The overload of stimuli could send them into madness. It was insanity to think they would all make it to her estate without mishap. How would Ryland Miller survive without her to shield him from the rest of the world, even for a short period of time? It would be so easy for him to be separated from the others. He would send the weaker men with Kaden and protect their backs. She knew that, accepted it. Ryland would guard the others before he would think of his own safety. It was that trait in him that appealed so strongly to her.

If she'd left them in the laboratory the men would have no hope of finding peace. They would be used, observed, treated eventually as lab rats, not humans—she had already noticed the guards and techs were depersonalizing them. Colonel Higgens obviously wanted them dead, and she believed he was arranging "accidents" for them during testing. At least she could provide money enough to find a place to live in freedom, in seclusion maybe, but still living. They would be safe. And both Peter Whitney and Ryland Miller had thought the risk was worth it. She had to be content with that.

When the ferocity of the storm had eased, she headed for her car. The compound was in an uproar, guards scrambling in all directions, lights shockingly bright in the night as they swept continually along the shadows of buildings, seeking prey. The drizzle of rain couldn't mute the shocked shouts and blaring noises as the word spread that the GhostWalkers had escaped. The cages were empty and the tigers were out. Fear spread like a disease. Lily could feel waves of it shimmering off the guards as they scurried around her. The post was on lockdown and there was no way for her to leave.

The emotions running so high were overwhelming. She could only hope Ryland and his men were safely away. As it was, her own barriers were flimsy, battered by the high levels of fear and adrenaline broadcast by the guards and technicians. She waited it out in her office, her hands over her ears to muffle the sound of the screaming sirens. She was glad when, after a time, the noise stopped abruptly. The sudden silence was a mercy to her throbbing head. Lily took a long shower in her private bathroom and put on a change of clothes she kept for the many nights she spent working.

She was not surprised when two guards asked her to accompany them to the office of the president to meet with a military liaison and the executives of Donovans. With a small sigh conveying her reluctance, she complied. She was drained physically and emotionally and was desperate to hide from the world.

Thomas Matherson, aide to Phillip Thornton, was waiting to fill her in. "General Ronald McEntire happened to be here tonight visiting the compound. He called General Ranier, Colonel Higgens's direct commander, and insisted on being brought on board." The aide opened the door for her and gestured for her to precede him.

Lily couldn't believe her good fortune. A general who had no knowledge of the experiment. If she could find a way to talk to him alone, she could tell him her suspicions about Colonel Higgens. The terrible knots in her stomach began to ease.

The large room was dominated by the enormous round table. Every chair was filled and all heads swung to look at her. Most of the men half rose when she entered, but she waved them to their seats.

"Gentlemen." She spoke softly, her voice filled with her usual confidence. She knew her expression was absolutely serene, she'd practiced it often enough.

It was a measure of his upset that Phillip Thornton performed the introductions himself. He nearly always left what he considered menial tasks to his assistant. "Dr. Whitney has just agreed to take over where her father left off. She's been siphoning through his data, trying to make sense of it for us."

Barely acknowledging the introduction, the general glared at Lily. "Dr. Whitney, fill me in on this experiment." It was an order, sharp and clear, the general's eyes betraying his anger.

"How much do you know?" Lily was cautious. She wanted to be careful, feel her way with him. To stall. To give the men time to find their escape routes and use them. Surreptitiously she glanced at Colonel Higgens, raising an eyebrow in inquiry.

His nod was slight, almost imperceptible, giving approval.

"Let's say I know nothing."

Matherson pulled out a chair for Lily close to the general and across from Phillip Thornton. With a grateful smile to the aide, she took her time seating herself. "I trust that everyone in this room has the proper security clearance?"

"Of course," snapped the general. "Fill me in on these men."

Lily's gaze settled on his face. "The men were drawn from all branches of the service. Dr. Whitney, my father, was looking for a particular type of man. Green Berets, Navy SEALs, Special Forces, Rangers, men highly skilled and able to endure in difficult circumstances. I believe he pulled men from the ranks of law enforcement also. He wanted men of superior intelligence and officers who had come up through the ranks. He wanted men who could think for themselves if the situation demanded it. Each of the men had to test high for a predisposition for psychic ability."

The general's eyebrow shot up. He glared at Colonel Higgens. "You knew about this nonsense and you approved it? You and General Ranier?"

Higgens nodded. "The entire experiment was approved from the beginning and it had merit."

There was a small silence while the general seemed to take it in. He turned back to Lily. "And how would they test them for psychic ability?"

Lily looked at Higgens as if for help. When none was forthcoming she shrugged. "The screening part was easy enough. Dr. Whitney, my father, that is, developed a questionnaire that highlighted the tendencies toward the clairvoyant."

"Such as . . . ," General McEntire prompted.

"The ability to remember and interpret dreams, frequent déjà vu, the sudden urge to call a friend, just when he's in trouble, even the tendency to accept the idea of clairvoyance because 'it feels right' is positively associated with the talent."

The general snorted. "Utter nonsense. We dropped those programs years ago. There's no such thing. You took good men and brainwashed them into thinking they were superior to the rest of us."

Lily tried to be patient, wanting the general to understand the enormity of what had been done to his men. "Of course, there's a lot more we don't understand about the neurobiochemistry of clairvoyance than we actually know, but recent advances in neurobehavioral psychology have strengthened some hypotheses. We know, for instance, that the capacity for clairvoyance is genetically determined. We all have heard of a few individuals doing remarkable feats in the paranormal sphere. These are psychic geniuses." Lily groped for a way to make him understand. "Like an Einstein in physics or a Beethoven in music. Do you understand?"

"I'm following you," the general said grimly.

"We know that most master physicists are *not* geniuses, nor are most concert-level musicians child prodigies. My father put together a program to screen potential candidates for an aptitude for clairvoyance, then he developed a program to train and enhance their potential. Think of a bodybuilder. He is a result of genetic potential, strict training, and . . ." She trailed off, hastily censoring the "probably designer drugs." The less they got into that part the better.

She had no intention of being specific with any of these men, least of all Philip Thornton and Colonel Higgens. Her father had been meticulous about not allowing his formula to fall into anyone's hands; she wasn't going to give it away to the very crowd she suspected of his murder.

The general heaved a soft sigh and sank into the chair behind the desk. Rubbing his temples, he looked at her. "This is beginning to sound too plausible. How did he get it to actually work? They've tried this type of thing in every country for years and had nothing but failures."

"Dr. Whitney used more than one route." She tapped her foot, trying to think of a way to explain in layman's terms. "Every object above 273 degrees Celsius or zero degrees Kelvin emits energy. Biological organisms tend to focus on certain frequencies, while screening other frequencies out. That requires energy." When the general frowned, Lily leaned toward him. "Think of a refrigerator. One often doesn't even notice the motor is running until it shuts off, then suddenly it's a relief. These 'filters' are guided by the autonomic nervous system and commonly thought to be out of conscious control. Am I making sense to you?" When he nodded, she continued. "However, there are several examples of stunning control of the autonomic nervous system. Biofeedback techniques can lower heart rate, blood pressure, and body temperature. Zen masters and yogis are legendary. Even prolonged sexual performance by males is an example of somatic intervention over the autonomic nervous system."

The general had a scowl back on his face.

"The point is that the energy that is important to paranormals is usually filtered to pathetic levels in adult humans and these filters are under autonomic control. Dr. Whitney found a way to decrease the filtering system, using mind-body control techniques taught by the Zen masters."

The general rubbed his hand over his face, shaking his head. "Why am I beginning to believe you?"

Lily stayed silent, willing him to understand, wanting him on the side of the men. She thought of Ryland and the others out there in the storm. She sent up a silent prayer that they were all safe.

"Please continue, Dr. Whitney." The general began to tap a pencil on the desk in agitation.

"Using PET scans of working clairvoyants, my father found that the areas in the brain most important for clairvoyance were the same areas responsible for autism: the hippocampus, the amygdala, and the neocerebellum. He found other links as well. There is a higher level of psychic ability in autistics in comparison to the general population. Moreover autistics are on sensory overload; they probably have a filtering defect. Reducing the filters, then, just gives you noise, like an untuned radio. You don't produce psychics, just autistics."

"So there were problems I take it."

Lily sighed with regret. "Yes, he encountered problems. At first the men were housed in regular barracks together to promote unity. The idea was to form an elite unit that could use their combined skills for certain high-risk jobs. The unit was given field training as well as lab training. They went far beyond anyone's expectations. Most of them proved capable of telepathy on some level."

"Elaborate for me."

"They had the capability of speaking together without speaking aloud—sending thoughts to one another, for lack of a better way to explain. Dr. Whitney hooked them up to the scans and the actual brain activity was unbelievable. Some of them had to be in the same room to communicate that way while others could be completely across the compound." Lily glanced again at Colonel Higgens. "You can see how such a talent would be useful on a mission. Others were also able to 'hear' thoughts of people in the room with them.

"The variety of skills is documented, sir, videotaped and recorded if you care to see for yourself. Some of the men were able to hold objects and 'read' them. The talents were varied. Psychometry. Levitation. Telekinesis. Telepathy. Some only had one, others tested strengths in several to varying degrees."

Lily took a deep breath, let it out slowly. "The problems that were encountered were not foreseen and Dr. Whitney couldn't solve them." There was real regret in her voice. Lily cupped her hands around the warmth of the teacup that Matherson had placed in front of her. "There's a reaction called tachyphalaxas. The body senses too much action at the receptor and down-regulates them. Suddenly the radio is nothing but static again. There were some who experienced unrelenting seizures from hyperstimulation. One went insane—autistic, really. One other died of cerebral hypoxia, or intracranial bleed, from head injuries." That wasn't exactly the truth; she felt there was another explanation for the intracranial bleed but wasn't going to venture a hypothesis.

"My God." The general shook his head.

Higgens cleared his throat. "There were psychotic breaks, sir. Two became violent. Uncontrollable. Even the others couldn't help them."

Guilt ate at Lily's insides, churning her stomach. "As soon as Dr. Whitney realized what the problem was, he attempted to create a calming atmosphere that was soundproof, a place that could insulate the men from the constant torment of people around them. He regulated the atmosphere, used lighting and soothing natural sounds to relieve the continual assault on the brain."

"Can these men really give suggestions to others and force obedience?" General McEntire demanded. "Could these men have given your father some kind of posthypnotic suggestion? His car was found down by the docks and there's been some speculation that he's at the bottom of the sea."

Lily gasped. "Are you implying these men had something to do with my father's disappearance? He was the only one capable of helping them."

"Maybe not, Dr. Whitney. Maybe you are," Colonel Higgens pointed out. "It could be that Ryland Miller figured that out. He heard your answer when I made the mistake of asking you in front of him if you could read your father's code."

A shiver shook her frame as certain knowledge blossomed. The moment she had answered in the affirmative, she had sentenced her father to death. She remembered how Higgens had suddenly changed, how he had ceased arguing with her father and looked at her with speculation instead of hostility.

"I'm sorry this is necessary, Lily," Phillip Thornton said. "I know you're grieving and you've been up long hours trying to figure this out for us."

Lily forced a smile and waved his concern aside. "I don't mind doing what I can to help, Phillip. This is, after all, my company too." She owned a large block of shares and wanted to remind him of the fact. "Have you any idea how this could have happened? I spoke with Captain Miller at great length this morning. He appeared quite cooperative and even was considering the possibility that one of the side effects of the experiment might be paranoia. He spoke so highly of Colonel Higgens, then would suddenly become hostile toward him. I pointed that out to him and he definitely was considering the possibility. He has a quick, logical mind."

"He did ask to see me," Colonel Higgens admitted. "I went to speak with him and he did say something along those lines." He rubbed his forehead. "The cage was securely locked when I left that room. The cameras will bear me out on that."

"The cameras were on the blitz again," Thornton said.

There was a sudden hush in the room. All eyes were on

Colonel Higgens. He sat back in his chair, glaring at them. "I'm telling you the cage was locked. I wouldn't have unlocked it with or without an armed guard present. In my opinion Captain Miller is a dangerous man. With his team, he is nearly invincible. We're going to have to send everyone we have against him."

"I hope you're not implying that we should terminate these men." The general stared hard at Higgens.

"We may have no choice," Colonel Higgens replied.

"Excuse me, gentlemen," Lily interrupted. "There is always a choice. You can't abandon these men because they did something in desperation. They were under tremendous strain. I think we need to step back from this situation and try to figure out how we can help them."

"Dr. Whitney, do you have any idea how long they will be able to survive without insulation from the noise and emotions of people around them?" Phillip Thornton asked. "Are we sitting on a time bomb?"

Lily shook her head. "I don't honestly know."

"What will happen if these men turn violent?" the general asked. He was twisting a pencil in his fingers. He tapped the lead on the table, the pad of his thumb striking the eraser, as if that would somehow stop what he was hearing. "Is that a possibility?" He looked around the faces at the table. "Is that a viable possibility?"

Lily twisted her fingers together tightly. "Unfortunately these men are highly skilled in combat conditions. They have had every advantage the military could give them through special training. There was an incident the first year of field training involving one of the men. I viewed the training tape." She took a cautious sip of tea.

"I don't think I'm going to like what I'm going to hear," General McEntire said.

"One of the trainees became disoriented during a mission in Colombia and along with the targets, he went after some of the innocent populace. When Captain Miller attempted to restrain him, the trainee turned on Miller. The captain was given no choice but to defend his own life and protect the other members of his team. They were friends, close friends, and he was forced to kill." She had watched the attack on the film and it had been gory and grim.

Even worse had been the tapes of Ryland Miller afterward. Although she was watching film she could almost absorb his emotions. The guilt, the frustration, the anger. He had been despondent, hopeless. "You have to understand, sir, paranormals are subject to and respond to different stimuli than we can sense. They live in the same world, but in a different dimension, really. So, the line we draw between clairvoyant and insane is very thin and sometimes nonexistent. These men are unlike any soldiers you've ever trained. You have no idea what they're capable of."

Lily took another sip of tea, savored the warmth as it settled in her stomach. The general couldn't conceive of the power the men wielded. But she knew.

"Why would they want to leave if they knew the risks in leaving?" The general scowled at them all, his eyes raking the room. "What conditions were they living in?" The implication of abuse was there and Lily fought down the urge to blurt out the entire story to him. How the men were isolated, even from one another, cut off from their command, studied like animals in cages. Subjected to continual tests.

The pencil between the general's fingers snapped in his fingers, one end sailing toward Lily, the other still in his hand.

Lily caught the end of the pencil before it rolled off the table, her thumb sliding over the eraser, automatically absorbing the textures, absorbing the heavy emotions. She stiffened, her gaze sliding to touch the general, then away. She wasn't telling him anything he didn't already know. He was tamping down his fury that Ryland Miller and his team had escaped. There was money to be had. Ryland stood in the way.

The emotions swirled together, a mixture of violence and impatience over a thwarted plan. General McEntire was up to his bushy eyebrows in deceit and treachery. Lily folded her hands carefully on the table, looking as serene and confident as she could when she wanted to leap at McEntire and brand him a traitor to his country and demand what he knew of her father's death.

"The living conditions, Colonel Higgens: Why would these men feel they needed to escape?"

"They were isolated from one another." Lily forced her voice to work.

"For their own good," Higgens snapped. "They were growing too powerful together, they could do things we didn't expect. Not even your father expected their combined powers to be what they were."

"That was no excuse for forgetting dignity, Colonel. They are human beings, men who were giving service to their country, not lab rats," Lily objected coolly.

"Your father was solely in charge of this experiment," Colonel Higgens shot back. "He's responsible for the results."

"As far as I can ascertain," Lily said calmly, "my father, Dr. Peter Whitney, conducted the experiment in good faith. When it had become apparent it was harming the men, he immediately called a halt to enhancing the rare talents, immediately trying to find ways to help them cope with the repercussions. He sought ways to make the men more comfortable. Unfortunately, no one listened to him. I read your direct orders, Colonel Higgens, and Phillip Thornton signed those orders, insisting the men continue. On your say-so, Colonel, Captain Miller ordered his men to follow your command and he and his men did so. Your orders, sir, were to continue training under a variety of conditions and the men, being who and what they are, followed orders despite knowing they were deteriorating rapidly, their control unraveling even as they grew in power and ability. It is well documented that my father objected, that he laid out the repercussions, and that when you ordered the men to be isolated from one another he told you they would have a much more difficult time. You ignored everything he said and you have the results of your own foolish decisions."

"Your father refused to provide me with the data I needed." Colonel Higgens turned bright red he was so angry. "He wanted to reverse the process and throw out everything because of one or two acceptable losses."

"My father tried to find a way to restore filters and deactivate the part of the brain he had stimulated. He could not. And there were no acceptable losses, Colonel; we're talking about human life."

Phillip Thornton held up his hand. "This is a discussion best left for later when we all have cooler heads and more sleep.

Right now we have to find a way to contain this situation. Dr. Whitney, you've given us quite a bit of information, but we really need to know exactly what was done to these men. We have access to some of the greatest minds in the world to help us, if we knew exactly what your father did, and how he did it," Thornton pointed out. "Can you explain it, step by step, to us?"

"I'm sorry, sir, I can't. I can't find his original data. It wasn't in his office here or at home. I tried both computers and I'm going over his reports now to see if I can spot anything that will help me to figure it out." Lily allowed her extreme fatigue to show, pushing her hands through her hair. "I've given you all the information I know at this time, but I'll continue looking."

Higgens snorted his disgust. The general shoved his coffee cup across the table, splashing dark liquid onto the highly polished surface. "Who knows about this?" The general continued glaring at those in the room.

"It's classified, only a few people," Colonel Higgens answered. "Aside from those of us in this room, General Ranier and the techs here at the lab."

"Keep it that way. We need to contain this and mop it up as soon as possible. How the hell could this happen? Can any of you tell me that? With all the security, how could they have pulled this off?"

There was a small silence. Again it was Higgens who responded. "We believe they've been testing the security, setting off the alarms, shutting down the cameras, and manipulating the guards, practicing for the last couple of weeks."

The general exploded with rage, his hands curling into two tight fists. "What do you mean manipulating the guards?" he roared, his face so red Lily feared he might have a stroke.

"I've already explained it, sir. It's part of their standard training," she explained patiently, "planting a suggestion to look the other way. Very useful when infiltrating enemy and terrorist camps and in hostage situations. They are capable of unbelievable feats. They use their minds to coerce the enemy without the enemy knowing."

"And these men are out there somewhere right now? Walking time bombs, men who very well could become mercenaries or, worse, who could go over to the other side?"

Lily lifted her chin at the man. "These men were chosen for

their loyalty, their patriotism. I can assure you, sir, they will never betray their country."

"Their loyalty became a question the minute they became deserters, Dr. Whitney, and make no mistake, that is just what they are. *Deserters!*"

EIGHT

THE wind tore through the trees, bending trunks nearly double, sweeping branches along the ground. The chain-link fence loomed and Ryland leapt up, catching the links, scrambling up and over in one smooth move, landing on his feet in a crouch. He remained low to the ground and silently signaled to the man on his left.

Last man clear.

Raoul "Gator" Fontenot dropped to his belly and scooted along the ground toward the sound of the baying dogs. Telepathy was one of his weakest talents, but he could tune in to animals. It was his job to direct the guard dogs away from the other members of his team. Knife in his teeth, he moved through the grass along the fence line, willing the lightning to stay in the clouds. Too many guards were swarming along their escape route, and even with Ryland's tremendous control, to manipulate all of them was an impossibility. It took a collective effort and, through necessity, they were scattered.

Waves of fear and aggression poured from the guards, compounding the danger to the team. All of them were feeling ill from the tremendous energy being generated.

Coming up on you now, Gator.

Gator glanced back toward Ryland, caught the swirl of his

fingers, and nodded in understanding. He transferred the knife to his right hand, blade flat along his wrist to hide the telltale glint of steel, and dropped all the way down on his belly, breathing softly, inaudibly, willing himself to be a part of the earth. The dogs were eager, rushing toward the fence, toward his comrades. The enormity of his task shook him for a moment. He had to lie there in plain sight, trusting his captain to keep the guards looking the other way while he directed the dogs to a false trail. One slipup and they were all dead.

The rain beat down on him, a steady assault. The wind howled and moaned as if alive and protesting the unnaturalness of what they were doing. Of what they were.

Captain. It was the best he could do with his lack of telepathy, a one-word protest against having the lives of so many in his hands.

This is a piece of cake for you, Gator. A pack of hounds dogging our heels is nothing to you. That was Captain Miller, coming through. Gator's stomach settled a bit.

A walk in the park. Kaden threw in his two cents, laughter in his voice, as if he were enjoying the adrenaline rush after their forced confinement. Gator found himself smiling at the thought of Kaden loose on the world.

At once he felt the movement of the others and knew Ryland was so tuned in to him that he was already directing the rest of the team forward. The men would be ghosts moving through the storm, but he couldn't worry about them. And he couldn't worry about being seen or captured. Gator put his fate in the hands of his team leader and narrowed his world to the approaching dogs.

Ryland strained to pierce the dark veil of the rain-swept night, watching for the guards and dogs as their pursuers neared the fence. He trusted Kaden to keep the other men moving. His job was to protect Gator and the two men behind him. Ryland was worried about Jeff Hollister. Hollister was in bad shape, but game enough, struggling not to slow the team. He had barely made it over the high chain-link fence with help from Gator and Ian McGillicuddy. McGillicuddy lay beside Hollister somewhere behind Ryland, holding position to protect the weakest member of his team.

The dogs were acting frenzied now, picking up the scents,

rushing toward them. Almost abruptly they stopped, sniffed the ground, turned in circles, not obeying their handlers to move forward. One large shepherd took the lead, swinging south, away from the escaped prisoners. The other dogs rushed to follow, baying loudly.

Gator pressed his throbbing forehead into the soft, wet earth in an effort to alleviate the pain brought on by such intense concentration and use of energy. The fear emanating from the guards was like a disease spreading and infecting everyone it came in contact with. The guards had been told the men were dangerous killers and all of them were extremely nervous.

Mass hysteria. Ryland's voice was soothing in Gator's pounding head. *I know you're all comfortable there, but don't go to sleep.*

Gator rolled toward Ryland, judging his position and working his way back as soundlessly as he could. The misdirection of the dogs wouldn't hold for long, but it gave them a few more precious minutes to cover their tracks and get to safety.

Ryland reached out and touched Gator to let him know his tremendous effort was appreciated. They began inching their way forward across the open meadow, flanking Hollister and McGillicuddy.

Clear. Kaden reported his group had made it to the other side of the meadow without incident.

Take them forward. We're right behind you. Gator cleared our back trail but it isn't going to last. Ryland was uneasy. He glanced toward Jeff Hollister. The man's face was etched with pain. Even with the black swirling clouds and vicious rain, the darkness of the night, he could see the lines there. Cursing Peter Whitney silently, he slowed the pace even more. The agony in Jeff's head radiated out of him to touch every member of the team. Jeff needed the medication Ryland had ordered them not to take, fearing it was too dangerous. Now he wondered if he had given Hollister a death sentence with that order.

Hang in there, Jeff. You're almost there. I've got meds lined up to help you out.

I'm slowing you down.

Don't communicate! Ryland protested sharply. *You can't afford the effort.* Ryland feared Jeff would have a seizure if the assault on his brain continued. Unease was growing in him.

Fear for his men, the sudden chilling premonition of danger. *Ian?* Ian McGillicuddy was a human antenna for trouble. He could sense danger coming.

Oh yeah, we've got trouble. It's coming fast.

Ryland scuttled forward on his belly, angling once again toward Gator. *Move it, Jeff. Get him up, Ian, run flat out toward the cars. Wait no more than five minutes and then get Jeff clear.*

We're not leaving you behind. Jeff's voice was unsteady, harsh with pain.

Ryland's heart swelled with pride. Even as ill as Jeff Hollister was, he put the members of the team first. *That's an order, Jeff. You and McGillicuddy clear out in five minutes.*

Ryland felt it then, the burst of malignant energy pouring over him. Instinctively he rolled to protect Gator, covering the man's back even as he faced upward. His hands met the solid bulk of flesh and blood.

He didn't see the knife so much as he felt it as it came swiftly toward him. It was reflex and training that saved him, his hand closing solidly around his assailant's wrist to control the weapon. Recognition crowded in. Russell Cowlings had come out of the night and attacked them. Ryland rolled away from Gator, taking the heavier man with him. Planting his foot squarely in Cowling's chest, Ryland launched the man over his head.

Cowlings landed with a soft thud, rolled, and came up in a half crouch. Ryland leapt to his feet, his hand slapping away the darting knife as the man came at him a second time. They circled each other cautiously.

"Why, Russell, why would you betray us?"

"You call it betrayal, I call you deserters." Cowlings feinted another attack, threw himself forward when Ryland stepped to the side, going in low and mean, blade up to do the most damage to the soft parts of the body.

Ryland felt the tip of the knife slice his heavy shirt, belly level. He was already whirling around, catching Cowlings's wrist and taking him down so that Cowlings's legs flew up and he landed hard. Counter-moving, Cowlings turned his wrist to get control of the blade of the knife. He yelled as he did so, calling out to the security guards for help.

"Go, Gator, get clear," Ryland ordered as he locked Cowlings's arm, pointing his little finger back behind him so the man's body followed. Cowlings was forced to drop the knife or allow his hand to be broken. The knife dropped to the ground and Ryland kicked it hard, sending the weapon spinning some distance away into the taller grass.

Man down. Jeff is down. He's having a seizure. Ian Hollister reported in his usual calm voice.

"Gator, go," Ryland repeated. *Help Ian get Jeff clear.*

Cowlings tried to lash out with his legs, scissor-kicking in an attempt to bring Ryland down. "Yeah, send him away," Cowlings spat. "It won't matter, you know, they'll all die."

Ryland moved to the side, planting a vicious back kick squarely on Cowlings's thigh. "Is that what Higgens told you? Is that why you sold us out, Russ? Did Higgens convince you we were going to die?"

Cowlings swore and spat on the ground. He turned his head to glare up at Ryland. "You're just so bullheaded, Rye. What's wrong with using our skills to make money? Do you know what Peter Whitney is worth? What that daughter of his is worth? Why should they get all the money while we take all the risks? The employees at Donovans make more money than we do."

Cowlings came in fast, smashing two hard jabs at Ryland's jaw. Both punches were blocked and Ryland retaliated with a body blow going straight up toward the throat. Cowlings managed to reel backward, barely escaping the lethal attack.

Ryland was aware of the dogs again, the sounds of excited voices getting closer. "This is about money, then, is it? It's about your greed, Cowlings, not death?" Ryland snapped. "You aren't afraid of dying, are you? Why is that? Did Higgens give us all something to cause these seizures?"

Cowlings laughed. "They're all going to die, Miller. Every last one of them. You can't save them and then who is going to be valuable? Higgens will need me."

"You're dancing with the devil, Russ. Do you think the colonel is acting in the best interest of our country? He's selling us out."

"He's smart enough to see that money can be made. You're in the way, Miller, you were from the start with your Boy Scout attitude. Hell, we tried twice to kill you and you just won't die."

"Higgens will get rid of you the minute he doesn't need you."

The sound of the dogs was getting closer. Someone had heard Cowlings yell and had turned the pack around.

"He'll always need me. I can tell him things no one else can. He knows it and he's not going to kill the golden goose."

Ryland moved in fast, using the speed he was known for, a blurring motion of hands and feet, driving Cowlings backward. He didn't feel any of the blows Cowlings managed to land, his adrenaline protecting him. His world had narrowed, focused on his opponent. There were few who could defeat him in hand-to-hand combat. Ryland was in a life-or-death battle. Russell Cowlings wanted him dead.

Cowlings grunted as Ryland landed a round kick to his ribs, smashing into bone. The air whistled out of his lungs and he dropped like a stone, fighting for breath. The security guards and the pack of dogs were already too close, coming toward Ryland at a dead run, with only the fence separating them. Ryland kicked Cowlings hard in the head, hoping to knock him out. He spun around and sprinted across the open meadow away from Gator, Hollister, and McGillicuddy.

Ryland's boots slapped the mud hard, making noise, drawing the attention of the dogs. The animals bayed wildly, dragging at their leashes until their handlers allowed them to slip free. At once the dogs ran to the chain-link fence and began tearing at it in a frenzy. Some dogs tried to leap it, others to climb, still others to dig.

Small circles of light danced and wavered in the sheets of rain, the guards' vain attempt to illuminate the area. Ryland zigzagged across the grass, making more noise so that the guards might hear him even over the loud barking of the dogs. It took a moment for the men to react, but they did as he wanted, running along the fence toward his position and away from his men. As long as they were running parallel with him, no one thought to stop and cut the fence to let the dogs through. It gave Ryland a few more precious minutes to cover more ground so his men had time to get their downed comrade clear.

He was grateful for the strong winds and pouring rain, for the thunder and lightning rocking the skies. It would be a while before a helicopter would be put up in the stormy skies in an attempt to track them. His men would be safely away in the cars Lily had waiting for them. Her security man, Arly, had left the various cars parked at different points at least two miles from the laboratories.

Ryland heard the warning rattle of the fence and turned away from it, sprinting toward the nearest group of buildings. One of the guards snipped the fence, widened the opening to allow the dogs to pour through. They rushed in a pack toward Ryland, eager to hunt their prey. The guards followed, ducking through the fence in hot pursuit.

Ryland's boots smacked the pavement loudly as he raced across the street and leapt up on top of a parked sedan. He jumped, his fingers catching hold on the edge of the eaves of the storefront. It was a poorer section of town and the buildings were old and run-down, but the wood held up as he dragged himself onto the roof.

We're clear. Ian indicated they had located one of the cars and were safely away. *We can circle around and pick you up.*

Jeff? Ryland wanted medical care for the man as soon as possible. There was no telling what was going on in the over-stimulated brain. He raced across the roof and leapt to the covering of the next building. It was slick from the rain and he slid precariously, fell on his backside just as a barrage of bullets whistled by him.

He needs medical attention. Give us your position.

Ryland crawled across the roof, not taking a chance on skylining himself with trigger-happy guards. If Cowlings was telling the truth and he'd already been a target twice, chances were good the guards had been ordered to shoot to kill. The roof had a door leading to a small stairwell. *I'll make it to you. Stay in position. Shots have been fired. Stay out of the area.*

The door was locked. Ryland didn't waste time, he simply crawled to the far side of the building and peered over into the street. There was a small overhang to shade the entrance to a store. Ryland dropped onto it, fought for a purchase in the rain-soaked wood, slid a few inches before he caught himself. From there he jumped to the sidewalk. The landing was hard, jarring him.

There was an alley a few feet to his right but he didn't trust that it would bring him to the street he needed. He forced air into his body, slowed his breathing, and melted into the shadow of the building. There was only the sound of the rain as it poured from the skies. The roar of the wind as it showed its fury. Clouds boiled overhead, black cauldrons of spinning dark angry threads spawning veins of lightning arcing from cloud to cloud. Ryland's luck held and the lightning didn't flash close to him, allowing him to slip silently through the street to the corner where the car was waiting with the motor running and the passenger door open.

He leapt into the seat, slamming the door closed as Gator took off so fast they fishtailed in the rain-soaked road. Ryland turned to look at Jeff lying so quiet and pale on the backseat. "Is he alert?"

Ian shook his head. "He's been down since the seizure. Gator and I carried him to the car, but we couldn't bring him around. I hope the lady doctor knows what she's doing or we're going to lose him."

There was silence in the car. Too many had been lost already. None of them knew if it was inevitable or not.

LILY stared out the window as the limousine glided through the rain-wet streets. She'd left her little car in the parking lot and was thankful that John had come to get her. Where was Ryland? Had he made it to the house yet? She felt almost numb with terror for him. She didn't expect to feel this way. She couldn't think of her father, or the conspiracy. She couldn't think about the other men somewhere out in the ferocious storm fighting their way to freedom. She could only think of him. Ryland Miller.

She ached for him. She closed her eyes and he was there, behind her eyelids, sharing her skin. It was revolting and juvenile and illogical, but none of that mattered. She couldn't force her thoughts away from him. She had to know if he was alive or dead. If he was injured. It frightened her how strong her need was to see him, to touch him, to hear the sound of his voice. She didn't dare reach out to him telepathically, not when the stakes were so high and his total concentration was needed where he was.

The garage door opened smoothly and the limousine rolled

into the huge garage. To her relief there were several other cars parked in the garage. For a moment she laid her head against the headrest and let her breath out slowly. The limousine halted and her chauffeur turned off the motor.

"John, thanks for coming to get me in this awful storm. I'm sorry for dragging you out, but I was so tired and I didn't want to stay at Donovans overnight." Nothing could have induced her to stay at the laboratories now that Ryland was no longer there. It was strange, almost terrifying, how bereft she felt.

"I'm glad you called me, Miss Lily. We were all worried about you. Why were there so many guards poking through the car? They've never done that before." The chauffeur turned to look at her with a raised eyebrow, but he refrained from saying a single word about the disappearance and reappearance of storm-drenched cars in their garage.

"I'm sorry, John, it's a classified thing to do with the military." She slid from the car, swaying with weariness. She could hear the wind howling at the doors of the garage and she shivered. "What a ghastly night."

He glared at her as he opened the driver's side door. "You didn't eat today, did you? Not a single thing."

Lily leaned over and kissed the top of his head. "Stop worrying so much about me, John. I'm a sturdy woman, not a delicate waif."

"I have a feeling I'll always worry about you, Lily. This thing with your father . . . I'm damnably sorry." John shook his head. "I thought he might be found, but he'd never stay away from you this long. And if it was a kidnap for ransom, or even secrets of some kind, we would have heard."

Lily could see the lines of age in his face, the tinge of gray to his coloring. She put her hand on his arm. "I know how much you loved him, John. I'm sorry for both of us." His sorrow was beating at her, profound and deep, slashing at her unprotected mind.

Lily closed her eyes for a moment, worried about Ryland Miller and his men. She wanted to check with Arly and make certain they had arrived and were safe within the thick walls of her home. Compassion welled up as she studied her chauffeur. John suddenly appeared fragile and looked his age. It caught her by surprise. She didn't want to lose John.

"He was my friend, Lily, my family. I knew your father when he was a boy. My father worked for his family. I think I was his only friend growing up in that house. His life was hell in that house. His parents and grandparents had been carrying on some sort of experiment to have a child of great intelligence. He was unloved, merely a product of breeding the right genes. His parents never talked to him unless it was to insist on his studying. He wasn't allowed to play sports or play with toys or even associate with other kids. They wanted a highly developed brain and everything he did even as a child was to that end. And when you"—he hesitated—"came along," he improvised, "Peter vowed he wouldn't be like his parents. I talked to him many times about his absentmindedness. I know it hurt you when he couldn't remember your important events." He shook his head sadly. "He did love you, Lily. For all his strange ways, he did love you very much."

But Peter Whitney had been like his parents. Exactly like his parents. He had followed in their footsteps until something had opened his eyes. Lily put her arms around John as he got out of the car, hugging him. "Does everyone in the household know I'm not his biological daughter?"

John Brimslow stiffened, jerked back to glare down at her. "Who told you that?"

"He did," she said. "In a letter."

He passed his hand over his face, then gripped her arms. "You were everything to Peter." He cleared his throat. "And to me. To all of us. You brought sunshine to us, Lily. Rosa could never have children. Arly dated a multitude of women but he never could tolerate anyone's company but his own for very long. We're a family of misfits, Lily. You've always known about me, I never hid who I am from you. We built the family around you."

Lily smiled at him, grateful for his words. "John, do you know how my father came to adopt me?"

John shifted uncomfortably. "Your father went overseas. Some people might say he bought you, Lily, I don't know how much money was involved, but does that matter now? You didn't have a family and neither did we."

They walked together through the entrance hall leading from the garage to the house, Lily's hand tucked in the crook of

John's arm, as he continued, "Rosa was young back then, she barely spoke English, but she was a nurse and she needed a job to stay in the country. Peter snapped her up as your nanny and eventually she ran the house for us." He grinned at her. "She frowned on my lifestyle at first. I had already met Harold by then and we were life partners. Peter never judged me, but Rosa was afraid I would somehow damage you with my perversions."

"John!" Lily protested. "She has never, ever indicated in any way, by word or action, that she disapproved of you. Rosa speaks very highly and affectionately of you."

"That was in the old days when you were just a little thing. She's come to accept me and she nursed Harold devotedly at the end. I don't know what I would have done without her." He patted her hand. "Or you, Lily. I'll never forget you standing next to me at the grave site with your arm around my waist and sobbing right along with me."

"I loved Harold, John. He was as much a part of our family as you and Rosa and Arly. I still miss him, and I know you do too." She stopped walking just outside the kitchen where she knew Rosa was waiting for her. "Have you had a physical recently? I want you to rest and take very good care of yourself. I can't afford to lose anyone else in my family."

He lifted her chin and brushed a kiss over the top of her head. "I'd like you to remember how important you are to us, Lily. You have enough money and a beautiful home, you never have to work if you don't want to. Don't get into whatever Peter was into. I know he was more distracted than usual those last few weeks."

Rosa burst through the kitchen door and flung her arms around Lily. To Lily's horror, she was sobbing. "I paged you over and over, Lily. Why didn't you call me? You didn't say you were going to be late and when I called Donovans they wouldn't tell me anything except there had been trouble."

Lily held her close, astonished that the unflappable Rosa was so distressed over her being late. "I left my pager in my locker. I'm really sorry, Rosa, I should have called you. It was so thoughtless of me."

"The storm was so wild, I thought you must have had an accident." Rosa clung to her, alternating between hugging and patting Lily's back.

"Didn't Arly tell you I asked him to send John for me?" Lily looked up at her chauffeur for help. Rosa was prone to outbursts of temper, chasing people around her kitchen with tea towels, but she never wept as if her heart were breaking.

"When the police didn't call about an accident I was afraid someone had kidnapped you. Oh, Lily." She turned away from the younger woman and covered her face with her hands, sobbing uncontrollably.

John put his arm around her, frowning as he did so. "Rosa, dear, you'll make yourself ill. Sit down, I'll make tea for you." He helped her to the nearest chair.

Rosa put her head down on the table and continued crying. John put on the kettle to boil water. Lily stood close to the older woman, puzzling over her behavior. "Rosa, I'm perfectly fine. Don't cry anymore. I promise I'll be better about calling you."

Rosa just shook her head. Lily sighed. "John, perhaps I should speak to Rosa alone, do you mind?"

John kissed the top of Rosa's head. "Don't make yourself sick. It's been a difficult time for all of us."

Lily waited until the kitchen door swung closed. "What is it, Rosa? Tell me."

Rosa continued to shake her head, refusing to look at Lily.

Lily took the time to make the tea, first heating the small pot with a little water from the kettle, then discarding the water before measuring out the tea leaves and pouring on the boiling water to brew. The simple ritual cleared her mind and allowed it to work as it preferred, coming at the puzzle from various angles. She waited for the worst of the storm of tears to pass before placing a teacup in front of Rosa. All the time her mind was working, putting together the fact that Rosa was a nurse and Peter Whitney had brought her into the country.

"Does this have anything to do with the fact that you were my nurse when my father brought me here with all those other little girls?" She asked the question very softly, without inflection, not wanting to sound accusing.

Rosa cried out and stared at Lily in shock. There was guilt in the depths of her eyes. Guilt and sorrow and remorse. "I should never have agreed to do it. I had nowhere to go, Lily, and I loved you so much. I couldn't have children of my own. You have been my daughter."

Lily sat down abruptly. "Why didn't you ever tell me about my father, Rosa? Why didn't you tell me about that horrible room and all those other poor little girls?"

Rosa looked around in fear. "Ssh, never speak of such things. No one can ever know about that room or those poor children. Dr. Whitney should never have told you. It was wrong. He came to see that and he tried to find those girls good homes. What he did was evil, unnatural. His eyes were opened when you were nearly killed."

Lily took a cautious sip of tea. Rosa obviously believed Lily's father had told her everything. "My leg," she said, as she set the cup in the saucer. "I had so many nightmares and Dad would never tell me."

"It was a terrible accident, Lily. Your father was devastated. He promised me he would never make you do anything like that again." Rosa was whispering, obviously fearful of being overheard.

"Did John know about the other girls? Did he know about the experiment?" Lily couldn't look at the woman who had raised her. Couldn't look at the tearstained face, which plainly told her there was so much more she didn't want to hear.

"Oh no, Lily," Rosa protested. "He would have beat Peter within an inch of his life and then he would have quit. Peter needed John to keep him human. Your father only had a few people he allowed into his world. John was a big part of that world. They were boyhood friends and John never minded Peter's eccentric ways."

Lily was watching Rosa's face closely. "Why are you so upset, Rosa? Tell me. All of this was a long time ago. I would never blame you for something my father did. You're a victim as much as I am."

"I can't tell you, Lily. You'll never forgive me and you're the only family I have. This is my home. John, Arly, you, and your father are my entire world."

Lily reached across the table to take Rosa's hand. "I love you. Nothing can ever change that. I don't like to see you so upset like this."

"Arly told me someone broke into our house. He said they knew exactly where your office was and where your father's office was. He said they had the house codes." Rosa stared miserably into her teacup.

Lily allowed the breath to leave her lungs in a little rush. She remained silent, simply waiting. Her fingers tightened around Rosa's hand in reassurance.

"They threatened me Lily. They said they could make me leave the country. They said they could make a problem with my citizenship papers. They said I would never see you again."

"Who told you that?"

"Two men stopped me as I was getting out of my car at the grocery store. They had badges and wore suits."

"Rosa, you know you're independently well off and my money is your money. Our lawyers would never allow anyone to send you away. You've lived in this country for years. You're a citizen, legally here. How could you think we would ever allow you to be taken away?"

"They said they would just take me off the street and send me away and no one would ever know what happened to me. Then they said they could make you disappear, too. I should have told you but I was so afraid. I thought Arly would catch them whether or not they had the codes. He has all those silly gadgets he loves so much."

Rosa had never paid attention to life outside the Whitney home. Coming from a poor background, coupled with the guilt she had always felt over her part in using little children in an experiment, had aided in keeping her segregated from the outside world. "Did you tell them about the laboratory?"

Rosa squeaked in terror. "I never speak of that unholy place. I try to forget it exists. Your father should have destroyed it." She raised her stricken gaze to Lily's. "I'm sorry, Lily. I copied some of your father's papers off his desk. I tried to give them things that didn't matter but I didn't know what was important."

There is a traitor in our house. Lily leaned over and kissed Rosa. "You have no idea what a relief it is to hear this. I knew someone in our home was supplying information and I thought it was a matter of money or politics. These people can't touch you, Rosa." Rosa was no traitor, just a simple frightened woman who had done her best to feed information of little consequence to those threatening her. The relief was overwhelming. "If they contact you again, let me know or tell Arly."

"I don't leave the house anymore, Lily. I have our groceries delivered. I don't want to see these men." She leaned toward Lily, a fresh flood of tears swimming in her eyes. "What if they are the men who made your father disappear? I'm so ashamed of myself. I should have told Arly but I didn't want him to know I even spoke to those men. What if they take you away from me? I'm so afraid."

"No one is going to harm me, Rosa. And if you ever disappeared, I would move heaven and earth to find you. I need to know a few other things about the time when my father first hired you."

Rosa shook her head and clambered to her feet, taking her teacup to the sink. "I don't speak of that time. I won't, Lily."

Lily followed her. "I'm sorry, Rosa, but it isn't just idle curiosity. There are other things going on and I need to find a way to fix them. Please help me."

Rosa crossed herself and turned toward Lily with a helpless sigh. "If we do evil, it will haunt us always. Your father did things that weren't natural and I helped him. No matter what we do now, we have to pay for what we did then. That's all I'll say on the subject. Go to bed, Lily. You look so pale and tired."

"Rosa, what did I do that brought me to Peter Whitney's attention in the first place? What set me apart from the others so much? There must have been others who could do the things I did."

Rosa hung her head. "The things he did were wrong, Lily. I've tried very hard to make up for helping him. I don't want to think about those times."

"Please, Rosa, I need to know."

"Even as an infant you could make things fly in the air. If you wanted your milk and we were too slow you could bring it to you. It is no good to think of these things. We have a good life, long past those times. Go to bed now and sleep."

Rosa kissed Lily and walked out of the kitchen, leaving Lily staring after her. Lily put her head down on the sink and growled in sheer frustration. Rosa had always been stubborn over the strangest things. Pressing her for more information was useless. Lily pushed away from the counter and made her way through the darkened house to the stairway.

Lily wrinkled her nose when she saw Arly waiting for her on

the bottom stair. She should have known he'd be there; her family had a tendency to hover.

"I didn't think you'd ever get here. You left me in a mess, Lily."

Lily scowled at the annoyance and accusation in his tone. "Well, I've had a few little problems to deal with tonight, Arly. I'm so sorry if you were inconvenienced and missed your beauty sleep."

"You're in a foul mood tonight."

"Did they make it?"

Arly stood up, towering over her. "Now you want to know. The trouble with women is they never have their priorities in place."

"If you give me any trouble tonight, Arly, I swear I'm going to smash you one. I am not in the mood to pander to your over-inflated ego, soothe your ruffled feathers, or listen to you expound on your pet peeves."

"I always told your father you had such a penchant for violence. Why couldn't you be one of those seen-and-never-heard children?" Arly groused.

"I made up my mind after the first five minutes in your company I was going to be the plague of your life." Lily leaned her head against his chest wearily and looked up at him. "I am, aren't I, Arly?"

He kissed the top of her head then ruffled her hair as if she were still a child. "Yes, Lily, you're definitely the biggest plague of my life." He sighed. "One of the men is in bad shape. They said he had a seizure and all of them are worried about a brain bleed."

Her heart dropped to the floor. Her legs turned to rubber. She clutched at Arly's sleeve. "Who? Who is it?"

He shrugged, his gaze narrowing as her agitation registered. "I don't know, someone they call Jeff. He's out like a light."

Lily breathed a prayer of thanks that it hadn't been Ryland. "Take me to them, Arly and I'll need our medical kit."

"Are you certain about this? If these men are caught here, we could get into a lot of trouble. Are you prepared for that?"

"Are you prepared for the alternative?"

NINE

RYLAND met her at the door, his silver gaze devouring her face, taking in every shadow, noting how pale she was. Without preamble, he pulled her into his arms. Needing her. Needing to feel her against him. Needing to run his hands over her body and assure himself she was unharmed. "Why the hell are you so late? Didn't you think I'd be worried about you? I didn't have the energy for wave communication." He gave her a little shake.

Lily rested against the hard strength of his body, grateful he was alive. His heart was reassuringly steady and his muscles were solid beneath her hands. "I was so worried about you, Ryland. I was held up at the laboratories. I had to talk with General McEntire. He was there when the escape took place and Higgens and Thornton asked me to join them in explaining everything." At that moment she didn't care to reason out why it was so important to her that Ryland was safe, it only mattered that he was. That her world could continue and she could breathe again.

Lily found that her fingers were curled possessively in Ryland's hair. She *had* to touch him. She wanted to weep with relief. "Arly tells me someone had seizures." *I was so afraid for you.* She was revealing too much of her feelings but she couldn't stop herself.

"Jeff Hollister. We haven't been able to wake him." He clasped both her hands in his, brought her fingers to the warmth of his mouth, all too aware he wasn't alone with her when he needed to be desperately.

"Do you know whether he was given anything to sleep last night?"

"He was hurting bad. Telepathic communication is difficult at the best of times and he was already worn down. I was trying to sustain the bridge myself for everyone but I . . ." He trailed off, guilt riding him hard. He had been selfish. He had wanted to dreamwalk. Wanted to comfort Lily. Be with Lily. In using up his energy that way, he had been unable to provide as much for the others.

Lily tightened her fingers around his. "Ryland, you aren't responsible for everyone. You're not."

There was too much compassion in her eyes. Lily could so easily turn him inside out. Just the way she looked at him made him feel different inside. He liked her. He liked being with her, hearing her voice, watching her expressions. She was burrowing into his heart, he could feel her there.

"Sure he is." The voice was deep and edged with humor.

Lily whirled around to face Kaden, ready to battle for Ryland. Kaden was tall and thick with muscle and sinew. A man with cold eyes and the face of a Greek god. And he was grinning at her.

"Just ask him. He thinks he's responsible for the entire world." The flat black eyes swung to taunt Ryland. "And you're making a damn fool out of yourself looking at her all goofy that way. You're making the male gender look bad."

Ryland's eyebrow shot up. "It's an impossibility for me to look goofy at anyone."

"He talks about you all time too, we can't shut him up."

"Do you make it a habit to sneak up on people?" Lily was trying not to laugh. He'd deliberately made her blush. She tried to control the faint color but his hawklike gaze had definitely spotted it. Arly stared at her as if she'd grown two heads. She resisted the desire to kick him in the shins, struggling for serenity instead.

"Yes, ma'am, now that you mention it, I'd have to say that's one of my specialties." Kaden looked unrepentant.

Lily rolled her eyes. "Where did you put Jeff Hollister? I'd like to take a look at him. And did any of you think to bring out those sleeping tablets so I can run an analysis on them?" She fell back on what she knew best. Science. Logic. Knowledge. Anything but men.

"Close your mouth, geek boy," she hissed as she swept past Arly with her head held high. "You're catching flies."

Arly stomped after her, hurrying to catch up. He leaned over to whisper overly loud in her ear. "We didn't raise you to be a little hussy."

Ryland saw her lips curve for just a moment, but she managed to keep a straight face, looking down her patrician nose at him. "I don't know what you thought you saw, but I've been meaning to tell you for some time to use the new insurance plan for glasses. Thick Coke-bottle glasses might be helpful."

"Oh, you'd like me to believe you weren't petting him like a favorite cat. My face turned red watching you. Where'd you learn to behave like that?"

"You know those movies you watch all the time, no one's supposed to know about?" Lily said sweetly. "You accidentally played them on the wrong channel. It's amazing the education one can receive."

Arly kept pace beside her, not even breaking stride. "Do you even know his name? I'm going to tell Rosa."

"Go ahead. I'll tell her about your movie collection."

Ryland laughed softly. "You two sound like bickering siblings."

"She's always been jealous of my superior intellect," Arly explained.

Lily tossed her head. "Ha! The only thing I've ever been jealous of is your skinny body."

Ryland pushed open the door to the injured man's room. Although Lily had had the room outfitted with blue lights, they had been dimmed and it was difficult to see Jeff Hollister at first. Lying so still, his face pale and his hair platinum blond, he looked like a wax statue. She heard the CD playing soft strains of music over the sound of the rain; even with the thick walls of the house, this was needed to provide a soothing respite for the men.

"Jeff is from San Diego, California. He's a champion surfer," Ryland said, leaning down to pat the man's shoulder. "He talks like an idiot, mostly slang, but has a high IQ and a degree from MIT. His family would be devastated if anything happened to him. His mother sends him cookies every month and he gets letters from every brother and sister he has."

Lily was watching the way Ryland's large hands, scarred from numerous fights, were so gentle on Jeff Hollister's shoulder. The lump in her throat grew. Ryland would be just as devastated as Jeff Hollister's family if she couldn't find a way to save him.

"You'll have to let me examine him. Rosa, my housekeeper, is a nurse and if necessary, I can call in a doctor who would be discreet."

Arly cleared his throat. "Lily, you can't bring Rosa in here. She can't know about this. She's . . . strange."

"She's not strange," Lily defended immediately. "She just doesn't believe in experiments." She frowned at Arly.

"I wasn't saying anything against her, hon," Arly said, touching her shoulder in a brief gesture of solidarity. "You know the way Rosa always talked about her family—very religious."

Lily leaned into him just for a moment, then bent to examine Hollister.

Ryland shook his head. "We can't chance bringing a doctor here. If he needs medical care beyond what you can give him, we'll take him elsewhere. I won't compromise your safety any more than we already have."

Lily glanced up at his face, and noted the glint of steel in his eyes. The absolute resolve. The regret that flickered across his face and was gone.

"Fine. Who witnessed what happened to him?"

"That would be me, ma'am." The voice came out of the darkest corner of the room and nearly made Lily jump out of her skin. She whirled around to see a large man stirring, slowly standing until it seemed a giant was in the room with her. He was tall and heavily muscled, with chestnut hair that gleamed red in the faint light from the lamp. She was shocked at how silent he was as he crossed the room to reach her side. "Ian McGillicuddy, ma'am. Remember me?"

How could she forget? She had read his profile before going to see him but nothing could prepare her for the sheer power radiating from him. His eyes were a dark brown, piercing and intelligent. He moved with a speed and silence that seemed impossible for such a big man. "Yes, of course. I'm glad you're safe, Mr. McGillicuddy."

From somewhere in the darkness there was a humorous snort at her formal use of his name. Lily realized the men were all keeping vigil over their fallen comrade.

"Call me Ian, ma'am. I don't want to have to give any of these boys a lesson in manners."

She looked up at him, at the amusement dancing in his dark eyes. "No, I guess we can't have that. Call me Lily and I'll drop the 'mister.' You want to describe everything you can remember about his condition?"

"He was very pale. Jeff was always outdoors and he had a tan that never went away. We've been locked up and I haven't seen him, but it was a shock to see him so white. He was sweating and he felt clammy to me. He said his head felt like it was going to explode. He kept touching the back of his head when he said it. I could tell he was afraid, and Jeff is fearless. He's one of those kamikaze types that just goes for broke."

"Did he say whether or not he took a sleeping pill?"

Ian shook his head. "No, but he said he just wanted to sleep to escape the pain and dreaming of sand, surf, and home was better than knowing you were dying of a brain bleed. He was worried about slowing us down and kept telling me to leave him."

"Did any of you take a sleeping pill?" Lily asked.

"Hell no, ma'am." A tall man with dark skin and black eyes stepped out of the shadows. "The captain said not to touch anything and we didn't."

"You're Tucker Addison." She remembered his profile. He had served in an antiterrorist unit and had earned several medals. "I need to look at his neck and the back of his head. Would you mind helping Ian roll him gently over?"

"I just wanted to say thank you, Dr. Whitney, for letting us set up a command post and camp here in your home." His hands, as he assisted Ian in turning over Jeff Hollister, were incredibly gentle. He handled the man as if he were a baby.

Lily bent over Jeff Hollister, running her fingers over his skull. His breathing was normal, his pulse steady. His skin was cooler than normal, and the pulse beat hard in his temple, but he appeared to be asleep. She gently pushed the hair from his neck and examined his skin. She couldn't see any visible signs of swelling or outward ruptures. Then the pads of her fingers found the scars: Jeff definitely had receptors behind his ears.

Lily hissed out a swear word as she straightened. "Was he taken to the clinic recently? Had someone other than me visited with him alone?" She was furious. *Furious.* Her fingers curled into a tight fist. Her father had a lot to answer for.

Ryland stepped up quickly and ran his fingers around Jeff's skull, finding the same scars, feeling his way behind the man's ears. A muscle jerked in his jaw as he stepped back.

Tucker and Ian carefully laid Jeff Hollister back on the sheets. "What is it? What did you find?" Ian asked.

Ryland reached out, and right there, in front of all his men, began to uncurl Lily's fingers. "Jeff was complaining of severe headaches and a couple of days ago they took him to the clinic and supposedly treated him. Jeff said the headaches came back worse than before. He stopped using any form of telepathy. We carried him on the wave to keep him in the loop but told him not to respond unless it was imperative." Ryland carried her hand to his mouth, breathed warm air into the center of her palm. "What is it, Lily? What do you think happened here?"

She pulled away from him abruptly, paced across the room, not appearing to notice as men scattered out of her way. Ryland started to protest but Arly shook his head slightly, indicating the need for silence.

Ryland watched her, the quick, restless movements of her body, the frown on her face. She was far away from them, computing data. While she was busy he took the time to examine his men, running his fingers carefully over every head, searching for telltale scars. He even checked his own head. When he found everyone else was clean, he breathed a small sigh of relief.

"I need to know his talents. What can he do?" Lily asked.

"Jeff can move objects. You have keys to the jailhouse, don't leave them hanging around because he can lift them as sweet as you please," Tucker said. "And he can do the mojo thing."

Startled, Lily blinked, focused on Tucker. "I'm sorry, I'm not familiar with the mojo thing."

Tucker shrugged. "He can levitate."

"No, he can't," Ian denied quickly. "No one can really do that. It's a party trick or something and he just likes to gloat."

"He can levitate?" Lily looked to Ryland for confirmation. "How in the world does he do that? And how does that fit in with your abilities?" She had watched the earlier videotapes of the young girls. None of them had ever achieved levitation and she hadn't considered the possibility, or what it could be used for. "What, he just floats in the air?"

"A few inches from the ground. If he lifts any higher, it hurts his head. He gets migraines for days," Ryland explained. "Some of the abilities aren't worth the effort needed to use them."

"How much actual practice did all of you put into using your talents?" Lily asked.

It was Kaden who answered. "We trained together as a military unit for several months while Dr. Whitney, your father, put us through a battery of tests. We began training as a psychic team under military conditions. I was a member of the Special Forces—in fact, I went through training with Ryland—but now I'm a civilian, a homicide detective in the police force. I met the criteria, spoke at length with Ryland, and decided to join. Once our abilities were strengthened, we worked well together for some time." He looked at the others for confirmation.

"About three, four months," Ian agreed. "It was amazing. We could do all sorts of things. Talk about a high."

"But were you given exercises to do to shield yourselves from unwanted information and emotion," Lily persisted.

"At first we were doing a tremendous amount of mental exercises but then Colonel Higgens demanded quicker results. He wanted us out on training missions, pitting us against nonpsychic teams," Kaden explained.

"Unfortunately, we wanted the action. Sitting around a little room with wires on our heads was boring," Ryland said. "Your father warned us it was too soon. There were several meetings and in the end, we all compromised. We spent three days out in the field and two with electrodes recording our every move."

Lily paced across the room again. Ryland was beginning to recognize the pent-up emotion in her quick steps. She probably didn't realize she was angry, but her body betrayed the depths of her emotions. "I can't believe he would allow you to get away with that. He knew better than to compromise on safety, especially when he had earlier data."

"Earlier data?" Kaden echoed.

Lily stopped in her tracks as if she'd forgotten they were in the room with her.

Arly deliberately turned the attention away from the subject. "That's what you get for talking to yourself all the time. You think you're having a conversation with yourself."

Lily made a rude noise, easily following his lead. "Does anyone know if Hollister can dreamwalk?" She studiously avoided Ryland's gleaming eyes.

There was a small silence while the men exchanged looks. "Dreamwalking is considered weird mojo just like levitation," Kaden said. He looked around the room, his gaze piercing the darkness. "It's a useless talent."

Ryland shrugged. "Dr. Whitney—the senior Dr. Whitney—said entering into a dream with another person could be dangerous and discouraged us from exploring it."

"You've tried it?" Kaden asked. "You should have told me, Ryland. You know the number one rule is to always have an anchor. Whitney drilled that into us. You drilled that into us."

"Talk about weird mojo," Tucker murmured.

Ryland sighed. "I discovered I could do it by accident. I talked to Dr. Whitney and he was adamant that it was too dangerous to bother with. At the time I asked him if any of the others could walk in dreams and he said one or two." He looked around the room. "Has anyone else tried it?"

There was a faint movement in the corner on the far side of the room. All eyes turned to confront the man sitting silently in the deepest shadows. She had the impression of darkness and raw strength. Of something lethal stirring dangerously. She tried to see his features, but the dim light from the lamp couldn't quite reach him.

"Nico?" Ryland prompted. "Are you able to walk in dreams?"

"I have always been able to walk in dreams." The voice matched the image, sending a shiver of fear trailing down Lily's spine. She knew who he was. Nicolas Trevane. Born and raised on a reservation until his tenth year. Lived another ten years in Japan. A sniper for the military with more medals than she could count and more kills than she wanted to know about. She remembered his eyes tracking her as he sat perfectly still in the center of his cage. Even behind bars he had unnerved her, giving the distinct impression of a dangerous predator simply waiting his chance.

"My father said 'one or two' others. If Ryland and Mr. Trevane can both walk in dreams, and no one else is admitting to it, there's a possibility that Mr. Hollister can also walk in dreams," Lily mused aloud. She was already moving toward the door, pushing her way through the group of men.

"Lily," Ryland said sharply, "where are you going?"

She stopped, surprise blossoming. "I'm sorry—watch him, his pulse is strong and he's breathing normally. I need to do a little research. I don't want to chance trying to wake him if it isn't safe. So let him be, just watch him closely."

Ryland went out the door with her, following her down the hall. "Talk to me, Lily—what's going on with him? What do you suspect?"

"I think someone may have pulsed electricity into his brain, delivering a concentrated surge on a small spot." She walked quickly, her mind turning over the various possibilities. "I have to have more information to make any kind of a logical assessment, but I've had my suspicions. Brain bleeds are a side effect, although rare."

Ryland caught her arm, halting her progress, forcing her to face him. "Stop a minute and explain this to me. I'm sorry I'm not keeping up here, but if you think someone is shocking my men, giving them some kind of electric lobotomy, I think it's important for me to know." Ryland gave her a little shake. "What have they done to my men?"

"I don't honestly know, Ryland. I have a few suspicions but what's the point in making unfounded accusations?"

"Where are you going?" His silver eyes were glittering with

a turbulence that suggested a storm was brewing just beneath the surface.

Lily waited a heartbeat before answering, disturbed by his tone. "I just told you, I need more information. I intend to consult my father's notes." She tried to keep annoyance out of her voice, acknowledging he had every right to be upset over further potential threats to his men. She knew she was often abrupt and clipped when her mind was elsewhere. Arly reminded her often enough and had pointed out the same behavior in her father.

Ryland's palm curled around the nape of her neck and he drew her close against his hard strength. "I'd like some sort of explanation whether it's technical or not. I'm not a complete idiot, Lily, and I have the right to assess the threat to the men."

Lily let her breath out slowly, took his face between her hands. "If I gave you the impression that I didn't think you could understand, I apologize. I have a tendency to get lost in my work and forget what's going on around me. For that matter, anyone or anything around me."

Ryland simply bent his head to hers and took possession of her mouth. Time stood still. The walls fell away as he whirled her out of the boundaries of the world and into the stars. Her arms circled his neck, her body molding immediately to his.

"I always thought," Arly said loudly, coming up behind them, "that making out in a hallway was the kind of thing teenagers do."

Ryland took his time, making a thorough job of kissing Lily. When he reluctantly lifted his head, his gaze shifted to Arly. "Interesting point of view, but in my opinion, kissing Lily anywhere, anytime is a must."

Lily made a face at Arly as she moved past him toward the long winding staircase that led to the lower stories. "I wouldn't know, Arly, never having gone to school as a teenager and never having kissed in hallways."

Ryland kept pace with her. "For someone without the necessary experience I'd still have to rate you excellent at kissing in hallways."

"Thank you," Lily replied demurely. "I'm certain I could have done much better had Arly given me a few more minutes."

"Oh, no, you were fine," Ryland reassured her. "I was just

reminding you I was around. Hallway or not, I wanted you to remember my existence."

Lily laughed softly, but her smile was already fading as she turned to hurry down the stairs.

Ryland watched the distant look return to her face and sighed. Arly shook his head. "She's brilliant, you know. She's like a machine if you feed her data. There are very few people in the world who can do that."

Ryland nodded his agreement but his frown remained. "It's a little hard on a man's ego."

"She's someone special, Miller. Different in ways you can't imagine. And she's chosen you." Arly looked the man up and down. Took in the battered, scarred hands, evidence of fights, the muscular, stocky body and rough-hewn face. "Aside from the fact that you're probably on the FBI's most wanted list, do you have any other qualifications I might want to know about?"

"Qualifications?" Ryland echoed. "Are you asking me in a roundabout way my intentions?"

"Not yet." Arly was honest. "First I wanted to find out if I even want you to state your intentions. I haven't decided. I might still throw you out."

"I see. You have something against the military?"

"Aside from the fact that you're probably an adrenaline junkie or you wouldn't have gone anywhere near the Special Forces or Dr. Whitney and his crazy experiment? Or that guys like you wind up dead because you never learn enough is enough? Or that you go through women like water?" Arly indicated Ryland's hands with his chin. "And that you've probably seen the inside of more than one jail because you get in fights."

Ryland whistled softly. "Tell me what you really think, don't spare my feelings."

"I had no intention of sparing your feelings. Lily is like a daughter to me. She's my family. You'll find the members of this household love her and will go to any lengths to protect her. And she's rich beyond your wildest dreams. She doesn't need a gold digger trying to waltz in and sweep her off her feet with a few practiced kisses."

"Now you're getting on very thin ice," Ryland warned. "I don't have any desire for Lily's money. As far as I'm concerned she can give it away to charity. I'm perfectly capable of providing for us."

Arly's eyebrow shot up. "You're arrogant on top of everything else. Great. That's going to mesh really well with her delightful personality." He was silent for a few steps, obviously debating how to say his piece. "Lily isn't like everyone else, Miller. She has special needs and her brain requires constant information to work on. Without it, she doesn't do well. Just as your men all will require special circumstances in their choice of homes and work environment, so does Lily. I'm telling you this because when all's said and done, I think you really are sincere and she's so damned stubborn I couldn't persuade her away from you if she's made up her mind."

"I know she's going to require care."

"Not care, Miller. This house. These walls. People like me around her, who don't drain her energy and batter her day and night with unwanted emotion. She thrives because her father saw to it that she would. You can't take her away from here for very long."

"She said there were others. They would be women now, what about them? How did they survive without the benefits of Whitney's money and his protected environment?" Ryland asked curiously.

Arly swallowed several times before replying. Finally he shook his head helplessly. "I have no idea about any other women. I look after Lily and that's all I can handle."

They had to hurry down the stairs and through the maze of corridors to catch Lily. She had halted at the door to her father's office. Lily punched in the code to unlock it and hesitated, looking around carefully. "Are you certain no cameras were placed in this area, Arly? And you did a sweep of my father's office again, didn't you?"

"A few hours ago, after the day help went home," Arly admitted. "That's where we're most vulnerable. We need the staff, but they aren't necessarily loyal to the estate. It won't matter how much we pay them, if they're offered more, they'll give out information and maybe even go so far as to snoop in the areas off limits or drop little listening devices."

"I've set up a command post on the third floor," Ryland said. "We mapped out several escape routes, going up to the roof and down to the tunnels. Thanks for the motion detectors, Arly. Those certainly make the men feel more secure."

"You can't leave the parameters I gave you," Arly cautioned. "We can't guarantee safety if you do. Lily tells me she's going to work with you and the others to prepare all of you for the outside environment and hopefully minimize the risks of complications. In the meantime, you'll have to realize the day staff is our greatest security risk."

Lily stepped back to allow the two men to precede her into the office. She wanted to ensure the door was locked. Arly had changed the security code on the off chance another intruder might get into the house.

"I'm going to monitor the house from my rooms," Arly announced. "Will you be all right?" He pointedly ignored Ryland to ask the question of Lily.

"I think Captain Miller knows all sorts of hand-to-hand things," she quipped.

"That's what I'm afraid of," Arly said. In a rare show of affection he leaned down to kiss her cheek. "You aren't wearing your watch. And you're looking tired. Maybe you ought to sleep for a few hours before getting involved in your research, Lily."

"This can't wait, Arly, but thank you for worrying. I'll go to bed as soon as I can and I'll sleep all day."

"And wear your watch."

Lily hugged his thin body close to her. "Don't worry about me, Arly."

Ryland watched the older man go. "He's a tough guy when it comes to you. He gave me the second degree. I had the feeling he might turn me in himself if he thought I was up to no good." He watched with interest as Lily went to the grandfather clock and did something he couldn't see with the hour hand. To his astonishment the front of the clock moved forward to reveal a hidden chamber in the wall. Then he found himself staring at an opening in the floor.

"Does the house have many of these rooms?" He followed her down the steep, narrow staircase. His shoulders brushed the walls on either side.

"Well, if you mean are there passageways, yes, and hidden rooms, but there is no evidence of this stairway. It's sandwiched between two of the basements' walls. It leads beneath the basements underground and I don't believe it was in the blueprints, so my father's laboratory is very secret. He has up-to-date equipment in it along with an entire library of documentation on his earlier experiment as well as with you and your men."

"Explain to me about the electricity pulses, Lily. I need to understand what Jeff is up against." Ryland stared around the laboratory, amazed at the meticulous detailing of Peter Whitney's private lab. He shouldn't have been. Research was Whitney's life and he had the money to indulge his needs, but the equipment could only have been found in the best research centers.

"The entire idea of brain bleeds as a side effect bothers me," Lily said as she began to scan dates on the neat collection of disks. "Everyone seems to accept it as normal but it isn't. It would be incredibly rare. Seizures would have to be massive and continuous to cause the bleeds. And what's bringing the seizures on? Prolonged exposure to highly emotional waves of energy? Using telepathy without an anchor, or a safeguard? That could happen, the brain is overtaxed, too much garbage getting in, but it would more likely produce severe migraines. I've been functioning for years overstimulated by emotions and unwanted information. Yes, I get migraines and it's very draining but I don't seize and I don't have brain bleeds."

"I still don't know what that means. We've lost two men to brain hemorrhages; at least that's what we were told happened to them."

Lily inserted a disk into the computer. "My father tried using small pulses of electricity to stimulate brain activity in his initial experiments. He surgically planted electrodes directly on the areas he wanted enhanced. The microelectrodes recorded action generated by individual neurons. The electrical signals were amplified, filtered, and could be displayed visually and even converted to sounds through an audiometer."

"He was watching the brain waves react?" Ryland watched the data flashing over the screen at a rate he couldn't follow but even while talking, Lily seemed to be computing it. He watched the expressions chasing across her face, interest, a frown, a slight pause as she shook her head, then more data.

"And listening to them. Neurons have characteristic patterns of activity which can be both visualized and heard." She murmured the information absently, peering more closely at the screen.

"Damn it, Lily! Are you telling me we have something planted in our brains along with everything else done to us? No one agreed to that." He rubbed his throbbing temples, fury swirling in his gut.

"Jeff Hollister has evidence of surgery. But I can't imagine Dad repeating such a terrible mistake—one of the rare side effects he found long ago was brain bleeds and he determined it wasn't worth the results."

"So you think we all have these things implanted?" He couldn't help rubbing his hands over his head again and again searching for scars. The idea sickened him.

Lily shook her head. "It's a complex procedure. They would have had to fit him with a headframe which they'd attach to his skull and to a table. It has to be done with the patient awake, so he would have known it was being done. A computer is used for the exact imaging. It's very precise, Ryland, someone would have to know what they were doing."

Ryland swore again under his breath, pacing away and then back to her.

"If someone were arranging accidents or trying to make the psychic experiment appear a failure, they could have done something to any of you in the surgery unit at Donovans. They're certainly equipped for it."

"What? Sabotage?" Ryland swept a hand through his hair. "Damn them."

Lily shrugged. "Most of the time this type of conspiracy involves money. Or politics. If it could be made to look as if all of you were at risk on the outside, and you couldn't be used for military purposes, but in truth, the enhancement worked without too many complications, the information could easily be sold to a foreign nation."

"How would someone know about electrodes in the head causing brain bleeds? I didn't know," Ryland admitted. "If Higgens is behind this, how would he know?"

"Thornton would know." At his puzzled frown she explained. "The president of Donovans. A few years ago doctors began research on a project using deep brain stimulation for

Parkinson's disease. The idea certainly has merit and other researchers were very interested to see what else the process might be used for. Thornton and I had a long discussion about it a few months ago. I remember because he was so interested in the procedure and its uses. And if Dad mentioned he'd thought of it and dismissed the idea as too dangerous, that might have triggered interest right there if they were looking for a way to sabotage the experiment."

She sounded so fascinated it annoyed him. "Damn it, Lily, is there a possibility we have electrodes in our brains and we can't feel them? And if we do, how are they messing with us?"

"There would be evidence, Ryland. Also, Dad stated absolutely he wouldn't risk repeating the problems associated with the first experiment, even though now he would be able to map a target site with pinpoint accuracy." She looked at him. "The autopsy report was done at Donovans and Dad didn't believe it. He suspected someone was tampering with you and your men, but he wasn't certain. Look at this, Ryland." She peered at the screen. "Dad tried repeatedly to speak to General Ranier, in fact, had several conversations with his aide, apparently recorded on Dad's side, so the tapes are here somewhere. Ranier never called him back. Dad sent four letters and various emails to him and not one was answered." She tapped the computer. "It's all right here in his journals. General Ranier is a family friend. I had no idea Dad tried to contact him so often."

Ryland paced across the floor, swearing under his breath. Lily was swaying with exhaustion, the dark circles under her eyes more pronounced than ever. He wanted to gather her into his arms and hold her to him. Carry her to her bed and curve his body around hers protectively. His hands came down on her shoulders in a soothing massage. "You need to lie down for a while, Lily. You should go to bed. If Jeff is safe for the time being, then you should just get some sleep."

"I am tired," she admitted. "I just have a few more things to look at here and then I'll check on Jeff one more time."

"How would they deliver the electricity?" Ryland asked curiously.

She scanned the third disk quickly, stopping twice to silently absorb the more technical material. "If it was legitimate, you'd wear a small power pack, much like a pacemaker. You'd switch it on yourself. It's magnetic. The smallest pulse possible for results would be delivered. None of you have a power pack so if it happened to Jeff, the electrodes were placed without his real knowledge or consent of what they were doing and then he would have been subjected to a magnetic high frequency delivered by an outside source. I'm hypothesizing, Ryland, I'm not certain how or even if it could be done for certain."

"Why? What would be the point of doing that to him?"

"To kill him of course." Lily shut down the computer. "Come on. Let's go check on him. It's been a long night."

He took her hand. "And a longer day," he agreed.

TEN

*I*need *you.* Lily woke with a start, her heart pounding with fear, or maybe in anticipation, her eyes straining to pierce the darkness into the corners of her bedroom. The voice was clear and strong. Edgy with hunger. Not a dream this time. Ryland was in the same room with her.

She rolled over and peered under her bed. Laughing at her silliness, Lily lay back against the pillow, staring up at the ceiling. The sound of her voice helped to stifle the disappointment settling in her body. She ached. Inside and out, she ached for him. For Ryland Miller. The silver slash of his eyes. The temptation of his mouth. His body. She dreamt of his body. Of holding him close, of his hands and mouth touching her, tasting her. Of the feel of his skin. She woke burning and alone. Hollow and empty and moody.

After she had left him with Jeff Hollister, she had returned to her father's secret laboratory, wanting to read more of his journals. Lily feared doing anything that might harm Hollister but Ryland had been adamant that they not bring in medical help. She worked most of the morning and into the afternoon, falling into bed just before five. Obviously she had slept into the night.

She was not going to search Ryland out. Thinking about him

interfered with her ability to concentrate on helping him. It was far more important to find answers. She had supplied him with a safe refuge and plenty of food. Getting involved with him any further could jeopardize everything, she told herself firmly. The best way to help Ryland Miller and the others was to find out everything she could about how her father had managed to open their brains to the waves of energy.

Lily shoved a hand through her thick mass of hair tumbling around her face. She could never live up to the erotic dream they'd shared. It was easy enough to be completely uninhibited in a dream, but she had no idea how to behave with a flesh-and-blood man expecting a siren. *Why* had she ever shared that dream with him? She blushed a vivid scarlet, groaned, and hid her face in her hands.

"Think of something else, Lily. For heaven's sake, you're a grown woman. It's imperative to find the answers. Stop thinking about him!" Lily tried to be firm with herself, forcing her mind to consider other things besides raw, hot men. Man. She sighed. "Okay, Lily, focus here. Colonel Higgens is bound to eventually become suspicious of you. Sooner or later he'll find a way to penetrate security. Arly only *thinks* he's a miracle worker."

Lily threw back the covers and padded across the room to the tiled bathroom on bare feet. She wore only a long shirt. Ryland's shirt. It still held his scent, enfolding her in his presence like an embrace. She had stolen it, a pathetic impulse she was slightly ashamed of, but eternally grateful she had acted on. It had been left in the laboratory along with his other clothes, ready to be sent out to the laundry. She couldn't believe she had been reduced to stealing a shirt. It was more than pathetic, it was truly wretched.

Taking her time as she washed her face, using the opportunity to give herself a stern lecture, she peered at her face in the mirror. "You don't want him anyway, Lily, you want to be loved for who you are, not because you have great chemistry." Her eyes were too large for her face. She was too pale. Drooping. Why hadn't she been born model thin and gorgeous? With a perpetual tan?

Great chemistry works for me. The voice slipped into her mind. Slid over her body like a physical touch.

Lily stiffened, her fingers curling around the edges of the sink. Using the mirror she searched the room carefully. It was one thing to dream of him, quite another to face him alone and vulnerable in the privacy of her rooms. The connection was too strong between them. She didn't trust it . . . or him. "Are you here in the room with me? Because you'd better not be. You have a designated area of safety and my private rooms are not included." She asked the question aloud, wanted him to answer aloud. It was far too intimate an exchange with him in her mind. Her thoughts. Her fantasies. The color wasn't just in her face anymore, it was creeping up her entire body.

I like your fantasies. Ryland's voice purred. Like a great contented cat. Purred so that it vibrated through her body, set her on fire.

He couldn't be in her room. He'd better not be in her room. Her heart was pounding with a mixture of fear and excitement. She wanted to see him, but dreaded being alone with him. And she was wearing his shirt. . . . It was possible she wanted him so much she was imagining things. She closed her eyes. Imagination had already gotten her in trouble once; she wasn't about to allow it to happen again.

Hands whispered up her thighs, pushing aside the long tails of her shirt, slid over the curve of her hips, framed her rib cage, and moved up higher to cup the weight of her breasts in rough palms. Lily's eyes flew open to stare at his face above her own. Real. Ryland crowded close to her. His body, hard and hot, pressed against her back. His hands, beneath the thin material of her shirt, were possessive, his thumbs stroking her nipples into taut peaks.

Ryland watched her face in the mirror. Fear blossoming. The shock. The pleasure. He slowly bent his head so that his lips skimmed her neck. "Don't worry, Lily, I know you. I know what you want. I know what you need right now. I need it too. The rest will come later."

Desire was a hot heat spiraling through her body, every nerve ending alive. Lily gasped, her fingers tightening around the edge of the sink. She should have been screaming a protest; instead she stood very still absorbing the feel of his hands on her body. "Are you crazy? How did you find me? You shouldn't be here, Ryland." She wanted him more than life itself. But she wasn't what he thought. She could never match the erotic fantasy they had woven together.

Ryland's teeth scraped gently over her neck, sent fire racing over her skin. "Did you think anything could keep me away from you?" His hands were possessive around her breasts. "Don't be afraid, Lily. Anything we do is going to be perfect between us."

She couldn't help the thrill of excitement that raced through her, even if her mind taunted her with her lack of actual experience. Their eyes met in the mirror. She could see his hunger. Stark and raw. There were lines etched into his face that hadn't been there before. There were shadows and a certain edge to the sensual cut of his mouth.

Lily drew in her breath to tell him it was wrong, they didn't love one another, it was a chemical reaction, anything to drive him away, but he drew her closer to him, fit her body snugly against his. She could feel the hard bulge pressed against her, evidence of his body's urgent demands. She felt as if she belonged to him. With him. No longer Lily but a part of Ryland. As if there would be no Lily without him.

"It's been hell without you, Lily. I can't explain it any other way. With you, I can function. I can control what's happening to me."

"You aren't controlling yourself now." She wasn't entirely certain she wanted him in control. One hand was sliding lightly over her stomach, his fingers moving in a massaging caress impossible to ignore. She closed her eyes against the sensation and unexpectedly tears burned behind her lashes.

Immediately his hand stopped moving. His breath hitched in his throat. "Don't do that. Don't hurt like that." His hands reluctantly left the refuge of her body. He turned her into the shelter of his chest, his arms enfolding her close. His body was protective, his hands tender as they stroked her silky hair. "I know you're confused right now. I know you don't think what's between us is real or that emotion plays a part in it, but you're wrong, Lily. I think of you all the time, how you are, what you're feeling. I love the sound of your voice, your smile. It isn't just sex."

"It isn't that." Lily turned her head to rest it over the precise spot where his heart beat so steadily. It was happening all over again. Each time she was near him she could deny him nothing. She couldn't look at him. She wasn't certain she could ever look at him again. "I don't want you to be disappointed."

Ryland stood very still. It was the last thing he expected. Lily was the epitome of confidence. She was beautiful and perfect and her mouth was a total sin. "Lily, honey, look at me."

Mutely she shook her head. Ryland stroked her hair, crushed the thick strands in his fist. He bent his head, inhaled her fragrance. Inhaled her scent. *Lily.* His Lily. "It would be an impossibility for me to be disappointed in you."

She pushed away from his warmth, from his solid body. "You shouldn't be here. And I don't want to talk about this." It was too humiliating. She was already making a complete fool of herself. Lily thought to put distance between them, but they were in the confines of the bathroom and her back was up against the sink. Ryland was a large man, his broad shoulders filling the room, his body blocking the doorway. She faced him, shaking her head, her blue eyes sad. "You're going to be expecting me to be like . . ." She frowned, waved her hand around, settled on one word. "Her." *Your hot little fantasy woman that can do everything. Anything.* She blushed a vivid scarlet again, hoping the darkness would cover what was an appalling shade on her.

He reached out, laced his fingers through hers, and tugged until she reluctantly followed him into her darkened bedroom. "I think we need to have a little talk, Lily."

Her heart jumped wildly. She allowed him to pull her toward the wide armchair beside the tall lamp. It was utterly ridiculous how helpless he could make her feel with just the velvet tone of his voice. Her body went into meltdown and she couldn't think clearly.

He seated himself comfortably, tugged on her hand until she fell against him. He settled her on his lap, all too aware she wore nothing beneath the shirt. His shirt. It pleased him that she wore his shirt. "I don't think a little talk is going to help, Ryland. I can't be that woman in our dream. I've never really been with a man. It was all imagination and reading."

"I want to read the books you've been reading." His hands seemed to have a mind of their own, sliding over her bare thighs, long, gentle strokes to feel the petal soft skin of her. He had always known her skin would feel as it did. It was impossible to keep his hands off of her.

His hands followed the path of her thigh, slid around to cup her bare bottom, massaging and stroking until she thought she might go out of her mind.

"Ryland, it won't be the same as it was in the dream." She felt as if she were pleading with him, but she didn't know if it was for him to believe her, or persuade her.

"I hope not. I want it to be real. I want to be deep inside your body. I want your hands really touching my skin. It isn't going to matter that you're not experienced, Lily. It only matters that we want to please one another, enjoy one another."

She hated herself for being such a coward. They would be spectacular together and then he would walk away and leave her. "Do you think you're making this any easier for either of us?" Lily leapt up as if his touch were burning her. It was burning her. Her breath was coming in ragged gasps. She paced across the hardwood floor, back and forth, confused and slightly disoriented. "And what do you think is going to happen if we . . . if I let you . . ." She glanced at him from under long lashes. "Afterward . . ."

His legs were stretched out comfortably and he was watching her, his gaze moving slowly, hotly over her body. Devouring every inch of her. At once she was aware of her naked body moving restlessly beneath the shirt. Her breasts ached and her body felt heavy, throbbed for release. For him. "Afterward, I hope to start all over again. And again. And again. It will never be enough for me."

Lily shook her head and backed away from him. "We both know you'll have to leave me eventually. It will be that much harder when you go."

He rose in one fluid movement, stalking her right across the bedroom floor. Lily backpedaled hastily to elude him. "It can't get much harder than it already is, Lily." His voice found its way into her bloodstream, creating a molten river. He reached out with his incredible speed and shackled her wrist with his fingers.

At once she went very still, her stomach somersaulting. She ached for him. If she closed her eyes to block out the sight of him, it wouldn't matter. He was already deep inside of her. And which would be worse? Having him and watching him walk away from her? Or never having him and feeling empty for the rest of her life? She would rather have the memory of a real experience than a dream.

"Lily?" His voice was velvet soft like the night itself. The fingers wrapped so loosely around her wrist like a bracelet suddenly tightened, brought her up short. "Lily, what am I feeling right now?"

She forced her gaze to meet his. Allowed herself to absorb his raw emotions. Desire. It was hard-edged. Dangerous. Primal. The force of his hunger for her body shook her. He didn't flinch away from the knowledge in her eyes.

"How can you think there's separation from your body and your mind and heart? I need you. Want you. Every square inch of you, Lily. Is that such a terrifying thing? Are you so afraid of me? Of being with me?"

Was there a note of hurt in his voice? He always sounded so in command, in control, yet there was a curious vulnerability in him when he was with her. She continued to look up at him, unable to break away from his mesmerizing gaze. From the stark desire she saw there.

Ryland moved then, slowly lowering his head to hers. Inch by slow inch. All the while holding her captive with the power of his glittering eyes. Her pulse, beneath the pad of his thumb, raced wildly. His lips moved against hers. Gently. Skimming. Barely touching. "You've forgotten to breathe." His breath was warm on her skin, on her mouth, breathing for her, sharing the very air in his lungs.

His lips were soft. Velvet soft. Heat curled in her stomach, pooled into a sweet ache. Ryland leaned closer, his lips rubbing over hers, teasing at the corners of her mouth, small little nibbles. An enticement. A temptation. His tongue traced the line of her lips, a gentle persistence completely at odds with the tremor of intense hunger that ran beneath the surface of his body.

His hands were gentle, tender even, as one curled around the nape of her neck to hold her still. The other followed the line of her back, the curve of her hips to rest possessively on her bottom.

A flame shot through her bloodstream, wild and hot and all at once out of control. The sensation was shocking when he was so gentle, coaxing her response rather than demanding it. Lily felt weak with wanting him, tired of fighting the attraction between them. The temptation of heat and fire stole her good sense. Her mouth moved under his, her lips soft and pliant and welcoming.

His mouth hardened, became hot and dangerous, compelling her to open for him, her dark sorcerer claiming his rights. At once she was swept into another world, one of pure feeling, of colors and sensations. Tongues of fire raced along her skin. Every nerve ending came alive. Her blood was thick and hot with need. Her body craving, *craving,* until her arms crept around his neck and her body molded itself to his.

Her breasts ached, her body throbbed. His hands cupped her bottom, lifting, pressing her against the thick evidence of his arousal, rubbing her close until the friction was almost too much to bear.

Ryland groaned, a sound of stark need. "I'm losing my sanity, Lily. I burn for you, day and night." The words were whispered against her open mouth. "It's not comfortable or pleasant, it hurts like hell. Put me out of my misery, honey. Help me, Lily. I can't think with wanting you."

"Want" was such an insipid word. How could he explain to her what it was like for him? Day and night thinking of her, dreaming of her, a drug in his bloodstream, a craving that couldn't be sated. His body was always hot and unmercifully hard. There were no words adequate enough, intense enough, to describe the nights of sweat-soaked sheets and days with his jeans stretched so damned tight over his hard body he thought he might never be able to take another step without pain again.

His hands on her bare bottom cupped her firm muscles, began a slow, intimate massage, deliberately, wickedly enticing her.

Lily couldn't breathe with wanting him. His mouth fastened to hers, devouring her, the gentle coaxing manner lost in the inferno building between them. She let her body answer for her, without words, giving consent with her hands, sliding possessively over his body, while her tongue dueled with his.

Ryland groaned softly, low in his throat, somewhere between a growl and a purr. Lily was trembling beneath his hands. He didn't want her to be afraid or nervous, not even for a moment. "I dreamt of this moment, Lily." He lifted her easily, casually, his mouth roaming her face and throat as he carried her to the bed. "So many times, I dreamt of this."

Lily could feel the coolness of the sheet against her back as he pressed her into the mattress. His hands were strong, determined, possessive even as they roamed over her body. His face was etched with deep emotion, his eyes burning. He swept away the shirt, dropping it carelessly on the floor. She heard him gasp, the hitch in his breath, the husky sound in his throat. His palms trailed over her skin slowly from her shoulders, over the swell of her breasts, along her narrow rib cage to her tucked-in waist and the flat expanse of her stomach. "It's amazing how soft your skin feels."

His touch was exquisitely gentle, completely at odds with the terrible hunger burning in his eyes. He bent his head slowly to her breast. His breath reached her skin first. Warm. Moist. His lips were soft.

Lily jumped under his seeking mouth, all at once so sensitive even the brush of his hair was erotic against her skin.

Ryland was determined to go slow, stay in control, hold his terrible hunger for Lily under some sort of rein. The last thing he wanted to do was frighten her. There was plenty of time for wild cravings—right here, right now, it was all about pleasing Lily.

Go slow. Go slow. The words beat like a litany in his head. His fingers trembled as they stroked her breasts. Worshiped her. He closed his mouth around the soft mound, a tight wet bond, his tongue dancing over her taut nipple as he suckled.

Lily cried out, arched into him, craving his touch, needing more. Always more. "Take your clothes off, Ryland," she pleaded, "I want to touch you, look at you." Her voice, hungry with urgency, hungry for him, shook him. She had known the moment she laid eyes on him that she wanted him and she had immediately begun to educate herself, learning as much as she could about sexual appetites, wanting to know how to please him. Nothing she read or watched had prepared her for what she was feeling.

She had thought she would be embarrassed and afraid to be naked in front of him, but instead she reveled in the way he looked at her. The way he touched her. The way his gaze burned over her so possessively.

Ryland lifted his head, studied her cloudy eyes, her soft mouth swollen from his ravaging kisses. "I'm trying to be gentle, honey." He attempted to explain, but the words were trapped in his heart. His hands were already pulling off his clothes, flinging them aside. His heart beat like thunder. He had fantasized this moment so often, his body in a continual state of arousal for so long, he feared anything he said could never describe how he felt about her. There were no words. She was a fever in his blood, a craving, obsession, she was his heart and soul. How could he say that to her? "I swear I won't hurt you." He meant ever. Not with his body and not with his mind.

Lily stared up at him, lying in the darkness, mesmerized by the dark passion etched deeply into his face. He took her breath away. Every muscle in her body was weak with wanting him, every cell on fire for his touch. She should have been afraid of his craving, the intensity of his terrible hunger, but within her body, in the shadowy corners of her soul, she found her own secret desires.

There was no ice running in her veins, there was molten lava. Deep inside of her stirred a volcano, hot and thick and ready to erupt, swirling to the surface to meet his every demand. Eagerly. Wantonly. She reached for him. "I'm a woman, Ryland, not a porcelain doll. I know exactly what I want."

Their mouths fused together, electric and hot. Her hands moved over him, needing to feel every muscle, just as he needed to explore her body. He kept to his plan, using slow torture to arouse her to a frightening pitch. He suckled her lush breasts, his tongue teasing, his teeth scraping gently, his mouth hot and moist. He traced her ribs, the flat of her stomach. The curve of her hip, every hollow. He wanted every one of Lily's secrets. He wouldn't take anything less.

"Ryland, please," Lily's body was so sensitive she was afraid she was going to cry with wanting him. She was aching and heavy and beyond reason.

"Look at me, baby," he said softly, directing her gaze to the heavy erection. "I'm a big man and I'll be damned if I'll hurt you, even a little."

His finger stroked into her damp heat and she nearly rose off the mattress. "You're torturing me," she said, but she couldn't stop herself from pushing against his hand, desperately seeking relief.

Ryland encouraged her to thrust against his hand as he slowly pushed his finger into her tight channel. She was hot and slick but far too tight to take his thick arousal. It was obvious she hadn't been with anyone else and the idea that he was her only, that he would be the one teaching her was even more exciting. Lily was passionate, abandoned, willing to do what came naturally to her.

"I'm going to stretch you a little more, honey; just relax for me. You trust me, don't you, Lily?" He withdrew one finger, slowly inserting two, watching her expression closely for signs of discomfort as he pushed deeper into her body.

The sensation was so pleasurable it was alarming. Lily fought for breath, fought for control where there was none. She never wanted Ryland to stop. He thrust deeper, the friction electric, shocking in its intensity. He was doing things deep inside her, stroking and teasing and making her crazy so she couldn't lie still. Her hips surged against his hands wantonly.

"This shouldn't hurt, Lily, I'll make it good for you," he whispered, pushing her thighs apart, settling his weight there. "Look at us, honey. We belong together." Ryland took his erection in his hand, pressed the engorged head to her moist entrance.

He was far thicker than she had anticipated and he stretched her body, slowly, pushing his way through her hot folds, forcing her tight muscles to allow him entrance. She cried out as he went deeper, stopped at the thin, almost nonexistent barrier, then deeper still in a harder thrust, filling her to such a fullness she burned and throbbed and unexpectedly plummeted over the edge.

Neither expected the reaction, the waves of enchantment rippling through her, spreading like a tidal wave. Her body gripped and suckled at his, so tightly he was gritting his teeth, the pleasure so intense it bordered on pain. Her orgasm bathed him in hot heat, so that he slipped in another couple of inches.

Lily looked up at his face and his male beauty took her breath away. She wanted everything with him, too. She trusted him inexplicably. And she wanted every moment with him. "I want to be your every erotic fantasy." The words came out of nowhere. Said into the night. "Teach me how to please you, Ryland."

The honesty in her voice shook him, ripped his heart right out of his body. He withdrew, pushed deep again slowly, feeling his way, wanting it right. Wanting it perfect for her. His hands tightened on her hips as he began a slow, steady rhythm. He urged her body to move with his. "Everything, honey. We'll have it all. I want to know your body better than you know it. I want every square inch of you to belong to me."

He caught her hips in his hands, holding her firmly, tilting her body while he went deeper still, wanting her to take all of him. Lily gasped as the heat engulfed her, as he filled her completely. Ryland began to move again, long slow thrusts, deep and perfect.

She cried out again, low, in her throat, as he changed speed, driving harder, faster. "We're just getting started, Lily," he promised. "This is just to take the edge off." He let himself go, his hips surging deep into her tight channel over and over, taking them higher than he ever thought possible. His head roared and his body clenched and burned, but he didn't want the ecstasy to ever end.

When his orgasm came, it was explosive, ripping through his body with gut-wrenching force, shaking him, nearly taking off the top of his head. Her body was so responsive to his, following his every lead, he had never experienced anything remotely like it. He was staggered by the intensity of pleasure she had given him. And he had given back to her.

Ryland collapsed beside her, holding her in his arms, his face buried against the softness of her breast, his body still deep in hers. He had known he wanted her, that it was for all time, but he hadn't realized what was between them. A priceless gift, a treasure beyond his dreams. She was wrapped so tight inside of him, he knew it was more than his body and mind. More than his heart. She was entrenched in his soul.

"I thought it was painful for women their first time," she said. "I expected it to be so different. You having all the fun and me being disappointed."

"Did you?" He was smiling, joy spreading through him. That was the Lily he knew, analyzing her data. "I guess you were thinking about some other man making love to you." Deliberately he drew her breast into the heat of his mouth, knowing each time he sucked strongly or lapped with his tongue, the shock waves rippled deep inside of her, doubling her enjoyment.

Lily closed her eyes, pleasure washing through her. "Is it always like this? I read all those manuals but . . ." Her voice hitched as his tongue swirled.

"Manuals?" Ryland lifted his head, grinning at her in the darkness. "That's so you, Lily, reading a book to experience life. If you were wanting to know something why didn't you just ask me?"

Her fingers found the silk of his hair, tunneled, and held. "I might have been embarrassed. It isn't easy to talk to someone of experience about intimate matters."

She was frowning, he knew that she was. Everything about her made him smile. Her tone was so scientific, yet he could feel her body trembling, the little aftershocks still rocking her. "We've always talked about everything, honey. I didn't exactly make it a secret that I wanted you. You could have told me you were inexperienced. I might have toned down our very erotic dream."

"I liked your dreams. The visuals were astounding, much better than the lifeless manual. I wasn't actually certain it was physically possible to do the things the books talked about."

He cleared his throat. "Where exactly did you get these books?"

"Off the internet. They have very explicit information and people willing to answer all of your questions."

He groaned aloud. "I'll bet they do. I think I'd like to see these books of yours. I was a little concerned you might tell me you were really watching Arly's movies."

She laughed wickedly. "I'm not certain he has any movies but if he does, he's probably putting some sort of security device on them to keep me away."

"You have a mean streak in you." Ryland leaned down to nip at her enticing breast. "You smell so damned good, Lily." His body was still locked with hers. He could feel every ripple in her muscles. He discovered just breathing on her taut nipples caused an answering contraction in her deepest core. She bathed him in liquid heat and sent pleasure coursing through his body. "I noticed that immediately, how wonderful you smelled."

She rubbed her face against his throat. "I love the way you feel." And the way he cared about his men. And the way he loved his mother. And the way one unruly curl fell across his forehead no matter how he slicked it back. It was appalling how much she loved about him. She couldn't help running her hands over his back to feel the defined muscles there. "I used to wonder about miracles."

"Miracles?" He echoed the word, shaken by the naked emotion in her voice. She turned him inside out with a tone.

"Well, yeah. Miracles. What could be considered a true miracle, that sort of thing. It's an interesting puzzle that so many people around the world have a form of worship and belief. But actually . . ." She trailed kisses along his throat, over his jaw to tease the corner of his mouth.

Rather boldly for a woman of no experience, but his body reacted, growing hard when it should have been impossible. Ryland kissed her because he couldn't stop himself from tasting her. From just fusing them together and wanting to remain that way, locked with her in a private world of heat and passion. His hands moved over her body, memorizing every line, every hollow. The texture of her skin. The way she reacted, her muscles contracting around him and her breath leaving her lungs in a rush of pleasure.

She was his miracle. In the midst of a hell he had helped to create, he had found her. Lily's lush body was paradise. Her smile, the sound of her voice. Even the way she moved and could look so haughty with her tempting mouth and cool blue eyes. He raised his head to look down at her.

"Lily, from now on, if you have any questions on sex, ask me." He caught her waist as he rolled onto his back, not wanting to break contact, wanting to stay buried in the tightness of her hot, slick body.

Lily gasped as she found herself sitting up, astride him, his body deep within hers. Her hair fell in a tousled cloud around her, the silken strands teasing her sensitized skin. It was impossible to be embarrassed when he was obviously enjoying the sight and feel of her body. His hands came up to cup her generous breasts, his fingers stroking and caressing.

Lily closed her eyes and gave herself up to the sheer pleasure of experimenting. She moved her hips, slid over his body, tightened her muscles. She felt him deep inside her, growing, thickening, responding to her movements. She began a slow ride, arching back to give him a good view of her breasts swaying in temptation. It was an amazing feeling to just indulge herself in every sensation. She moved slowly at first, judging his reaction, getting used to taking the lead. Then she became bolder, trailing her fingers along his muscles, swirling fingernails over his flat belly and teasing dark curls of hair. She experimented, tightening muscles as she rose up, as she slid along the length of him, moving faster and harder until she had to open her eyes and see the naked passion on his face.

She loved his rough, weathered features. The dark shadow along his jaw. The brilliance of his silver eyes. He took her breath away and sent her body into meltdown. She reveled in his watching her, touching her. The way his gaze was so hot, so intense, electrified her, brought her body to a life of its own.

Ryland couldn't take his gaze off of her. Lily's body was flushed with the fever of passion. Her breasts moved invitingly with every surge of her hips. She rode him hard, incredibly uninhibited, showing her enjoyment of his body with her every touch, every gesture. Her eyes clouded over, her breath hitching. A soft sound escaped her throat. At once he caught her hips in his hands, holding her while he took over the pace, surging into her, guiding her movements so her body fisted around his. Velvet soft, fiery hot, a liquid flame wrapped tightly around him.

Lily threw her head back, cried out his name, a gasp of wonderment, of awe, while her body rippled with strength and life around his, driving him over the edge with her.

"You're unbelievable," she whispered, bending to kiss him. The action tightened her muscles around him, mashed her soft breasts into his chest.

Ryland was amazed at how masculine the simple action made him feel. And he was really amazed at how bereft he felt when she slid her body from his and lay beside him. He longed to stay deep inside of her, filling her, joined with her, sharing the same skin with her. "Oh, we're just getting started, Lily. There are all kinds of ways to make love and to enjoy one another. I've got plans."

She looked at him suspiciously. "What kinds of plans?"

He took her hand, brought it to his lips, and used his tongue to lap sensuously around her finger before drawing it into the moist beat of his mouth. Her eyes widened at the way her body reacted when he sucked on her finger, and used his tongue shamelessly in a simulated mating.

Lily blushed a vivid scarlet, but her body burned hot and wild, a reckless promise of pleasure. "My brain already melted, Ryland, it's too late." Her voice was breathless with wanting whatever they could share together, but she was exhausted and she knew it.

He found the down comforter on the floor where it had fallen and drew it up to cover them both before wrapping his arms firmly around her. "We have time, Lily, I'm not going anywhere. Go to sleep, honey, you need your rest."

ELEVEN

LILY felt Ryland's arms around her, his hands cupping her breasts possessively. Ryland was curved around her body, pressed tight against her, his body so hot there was no need of covers. "Go away." Her voice groaned the order. "I can't possibly move. Not ever again. Can someone die from making love too many times?"

His teeth nibbled on the nape of her neck. "I don't know, but I'm willing to try if you are." It was sheer joy to wake up with Lily in his arms. "I want this for the rest of my life." He'd had no intention of saying it out loud, but it slipped out anyway.

Lily turned in his arms, her soft breasts brushing his body intimately. Her blue gaze drifted over his face until he felt her stirring inside his body, whisper soft, like butterfly wings. "I do too, Ryland, but I don't honestly know whether or not what we feel is real or contrived by my father. Could he have done something to enhance what we feel? What if we find later he did?"

"Do you think it's possible?"

She frowned in thought. "I honestly don't know. I can't imagine how, but we react so violently to one another. I can't keep my hands off you. I really can't. I'm not like that, Ryland.

I know myself very well, and I just never thought about sex the way I do now."

"Suppose we find out he did, Lily?" His thumb strummed her nipple just so he could feel her shiver in reaction. He inhaled the fragrance of her hair. "What difference would it make? He may have found a way to manipulate sexual feelings, although I doubt it, but it would be impossible for him to force someone's emotions. If I couldn't have your body, Lily, I would still want you."

"Why? What do you think is so special about me that you would want to spend the rest of your life with me?" Her voice was very low.

"Your courage, your loyalty," he answered instantly. "You think I can't see those things in you? I'm *trained* to read people. You defend your father even with all the things you've learned about him. I see the way you touch Jeff, a virtual stranger, yet with gentleness and caring. I see the love you have for your family. You're so willing to help us when you didn't have to open your home to us. Hell, Lily, you could have turned your back on us, you probably should have. You don't think I can see you running yourself into the ground, so exhausted you want to crawl into a hole, but you keep going for others, to make it right for others. Who wouldn't fall in love with a woman like that?"

She shook her head. "I'm not like that. I'm just me, Ryland."

He kissed the frown on her mouth. "You're exactly like that. Little things can come in time, but the important things I already know. You have a great sense of humor. And you can carry on an intelligent conversation." He grinned at her. "I might not know what you're saying part of the time, but it sounds good."

There was a silence while she studied his expression. How could she be uncertain of him? He'd taken his heart right out of his body and gift-wrapped it for her. His gut churned in an agony of sudden fear. "Would finding out your father did something to us make a difference to you, Lily? Is that what you're trying to say to me?"

"Did you really look at me last night, Ryland? It was dark in here. Did you really look at my body, because I'm not beautiful at all like you think I am." Lily sat up, determination plain on her face. "There's a lot of things wrong with me. Flaws. You must have noticed them."

Ryland sat up too, rubbing his mouth to hide amusement he couldn't push away. Lily was a woman, all right. Last night she had come apart in his arms, unashamedly riding him, showing off her body, but now, in the light of day, she was resolutely going to tell him about her "flaws." "Flaws, plural?" He rubbed his chin this time, still carefully covering his mouth. "You have more than one? I did notice your tendency to be a little haughty."

The full power of Lily's blue eyes turned on him. Glaring. "I am *never* haughty."

"Sure you are. You have that princess-in-the-castle look you give the mere peasants when we get out of line," he said cheerfully. "I noticed it, but it's such a minor flaw I can live with it."

"My leg, you imbecile. I was talking about my leg." She thrust it out for him to see. Scars marred her calf, which was sunken in and shiny where part of the muscle was obviously missing. "It's ugly. And I limp when I'm tired. Well, I limp most of the time but I really limp when I'm tired." She was watching his face closely for signs of repugnance.

Ryland leaned closer to inspect her calf. He took her leg in both hands, ran his fingers in a long caress from ankle to thigh. She jerked, retreating, but he held her firmly, bending to kiss the worst of the scars. His tongue traced the strange pattern. "This is not a flaw, Lily. This is life. How the hell do you manage to get your skin so soft?"

She tried glaring and even considered her so-called haughty look but a smile broke through all the same. His voice was sincere and his gaze rock steady. "I think you're still thinking about sex, Ryland. We're supposed to be talking seriously." She was reluctant to pull her leg away from his caressing fingers. There was a soothing quality to his touch. He made her feel beautiful even when she knew she wasn't.

"And I'm not exactly a model. I'm fat in places and skinny in others."

His eyebrow shot up. "Fat?" His gaze was hot as it ran possessively over her body.

Lily crossed her arms over her generous breasts. "You know very well my hips are enormous and so is my top. I look like

I'm tipping over. And my legs are skinny so I look like a chicken."

"I see I'll have to do an inspection," he replied good-naturedly. "Here, let me take a look."

Lily slid away from him, dragging his shirt to her to cover her body. She gave him her coolest look, but her eyes were dancing. "You are impossible. I have to check on Jeff Hollister."

He grinned at her as she stood up, backing away from him. "I don't know, honey. I like the way you look but I have a jealous streak. I don't think my heart could take you walking around in front of my men covered only by my shirt."

She stuck her nose in the air. "I'm taking a shower and getting dressed first." She tried to sound snippy, nearly ruined her perfect performance by laughing, but she managed to control herself.

Ryland padded after her completely naked. Lily didn't hear him behind her and nearly jumped out of her skin when his body crowded against hers in the glass shower. "We weren't finished conversing, were we?" he asked innocently.

She did look down her nose at him, every bit as cool and haughty as he'd called her. "We are more than finished. Go away."

Ryland laughed and rushed her, scooping her up and turning on the water so it cascaded over both of them. His mouth was on hers, stopping protests before she could start them. Heat flared instantly between them, hunger, sharp and elemental.

"We can't," Lily gasped, her arms sliding around his neck to cradle his head as he lapped the water from her breasts. He made her legs weak, her body soft and pliant, aching with need instantly.

"We have to," he countered and closed his mouth over the temptation of her breast. "I want you so much I can't stand it."

"Well, I think I'm going to fall down if you keep doing that."

"You're as hot as I am." His hands were stroking and caressing, already exploring possibilities. "Put your arms around my neck. I'm going to lift you up and you just wrap your legs around my waist."

"I'm too heavy," she protested, but she obeyed him because

he was so tempting she couldn't resist him. She would never be able to resist him.

Lily cried out as she settled over him, forgetting every protest, wanting nothing but to have him fill her. To be with her always.

Neither had any idea of time passage, finding pleasure in being together, rapture in making love. They washed one another, talked softly, laughed often.

As he turned off the shower and tossed Lily a towel, he caught her frowning. "You're not really worried about some other nonexistent flaw you have that you think I should know about," he asked as he ran a towel over his body.

Lily tried not to stare at his body in utter fascination but his muscles really did ripple beneath his skin. "Do you realize I don't even know what kind of music you like?"

Ryland grinned and snapped the towel at her before padding across the floor completely naked without the least bit of modesty. "Does it matter?"

"Of course it matters. I'm pointing out we don't know very much about one another." Why in the world were her eyes glued to his butt? No matter how hard she tried, she couldn't make herself look away. And he was laughing at her.

"I love all kinds of music. My mother listened to everything and insisted I listen too. She also made me take dance lessons." He made a face as he pulled his shirt over his head.

Lily had to laugh at his expression. She could imagine him as a young boy with his curly hair tousled and unruly, spilling into his face while he scowled at his mother in protest. "I took dance lessons," she pointed out. "Private ones, here at the house, in the ballroom on the first floor. I had all kinds of instructors. It was fun."

"When you're ten and a boy, you think it's the end of the world. I had to defend myself and beat up every boy in the neighborhood for two years before they left me alone." He grinned at her as he dragged on his jeans. "Of course, by the time I was in high school, I discovered knowing how to dance was a good thing because girls like dancing and I was very popular. My friends quit sneering pretty fast."

She could imagine him popular with the girls. He looked a

rogue with his black curls and his slashing eyes. "Your mother sounds so interesting."

"She especially liked Latin dancing. She would laugh and her eyes would sparkle. I really didn't mind nearly as much as I wanted her to think. I loved watching her dance, she always had so much fun. We didn't have the money for the right clothes or the right shoes, but she always found a way to get us lessons." He looked at Lily. "Did your father dance?"

"Dad?" Lily burst out laughing. "Heavens no. He wouldn't have ever thought of dancing. Rosa was the one who insisted I learn to dance and she got her way because Arly had insisted I learn martial arts and Dad approved of that. She used the well-rounded-education approach. Instructors of just about everything were brought here to the house. I had art teachers and music teachers and voice teachers. I learned to shoot a gun, use a bow and arrow, even a crossbow."

Ryland was fascinated with her lacy scrap of underwear, a sheer red thong she donned not having the least idea that his body was growing hard just watching her.

"Arly danced with me. Arly and John were very much like fathers or uncles. They had nearly as much say as I was growing up as my father, maybe more. Dad was absentminded about parenting. He didn't remember I existed for days at a time if he was working on something."

"You didn't mind that?" Her voice was so matter-of-fact it astonished him. His mother had been interested in every aspect of his life. He couldn't remember a subject they hadn't talked about.

"That was just Dad. You had to know him. He wasn't all that interested in people. Not even me." She shrugged as she drew on a pair of dove gray trousers that molded to her hips. There wasn't a single line to mar the way the material lovingly hugged her bottom. "He was good to me, Ryland, and I felt loved, but he didn't share time with me unless it was something to do with work. He had exercises he insisted I do on a daily basis to strengthen the barriers in my mind. I intend to teach them to your men. I live in a protected environment, but I'm able to function out in the world when I have to. I'm hoping to at least provide that for you and the others."

She had slipped on a silk blouse over a wispy lace bra. Ryland reached over to button the tiny pearl buttons because he had to touch her. His knuckles brushed her breasts and her nipples tightened immediately in response. Her vivid gaze met his and they stared at one another in helpless hunger.

Holding the edges of her blouse together, he bent his head slowly to hers and took possession of her mouth. He wanted to put his mouth right over that silk and lace and suckle her breast, nip and tease and see her eyes cloud with passion and her skin flush just for him, but he contented himself with thoroughly kissing her instead.

"Ryland." Her voice was shaky. "Is this normal?"

"I've never felt this way about another woman. How the hell would I know if it's normal or not?" He kissed her eyelids, the corners of her mouth. "Whatever it is, it seems normal for us and that's good enough for me." Resolutely he finished buttoning her blouse, bending his head for just one moment to plant a kiss on the tip of her breast, nuzzling her through the silk.

Lily had the mad desire to grab the nape of his neck and force him to her aching breasts, just hold him there, while his tongue and teeth and the heat of his mouth worked their magic on her. Her body was sore, but deliciously so, reminding her continuously of his possession.

"Lily." He said her name and she blinked up at him, coming out of her daydream, realizing her hands were tracing the definition of his muscles, sliding over his body as if it belonged to her. "Don't we have work to do?"

"Try not to be so distracting," she ordered. "I have an idea that might help Hollister. Being here, in this house, should provide relief for all of you. The walls are extra thick and each individual room is soundproof." She looked at him soberly. "That's the other flaw, you know, Ryland. I'll never be normal. I need this house in order to survive. Everything here is designed to keep my world protected. The amount of land surrounding the house. The day staff is in and out in a matter of a couple of hours and I never come into contact with them."

Ryland caught her face in his hands. "I don't care what you need to exist, Lily, as long as you do. That's all that matters to me. We're all counting on you to teach us how to live in the world again. You have a job, you're a contributing citizen. We're hoping you can do that for us. Allow us to live again."

She looked at him, completely unaware her heart was in her eyes. "I hope so, too, Ryland."

Lily had expected rejection. It made him crazy to think that she wouldn't know her worth. He could feel her pain simmering just below the surface and his heart ached for her. She had just lost her father and she was discovering more about him and about her life than she could handle all at once. And he had brought her even more trouble, allowing her to risk everything by hiding fugitives in her home.

He swept a hand through his hair, turning away from her. "I'm sorry, Lily, I had nowhere else to bring them." He sat heavily on the bed, reaching for his shoes.

Lily dropped her hand onto his head, her fingers tunneling in his damp hair, connecting them. "Of course they have to be here. I'm going to lay out exercises that must be done several times a day. I have all the recordings of the earlier work done with the girls, with me. I think that's a large part of the problem. They were all so eager to use you in the field, they didn't prepare you properly for the assault on your brain. They opened the floodgates and didn't give you even the flimsiest of barriers to protect you. You all relied on your anchors. And once you were separated only the anchors could exist without continual pain."

He was listening to the tone of her voice. She had switched on him again, almost musing aloud rather than conversing. Her mind was turning over the problem, examining it from every angle and coming up with solutions at a rapid rate. It made him smile. His Lily. He savored that. *His.* She belonged to him in every way.

"Depriving you of your anchors set all of you up for continual trips to the hospital. I have to get in there and look over the records, see if the same people were working each time."

"Wait now, Lily." She was walking briskly out of her room toward the kitchenette that seemed to accompany every wing of the house. Ryland followed in her wake, his heart in his throat. "You damn well aren't going back to that place."

She looked at him with cool eyes. "Of course I am. I work there. I own stock in the company. The research I've been working on for the last four years could save lives." She stalked across the marble tiles to the gleaming refrigerator. "Whoever murdered my father is at Donovans and I'm going to find them." There was no challenge, no defiance, only a calm, quiet statement. She handed him a glass of milk, drank one herself.

There was no point in arguing with her when she was in her present mood. Ryland quirked an eyebrow at her. "This is it?" He stared at the white liquid. "No coffee? No breakfast? I give you a night of unbelievable sex and you give me a glass of milk?"

Lily smirked at him. "Get it straight, Miller. *I* gave *you* an unbelievable night of sex and I don't cook. Not ever."

"Oh, I see how it is. The incredibly intelligent woman doesn't know how to cook. Admit it, Lily."

Lily rinsed her glass in the sink. "I was given gourmet cooking lessons by one of the top chefs in the country." She waved her hand at the cupboards. "Feel free to fix yourself something. Rosa keeps it stocked with things in hopes I'll eat more."

"I'm intrigued. You really can cook?"

Lily found the mosaic tile on the counter interesting. "I didn't say that, exactly. Only that I had the lessons. The man may as well have been speaking Greek." She grinned at him. "Well, not Greek, I can speak Greek, but I couldn't understand a word the man said. It's an art form and I have no creative talents whatsoever."

He put his arm around her, pulled her beneath his shoulder. "Fortunately I'm a great cook." He kissed her temple, a mere brush of his lips but he felt the answering tremor in her and it pleased him. "I think you have the potential to be very creative," he whispered suggestively. "You just chose the wrong art form."

Lily found herself blushing. Even his tone of voice slipped under her skin and heated her blood. She suddenly found she was a lot more creative than she had ever imagined. She shook her head firmly. "Stop trying to tempt me. I have work to do with Hollister and the others."

His hand slipped from her shoulder, trailed down the neck opening of her silk blouse to skim along her bare flesh. Lily sucked in her breath against the trail of flames he left behind on her skin. "Am I tempting you, Lily? You always look so cool. I always have a mad desire to melt the ice princess."

She *never* felt cool around him. She didn't reply, forcing her mind to consider the facts. "Ryland, maybe we're looking at this the wrong way. Let's turn it around. Let's say the experiment had a high degree of success. There were several deaths and the men were suffering seizures and brain bleeds."

"I'd say that wasn't a high degree of success." He kept pace with her, a scowl on his face. "Don't go scientific on me. These men are human beings with families. They're good men. We're not just writing them off as lab rats."

Lily sighed. "You're too close, Ryland. You have to learn how to step back. They're expecting that reaction. It's human nature. A few deaths, call it off. The results aren't worth the price."

"Damn it, Lily." He could feel his temper rising. His palms itched to shake her. Her tone was impersonal, a computer calculating. "A few deaths aren't worth the price."

"Of course they aren't, Ryland. Put emotion aside for just a few minutes and consider other possibilities. You said yourself that the first year everything went fairly smoothly. You were used in training missions and your team performed well."

"There were problems," he said, reaching past her to open the door to Jeff Hollister's room.

Lily could see the gathered men, still holding vigil over their fallen companion. It wrenched at her heartstrings the way they guarded him. Big, tough men, capable of being lethal should the occasion call for it, but talking soothing nonsense to a friend when he was down and sitting up when they had comfortable beds, just to see to his needs.

"Any change?" she asked Tucker Addison. In the light of day, the man looked like a linebacker to her. She couldn't imagine him going unnoticed in an enemy camp, but his hands, as they tucked the blanket closer around Jeff Hollister, were gentle.

"No, ma'am. Last night, on and off for about ten minutes he seemed restless, but then he settled back down again."

Lily made a second examination of Jeff Hollister, paying particular attention to his skull. "Feel this, Ryland, he definitely has evidence of surgical scarring."

"Well, he did have surgery. He was rushed to the hospital to relieve swelling about three months ago," Ryland said. "They drilled a hole in his head."

Lily's gaze was cool and assessing. "I doubt they were relieving pressure in his brain; more than likely that's when the electrodes were planted." She stood for a moment looking at Ryland. "I know you did it yesterday, Ryland, but if no one minds, I'd like to examine all of the men. I want to be absolutely certain."

Gator leapt up. "Raoul Fontenot volunteering, ma'am." He grinned at her engagingly. "We could use my room, a couple of doors down and to the left."

"Thank you, but that won't be necessary," Lily answered, running her fingers over his skull while several of the men snickered. "You're fine."

Ryland took the opportunity to smack Gator on the head. "Your only problem is your skull's too thick."

One by one, Lily examined the rest of the men. Only Jeff Hollister showed signs of surgery. "Have any of the rest of you had seizures?"

"I did, ma'am," Sam Johnson, the only other African American besides Tucker Addison in the room, admitted. He was a big man, light on his feet, a man renowned for his hand-to-hand combat. Few could surpass him in a physical fight. He had been an instructor in the Special Forces team. "I was out in the field and had a small seizure during a mission. The video and voice feed on my camera and my partner's camera weren't working that day so there was no data on it. That's why it didn't show up in a report."

Ryland spun around. "You never verbally reported it?"

"No, sir," Sam said, glancing into the deepest corner where Nicolas sat so silently. "We talked it over and decided we'd better not. The men who went to the hospital all ended up dead within a few weeks. If it happened again, I was going to report it."

"But it never happened again," Lily finished for him. "Do you recall whether or not you had suffered a migraine prior to the seizure, maybe a day or so before it?"

"I had a hell of a migraine afterward, ma'am. I thought my head was going to explode, but I didn't dare go to the hospital so I rode it out with a little help from my partner. He knew some mumbo jumbo, cures from the old ones, and damn if they didn't work too."

Lily knew immediately the partner who knew "mumbo jumbo" was Nicolas. He apparently had an extensive knowledge of healing plants. She glanced at the man but he was staring straight ahead as if he didn't hear a single word.

"What about before that?"

"We'd trained for a couple of days and I was separated from Nicolas. He's an anchor, and I couldn't block out all the garbage coming at me. My brain felt like it was on fire. I started vomiting that night and couldn't see so I asked for medication."

"Who separated you from your anchor?" Lily asked.

"Orders came down," Sam said. He looked to Nicolas. "From Captain Miller."

Ryland shook his head. "I never have given an order separating anchors from the men assigned to them. It would defeat the entire mission." His gaze found Nicolas. "You thought it was me."

"I wasn't certain, Rye, and I wasn't going to take chances with his life. I watched you and waited. If it had been you . . ." Nicolas shrugged his shoulders casually.

Lily shivered as the flat, cold eyes moved over Ryland. Nicolas didn't have to voice a threat, it was there in his eyes, in his casual shrug.

"Russell Cowlings delivered the order," Sam admitted. "There was no reason to think you hadn't given it."

"The snake," Gator said. "He attacked us and tried to kill the captain."

"If I'm getting this right, Gator," Tucker said, "Russ did more than that. He set Sam up to die. Isn't that what you think, ma'am?"

"I think he did, yes. I think Sam had a violent headache after being separated from his anchor and when he asked for medication, he was given something that triggered a seizure. I don't think the seizures are caused by the enhancing process, or if they are, it's a rare side effect. And I don't believe the brain bleeds are caused by severe seizures. I believe the men you lost to those complications were at some time taken to the hospital and, under the pretense of relieving swelling, I think the men underwent surgery and electrodes were planted in specific parts of the brain. Eventually the men were subjected to magnetic fields of extremely high frequency. The heat generated tissue damage and caused hemorrhage."

"How could they get away with something like that?" Ryland demanded.

"They performed the autopsies, didn't they? They determined the cause of death. What better way to sabotage a project than to pick off members of the unit one by one and make it look as if they were dying from complications or side effects?"

Tucker swore aloud, turned away from her to stomp across the room in frustration and anger. He was a big man, very muscular, and he gave off the impression of immense power and raw strength. "What the hell do they have to gain?" he asked. "I don't understand, what do they have to gain?"

Ryland sighed and raked his hand through his hair. "Money, Tucker. A fortune. What we can do is worth a fortune to any foreign government. Even terrorist organizations would be willing to pay for the information. We can whisper and have guards look the other way. We can disrupt security systems. The possibilities are endless. They convinced us to be afraid of strengthening and using what we have in order to slow us down."

"Let's be careful here. I'm not saying I'm right," Lily cautioned. "Peter Whitney was my father and I loved him very much. I would prefer to think he conducted an experiment in good faith and that he went forward with it until he became aware of the deliberate sabotage. I could be completely wrong."

"So what do we do for Jeff?" Ian McGillicuddy asked.

"First we have to wake him up and then he has to be taken to a surgeon. I know someone who will help us." Lily looked at Ryland. "I believe Hollister is a dreamwalker. I think he took medication of some kind. . . ."

Ian shook his head. "Ryland said it wasn't safe. He wouldn't go against orders."

"But this pill was probably given to him much earlier, when he was in the hospital, so he believed it to be safe. He didn't consider it disregarding an order—he didn't touch the one given to him that night."

"How do you think we can wake him without harming him?" Nicolas asked. His voice was very low, but it carried through the room and silenced the whispered conversations between the men. "I tried to wake him the old way but he was resistant."

Lily was all too aware of the sudden silence in the room. All of the men stared at her expectantly. She let out her breath slowly. "I think we have to go into his dream and bring him out. And I think we can expect trouble."

Ryland moved closer to the bed to study Jeff Hollister's pale face. "What do you mean, trouble?"

Lily was watching Nicolas. His expression never changed. He remained still, but his black eyes were fixed intently on her face.

"Lily"—Ryland was insistent—"what are you thinking?"

"She's thinking Jeff Hollister is a trap." Nicolas answered in his quiet, even voice. "And I think she's right. I feel it. When I try to connect with him, I feel his spirit warning me away."

Ian looked from Lily to Nicolas and then to Ryland. "I'm not certain what you're talking about. How could Jeff be used as a trap?"

Lily patted Jeff's shoulder as he lay sleeping so peacefully. "If I'm correct, he took a pain pill he received from an earlier hospital stay. I think it knocked him out long enough for someone to go into his cage and create a magnetic field of such high frequency the electrodes reacted. My belief is that it was an attempt on his life. The electrical pulses were too strong and caused a brain bleed. Hollister hung on, probably through sheer guts, while you made your escape. He seized, knew he was in trouble, and put himself out, using his ability as a dreamwalker."

"So he's somewhere else."

"It was probably the only thing he could do to save himself. If I'm correct someone else has the same ability to dreamwalk and they're using him as a lure for the rest of you. Don't ask me how. I'm guessing. If we manage to wake him, we'll have to assess any damage done. I want to call Dr. Adams—he's a renowned brain surgeon and he would be willing to help us."

Ryland shook his head. "We're fugitives, Lily. By law he has to turn us in."

"Yes, well," Lily hedged. "Hollister needs medical care immediately. I'll guarantee Dr. Adams's cooperation. In the meantime, we have to bring Jeff out of his dream."

"Lily, stop saying 'we.' You can't come with us," Ryland said firmly. "And before you protest, listen to me. If you're right and Jeff is being used to trap us in some way, then we need you here as an anchor with Kaden. More importantly, if someone else is lying in wait for us, you can't be identified. This house is our only haven. My men need to learn those exercises you keep talking about. We have nowhere else to go."

Lily had to admit he was right, but it didn't make it easy for her. She had a bad feeling, a portent of danger that wouldn't go away. And Nicolas felt it too.

"We'll need everyone to tap into the wave of energy just in case," Ryland added.

The men agreed without hesitation. Once again Lily was moved by the camaraderie the men had for one another, their willingness to put their lives and mental well-being on the line.

Nicolas sat tailor fashion right there in the middle of the floor, closing his eyes and centering himself. Ryland positioned himself on the bed beside Jeff Hollister. Lily watched as they sought inside themselves, a meditative practice essential to anyone who had to deal with psychic spillage. She knew the instant both men went under, by their slow, steady breathing.

RYLAND looked around curiously. He was on a sand dune, looking toward the ocean. Of course Jeff would choose a familiar place. The dunes stretched endlessly, and the waves pounded the shore, rushing toward him and breaking over the rocks, sweeping into the tide pools.

He began walking down the beach, knowing Jeff had to be close. Nicolas appeared briefly to his left, sprinting over the dunes away from him, shading his eyes and looking out to sea.

"He's out there"—Nicolas waved toward the ocean—"riding the waves. And he doesn't want to come back."

"Well, that's too damned bad. He has a family to think about," Ryland said. *I don't like the feel of this.*

Neither do I. I'm getting into position.

The water swelled, the wave growing larger and larger and beginning the rush toward shore. Ryland spotted Jeff on his surfboard gliding toward them as the wave began to curl, forming a long pipe. For a moment he was caught by the sheer mastery of Jeff's athleticism, the way he seemed a part of nature itself, anticipating the wave so that he shot through the pipe and came out just as the wave collapsed.

Ryland pulled his fascinated gaze away from Jeff and began scanning the water for possible threats. He was on full alert, his probing gaze taking in the sky, the sea, and the sand dunes. He knew Nicolas would be doing the same. He didn't have to check—Nicolas was first and always on alert. He spent months alone behind enemy lines, months tracking a single target. Men like Nicolas were never ambushed, they did the ambushing. Ryland was glad to have the man guarding his back.

Nicolas put his fingers in his mouth and whistled, a peculiar high-low sound that carried on the wind. Ryland spun around and ran to his right, toward the shore and Jeff.

Jeff Hollister immediately glided for shore, hitting shallow water on the run, automatically scooping the board beneath his arm as he ran toward them. "What are you doing here?"

"Bringing you home." Ryland indicated the relative cover of the nearest cliffs, away from the open dunes. He dropped two paces behind Hollister, covering his back.

"Cowlings is here somewhere, I've spotted him twice watching me." Hollister flung the board out of the way, sprinting barefoot down the beach. "You shouldn't have come, Captain, I can't go back. I don't want to live my life brain dead."

"Save your breath," Ryland snapped. "And run like hell."

The whistle cut through the air a second time, a single note this time. Ryland leapt on Jeff, tackling him, throwing his body onto the sand. Ryland landed on top, shielding him as bullets thudded into the sand just ahead of them. He had no idea of the effect of dream death on the physical body—but he feared the results. They both rolled toward the pounding waves and came to their feet on the run. Neither looked back, they sprinted, zigzagging to make themselves more difficult targets.

"Now!" Ryland gave the order just as the whistle cut through the air again. Both men were immediately in the sand, scooting forward, scrambling on their bellies toward cover. Bullets tore chunks out of the boulders just over their heads.

They dove behind the rocks and sank down, forcing their

lungs to slow. "You're not brain dead, you idiot," Ryland said, affectionately slugging Jeff. "You're caught in a dream." He looked around. "Where's the girl?"

Hollister laughed. "She was here until I spotted that frog Cowlings. I knew something was up when he didn't make his move on me. I realized he was here to kill me. When he waited, I figured he thought you'd show up."

"He didn't count on Nicolas." Ryland grinned, pulled a gun from inside his shirt, and handed it to Jeff. "If you had a brain in the first place, you would have realized you couldn't be brain dead or you wouldn't have been able to figure all that out."

Jeff bellied down and wriggled through a shallow depression between two rocks to take a cautious look. "Look who walked into a trap." He fired off three rounds quickly and used the time to secure a better position behind a larger, flatter boulder that afforded him more of a view.

Ryland was watching him carefully. They were in a dream, but Jeff was no longer remembering he was dreaming and he was dragging one leg.

"It isn't an ambush if you know they're waiting. No one escapes Nicolas when he's hunting. We just have to picnic here for a short while and let him do what he does. Cowlings didn't know Nicolas could dreamwalk." Even as he was speaking, Ryland was crawling away from Jeff Hollister to put distance between them. The trap had been set for Ryland. Had Ryland not come to bring Hollister back, Cowlings would eventually have made his move against Hollister.

Bring Jeff out, Kaden. Pull Jeff out. Ryland gave the order through the telepathic link with his second-in-command. Jeff had created the dream so his leaving would add the burden of sustaining the dream to Ryland.

Hollister let out a small cry of protest, but the combined force of all the men was stronger than his will. Jeff felt the soft mattress beneath his back and waited for the mind-numbing pain. He opened his eyes cautiously. Lily Whitney bent over him, speaking softly, asking him a dozen questions, all the while occupying his mind to prevent him from thinking about the possibilities of brain damage.

Can you take him out, Nicolas? Ryland felt a sudden surge

of energy in the air around them. *Watch yourself, he's trying to project.*

I need to get closer.

He's on the move. He's running. The wind rose suddenly, ferociously, creating an instant sandstorm. Ryland swore and scuttled across the ground, changing positions quickly, the sand stinging his skin. He kept his eyes closed, but allowed his senses to flare out across the landscape, searching for waves of energy indicating "hot" activity.

He heard the whine of a bullet but it thunked into the rocks where he had been. At once there was the sound of running steps in the sand. Ryland lifted his head to peer cautiously over the short boulder he was using as cover. Sand stung his eyes but he caught a glimpse of Cowlings running toward what looked like a door. Just before he reached it, Nicolas rose up from the dunes, a knife in his fist.

Ryland felt the instant surge of pure energy, and Cowlings simply disappeared. *Kaden! Bring us out now. Now! Nicolas, wake up!* He hesitated just long enough to make certain Nicolas obeyed him before following. Behind him the world turned to hell, fire raining from the skies and blowing across the sand, a boiling cauldron of orange and red flames.

NICOLAS and Ryland looked at each other across the safety of the room. "Did you feel that?" Ryland asked the others.

"What was it?" Kaden asked.

"It wasn't Cowlings. He couldn't produce that much energy. His telepathic powers are nowhere near that strong," Ryland said.

There was a short silence. Nicolas stood up, stretched, and went to Jeff Hollister's side. As he passed Kaden, he clapped a hand on Kaden's shoulder in a salute of thanks. "What do you think it was?" Nicolas asked Ryland.

"I think someone used Cowlings as a conduit. We're dealing with energy. There are all kinds of energy." Ryland looked at Lily. "Who would know how to manipulate wattage or voltage massing in the air?"

Lily sighed. "Someone at Donovans."

TWELVE

"A RE you certain you want to go back here, Lily?" John Brimslow asked. He didn't shut off the motor, hoping Lily would tell him to turn around and drive her home.

"I have so much work, John," she said. "I can't fall too far behind. And don't worry about picking me up because I left my car here and I can drive home."

John sighed. "I'm not one to tell you what to do, Lily, but I don't like this. It doesn't feel right to me. I know you've spoken several times with the investigators regarding your father's disappearance. . . ."

"He's dead, John." She said it quietly.

"What did they tell you?"

"I know he's dead. I 'felt' him die. He was murdered. Thrown off a boat into the ocean. He'd been bleeding heavily so he was nearly gone, but he was still alive when he went into the cold sea." She rubbed her hand over her face. "Someone from here"—she waved toward the sprawling complex of buildings—"had something to do with his death."

John's face flushed dark with anger. "That does it, Lily, you can't go back into that place. We have to talk to the police."

"And what are we going to tell them, John? That my father conducted experiments on human beings and opened up a psychic floodgate he couldn't close? That I connected with him as he was dying and he told me before they threw him overboard that someone at Donovans was responsible? Do you think they'll believe me—or lock me up? I'd be the hysterical daughter or, worse, the daughter who inherited a fortune when her father disappeared."

"You already had the fortune," John pointed out, but he was shaking his head sadly, knowing she was right. "What do you mean conducting experiments on human beings? What are you talking about with psychic floodgates?"

Lily let out her breath slowly to regain her normal calm. "I'm sorry, John, I shouldn't have said that. You know Dad did research for the military and he often became involved in projects with a high security clearance. I should never have even mentioned that. Please forget it and never say a single word to anyone about it." It was a measure of her fear and distress that she had made such a blunder. There was a certain innocence, a frailty about John that made her always want to protect him.

"Does Arly know about all this?"

Lily leaned against the seat and looked at the older man, studying his features. Since the disappearance of her father, he seemed older, thinner. "John, you aren't staying up nights, are you?" she asked suspiciously.

His gaze wavered, fell away from hers. "I've been sleeping in the old chair at the bottom of the stairs leading to your wing. I have a gun," he confided.

"John!" She was startled. She couldn't imagine John shooting anybody. He might fence with them, an elegant swordfight. She could see him slapping somebody with a white glove and challenging them to a duel, but she couldn't picture him pulling a trigger and taking a life. "What in the world are you thinking?" She was touched by his devotion. "Arly has that house so secure, spiders are afraid to spin a web. You can't be doing that anymore."

"An intruder got in once, Lily, and I'm not going to lose you. Someone has to look out for you now, and I've been doing it nearly thirty years."

"I love you, John Brimslow, and I'm eternally grateful you're in my life," she told him. "There's absolutely no need to guard me. Truly, Arly went through the house again with all new gadgets. He has a rather large ego and it really upset him that someone made it past all of his little toys." She grinned wickedly. "I had a lovely time pointing it out to him too."

"Not nearly as good a time as Rosa had. She chewed him out in two languages and I believe the word 'incompetent' came up more than once." John managed an answering smile at the memory.

"I almost feel sorry for him, but any man thinner than me deserves to be taken down a peg or two. Wish me luck, John, and stop worrying. I'll be perfectly fine." Hoping it was true, she kissed his cheek, got out of the car, and walked toward the entrance.

Ryland had been furious with her when he'd learned she was coming to Donovans, arguing and threatening to break back into the facility to keep an eye on her. The man had an extraordinary temper, one that smoldered and burst to the surface like a volcano erupting. He could be intimidating if she was silly enough to let him.

Fortunately it was imperative to get Jeff Hollister to Dr. Adams. They all knew it. Hollister's right side was weak, one leg in particular unresponsive. There was some numbness in his face and tremors occasionally in his right hand. She couldn't detect any significant memory problems or speech problems, but she wanted a specialist guiding his therapy. And she wanted to know if the electrodes should be removed or if it was safer to leave them. Jeff needed brain scans and help beyond what she could give him.

"Dr. Whitney!"

She spun around, a chill going down her spine as Colonel Higgens hurried to catch up with her. "Let me walk you to your office."

Lily smiled at him. Polite. Ice princess. For some reason Ryland's teasing words comforted her. She didn't mind in the least being haughty or an ice princess around Higgens. "Thank you, Colonel. I'm surprised to see you here. I had an image of colonels always off doing military inspections and generally shaking everybody up." She went through the heightened security checks with some impatience. "Isn't this annoying? Just like Thornton to beef up security *after* the chickens have flown the coop."

"Thornton and I have been talking about the situation, Dr. Whitney, and he'd like to see you first thing in his office."

"I'm sorry?" She continued walking briskly through the halls toward her office. "What situation are you referring to?"

"The men who escaped."

"Did you find them?" She stopped walking to face him. "Were they able to function outside the protected environment of the laboratory?" Even with her barriers and her shields in place, she could feel the waves of dislike emanating from Higgens. It was more than dislike. Violence and avarice clung to him. He even smelled like rotten eggs to her. Her stomach rolled in protest.

"No one's found them. Why weren't you at work yesterday?"

Lily remained silent, her gaze steady on his face, one eyebrow arched perfectly. She waited until he squirmed visibly. "I'm not in the habit of explaining myself to anyone, Colonel Higgens, least of all a man who does not have any connection whatsoever to my work. The moment those men were allowed to escape, I no longer had anything to do with that project. I was called in as a consultant, which I did as a favor to my father and Phillip Thornton. I'm extraordinarily busy and have no time to devote to a project that is basically defunct." She gave him a polite, fake smile and swept into her office.

Higgens followed her, a dark scowl on his face. "Thornton's on his way here now. We think you could be in danger."

Lily slipped into her white jacket. "I'm in danger of not getting my work done, Colonel. If you don't have anything of great importance to impart, I'm going to have to ask you to leave. I appreciate your concern, I really do, but I have a very good security man."

Phillip Thornton burst into her office. She felt waves of fear, and realized he was terrified of Higgens. "Lily! I was worried. I called your house yesterday but your housekeeper refused to get you on the phone."

"I'm sorry, Phillip, Rosa doesn't want me to come to work anymore. She's been afraid for me ever since my father's disappearance. I often work at home, you know that. It didn't occur to me that you would worry about me. I'm trying to ease Rosa's mind and still get my work done."

"Rosa isn't the only one worried about you, Lily. Colonel Higgens and I both feel the danger is very real that Captain Miller and his team may decide to kidnap you."

Lily leaned her hip against the edge of her desk and folded her arms in annoyance. "Oh, for heaven's sake. I expect Rosa to become hysterical but not you, Phillip. Why would Miller want to kidnap me? I don't know anything about this project; I came in late and know less than both of you. I would think he'd want one of you."

"I still think we should put a team on you," Phillip said.

"A team?" Lily's eyebrow rose even higher. "My family would have been happy with a bodyguard. What do you mean 'a team'?"

"Captain Miller is the leader of an elite group of soldiers, all with backgrounds in Special Forces," Colonel Higgens said. "A single bodyguard isn't going to be able to protect you from them. I have a team of soldiers, highly trained, ready and available to help out."

"This doesn't make sense to me. Why would Miller come after me? He knows I don't know anything, I couldn't possibly help him in any way. And it isn't as if I'm in the military, I'm a civilian. You can't possibly justify the use of soldiers in guarding me. I think we're all overreacting to my father's disappearance. We're all a little on edge but I think asking soldiers to guard me is a bit much. Phillip, if you're really worried, to ease your mind, I'll ask Arly to find me someone. But I have to go through all the security here and having someone with me will be a major hassle."

"I can find you someone with security clearance," Thornton offered.

"Just let me get to work." Lily smiled to take the sting out of her words. "You know I appreciate your concern, I really do, but Captain Miller only saw me a couple of times. I doubt if I made any impression on him whatsoever."

Thornton knew when he was defeated. "I still want you to do your best with this thing, Lily, look through anything your father had and try to figure out what the heck he did. It's important."

"Everything is important. All right," Lily conceded with a

sigh. "In my spare time, as if I have any, I'll poke around and see if I can come up with anything."

Thornton ushered Higgens out of the office ahead of him, then turned back abruptly. "Oh, Lily, I totally forgot. The annual black tie fundraiser is Thursday night. Your father was going to give a speech."

Lily was looking at him, her face very still, her heart suddenly pounding hard. In that moment she knew for certain Phillip Thornton had been involved in her father's death. It was in the guilt swamping him. It was in the way his gaze slid away from hers. In the sudden smell of sweat on his body. Her fingers tightened around the back of her chair, holding her in place. She was afraid to move, afraid to speak, certain she would say something to give her sudden knowledge away. She had been suspicious, but now she knew. She had known Phillip Thornton most of her life. Lily managed a brief nod.

"You know how important this event is to our company and the individual researchers. More than sixty percent of our funding can come from this one event. We'll have some very important people and several generals there, including McEntire and Ranier, and I'll need you to help out. You know the drill, you've been to so many."

"I completely forgot about the entire thing, Phillip."

"It's understandable, Lily," he said, "and I wouldn't ask if it wasn't necessary. Everyone will expect you to be there."

She nodded. She'd been flooded with condolences, from the president to lab technicians. She knew she would be expected at such a public event. "I'll go, Phillip, of course I'll go."

"And you'll give a speech?" They both knew with her father's disappearance, her plea would bring in even more money than usual. Everyone was searching for a way to show support to Lily and she knew it would happen at the fundraiser.

"Sure, Phillip." She waved him out of her office. General Ranier would be there and he always asked her to dance. The fundraiser would give her the perfect opportunity to read the general and find out if he, like his colleague General McEntire, was involved. Lily had completely forgotten about Donovans's most important event of the year. It would be the first time she ever attended such a huge function without her father. The thought saddened her. She sat for a moment at her desk, mourning him, missing him.

Lily put her grief aside, not wanting to broadcast too loudly and risk making a connection with Ryland. If he thought she was upset or in danger, he would find a way to get to her. It surprised her that she was that certain of him, that she knew he would come.

She spent several hours working in her laboratory, losing herself in formulas and patterns. When she finally realized how much time had gone by, Lily was annoyed with herself. She hastily tidied up her notes and hurried through the halls to the elevator until she was on ground level. The hospital was small but had equipment that would make any hospital or trauma center weep with envy. Lily signed in, going through the security checks to access the records she needed. She read through every entry she could find pertaining to Ryland and his men. Then she began researching the staff, checking entries to find who had been on duty when each man was brought in, looking for a pattern. Lily always saw the patterns and there certainly was one. She scanned the pertinent entries, noting names, and hurried back down to the lower laboratories, this time heading for her father's office.

Lily could still smell her father's pipe just like in his office at home. No one had cleaned his desk, although his papers had obviously been gone through. She went directly to his desk and turned on his computer. As she drew the keyboard out she knocked the mouse onto the floor beneath the desk.

Hissing her annoyance, Lily felt under the desk with her foot, her gaze glued to the screen in front of her. Her toes hit a cement block hard enough to send a jolt of pain up her leg. Lily peered under the desk. The mouse was all the way to the back, close to the wall. She crawled under the desk to retrieve the item, dragging it toward her by the cord. Lily had started to inch out from under the desk when the corner of the cement block caught her eye. It wasn't flush with the wall.

Lily sat on the floor staring at it for a moment. She had to duck her head beneath the desktop as she crawled in deeper. It wasn't easy to pull out the cement block; it appeared to be wedged in tight, but she took her time, working it loose. When she finally managed to pull it free, she saw at once her father had hollowed out an area behind the block to create a small space. There was a miniature voice-activated recorder lying against the wall.

Without warning, alarms shrieked throughout the buildings. Startled, she half sat, bumping her head on the edge of the desktop. She could hear the guards running in the hall outside the office. Lily listened to the alarm for a moment but there was no announcement of danger so she ignored the commotion to pry the recorder away from the wall.

She let her breath out slowly as she curled her fingers around it. It was very dark beneath the desk but she felt a tiny disk, so small she nearly missed it. There was no covering, nothing to protect it from dust or grime. She could see a disk was in the machine already and Lily dropped the second small diskette into the pocket of her white coat as she crawled out from under the desk.

Lily's hands were shaking as she sat in her father's desk and bent close to the small recorder. Nothing happened when she tried to play back the disk. Muttering curses under her breath, she rummaged through the drawers for batteries. There were no batteries of any size in the top drawers. Lily clutched the recorder in one hand and bent to search the lower drawers.

She knew even before she turned, half rising to meet the impending threat, already knowing it was too late. She'd been so caught up in wanting to hear her father's voice, hoping for evidence against his murderers, that she hadn't paid attention to her own warning system. She swung her head, caught a blurred glimpse of a man. Waves of violence, of evil washed over her just before everything exploded. A large fist smashed squarely into the side of her temple. Everything went black and tiny shooting stars burst behind her eyes. Lily caught at her attacker, raking her fingernails across his face, tearing at his shirt as she went down. She couldn't see him, but she heard his vicious curse and felt the second blow snap her head back and then she collapsed on the floor.

RYLAND was uncomfortable with the plan. He'd been pacing most of the day, wearing a hole in the expensive carpets. He should never have allowed Lily to go back to the laboratories.

Her safety was more important than any illusion of normalcy she was attempting to create. He had to persuade her to take a leave of absence. Her father had disappeared and that was enough of an excuse for her to take time off work.

Darkness had fallen and it was their chance to move Jeff Hollister. Ryland didn't like taking him out of the house but Lily insisted her friend Dr. Adams had more advanced equipment set up in his home. She had a van and two cars left for them just inside the entrance to the woods and outside the estate itself. Arly assured Ryland the doctor would keep silent. Ryland wasn't about to take any chances with Hollister's life. They were going to proceed as if they were in enemy territory.

"Nico, I need you to scout for us. Use the tunnel near the woods. We don't want to travel too far a distance with Jeff. Pinpoint every possible position of the enemy."

"And if the enemy is found, sir?" The voice was quiet.

"Do not engage. We don't want any evidence we were anywhere near Lily's house, Nico."

Nicolas nodded in understanding. He bent close to Hollister. "I'm working damned hard for those surfing lessons you promised me."

Jeff lifted a trembling hand, clasped Nicolas's hand in his. "You'll be a great surfer, Nico, whether I teach you or not."

"I only learn from the best, Hollister, so you need to get on your feet." Nicolas gripped Jeff's hand hard, then just as abruptly slipped silently from the room.

Ryland signaled Ian McGillicuddy and they both went out into the hall. "We'll need two men guarding Jeff at the doc's place. I want you and Nico to see to his safety. We don't know anything about this doc. If Lily's paying him off, it means he can be bought. One of you stays awake at all times."

Ian nodded his assent. "Do you have any ideas how we're going to get out of this mess, Captain?"

"I want everyone working on the series of exercises Lily gave us. She says if we learn them all we have a good chance of being able to live in the world under fairly normal conditions. She thinks the experiment wasn't a failure, that it could have been very successful had we learned the things we were supposed to have learned."

"Does she think Higgens killed the others?" Ian asked

bluntly. There was ice in his voice, a merciless sheen to his eyes.

"Higgens is involved, yes, and General McEntire. It looks as if Ranier may be, too, but we have no proof. As soon as we master the shields we'll be able to hunt down the men responsible. Not only are they murderers, but they're traitors to our country," Ryland pointed out. "They have to kill us now. They have no other choice. Don't take your eyes off of Jeff, even for a moment. I'm not losing another man."

"You won't, Captain, not on my watch," Ian said. "And Nico never misses."

"Stay on Jeff, Ian."

"I'm all over him, Captain."

They went back into Hollister's room where the others waited expectantly. "As soon as Nico gives us the go-ahead, we're taking Jeff out," Ryland said. "Tucker, you're the strongest. I want you to carry Jeff out."

Tucker's teeth were very white as he grinned at Jeff. "Don't worry, I'll handle you like a newborn babe."

Jeff groaned. "I can't believe he's going to make you carry me."

Sam poked him good-naturedly. "I'll make sure he doesn't drop you more than once, surfer boy, although it might fix you right up if you landed on your head."

"You'll take their backs, Sam. I don't want a single hair harmed on that surfer boy's head. I'd have to face his mama." Ryland shuddered.

"We wouldn't be getting cookies anymore, that's for sure," Gator complained. "Nobody makes cookies like Jeff's ma."

"Not to mention"—Jonas Harper looked up from where he was sharpening a four-inch blade with loving care—"he's a chick magnet. Pretty boy Hollister walks down the street and we don't need to look for women, they just follow him around."

Kyle Forbes stretched out his legs and burst out laughing. "That's because he isn't always fondling a knife, Jonas. Women run when you walk into the room."

Sam hooted and jabbed at Jonas with his foot. "Throwing knives doesn't really impress women, Jonas."

"It did when I worked in the circus," Jonas said. "They thought it was sexy."

Jeff tossed his pillow at Jonas. "You wish they thought you were sexy. Didn't your last girlfriend dump beer over your head?"

Laughter erupted. Jonas held up his hand. "That didn't count. She caught me with the Nelson twins sitting on my lap. She totally had the wrong idea."

Tucker retrieved the pillow, incidentally bashing Gator over the head with it as he did so. "That's not what I heard, Jonas. I heard she caught you in bed with the twins."

"That's the way I heard it too," Kyle said, "except the twins were hiding under your bed."

More hoots greeted Kyle's comment. Jonas took it in stride, grinning sheepishly. "You all are full of it. Gator has that hot Cajun blood and Jeff just stands there looking like a doofus and the women faint at their feet."

"I know you didn't just call me a doofus," Jeff said. "You're feeling your oats, Jonas, because I'm stuck in this bed."

Jonas grinned wickedly. "I've been giving it some thought, Hollister. With you out of the way, I might just have a shot at those Nelson twins. Tucker, drop him on his ass out there in the woods, you'll be doing us all a favor."

Kyle raised an eyebrow. Normally an extremely quiet man, a genius with explosives, he entered into the fun to keep Jeff Hollister's spirits high. "Jonas, aren't you forgetting his sisters? You swiped his sister's pictures out of his wallet and you kiss them every damn night. You think either one of those girls is going to look at you if you don't deliver their darling baby brother home safe and sound?"

The pillow came sailing through the air again, smacking Jonas in the back of his head. "You're the one who swiped my sisters' pictures, you perverted knife-wielding nutcase. Don't you even look at my sisters. They're both going to be nuns." Jeff crossed himself, kissed his thumb.

We've got watchers, Rye. And they aren't civilians. Nicolas always spoke in the same low tone. No one had ever seen him excited or nervous.

Is it a go? Can we get Jeff past them? Ryland had complete faith in Nicolas's judgment. *We can't put Lily at risk.* It had been his decision to use telepathic communication in spite of Cowlings. The man had little telepathic ability and Ryland judged the risk of his being close enough to pick it up was minimal.

They aren't taking their assignment seriously. My best guess, Rye, they're here to watch the woman. They have no idea we're here and they sure don't think we're coming.

It's a go then. Signal when you have a clear. I'm sending Tucker out with Jeff. Sam's got their back. Ian's the driver. The rest of us will control the watchers.

They're susceptible. They're bored and not on high alert. I don't think we'll have too much trouble. Tell Tuck to come a-running.

"We're good to go, Jeff," Ryland said gently. He nodded toward Tucker. "Kyle and Jonas will go out ahead of you. Nico's waiting. We know they're out there, we know they're watching, but they can't know we're here. This is the real thing. Walk like the ghosts you are and get through their lines. We'll meet up at the doc's house. You stand fast until we check it out once we're there. Your only responsibility is to keep Jeff and yourselves alive. If the place is hot, pull out immediately and come back here. Watch your back trail."

He stood looking at them for a long moment. "Remember, all of these people, soldiers, civilians, all of them, think we're escapees, that we've committed crimes. Unless your life or the lives of this team are in danger, do not use maximum force."

Ryland gestured and signaled Kyle and Jonas. Both gripped Hollister's shoulder hard then followed Ryland from the room, heading quickly for the tunnel. It had been a long day, watching over Jeff, worrying about him, seeing the damage to his right side, but unable to do anything to help him. They had waited for the sun to go down and the darkness to spread. Their time. When ghosts were able to walk. At last they could actively do something.

Once the day staff was gone, they were able to move more freely without fear of discovery. They had all the technology available to them, but it would never take the place of their belief in themselves.

Ryland went out of the tunnel first, moving quickly, silently, slipping through the darkness, keeping to the shadows. He could feel the surge of energy building as the men began to project, whispering into the night, telling the guards to look at the stars, to see the beauty of the night. To be blind to movement and sound. To look the other way as Ryland signaled Tucker and Sam to bring Jeff Hollister out.

Tucker was as large as a tree trunk, carrying Jeff protectively cradled against his massive chest. Jeff was no small man, but he looked a child beside Tucker's bulging muscles. For a big man, Tucker Addison moved like the ghost he was, gliding over the uneven terrain without a sound. Sam kept pace behind them, his eyes moving restlessly, constantly, seeking out the watchers, his weapon in his fist.

Ryland directed the guards away from the path in the woods Tucker needed to take in order to rendezvous with Ian and the car. Ryland led the way, shifting toward the most resistant of the guards. He concentrated on "pushing" the man harder, planting the urgent need to converse with his partner. Ryland dropped to his belly and scooted closer to the guard. He was reacting to the mental push by rubbing his head, shaking it as if his head needed clearing. The guard began to pace restlessly back and forth, pressing his fingers to his eyes.

Ryland held up his hand, signaling Tucker to melt into the shadows with his burden.

I'm dropping back to cover you, Nicolas reported.

You get them away safely, Ryland ordered. *Stay on Jeff.* He closed the distance to the guard so that he lay only a scant few feet from the man. He gathered his energy, his strength. It had to look like an accident, a believable accident. Ryland whispered a prayer asking for forgiveness if anything went wrong.

Two kids coming. Teenagers, Nicolas informed him.

Ryland let his breath out slowly, relief spreading. Allowed his muscles to relax. *Use them. Send them this way, right up to the guard. They can create our diversion.* He concentrated on the connection, building the bridge to the young boys sneaking through the woods with a flashlight and pellet guns. They changed direction immediately, highly susceptible to the waves of energy prodding them.

The guard swung around alertly as the boys laughed loudly together at a joke one of them told. His light blasted the two boys in the face, temporarily blinding them. The guard's back was to Tucker and the others. Ryland signaled them forward as he began his own retreat, moving cautiously away from the guard, staying low and using the bursts of conversation as cover.

Tucker moved through the woods quickly, staying to the shadows, deep in the trees, somehow even in the darkest sections, avoiding twigs and leaves that would give him away. Sam ran parallel with Tucker and Jeff, keeping his body between the two of them and the guards.

They're away. Ian's got them. Clear out, Rye. Ian had removed the dome light from the truck so Tucker and Sam could put Jeff in carefully without the glow of the overhead light to give them away.

Nicolas slid into a car beside Kaden, who pulled away from the curb before the door was closed. *We're away. We're away.*

Ryland signaled Kyle and Jonas ahead of him, and dropped back to protect his men as they hurried out of the wooded area. Behind them, the guard was still haranguing the two teenage boys, firing questions at them with the deliberate intention of scaring them.

Ryland was the last man in the third vehicle, urging Kyle to get moving even before he was fully in the car. They were careful to obey every traffic law, not wanting to take the chance of a police officer pulling them over. Dr. Brandon Adams's house was several miles from the Whitney estate. It was a large beautiful house surrounded by manicured lawns and wrought-iron fences.

Kyle cruised by, went nearly a mile down the road, turned around, and drove past the estate again. He slowed enough to allow Ryland and Jonas to slip out before cruising past a second time. He found a small turnout just beyond the house and parked the car beneath the sweeping tree branches. Ryland and Jonas were already scouting, spreading out to cover more ground. Nicolas and Kaden circled the estate from the other side.

Ian? You have any bad feelings you'd like to tell us about? No. I say it's a go.

Ryland made the sweep with the same thoroughness he applied to every task. They circled the house, taking their time, checking every position where someone could be lying in wait to ambush them. No one was anywhere near the house. Kaden and Nicolas went up and over the high railing surrounding the wide porch. Kaden continued up the side of the house, gaining entrance through a second-story window. Nicolas went in on the bottom floor through the back. Ryland went in through a sliding glass door. The lock was a joke.

He moved through the rooms, getting a feel for the house. It was empty, just as Adams had told Lily it would be. He could hear the doctor moving around upstairs.

Clear. Kaden reported.

Clear. Nicolas added.

Bring him in. Ryland moved into position behind the stairs. The doorbell pealed melodiously. A tall, thin man hurried down the stairs. He was dressed in charcoal slacks and a white shirt, both of which screamed money. He opened the door without hesitation. Tucker didn't wait for an invitation, but carried Jeff inside. Sam and Ian followed, closing the door behind them and casually locking it.

"Bring him into the back. I recently closed my small clinic so I have all the equipment we need on hand." The doctor led the way through the spacious rooms. "I've prepared a room at the very back of the house and I gave my staff a few days off. Lily said to get him back to her as soon as possible."

"Did she tell you we'd be staying?" Ian asked. "We'll take turns sitting up with him."

"Suit yourself, but I doubt if that will be necessary. I think he'll do fine."

The room was large and airy with a tremendous view. Ian walked over and pulled the heavy drapes. Sam opened the closets and all adjoining doors. "It's very necessary, Doc, but don't worry, we won't get in your way. We're self-sufficient," Ian said as he put his pack on the table. "We brought our own rations."

Lily had made certain to send along more than enough food when she heard the men were going to be staying. She had also insisted they keep working on their exercises.

"We'd like to secure the house," Ian said.

The doctor's eyebrows shot up. "I don't know what that means."

"Your locks are standard issue," Sam pointed out. "A child could break in."

"I have a dead bolt on the front and back doors." The doctor was not really paying attention to the conversation. He bent over Jeff Hollister, leaning close to peer into his eyes. His voice was unconcerned. Dr. Adams had no interest at all in the subject of security.

"You don't mind if we beef up your security, do you, Doc?" Sam asked.

Adams waved his hand vaguely. "Do whatever you feel you need to."

The knots in Ryland's stomach loosened. Dr. Brandon Adams had a mind similar to Lily's. She understood him. He was interested only in his subject. Not Jeff Hollister, only his brain and what it could reveal to him.

It's all yours, Nico. We're clearing out.

Ryland gave the signal to the others and they left the house with the same stealth they'd used when entering. The doctor never knew they had even been there.

THIRTEEN

THE house was still being watched. Arly had security guards patrolling, but the men hiding in the shadows were no civilians. Ryland was uneasy having his team split. And he was disturbed over Lily. He had reached out to her over and over in the last few hours, but she hadn't responded. He hadn't realized how much he counted on that connection between them and it was disturbing that he couldn't touch her. Once he had gotten Jeff Hollister to safety, he had concentrated on Lily, but he had been unable to establish any kind of bridge.

Throughout the long afternoon and evening, Ryland had become increasingly worried. Ian had come to him twice, saying he "felt" danger but couldn't say why. Ryland tried to put it down to the obviously military team guarding the house. It didn't help that he couldn't touch Lily.

Frowning, Ryland moved as a GhostWalker, slipping through the lines to get a fix on the positions of their enemy. Once a radio crackled, the sound loud in the crisp night air. A guard lit a cigarette, shielding the red glow with his hand, but the smell floated on the wind. Ryland watched them for some time, observing their boredom. The night was going to be long and cold for the watchers.

Finally. He saw the headlights and then Lily's car come up the winding drive. She was home and his world was right again. The day had been far too long, his heart pounding in his throat

every time he thought of her alone at Donovans. Those people
had managed to murder her father, and Ryland feared, as time
went by and they could find no trace of the GhostWalkers,
Higgens would begin to panic.

Satisfied, Ryland moved like the wind, silent, deadly. He
blended into the mottled patterns of the trees and shrubbery
along the high fence line. Arly had told them the fence was
wired with sensors and throughout the grounds motion detectors crisscrossed the area. He gained the treeline just behind the
estate, using the larger tree trunks as cover as he moved into
deeper woods. Ryland slipped easily past two guards holding a
bored conversation near the entrance to the closest tunnel.

The long-stemmed rose he held in his hand was devoid of
thorns, he had seen to it personally. He wished he had dozens
of them for Lily, but he had done the most he'd felt it safe to do.
Bypassing security, he had entered a flower shop on his way
back from seeing Jeff, and left the money for the single perfect
rose on the counter to be found by a puzzled employee. He
didn't think taking a dozen would have allowed him to sneak
past the watchers unnoticed.

Ryland went swiftly through the twists and turns in the narrow tunnel. The passageway came out in the upper halls. The
day staff was long gone. Even so, he went through the door cautiously, ready for anything, all senses alert. Darkness greeted
him. Even the night-lights were off. It didn't matter; he moved
unerringly toward his goal.

Ryland went from shadow to shadow, gliding through the
enormous house quickly. He found himself directly under the
staircase leading to the upper stories and the wing of the house
where his men were waiting. He walked up the stairs but veered
to the right, toward Lily's private quarters.

Standing just inside her bedroom, the sound hit him first.
Soft. Muted. Lily, *his* Lily, was weeping. He stopped moving,
so shaken he trembled. The sound of it tore out his heart. His
fingers curled around the rose, a tight fist against such a wrong.
He drew a deep breath of air into his lungs, held it, let it out
slowly. Her crying was almost more than he could bear. It made
him weak and it turned his insides to mush. He reminded himself every day it was a loss of control, not very macho for a
Special Forces man, and most of all that Peter Whitney might

really have manipulated him in some way, but none of it seemed to matter.

More than anything he respected courage and integrity and loyalty, all of which Lily had in abundance. Not wanting to startle her, Ryland eased his way close. "Lily," he said her name softly, tenderly, with a blend of heat and smoke.

Lily's gasp was audible. She buried her face in the pillow, turning away from him, humiliated to be caught in such a vulnerable moment. "What are you doing here, Ryland? Arly told me you were gone, that you had gone to check on Jeff." There was an edge to her voice. He heard it in spite of the sound being muffled by the pillow.

"Lily, you weren't worried about me, were you? You can't be crying because you were afraid for me." The idea alarmed and pleased him at the same time. He reached for the bedside lamp.

"No." She caught his wrist to stop him. "Please don't."

Ryland stood for a moment hesitating, unsure how to handle her mood. He brushed the velvet flower petals along her tear-wet cheek before laying the rose carefully on the pillow beside her.

Lily shivered with awareness, turned her head to look at the rose, then shifted her gaze to his face. There was so much sorrow in her blue eyes it beat at him, weakened him. "I'm so sorry about your father, Lily, I know how much he meant to you." He sat on the edge of her bed, carefully removed his shoes, and then dropped his shirt on the floor beside the bed. Very slowly, so as not to alarm her, he stretched his length out beside her. With infinite gentleness he pulled her into his arms. "Let me hold you, honey, just comfort you. That's all I want to do right now. I never want you to cry like this again."

Lily burrowed close to him, buried her face against his broad chest, her body relaxing into the shelter of his. She put her mouth against his ear, her breath warm on his skin. "It isn't my father, Ryland. It's everything. A moment of weakness. Nothing."

Something in her voice warned him. Everything male and warrior deep inside him went still. Waited. He inhaled sharply and smelled . . . blood. "What the hell?" His hands tightened possessively. "What happened to you? Where are you hurt?"

Lily clung to him. "I was in my father's office, looking around, and I found a small voice-activated recorder. Someone came in and hit me hard. I fell backward and they nailed me again as I was going down. They took the recorder."

He stiffened, a tremor running through his body. Rage was swift, volcanic. He swore very softly beneath his breath. "I'm going to light a candle and look at you. How bad were you hurt and where the hell were those idiot security guards?" He hissed the question at her.

When she didn't answer, Ryland reached around her to find the matches on her nightstand. The flare was small, a soft hissing as he lit the aromatic candle. He dropped the match in the holder and caught her chin firmly in his hand, turning her face this way and that inspecting the damage. His gut tightened; something very dangerous welling up deep inside him roared for release.

"Damn it, Lily, did you see who did this?" he persisted.

"I was just turning when he hit me. I had a brief impression of him and then I was on the floor." She traced his frown with the pad of her finger. "I'm fine, a little stiff, but I'll live."

His hands moved over her head. He felt a large bump near her temple and she winced when the pads of his fingers gently examined her.

A dark, predatory expression crossed his face, shimmered in the depths of his eyes, a menacing threat that caused her to shiver. At once he leaned forward to brush her temple and cheek with the warmth of his mouth. "You were supposed to have guards at Donovans. Where the hell were those useless guards? Where were they when all this was happening? Why weren't they watching over you? I should never have allowed you to go back there. Damn it, I'm a military officer, and I let a civilian go unprotected into a dangerous situation." He let *her* go—*Lily*—and she was hurt.

His voice was so beautiful it seeped through her pores deep into her body. As always it moved her as nothing else could. Somehow her head throbbed less with his concern. She touched his face gently, wanting to soothe him. "You know it was my decision alone and no one could have stopped me." When she felt him stiffen, she hastily continued. "An alarm went off. The guards ran to see if security had been breached," Lily said tiredly.

She lay back, settling closer to the warmth of his body without being fully conscious of doing so. "When I first went in this morning, Colonel Higgens met me and walked me to my office. Phillip Thornton joined us there and they told me they wanted me to have military guards because they were afraid you might attempt to kidnap me. They implied you may have been the one to attack me."

There was a small silence until he could swallow his anger. Both men knew he wouldn't hurt a woman.

Deliberately his white teeth flashed, a wicked smile that had his eyes glittering silver. "Kidnapping you has a very erotic side to it," he teased.

A small answering smile curved her soft, trembling mouth in spite of the attack. "You're so outrageous, Ryland. Only you would think of something so kinky."

He nuzzled her neck. "I like kinky, honey, when you're involved." His teeth teased her earlobe.

"More interesting things to look forward to." Despite her game attempt to smile, she sounded infinitely weary.

His heart turned over. He drew her closer to him, felt her soft body yielding to his. Ryland fought down his body's reaction, knowing she needed comfort. He could feel the pain throbbing in her head. "Did you take something for your headache?"

"I wouldn't take anything from them, I waited until I came home. I'm not sleepy or tired so much as just wanting to lie in the dark and feel sorry for myself."

He brushed kisses over her face. Feather light. Tender. "You need a cup of hot chocolate. I'm going to call Arly and have him get a doctor here to look you over."

"No! You can't do that, Ryland, you don't know them. Arly, John, Rosa, they'll be crazy. I'm fine, really, just a bump and a headache. And it gives me a great excuse to miss work for a couple of days and no one here will think anything of it."

"I don't want you to ever go back there. There's no need."

"Don't, Ryland." She touched her finger to the sculpted perfection of his mouth.

"Don't what? Want to protect you? I'm sorry, Lily but there's no way that instinct is going to go away. I knew. That day you walked into the room. I knew right then in that heartbeat of time when my brain was going crazy and my skin crawled and my insides were knotted up so tight I was going to explode. You walked into the room, Lily, and you were so damn beautiful it hurt."

"I don't remember it quite like that."

He crushed her silky hair in his large hands, brought the strands to his face to rub them along his jaw. "You tore out my heart on the spot, lady. It's been yours ever since. Damn it, I can't do anything else, feel anything else, but wanting to protect you."

"Ryland . . ." She looked up at him, her heart in her eyes. "I feel the same way about you, but we're both enhancers. Anything we feel is just more intense."

He took the rose from her pillow and placed it carefully on the nightstand beside the candle. "I've thought about this, came at it from every angle. I don't believe what I feel for you has anything at all to do with enhancing, Lily. I'd walk through hell to protect you. I'm not one of the nice men you've always known in your protected world. Don't see me like that, because it isn't who I am. You're stuck with the man I am."

"I don't want you to be any different, Ryland." It was true. In spite of herself, she couldn't help but love the way he was so protective.

"You're magic, Lily, sheer magic. And you're mine, Lily, my everything. I'm drawn to you because you're Lily Whitney with more courage in your little finger than most people have in their entire body. You have a brain, a sense of humor, a smile that knocks me over, and every single time I'm near you, I want to tear your clothes off. And damn it, I'm not going to lose you."

"You're not going to lose me." Her lashes lifted to give him a glimpse of her startling blue eyes. "I knew you would get around to sex sooner or later."

His hands slipped around her to cup her breasts beneath the sheet. She fit into his palms, warm and petal soft. "I forgot to say you always smell good too." He inhaled deeply, taking her scent into his lungs where it swirled, a potent temptation. "Stop deliberately distracting me, Lily, I want to give you a lecture."

Her mouth curved, her intriguing dimple appearing. "I believe you have your hands on my body, Captain Miller, not the other way around."

He closed his eyes briefly, groaning aloud over the possibilities her murmured words conjured up for him. "The idea of your hands on my body is alarming, Lily. Then I start thinking about what might come next. You have such a beautiful mouth. The things you could do with your mouth might be interesting."

A small laugh escaped; she opened her eyes to look at his face hovering inches from hers. "Life with you would be exhausting. You know that, don't you?"

"*Deliciously* exhausting," he agreed.

"And sinfully wicked."

His grin was a satisfied smirk. "*Deliciously* sinfully wicked."

He was simply cradling her breasts in his hands, his fingers wrapped possessively, but she felt the heat begin to spread from his hands to her body. A slow smolder. A *delicious* smolder.

His breath caught in his throat. She was looking up at him without guile, without hiding anything from him. Her heart was in her eyes. Love. Acceptance. Unconditional. Lily Whitney was on his side always. And that was both good and bad. Good because she belonged to him. Bad because she believed she had to protect him. She could make a tough man fall hard.

The flickering candlelight flared, the light spilling across her bruised face. She winced, looked away from him. "I feel so stupid. My father spent a fortune on the best self-defense instructors in the world. Worse, the minute the alarms went off, even before the alarms went off, I knew there was going to be trouble."

He remained silent, knowing she needed to talk about it. She was trembling, her soft body very close to his. His gut was still churning, all too aware she hadn't reached out to him at the time of the attack. His reaction swung back and forth between hurt and anger.

"I was looking through Dad's office, hoping to find something that might point me in the direction of whoever killed him. I've been through his office a dozen times and I know Thornton had to have gone through it thoroughly, but I keep thinking I'll find something."

He kissed the bump over her temple, feathered kisses down

her face to her swollen cheek. "It's natural to want to find the people who murdered your father, Lily. And we will."

"I found the recorder behind a loose brick of cement. I stubbed my toe when I was pulling out the chair to sit down at the desk. When I grabbed at the desk to steady myself, I knocked the mouse onto the floor. So I got down on the floor and had to crawl under the desk to pick up the mouse and I could see the brick wasn't flush with the wall. There was a hollowed-out area and I just pulled out the case."

"And of course, they must have a hidden camera in his office, so were watching every move you made. They probably figured the recorder either had the notes on the experiment that would tell them how your father managed to enhance our psychic abilities or it had something incriminating. Either way, they couldn't let you have it."

Lily slumped back against the pillow. "I knew they'd have a camera. I was always aware of it, but when I found the recorder, I was so completely caught up in finding out what was on it, I had tunnel vision."

"Let it go, honey. Anyone would have checked the recorder out." His lips skimmed the pulse beating in her neck, trailed to the hollow of her shoulder, and settled. "Are you thinking of falling asleep on me?" He knew she would lie there thinking about the attack on her, about the lost tape.

"Yes, I hurt everywhere. If you're staying with me, blow out the candle. I'd hate for the house to burn down."

"I'd like to stay all night with you, every night, but I don't sleep in clothes."

There was a small silence. "Fine, take them off."

Ryland shed his jeans quickly, not wanting her to change her mind and send him away. He lay back down, gathering her close, inhaling her warm scent, and trying to control his body when he fit his body protectively around hers. There was a small silence while his heart beat and his blood pounded through his body.

Lily sighed. "You're breathing too hard."

He laughed softly. "I have a plan, honey."

"Well, keep it to yourself for a while. And don't move so much, my head hurts."

She sounded drowsy, grumpy. Intimate. Warmth spread

through his body, did curious things to his heart. No one else saw her like this. Lily Whitney, so in control, so perfect at work or in public. With him she was different. Soft. Vulnerable. On fire. Grumpy. His smile widened until he was grinning like an idiot. Lily was wrapped so deeply in his heart and mind he knew she would never be out.

He concentrated on the candle, stirring the air until the flame was gone and the room was once more dark. Holding her was heaven and hell but he would take it. His teeth nibbled on her bare shoulder. "I'm hungry, Lily."

She made a soft, contented noise and snuggled deeper into his body. "You can be hungry tomorrow."

His smile was in his voice. "Do you realize you're a tiny bit grumpy when you're hungry? I've noticed it before."

He was massaging her skin, his hands warm and strong and comforting in the night. Lily's body was relaxing and her headache eased under his ministrations, but she sighed heavily. "You're going to pester me until you get your way, aren't you?"

His strong teeth teased her earlobe. "Absolutely, honey. I have to have food. And I know you haven't eaten a thing." He slipped out from under the covers.

"I wasn't feeling very hungry," Lily pointed out. Ryland took her breath away with how completely uninhibited he always was. He didn't seem to know the meaning of the word "modest." His muscles rippled and his body glided, fluid and powerful. She couldn't take her eyes from him. With a little sigh of regret for lost sleep, she threw back the sheet and followed him, dragging on his shirt without buttoning it.

"I'm starving." Ryland didn't turn around; he continued to walk, magnificently sensual, padding from her bedroom like a great jungle cat. As he walked through the open space of her hall, he caught up several candles from a mahogany shelf.

"You're always starving," Lily echoed. "You're going into the kitchen? You're crazy—it's the middle of the night." She hurried after him, the tails of the shirt teasing her bare thighs as she walked. "I wasn't kidding when I said I couldn't cook. I can't even microwave properly."

"I'm a good cook. Besides, I have plans for later on when you aren't hurting so much." He glanced back at her over his shoulder, his gray eyes glinting wickedly. His gaze moved over her body possessively, hungrily, caressing her soft curves openly. "I need to build up my strength."

"You do not need any more strength, Ryland." She sounded prim, but her nipples tightened under his hot look and deep inside excitement blossomed. "You're going to do us both in. And for your information, I have enough meds in me to numb an elephant."

"It didn't seem too numb when I was examining you."

"You pressed right on the bruise! Honestly, I'm fine."

"You'd better be telling me the truth." As they entered the kitchenette Ryland nonchalantly lit the candles and set them up on the counters to give himself light. He grinned at her. "Cooking by candlelight makes all the difference in the world. That's where your gourmet chef went wrong. He had no soul."

Lily burst out laughing. "You must have been a terrible little boy. I'll bet you got away with anything when you gave your mother that killer smile of yours." She leaned against the far counter and studied him, taking in every detail of his superb body. He was fit, each muscle defined. And he was moving easily around the kitchen, totally nude, semihard and unconcerned with it. His body fascinated her almost as much as his mind did. She loved his lack of modesty and the way it never seemed to bother him that he couldn't hide how much he wanted her.

Ryland enjoyed having her eyes on him. He bent to peer into her refrigerator, mulling over the contents, pulling out various items, all the while knowing she was looking at him. His body swelled even more at the knowledge of her perusal. He was content when she was near to him. Listened for the sound of her laughter. Needed to hear the quiet tone of her voice. He ached for her, to be with her, but not just a joining of their bodies; he wanted a commitment.

His shirt on her was far too large, draping her body yet gaping open to reveal intriguing glimpses of her soft breasts. He could see the shadow of the dark triangular thatch of curls at the junction of her legs. The edges of the shirt teased his senses with quick little glimpses then moved when she moved, hiding treasures.

"I was a wonderful little boy, Lily," he told her. "Just as our son will be."

Her eyebrow shot up. "Are we having a son?"

"At least one. And a couple of daughters too." He moved past her, slid his hand down her flat belly, caressing, stroking, his fingertips teasing the black curls at the junction of her legs before he moved on to the sink. "Lily! Look at this. You have bread dough here."

A shiver of excitement went through her. Her body clenched in reaction to his touch. "Rosa often leaves bread dough for me because I love fresh bread. I do manage to put it in the oven all by myself."

He paused in his movements to look skeptically at her.

Lily shrugged. "All right, fine, she wrote the instructions down and I keep them in the drawer right by the oven." She moved closer, wanting his touch again. "You want children someday?" The thought of having his child growing inside of her moved her. She placed her palm over her stomach, unconsciously guarding an unborn baby.

"Not someday," he corrected; "soon. I'm not getting any younger." He whisked the small tea towel off the rising dough. "Cinnamon rolls sound good, what do you think?" He reached over to turn the oven on preheat.

"With me? You want to have children with me, Ryland?"

He made a rude noise as he began combining ingredients in a bowl. "Try to follow along, honey, you have a high IQ. I know you can do it if you try."

Lily rubbed the pad of her thumb across her lower lip. "You must have been a monstrous child, Ryland. You must have been in trouble all the time." She made her way to the other side of the counter, watching him intently, a daring idea forming in her head. He was so sure of himself. And doing his best to ignore her while he worked.

She wandered around the counter to stand beside him.

Ryland looked up again. "I'm working here, and the candle-light across your breast is distracting. Go stand somewhere in the shadows."

Lily shook her head. "I think you could use some assistance." She was looking at his hands working the bread dough, not at him, but her voice had a husky, sensual rasp to it, exciting him, arousing him instantly.

Dark heat spiraled through him, robbed him of breath. He didn't dare speak, not wanting to break the sexual spell Lily was weaving. He began to whip ingredients together in a small mixing bowl, his movements sure and practiced.

Lily tugged at the roped muscles along his legs, forcing him to step back away from the counter. She pulled out a small shelf directly in front of him, a small board that had been used as a stepping stool when she was a child.

The air slammed out of his lungs. "I can't imagine how you're going to help me," he ventured, his voice so hoarse he barely recognized it.

"I used to stand on this when I was a little girl and wanted to get into the cupboards." She swung the board all the way out so he could see the legs unfolded on it. "I thought I'd just sit right here and watch you work. You don't mind, do you?"

"Sit." He gave the command gruffly. The one word was all he could manage.

Lily sank down slowly onto the small stool, seating herself directly facing him. His naked body was close and hot and hard. "I knew it would be the perfect height. You just work and let me see what I can do to keep you relaxed."

She had dreamt of this. Wanted this. It was too tempting to resist. His thighs were strong columns, and Lily brushed them carefully with her fingertips. He was already thicker, harder, anxious for the silken heat of her mouth. Her hands found his buttocks, stroked, urged him a step closer. "Are you certain I won't be distracting you?" Deliberately she prolonged the moment, stretching it out, her warm breath flowing over the thick, velvety, very engorged head. Before he could answer, her tongue danced in a single caress. "Because I wouldn't want to distract you. Cinnamon rolls sound very good. Warm and frosted and spicy."

Ryland's breath shot out of his lungs. "Lily." It was a command. Nothing less.

She laughed softly. "You have no patience, do you?" She wanted to drive him crazy, to feel powerful and in control, yet she had little experience and now that she'd insisted, she was afraid of disappointing him.

"I can read your thoughts, honey," he said tenderly. He bunched her hair in his hand, crushing the strands in his palms. "Everything you do pleases me. When we're both like this, it's so intense between us, it's easy enough to pick up what we want. Open your mind to me, the way you open your body for me. It's all there in my head, every erotic fantasy I've ever had about you. And every single one you've had about me."

"You have some interesting ideas," she admitted.

"So do you," he pointed out.

Lily leaned forward and took him into her mouth, hot and moist and tight, sucking gently, her tongue teasing and dancing all over so that the pleasure shot up his body and exploded like a volcano in his gut. A shudder ran through him as her mouth tightened and her tongue played, her hands urging his hips to find her rhythm. For a moment his mind wanted to shatter with the pulsing pleasure ripping through him.

Candlelight played over her face. She was so beautiful with her silky hair and the dark passion in her eyes. His hands stilled as he watched himself gliding in and out of her mouth, wanting the sight etched in his brain for all time.

This was the way it was supposed to be. Lily loving him, teasing him. Ryland giving her the same back. Their world. His fantasy. And he was determined to make every fantasy their reality. Lily needed him in her perfect world. She needed passion and love and to be shaken up now and again.

Ryland forced his hands to move, shaping the dough he was making, spreading it out on the counter in front of him. All the while, pleasure coursed through his body. He kneaded the warm mass, his hands rhythmic, his hips surging forward as her mouth tightened, going from playful to insistent. Her fingers were like the flutter of butterfly wings at times, then strong and demanding. She wrapped her hand around the hard length of him, tight, her hand following the rhythm of his, her mouth so hot flames were roaring in his belly.

A sound escaped his throat. "I think we've found where your creativity lies. You have wonderful form." His entire being, his very existence seemed to be focused in the heat of her silken mouth. He caught at her, stilling every movement before it was too late. "Too much, Lily, I want this time for you, not me." He dragged her off the small stool. Her body slid up his, soft and tempting. Ryland snapped his teeth together, biting off another groan as he lifted her onto the counter. "Sit there, don't do anything, just sit there."

"I was having fun," she complained, sweeping her tousled

hair out of her face. The action split the shirt wider open, so that her breasts were fully exposed.

He grinned at her. "I thought you said I was the impatient one." He quickly braided the dough, inserting the mixture from his mixing bowl. "We'll have plenty of time once I get this in the oven." He was already suiting action to words.

When he turned back to her, the look on his face set her heart pounding in anticipation. He moved toward her like a stalking tiger, all play gone, his eyes hot, burning with intensity. Watching him, Lily's heart accelerated. She couldn't have moved if her life depended upon it. He mesmerized her with his heat and hunger.

Ryland reached for her, pushing her legs wide to accommodate his larger body. He dragged her close, then bent her back, sprawling her on the counter. The candlelight played lovingly over the curves and hollows of her body, touching and caressing with flicking light. His hands were gentle as they shaped her, moved over her, following the playful light. "Do you know how beautiful you are to me, Lily?" Casually he dipped his finger in a small jar of strawberry jam and painted a line down the valley between her breasts to her belly button.

"I know I let you do outrageous things to me," she said, her breath in her throat. It was the way he stared at her. As if she were the only woman in the world. As if he were so hungry for her he might not make it through the night without her and he didn't care who knew it.

His hand caressed her moist entrance, long, slow strokes but never quite entering her. "We haven't even started with the outrageous things," he murmured and bent his head, his tongue following the trail of strawberries.

Lily shivered with pleasure, the cool air teasing her nipples into taut, responsive peaks. The feel of his tongue lapping over her skin, leisurely, casually, as if he had all the time in the world to enjoy her body, added to the anticipation. Her hips moved restlessly in invitation. He responded by pushing two fingers deep with tantalizing slowness.

She gasped as his teeth scraped her nipple, as his mouth closed over her breast, the sensation nearly lifting her off the counter. Then he was following the strawberries across her stomach, swirling around her belly button, dipping his head lower to catch the taste in her tight curls.

"You're killing me." Her hands found his hair, tangling deep into the curls.

He breathed fire between her legs. Pushed his fingers deeper, lifting his head so he could watch the way her eyes clouded. It heightened his own pleasure to see her response to him. As he withdrew, she pushed back, riding his hand, grinding deeper, seeking relief.

Her head was thrown back, her back arched, her breasts jutting temptingly as she moved, enticing him to fill her completely. He merely smiled, keeping the pace slow, blowing warm air against her heated mound. Before she could think, could reason, he withdrew his fingers entirely and replaced them with his tongue, stabbing deep.

She made a sound, somewhere between a scream and a moan, and her fingers tightened in his hair, dragging him closer. Her body erupted into quake after quake. Thinking she had relief, Lily took a breath only to be driven straight up into the clouds a second time as he caught her thighs firmly, holding her open to his seductive exploring.

He had wanted her like this, sprawled out in front of him, open to him, her taste and cries driving him wild. He had dreamt of it so many times, coming awake with a hard, painful arousal and no Lily to give him relief. He indulged himself, taking his time, taking her to the point of release only to stop, to ease back while she squirmed and pleaded. She was hot, a fiery inferno, and he knew what it would be like when he buried himself deep inside her. His hands moved over her body, exploring every secret hollow, every shadow, staking his claim, letting her know she belonged to him. The way he wanted to belong to her. All the while his mouth and fingers were taking her to the edge.

Lily was nearly sobbing with need. "Please, Ryland, I can't take any more." She meant it too. Her body was going up in flames and she was drowning, *drowning* in sensation.

"Yes, you can, Lily," he said softly, lifting his head, sucking the taste of her from his fingers, "you're going to take all of me deep inside you where I belong. I want you to know what no other man will ever do for you. I'm going to know you so intimately you're never going to think of leaving me."

He sounded so arrogant she smiled. She'd never thought of another man since the moment she'd laid eyes on him. And she certainly had never entertained the notion of doing *any* of the things she did with him, with some other man. "Stop talking and let's have some action," she pleaded.

He caught her hips, dragged her off the counter, and spun her around so that he could tip her back over the low shelf. She had a beautiful butt. He loved watching her walk, the sway of her hips was always such a temptation. One hand caught the nape of her neck, holding her in position while his rough palm caressed her buttocks. "Is this comfortable with your head down like this? I don't want you to hurt."

She laughed softly, pushing back against his hand. "I'm not thinking about my head right now, Ryland."

He felt her one last time, wanting to insure she was ready for him, his hand spreading her legs as he pressed insistently into her hot channel.

He was already on the edge of control and so was she. She pushed back again eagerly as he thrust hard. She was velvet soft, hot enough to burn him with flames, so tight it was as if a fiery fist gripped him and squeezed and suckled. She couldn't move, helpless in the position he had forced her into, and it gave him a heady sense of power. He drove into her again and again, filling her to the hilt, forcing her soft, yielding body to take every inch of him. She matched his rhythm, crying out softly as her body shuddered with pleasure. He kept pumping into her, hard strokes, moving in and out of her, thrusting deeply, a brutal passion seizing him, taking him ferociously.

Lily let go, the orgasm taking her like a freight train, ripping through her with immense strength. Her body shuddered, the sensation overwhelming so that she struggled not to cry from sheer pleasure. She hung there limply, exhausted, unable to move, Ryland buried deep inside her.

"Lily, tell me you're feeling what I'm feeling," he said, his mouth moving over the nape of her neck. "I didn't hurt you, did I?"

"Did I act like you hurt me, silly? But when you get your strength back, I expect you to carry me to bed. I'll never walk again."

His hands traced the line of her back, massaging, exploring, loving. "I don't know what I ever did to deserve this, Lily, but thank you."

She turned her head to smile at him, still too limp to move. Totally satiated, completely relaxed. The bump on her head was throbbing, but it didn't matter. He never stopped touching her, never stopped looking at her. He took what he wanted, but gave her so much more in return. "Has anyone ever told you how beautiful you are, Ryland?"

He cupped her breasts, his thumbs brushing her nipples, savoring the way her muscles clenched around him with every stroke. "No, but I don't mind at all if you'd like to tell me. Right now, you're looking pretty magnificent to me." And he meant it.

It was a long while before he managed to lift her into his arms and take her back to her room. They feasted on cinnamon rolls and jam before taking a long, very erotic shower together.

Long after Lily lay asleep in his arms, Ryland stared up at the ceiling. That part of him that was dark and dangerous had been aroused. Someone had dared to put hands on Lily. It was the wrong thing to do.

FOURTEEN

◆

LILY stared at her face in the mirror. The bruising around her cheek was too pronounced to ignore.

"I don't think you're going to be able to hide those bruises from Arly," Ryland said. "You look very . . . colorful."

"Oh, don't even say his name. I'm going to hide all day. Maybe you can lie for me and tell him I went to the laboratory." She frowned and touched the blue-black smudges. Her cheek was puffy and there was a distinct bump on her temple.

Arly and Rosa were going to go totally ballistic on her. And John, sweet John would probably get teary-eyed. But it was a good excuse not to go in to work.

"You try going near that place," Ryland challenged, "and I'll rat you out so fast to Arly, your little head will swim."

She made a face at him. "Your true colors are beginning to show. You have a mean streak in you." She peered at her face again. No amount of makeup was going to hide the purple and blue smudges. "I'm going to have to send Arly to Alaska on a mission of great importance."

"As long as you don't go back to Donovans today." Ryland handed her the phone, then stood watching her as she dialed and left a message for Thornton saying she would be working out of her home until the swelling in her face went down.

Lily handed Ryland back the phone. "Try not to look so smug," she told him, "I had every intention of calling in today, it had absolutely nothing to do with your bossy ways. I think giving orders to your men has gone to your head."

"Is this some kind of women's lib thing?" Ryland's eyebrow shot up. "Because if it is, look in the mirror again, lady."

Lily ignored him and twisted her hair into a tight chignon. Her gaze jumped to his when he made a sound in his throat. "Was that you growling? Do you have a kind of affliction you need to tell me about?"

"I wasn't growling. It was an involuntary protest."

"It was a growl, and what could you be protesting now? You're a high-maintenance person, aren't you?" Lily asked with a straight face and an aristocratic lift of her perfectly arched brow.

"High maintenance?" he echoed. "Lily, you're out of your mind. I don't think you have a clue what I do. Men obey orders because they trust me to know what I'm doing in high-risk situations." *Nobody* disobeyed or questioned his orders. Until Lily.

"Really?" She looked down her nose at him, princess to peasant. "*Men* obey your orders because of your rank. Women think things out and decide all by their little lonesome what to do." She patted his head, her fingers lingering for just a moment on a spiral curl. "Don't worry, now that I know about your little ego problem, I'll do my best to look all gushy when you pound your chest."

"Little ego problem? There's nothing wrong with my ego! How the hell did you manage to turn this around? Woman, you keep it up and you're going to find out just how kinky I really am."

Lily looked amused. "Of course. Sex. When losing an argument, man resorts to sexual implications. I have to assume you're referring to kinky sex for some kind of male caveman gratification. I did read about it, but, never having experienced kink, it didn't sound all that stimulating to me."

"Would you like me to remedy the situation for you?" Ryland offered in exasperation. "I'd be more than happy to give you an example. I want to see this book you keep referring to, and damn it, Lily, if you're laughing at me, I will turn you over my knee. Are you always this annoying?"

She leaned over to kiss his shadowed jaw. "I get worse if anyone tries to tell me what to do. Ask Arly. Even my father gave up after a while. He said I had problems with authority figures." Her hand stroked the slight stubble on his jaw and at once a delicious tingle began immediately at the junction of her thighs. She could feel the rasp against her skin all over again, heightening her pleasure.

His hand captured hers and he pulled her fingers into his mouth. One by one. Slowly. He suckled each finger. His tongue curled around her skin, laved and teased and danced. A slow burn started deep in her core, spread liquid heat like a fire through her veins. Lily jumped away from him. Eyes dancing. Skin flushed.

"You should be outlawed."

Ryland grinned at her, pleased with her response. "I am outlawed. And I don't mind you stroking my ego when it's genuine."

Her eyes widened. Her mouth opened but nothing came out. Lily shook her head. "Go away, I have work to do. I have to find all the tapes my father made on the first experiment and get every single exercise. What worked, what didn't."

His grin widened so that his silver-gray eyes lit up. "Lily falls back on science and work when she's losing."

"I didn't lose," she snapped instantly. "I *never* lose. I just don't choose to continue with this silly discussion when there's work to be done. Go away and bug your men. They're probably all ready for a chest-pounding session."

"It's not quite as fun when there's only a few of them. When do you think we'll hear from the doctor about Jeff's condition?"

"I'm certain he'll get back to me today." She pushed him away and walked toward the outer rooms.

Ryland kept pace easily. "I'm going with you, Lily. Two pairs of eyes are better than one."

She stopped in her tracks, not looking at him. "The day staff is here and it isn't safe, you might be seen."

"I can get by your day staff with no problem, Lily, that's not the reason you're so reluctant to let me go with you. You don't want me to see those tapes of your childhood."

His voice was so exquisitely gentle, so tender, Lily's heart turned over and she had to blink back tears. "I feel betrayed when I'm watching them, and if you're watching, I feel as if I'm betraying him. What he did was wrong, Ryland. It was bad enough that he did it to me, but there are other girls, women now, who didn't have the luxury of this house and the people in it. They had to have struggled, maybe even were institutionalized. That's not right. It will never be right and nothing I do will ever change it."

Ryland took her hand, pressed a small kiss to her open palm. "He learned to love through you, Lily. He learned right from wrong and morals through knowing and loving you. Don't feel guilty because you loved him. He tried to do right by you. He knew he was inadequate by himself so he surrounded you with others who would fill in the gaps. And he gave them a home, a sense of purpose, a family. Few people are all bad or all good, Lily. There are shades of both in most people."

She nodded. "I know that, Ryland, but this hurts. Going into that horrible room and having memories return. . . . Watching those tapes and hearing his voice. I didn't mean anything at all to him back then. You can hear the impatience when I don't perform to his satisfaction. Rosa—who was the nurse then—is a much younger woman, and looks very different, she tries to comfort me and he yells at her all the time." She pressed a hand to her head, still refusing to look at him.

"Lily, why should you put yourself through that?"

"I need the information for all of us. For your men, for those girls. When this is over, if it takes a lifetime, I'm going to find every one of those women, and I'm going to make certain each of them is all right."

"You don't need to be alone when you're watching the tapes." He tightened his fingers around hers. "We're partners in every sense of the word. I know you loved your father, and you don't need forgiveness for loving him, Lily. The man loved you and did his best to provide you with a home, a family, and the best education he could. There's no shame in that."

"The shame is in you seeing," Lily insisted. "He looks at me as if I'm a specimen. I don't want you to see that. I can't let you see me that way." She couldn't find the words to tell him it diminished her. It reduced her to that frightened, unloved child in a house of strangers. Ryland would see her like that. She couldn't bear that.

"I love you, Lily." He caught her chin, tipped her face up to his. "I'm going to love that little girl because she's in you."

Lily pulled her head away. "Ryland, don't. You don't know that. You don't know how you're going to feel about me when you view those tapes."

He started to protest, stopped abruptly when he noticed her hand trembling. He ached for her, felt her inner turmoil, pain swamping him, swamping her. "If I'm so shallow, Lily, that I'm not going to feel the same about you because you were mistreated as a child, then you should find out now. Do you really think that of me?"

She closed her eyes for a moment. "No, Ryland. It's just hard for me to sit there and watch it. To know it's really the truth. He never prepared me, I had no idea of any of it."

"Just keep in mind your father grew to love you. You gave him something all the money in the world couldn't buy."

"Isn't that the point, Ryland?" For the first time, her voice was bitter. "He did buy us and when everything went wrong he used his money to get himself out of trouble."

"At that time, Lily, he knew no other way." He slipped his arm around her, drew her beneath the protection of his shoulder. "Let's face it together. It won't be so difficult if we're together."

She remained stiff, holding herself away from him.

"I'm part of you. Whether you like it or not, I'm part of you. I feel what you feel. It's there, Lily, and it's always going to be there, whether we're separated or not. Take me with you."

Lily did look at him then. Her blue gaze moved over his face, studying him feature by feature. Looking for something. He sent up a silent prayer hoping she would find it. "You trusted me completely last night, Lily, this isn't different. You have to believe in me."

"This isn't just about me." She whispered it to him, wanting him to understand, wanting him to realize what he was asking of her. There were all those other little girls. She owed them something. Privacy. Respect. Protection.

His fingers massaged the nape of her neck, even as his body urged hers down the long hallway toward the winding stairs. "I know what it feels like to want to look after others. To *have* to look after others. It's born and bred in us, we can't help it. Share this with me and allow me to make it easier for you."

Lily already knew he would be going with her. She needed him there, because this time she had to look at all of it. She had an obligation to Ryland and to his men. The information on those tapes was invaluable to them. And perhaps to the girls on those tapes. She had to view all the records this time, she couldn't afford the luxury of spreading out that task over time.

Ryland was true to his word, slipping past the workers easily, waiting patiently while she unlocked the door to her father's office. He slipped inside, then stepped back to watch her lock it to prevent anyone disturbing them.

"Did you let Arly know where you were going to be?"

Lily made a face. "I'm staying away from Arly. He's going to smuggle more groceries past Rosa for your men. Fortunately he's always had a completely private suite in the house so he grocery shops all the time. I don't want Rosa to know about anything until this is over."

"In order to clear the men, I've got to find someone to help us. If not Ranier, then we'll find someone above him, Lily." He followed her down the stairs, noting she was limping more than usual. "Does your leg hurt?"

She glanced back at him, and his stomach clenched hard as he caught another glimpse of the swollen blue-black cheek and temple. The surge of rage, of the need for violent action, swirled to the surface. He had a sudden desire to wrap her up and lock her somewhere safe. "I didn't realize I was limping again. Sometimes the muscles knot up and it's painful. I don't pay much attention."

"How did it happen?"

Lily shrugged her shoulders as she entered the laboratory. "No one ever really talks about it. If I bring it up Rosa gets upset and crosses herself. She says not to speak of evil things."

"Your leg is an evil thing?" Ryland didn't know whether to be angry or to laugh.

"Not my leg, silly." Lilly burst out laughing, the dark shadows in the depths of her eyes instantly banished. "With Rosa anything has the potential of being evil. Falling on the floor could be evil if you land wrong. Who knows? I don't inquire too closely into Rosa's strange ideas." She waved her hand toward the far wall, where books and tapes and disks lined the walls. "They're in order. I think the earlier tapes have more of the exercises we're looking for."

It was easier facing that cold room with Ryland with her. Lily smiled at him, unable to put into words how she felt. How much it meant that he cared enough to insist on being with her.

Ryland watched her slide her hand over the library of videos. So many of them. He could feel her relaxing with him, but there was a definite apprehension in her as she pulled several videos from the shelf.

"Most of the tapes are narrated by my father, but he also has several notebooks that seem to go with each video where he's added more data and his thoughts on what he's found." Lily tried to keep her voice strictly neutral.

Ryland settled onto the long couch. Peter Whitney had obviously spent many hours in these rooms and must have used the sofa for sleeping. Lilly turned on the video.

Several little girls were sitting at desks. Each child wore her hair in braids and all wore a gray tee shirt over jeans. Ryland felt his heart twist as he realized the little girl to the left of the screen was Lily. He glanced at Lily; her expression was carefully blank and she was staring straight ahead at the screen.

Over the next three hours, Ryland watched the little girls carefully performing mental tasks. Peter Whitney seemed to forget the girls were children, berating them for slacking off, yelling at them in disgust if they cried. When one little girl complained of a headache, he told her it was her own fault for not working hard enough.

Lily remained silent through the first two tapes, carefully observing each exercise that Whitney gave the children and his comments on which ones appeared to work to strengthen shields and allow them some respite from the outside assault of sound and emotion on them.

Whitney had made the observation early that certain girls seemed to be anchors for the others, allowing them to function better. He removed the anchors and played various sounds and even had two nurses yell angrily at one another. The little girls collapsed, holding their heads, rocking back and forth, and eventually had to be sedated.

The third tape showed Lily as a child sitting on the floor in one of the small soundproof rooms. She sat for a long time, unmoving, no expression on her face. Suddenly the toys scattered around her began to come alive.

Lily sat up straighter and leaned forward, her gaze glued to the screen. The objects in the room were moving, the dolls dancing, the balls juggling in the air. Peter Whitney's voice narrated his observations on the tape. "Subject Lily is growing stronger in her ability to control objects. An orphanage nurse observed this phenomenon and, as an infant, subject Lily was branded a child of the devil. I was excited when I heard the stories of her mobile spinning and dancing in her crib and knew I had to acquire her. She is a strong natural talent and with the enhancement may prove to be the one to use for future generations."

Ryland stiffened, not daring to look at her. Damn the man. Damn him to hell for that. Lily had to know the implications of what he meant. She already believed Peter Whitney may have manipulated the strong physical attraction between them. Whitney's comment could reinforce that idea in her mind.

"This is such a prime example of history repeating itself." Lily swept her hand over her face. "Isn't it terrible how families perpetuate cycles of violence or criminal activity? In this case, experiments? Dad should have known better, he hated his childhood, yet he turned right around and did the same thing."

"In the end he learned, Lily."

"Did he? If he learned, Ryland, why was he still experimenting on you?"

The voice continued in the background. "I have encouraged her to play with her toys in such a manner and have found the talent has grown stronger and in fact she is refining it. The only way to obtain her cooperation was to isolate her from the other children. She showed little interest in playing with objects when the other girls were around. It took sixteen hours of isolation before subject showed interest in the objects provided for her."

"He's right," Lily said softly, "in the earlier tapes I controlled one or two dolls and the movements were jerky. Now nearly every toy in the room is moving with perfect control."

Ryland might have thought her absolutely calm, but he was

tuned in to her emotions, could observe her fingernails digging into her palms.

The child on the tape suddenly cried out and pressed her hands to her head. The toys fell to the floor and lay still. Whitney hissed in frustration and Rosa ran into the room to gather the crying child to her.

Ryland felt tears burning behind his eyes. He couldn't look at her as Lily changed tapes to view the next in the series. Peter Whitney had done nothing to comfort the child. He had only displayed his displeasure and frustration at the interruption of his experiment.

This time the child, Lily, was sitting alone in the same small observation room. Adult Lily fast-forwarded the tape until they could see action once again. The child shook her head stubbornly, her hands clenched in tight fists. Rosa stood in the background, her hand pressed to her mouth and tears running down her face.

"You're too little to do it, aren't you, Lily?" There was a sneer in Peter Whitney's voice, a taunting challenge.

Lily's chin went up and her eyes flashed. She leaned against the wall, her legs sprawled out in front of her, and she stared determinedly at the large box bolted into the corner of the room. One by one the bolts began to wriggle, spin, fly loose. The child pressed a hand to her temples but her gaze never wavered. Inch by slow inch, the box began to lift from the floor.

"Higher, Lily. Stay in control." There was a fierce eagerness in Whitney's voice, a wonderful triumph.

The box rose higher, dipping at one end, shaking unsteadily.

"Now move it across the room. You can do it, Lily, I know you can."

Ryland watched with his heart in his throat as the large box, obviously very heavy, rose even higher and began to float across the room. Telekinesis. He had no idea the weight of the box because they had fast-forwarded the tape but he had the feeling it was extraordinarily heavy. The child broke out in a sweat but her gaze remained resolutely on the box.

It was trembling visibly now, rocking in the air. It was high, nearly to the ceiling, but had only traveled a foot from its original position. Whitney made a sound of displeasure. The child winced. The box rocked more.

"Concentrate!" Whitney snapped the order.

Ryland was watching the child. Her face was white, her eyes enormous. Lines of strain appeared around her mouth. She was trembling with the effort to hold the box steady. Every muscle in Ryland's body was tense. He began to sweat as well. He remembered the tremendous concentration it took to hold an object and the pain suffered by all who were able to accomplish it. And they were grown men. Watching Lily's childhood unfold sickened him. He wanted to gather her to him and hold her protectively but Lily had moved a distance from him, her body posture screaming at him to leave her alone. Her arms were crossed protectively over her breasts and she'd drawn up her knees, hunching into herself.

Sickened, Ryland watched as the box began to make its way across the room, inch by slow inch. The closer the box moved toward Lily, the more control the child seemed to have. The box steadied, spun around, began to travel back.

Just that fast, the child was through. She slammed both hands to her temples, crying out in pain. The box dropped like a stone from its position near the ceiling. The crate hit Lily's leg, driving through flesh, tearing through muscle, pulverizing bone. Lily screamed hysterically as blood erupted and pooled around her. The wooden box splintered apart on impact, spilling weights onto the floor.

Rosa leapt past Dr. Whitney, reaching both hands to Lily's leg, clamping down hard and yelling instructions to her boss. The man stood in total shock, the color drained from his face, his eyes on the little girl writhing in pain.

"Dr. Whitney, help me!" Rosa barked the order, going from trembling shy girl to assertive woman in a crisis. "You did this with your meddling in God's ways. Now you have to fix it! Do as I say."

Lily's hand went to her throat, a protective gesture. "That's why Rosa would never talk about my leg. She always believed the things I could do were unnatural and should never be talked about. More than once she told me to make certain I never do anything 'unnatural' or God would punish me." Involuntarily she rubbed her aching leg.

Ryland couldn't watch anymore. He stood up abruptly and

turned it off. "I don't see why you would want any of these tapes, Lily. What good are they to us?"

That drew her gaze as he knew it would. She looked shocked, her eyes haunted. Troubled. "The tapes provide us with information we can compare against the data on you and the men. If any of the exercises were left off or not done on a daily basis, we can teach the men to do them. The entire point here is to allow all of you to rejoin society at some level. Hopefully as fully functioning people."

His gaze went to her hands. Her slender fingers twisted together, a certain sign of agitation. All of his men were doing their best to avoid any use of psychic talents, particularly telepathy, unless it was strictly necessary. Cowlings might be able to find them using the surge in energy if he happened to be close enough.

Lily had shields she had developed over the years and it was automatic on her part to use them. The house with its thick soundproof walls and setting away from the close proximity of others was a sanctuary to them, a respite from the noise of the world. They all were catching up on rest and diligently practicing the mental exercises Lily had given them. Just meeting her and knowing she was in the world had lifted all of their spirits. She was an example to them, a GhostWalker who functioned in society. The men knew it could be done and that she was willing to help them.

Ryland had not tried to penetrate Lily's shields once in the house. If her emotions spilled over to him when he made love to her, he accepted it gratefully and returned the heightened feelings to her. He wanted to touch her, to feel what she was feeling, to share her pain. It was bone deep, a sorrow he had no words of comfort to ease.

Ryland had watched Peter Whitney's face, studied his stunned expression as he stared down at the shattered child lying helplessly on the floor. That had been the defining moment—when Dr. Peter Whitney had realized the little girl was a human being. Lily's pain was too raw for him not to notice.

"Lily." Ryland reached out to her.

She stepped away from him quickly, holding up her hand to prevent him touching her. There was no way to explain to him how humiliating that scene had been for her. She hadn't been a child at all. She had been the lab rat Ryland had named himself the first time they met. "I can't, Ryland. I hope you understand."

He edged closer without seeming to move at all. "No, honey." He shook his head. "I don't understand. You aren't alone anymore and you don't have to feel sorrow or pain by yourself. That's what I'm here for." His fingers settled loosely around her wrist, a bracelet that tightened and tugged until her stiff body was brought up against his. "I can't make it go away, Lily. You have the right to grieve for that child. But I saw her suffering too. I saw a child who should have been loved and protected, exploited instead, and it sickened me that a man could do such a thing."

She averted her face quickly but Ryland caught her chin. "I also saw that man open his eyes and see for the first time that he was wrong. It meant something. That accident was the catalyst that turned his life around. I saw it on his face. When you're strong enough you can look again and you'll see what I saw. It was a terrible thing, Lily, but in the end, you made Peter Whitney into a humanitarian. Without you, without that accident, he would never have given to charities and worked to bring about change for the better. He wouldn't have even noticed the world needed those things."

"Then why did he do it again?" Lily burst out, tears shimmering in her eyes. "Why would he even think about it? He put you in cages, Ryland. He treated you with even less respect than he gave those children. Men who served their country. Men who go out and take chances to keep others safe. Men who track down murderers. He stuck you in cages and didn't protect you when he should have. Why would he ever allow any of you to leave the safety of the laboratories and your anchors, knowing you had no natural barriers left and you hadn't constructed new ones? How could he do that?"

"Maybe he had no choice, Lily. You saw him as all-powerful. His money and his reputation certainly gave him far more license than others have, but he was in bed with some pretty powerful people."

"Phillip Thornton is a troll. He's a moneymaker, that's why Dad backed him for the presidency of the company, but he's a wimp, Ryland. He's always been politically correct, seen with the right people, saying the right things. He would never go against my father. Never. He would be afraid to."

"He hated your father. He was afraid of him, Lily. Thornton came into the laboratory while we were working on some tests and interrupted us. Your father was furious and ordered him out immediately. I was standing across the room, but the wave of hatred and malevolence was shocking to me. It didn't show on Thornton's face. He simply apologized, smiled, and went out, but his eyes were flat and hard and focused on your father. If I had to guess that one man wanted your father dead, he would be my guess. Did he stand to gain anything?"

"Of course he did." Lily slipped out of the warmth of Ryland's arms and paced across the room, restless energy feeding her quick grace. "My father's vote counted for a lot. If he and Thornton had a falling out over something and Dad wanted him gone, he could make it happen. In any case I know Phillip is tight with Higgens. Between my father and me we hold the lion's share of stock in the company. Dad's influence counted a great deal among the stockholders."

"Do you inherit the stocks?"

"I inherit everything, but without his body, it will be complicated. The house is mine and has been for years. Dad gave it to me on my twenty-first birthday. I have a huge trust fund. Fortunately, my name is on everything Dad owned, all his companies, everything, so I can sign the necessary papers to keep things going. We took a few hits in the market when he disappeared but I authorized a publicist to work on shoring up our image of being solid and it seems to have worked. What about Colonel Higgens? He's my guess. He hated my father too."

Ryland shook his head. "No, with Higgens, it isn't personal. He's cold-blooded. I could see him getting rid of someone in his way, but it wouldn't matter any more to him than squashing a spider."

Lily pressed her hands to her head. "I think I need to start all those exercises again, Ryland. My head hurts."

Ryland led her to the couch and urged her to sit. His hands went to her shoulders in a gentle massage. "You're under a tremendous strain, Lily. It's only natural that you'd have headaches." He searched for something to take her mind off of her father. "It feels like we're all back in school, learning what we should have months ago. Everyone is complaining about your latest exercise. You should see Jonas controlling the pencil and blocking noises while Kyle does the chicken dance around the room."

Lily burst out laughing just as he knew she would. "I think we should record Kyle doing the chicken dance so we can blackmail him later on. And tell Jonas he's a baby. The pencil is just the beginning. He's going to be controlling much larger items, blocking noises while Kyle flaps his wings and carries on a telepathic conversation."

"We're going to have a rebellion."

"Men really are babies. I was doing that kind of thing at five. If you don't have a sufficient barrier how do any of you think you'll survive if you're caught and held in an enemy camp? Even working together on a mission, if you went in and Gator was separated from his anchor he would have to be able to function on his own." Lily reached back and caught at Ryland's hands, holding them tight. "If we fix this thing with the military and all of you are reinstated with no charges, you know Jeff Hollister will always have a weakness on his right side. And that's if we work hard with all the physical therapy Adams will recommend."

"I figured as much, Lily. I think he was afraid of it, too."

"It doesn't mean anyone will notice, but he will, and I doubt they'll allow him to function as a member of your team if they keep you all together."

"Kaden is a civilian. He joined to be in the antiterrorist unit only, called up when needed after training. He's a police detective and a darned good one. Probably because his intuition is a real psychic talent. It will be interesting to see if he's able to increase his arrest record and find the perps even faster. He was always remarkable. We went through training together years ago and have remained friends ever since."

"Did you know any of the others before this?"

"Nico. Kaden and Nico and I met up in boot camp and ended up in Special Forces training together too."

Lily shivered. "Nicolas is a bit scary, Ryland."

"He's a good man. You can't be in his business and not have it get to you. That's one of the reasons he agreed to come on board this project."

"Can you see him as a civilian?"

Ryland shrugged. "Nico is the epitome of a GhostWalker. He can disappear and never be found if that's what he wants to do."

"But he won't leave the rest of you."

"Not unless we got caught and then he'd go into hiding until he could break us out. He's loyal, Lily, and if you're his friend he'll go to the wall for you."

"He would have killed you had you been the one to give the order pulling the anchors. I saw his eyes, Ryland."

"I wouldn't have expected less of him, Lily," he replied quietly. "Somebody was killing our men."

She stood up in that quick, graceful way she had, completely unconscious of making his heart turn somersaults. "You live in a different world, don't you?" This time it was Lily who reached for his hand.

Ryland leaned into her, his body brushing up against hers. "I'm squarely in your world, Lily, and so are the others. Ghost-Walkers have no choice but to stick together."

Lily's sudden smile lit her face, drew attention to her enormous eyes. "Did Nico come up with that name?"

"You're beginning to know the men." Ryland was pleased.

"I'm beginning to know you." She rubbed her hand along his jaw. "You have a way of always making me feel better. I don't know what's going to happen in the future, but if I forget to tell you, I'm grateful you came into my life."

He kissed the palm of her hand. She didn't know Ryland Miller yet, but she would. Lily was his other half. He knew it with his heart and soul, with every breath he took. He didn't know the future, but he did know wherever it took them, they would be together. And more than likely the other men would be around. His men.

Lily caught his faint grin and her eyebrow went up. "What?"

"Just thinking about the kids."

"What kids?" Lily asked suspiciously.

"The ones upstairs.

FIFTEEN

◆

JEFF Hollister was smuggled back into the house the day of the fund-raiser. Lily spent most of her time working with the men, ensuring they did their mental exercises. She could tell she wouldn't be able to hold them much longer. They were men of action and hiding; even though the training they were doing was necessary, it didn't sit well with them. They groused, albeit good-naturedly, each time she raised the noise level and gave them multiple tasks to do.

"The lot of you are babies," she teased, looking around Hollister's bedroom where they all tended to congregate. She loved the way they all stuck together, never leaving their fallen comrade alone.

"You're a slave driver, Lily," Sam said.

She couldn't look at Ryland. She had spent the last two nights waking up in his arms in the middle of the night, crying like a baby. Even in the dark, when they were alone, she hadn't worked up the courage to tell him what she would be doing. She blurted it out in front of the others, hoping he wouldn't go ballistic on her.

"I can't remember whether I mentioned it or not, but I have to go out this evening and I'm already running late." She glanced at her watch for effect, trying to appear casual. "I still

have to dress. I'm giving a speech at a fundraiser for Donovans."

There was instant silence. All the men seemed to hitch forward, staring at her as if she had just announced she was preg-
nant. They looked from her to Ryland. He didn't disappoint
them.

"What the hell do you mean, you're going to some
fundraiser? You've lost your mind, Lily." Ryland's voice was
very low, clipped between clenched teeth.

Lily felt her heart jump. She would have preferred him raising his voice to her. The sudden tension in the room added to
her nervousness.

Ryland took a step toward her. "Thornton is involved up to
his eyebrows in this mess. He can't get to you in this house, so
he's luring you out into the open. If you don't start taking your
safety seriously, Lily, I'm going to have to do something about
it."

Lily patted Jeff Hollister's shoulder before straightening up
and turning to look at Ryland. She tried to appear unaffected by
his anger, but she was shrinking against the bed like a coward.
"I think you've been cooped up too long with Arly. Believe me,
I wouldn't dare not be aware of safety, he'd draw and quarter
me." She smoothed back Jeff's hair, hoping to change the subject. It bothered her that her hand trembled and Ryland's dark
eyes noted it. "Are you doing those exercises I gave you? I
know you're still weak, Jeff, but they're so important. If you
can build your mental shield, you can stand being out in public
and around other people for longer periods of time. It's no different than pumping up your body by lifting weights."

"It's a lot harder," Hollister objected, attempting to look as
pathetic as possible. "I just got back and the trip was rough on
me. That brain doctor poked and prodded in my skull. It's not
ready for all that muscle building."

"That muscle building is going to enable you to go home to
your family. Stop being a baby," she ordered. "Now, if you'll
all excuse me, I have to get ready for tonight."

An instant protest went up. Nico actually rose, a fluid rippling of muscle that caused her heart to beat faster in alarm. She
backpedaled toward the door. "Just keep working and behave.
All of you. I'll be checking in later and I'll tell you how it

went." She hurried out of the room. They were all looking dangerous.

Ryland followed her down the hall, his eyes glittering with menace. "I thought you had a high IQ, woman. Can't you see how risky this could be?"

"The fundraiser was planned months in advance. My father was giving a speech, and I'm going to give it in his place. Has it occurred to you that if I don't continue to act normal and go about my everyday life, I'll come under suspicion and then we'll all be in jeopardy?"

"For God's sake, Lily, you have a military team parked outside your fence, patrolling the parameters of the estate and trying to hear every word said using devices you wouldn't understand."

She turned to look at him, one eyebrow raised.

"All right, maybe you would understand," he conceded, "but damn it, you *are* under suspicion. You have to start keeping a lower profile."

Lily took the stairs two at a time, unconsciously trying to get away from Ryland. He was right, of course, and she knew it. There was some danger in doing anything Phillip Thornton wanted her to do, but it was a calculated risk and well worth it as far as she was concerned.

"Lily!" Ryland kept pace easily.

She paused just inside her sitting room. "I have to go, Ryland. I promised I'd give the speech and, believe it or not, funding is important. Several of the researchers need grants. Their work is important. My father never missed it and he detested parties and just about anything else that kept him from his work, yet he insisted I go too."

"I doubt seriously if he would think it was important enough to risk your life. You've already been attacked once, Lily."

"Because I found the recorder." She stopped dead in the middle of the bedroom. "There was another disk, Ryland. I slipped it into my lab coat pocket before I crawled out from under the desk. I bet they never even knew it was there. Why would they? How could I have forgotten? It's probably in my jacket pocket right now, hanging in my office." She looked at him. "I have to get it."

"Not tonight, Lily. You're making me crazy. It isn't worth

your life. You could have been killed." His fingers curled into a tight fist. His gut was churning with fear for her. "Why the hell do you have to be so stubborn about this? If you want the damned disk, I'll break into the labs and retrieve it for you."

"You will not!" The alarm showed in her eyes. He was certainly capable of doing such a thing. "Ryland, don't be crazy on me. I have to go to this event. I really do. It's very political. Congressmen, senators, everyone who is anyone influential will be there. Everyone is going to be represented, including the military. Don't you realize what that means? General Ranier will be there. I've known him since I was a child. When I see him I'll know if he's lying. If I talk to him on the phone I won't be able to tell."

Lily slipped into her dressing room where her dress was already laid out. She stepped into the shimmering gown, a stunning red that clung lovingly to her breasts and waist like a second skin but plunged daringly backless nearly to her buttocks. Along the curve of her hips, the dress began to flare, leaving her room to dance. Sparkling diamonds adorned her earlobes and a small diamond pendant hung nestled just above her breasts.

"The general has come to the fundraiser for the last three years and he's always danced with me. I've known him for years and we always considered him a good friend. It's the perfect opportunity to talk to him." She tilted her head to one side, studying her image in the mirror as she held her hair up to see which style best suited her dress. She met his gaze in the looking glass and laughed self-consciously. "I rarely do my hair or makeup for these things. Someone comes here to the house. I didn't want to bring anyone here this time in case it was used as an opportunity to slip someone into the house and put you all in danger. But I'm not very good at this."

She had spent an hour in the bath, another hour choosing her dress before going to see the men. Lily looked closer and frowned at her image.

"Wear it down." Ryland's voice was harsh, his expression intimidating as he came up behind her. "You look beautiful. Too beautiful to go to this thing alone." His hand brushed lightly over the curve of her bottom. "Do I have to worry about what you're wearing beneath this thing?"

She leaned back against him, fitting snugly into his body. "You're so obsessed with my underwear."

"Not your underwear, your lack of underwear. There's a difference."

"Well, look at it, Ryland, there's nowhere to put underwear, it messes up the lines." She smiled at him in the mirror. "Don't you prefer smooth lines?"

"It has no back. There's no material at all." His hand nudged at the edges of her dress, the clingy material cupping her breasts so lovingly. "You're going to start a riot in this dress."

"You do like the dress." Her eyes were beginning to sparkle.

"You're going to give the older men heart attacks." He brushed his knuckles along her swelling flesh. "And all the men are going to have painful hard-ons." He pushed against her so there was no mistaking his meaning.

Lily laughed at him, turning into his arms, her mouth seeking his. She gave herself up completely to his kiss, burning in his arms, feeding the flames in his belly so that every cell in his body hungered for her. Needed her. Craved her. Ryland tightened his arms around her. Why did he always feel as if she would flit away from him? One minute she belonged to him, shared his mind, his skin, the next gone so far he couldn't hold on to her.

Lily made a sound and he realized he was crushing her to him. "I'm sorry, honey," he murmured, brushing kisses over her face. "I don't want you risking your safety just so you can speak to the general, if he's a part of this thing, and it looks very much as if he is. . . ."

"Then I'll know, won't I? I've always been able to read him when we're dancing; even if we shook hands I could feel his emotions. He's too busy thinking about other people to protect himself." Lily slipped out of his arms. "I'll be fine. Stop worrying." She glanced at her image in the mirror. "Thank heavens a few days have taken the swelling down. At least I can tone down the bruises with makeup."

"Where is this thing?"

She shrugged. "Arly knows. He can get hold of me. It's the Victoria Hotel."

"Of course. The one with the glass dome and you have to be wearing a suit to get through the door."

"That's the one."

Ryland's hand curved around the nape of her neck and dragged her back to him, his mouth hard and demanding, feeding on hers, branding her his. Abruptly he turned and walked out of her room.

Lily stared after him for a long while, her fingers against her lips. The taste of him burned in her mouth, in her body long after she arrived at the hotel and had begun her circuit of greeting the other guests. It was strange how she felt Ryland with her, almost as if a part of him lingered inside her. And maybe it did.

THE music was loud and rhythmic, pounding out a beat that seemed to consume her. The room was enormous and still the crowd spilled over, into the halls and the dining room. There were so many people she felt crushed. It was difficult to keep her barriers erect and not be overwhelmed by the tremendous outpouring of emotional energy crackling in the air around her.

As Lily moved through the room, working the crowd, she went into automatic fundraiser mode. She read each person as she shook hands or exchanged hugs and fake kisses. Peter Whitney had drilled the importance of knowing the right people, getting them on her side. Now, more than ever, it was important to her. While they ate their exquisitely prepared meals she gave her impassioned speech on helping mankind and the need the researchers had for funding. She pledged a large sum to start the ball rolling and smiled with the right touch of confidence as they applauded her.

She drifted through the crowds, talking and laughing, saying all the right things, making her way to the ballroom. The muted lighting in the ballroom was much easier on her eyes. The pounding music managed to give her some relief from the excitement and sexual tension, the arguments flaring here and there, the undercurrent of affairs and conspiracies and corporate gossip.

Lily watched the women in their tight clinging clothes entice the men. Mere glances, a lift of an eyebrow, a whisper in an ear. The brush of bodies as they secretly touched, coming together for a stolen moment in the shadowed room and moving apart again. The looks. Assessing. Speculative. Sexy. This was the kind of place she would love to share with Ryland. Lily slid deeper into the shadows, watching the dancers. The music throbbed through her body, the beat hard and insistent. She had never noticed how the music could crawl inside one's body and heat the blood.

"Lily, dear." Phillip Thornton toasted her with his glass. "I want to introduce you to Captain Ken Hilton. He's been waiting to dance with you all evening. You look wonderful. Your father would have been proud of your speech."

"Thank you, Phillip." Lily ignored the sudden churning in her stomach, avoided touching Thornton by smiling up at the captain. "It's a pleasure to meet you."

The moment her hand slipped into his, Hilton swung her expertly onto the dance floor. He moved with complete assurance, his strength and confidence in his very hold. "I've wanted to meet the famous Dr. Whitney for a long time," he said.

Lily glanced up at him. "My father is the famous Dr. Whitney. I hide in the lab."

He laughed. "What a shame. No one as beautiful as you are should be locked up in a laboratory."

Her lashes fluttered and she whirled close to his body, then spun away from him. His hands guided her close and as he brought her back to him, he was more possessive. "You're an excellent dancer, Dr. Whitney."

"Lily." She smiled up at him. He thought she was an easy mark. A woman with too much money and vulnerable with the disappearance of her father. He was supposed to keep an eye on her and his duty just might have a few fringe benefits. She allowed the knowledge to wash through her before she raised her barriers and glided around the floor with him. He wasn't the first man to want her money and he wouldn't be the last.

"Are you here with Colonel Higgens?" She looked as wide-eyed as she could manage. "Or the general?"

"General McEntire," Captain Hilton said. "And call me Ken."

As he whirled her close to the shadows of the wall, Lily caught a glimpse of a pair of eyes watching them. Eyes as black as night. As cool as ice. Eyes that followed them around the dance floor while the body remained as still as stone. She nearly stumbled, had to cling a bit to recover. Naturally the captain thought she had done so on purpose.

What was Nicolas doing there? If Nicolas was there, did that mean Ryland was somewhere in the ballroom? Somewhere in the crowd? She couldn't concentrate on dancing, half terrified that he might really have been so arrogant as to come, and excited to think he really had dared such danger for her.

Even as she searched the darkest corners of the room, she smiled up at her partner. "Perhaps we should get a drink, Captain."

He gripped her elbow as if he were afraid of losing her in the crush of bodies. The lights were so dim it was nearly impossible to see. Hilton kept her close as he shoved his way to the bar, waving to get the bartender's attention.

A man in a dark suit fell into Lily, steadied her, murmured an apology, and moved back into the crowd almost before she could identify him as Tucker.

"Dr. Whitney?" Hilton sounded worried. His large body crowded closer to her. "Maybe this isn't such a good idea."

Her smile was brilliant. She should have known Ryland would be close. It should have made her angry, but she felt loved and protected instead. "A little jostling never hurt anybody. By any chance did Phillip Thornton ask you to look out for me?"

The captain froze in the act of dragging a glass toward them. "I wanted the chance to look after you. General McEntire and Colonel Higgens both thought you might be in danger of some kind. I volunteered for the assignment." Hilton swore under his breath as a woman in a flame-colored, nearly see-through dress brushed up against him as she slipped past, smiling seductively up at him.

"Ask her to dance," Lily suggested. "Live a little, Captain, she's much more your type."

The woman was staring blatantly at Hilton, fluttering her eyelashes, her ruby lips forming a kiss.

"She wants you," Lily teased.

Unexpectedly Captain Hilton grinned at her, the first genuine smile she'd yet seen on him. "She'd eat me alive, a woman like that. I can face a couple of men with guns and knives and never flinch, but I'd run if she looked twice at me."

Lily laughed. "You'd better put your running shoes on, Hilton, because she's looked more than once."

The captain shook his head. "I'll just stick close to you for protection."

"You can't. No one will ask me to dance if you're standing there all big and mean looking. And I promised General Ranier the next dance."

Lily patted his shoulder. The captain seemed confused, staring at the woman who seemed so blatantly to want to seduce him. Lily understood completely the collective energy pouring into the air around them, the whispers of command, the subtle influence on the captain and the predatory woman. "Go for it," she said, her voice low as she added her energy to that of the GhostWalkers.

Captain Hilton moved away from her, his eyes on the woman. Lily watched the long fingernails crawl up his arm, the scantily clad body rub up against his as the couple slipped into the shadows.

Lily looked around but she didn't see any more familiar faces. But she felt them. They were all around her. She was torn between fear and excitement, adrenaline heightening every sense. She made her way toward the front of the room, moving around the outer parameter of the dance floor. She couldn't stop her gaze from wandering into the shadows even as she smiled, nodded, and greeted people.

She spotted General Ranier and switched directions to intercept him. He was in the middle of a crowd of men including Colonel Higgens, Phillip Thornton, and General McEntire. As she approached them the colonel stiffened and his gaze searched the ballroom, obviously looking for Captain Hilton. Lily pasted on her party smile.

"Gentlemen," she greeted regally, sweeping past Higgens to tuck her hand in the crook of General Ranier's arm. "What a pleasure to see you all here. Quite a turnout this evening. Phillip, as usual you outdid yourself. I think the dinner and dance is a complete success."

"Thank you, Lily." Thornton beamed at her, instantly distracted by the compliment.

She rose up on her toes to kiss the general's cheek. "My favorite man. It's so good to see you again. You must come for dinner one evening."

"Lily." The general's hug nearly crushed her. "The disappearance of your father is a terrible blow. I've been traveling so much and kept missing you when I phoned. Naturally, I've been keeping up with the investigation. How are you doing? The truth now. Delia is here somewhere and she's been quite concerned about you."

"She sent me a lovely letter, General," Lily acknowledged, "inviting me to come and stay with you. That was so thoughtful of you both."

"We meant the invitation. You shouldn't be alone rattling around in that monstrosity of a house your father loved so much. Delia's worried you'll bury yourself in your work."

"I've gone to the laboratories a couple of times but mostly I work out of my home. Phillip has been wonderful." She tossed the president of Donovans a sweet smile and turned her full attention to General Ranier. "I would love to dance with you, sir, it's always the highlight of my evening." Lily dropped a graceful curtsey.

The general took her hand immediately. "I'm honored."

Colonel Higgens stared after them suspiciously as the general whirled her onto the dance floor. Lily looked right through him, not deigning to notice his boorish behavior.

The waltz provided Lily with the perfect opportunity for conversation. The general spun her across the floor, expertly guiding her through the crush of dancers, taking her out of sight of the group with whom he had been talking.

"Tell me the truth now, Lily girl, how are you really? And did I hear correctly that someone attacked you the other day in your father's office?"

Lily was trying to find some evidence of wrongdoing, of guilt or malevolence, but General Ranier was swamping her with concern. "Who told you?"

"Oh, I keep my ear to the ground when it comes to the well-being of my favorite girl. I've known you since you were eleven years old, Lily. You had the biggest eyes, very solemn, and you talked like a grown-up even then. I loved the sound of your laugh. Delia and I never had children after we lost our son and you filled that gaping hole for us. I bribe Roger to keep me informed. He calls my house directly so we don't have to go through my aide. The captain is a bright boy but a bit of a stuffed shirt."

Lily's gaze was searching the shadows. A couple spun dangerously close, lightly brushing Lily's arm. She caught the flash of teeth and the laughing eyes of Gator as he took his partner back into the crowd. The audacity of the GhostWalkers amazed her. She found herself laughing out loud.

"So you think he's a stuffed shirt too, do you?"

"Your aide? I've never met him, have I?"

"You were dancing with his brother, Lily. Captain Ken Hilton is my aide's brother. I thought you knew one another."

Lily turned the information over in her mind. "Were you aware my father called your office four times, as well as sent various emails, the week before his disappearance? And that he wrote you several letters detailing his concerns with the Special Forces team? He also called your residence repeatedly."

"He didn't leave a message. We were traveling, but I always retrieved my messages."

The general stopped dead on the dance floor. At once Lily felt the warning. *If he isn't part of the conspiracy, Lily, and they think he knows too much, they'll kill him. Get him moving, keep him calm.* Ryland's voice whispered over her skin, fluttered in her mind. She moved with the rhythm of the music, urging the General back into the dance steps. "Please, sir, you can't stop, you can't look as if we're discussing anything but light topics."

General Ranier responded immediately, throwing back his head and laughing as he took her deeper into the shadows and into the anonymity of the crowd. "What are you implying, Lily?" There was no uncle voice now, he was all commander, insisting on the truth. His dark eyes bored into her face.

Lily regarded him without flinching. "My father asked me to consult on the project. The day he disappeared I went down to the laboratories. The men were isolated from each other, depersonalized and living in cages where they had no privacy whatsoever. They had been sent out into the field against my father's specific instructions. He warned Colonel Higgens repeatedly that they needed stronger shields. There were three deaths I can't prove but suspect were murder and one attempted murder I can prove."

"These are serious allegations, Lily, do you know what you're accusing a respected officer of doing? Colonel Higgens is a respected man, a man of honor."

"It isn't just Colonel Higgens. General McEntire was aware of the project long before the escape of the men and his pretended demands to be included. Phillip Thornton is in on it too."

"On what, Lily? You're talking murder. Conspiracy. These are high-ranking officers in the United States . . ." He trailed off, his features hardening. A muscle ticked along his jaw. "My God, Lily, you may have uncovered the very thing we've been searching for. This is dangerous. Don't you talk to anyone at all."

"General, the men . . ."

"Lily, I mean it. You aren't to talk to anyone." He gave her a little shake. "If what I suspect is true, these men will kill you if they think you know something."

"They'll kill you too, General. They killed my father already. I'd be very careful of your aide if I were you. You're the only chance those men have."

The music ended and the general walked her to the edge of the dance floor. "Lily, tell me you had nothing to do with that escape. You don't know where those men are, do you? They could be in on this and they are dangerous. I've had reports."

"Just remember who wrote those reports, General. Think of the money other governments and terrorist groups would pay to get their hands on this ability. By making it look as if the experiment were a total failure, by discrediting the men and cutting them off from a legitimate chain of command, Higgens could easily control the situation. I'll bet he's in charge of finding them and he's branded them dangerous. . . ."

"Lily, they are dangerous. Do you have contact with these men?" His voice was gruff, demanding an answer. "I forbid you to put yourself in danger. Delia would be devastated if anything happened to you. I won't have it, Lily. I'll put you under house arrest at my residence and have you guarded day and night."

"How do you know for certain whom you can trust? I was afraid to talk to you about this because you didn't answer my father's calls or emails."

"I never received your father's messages or his letters, Lily.

You do believe me, don't you? I can't believe he's really gone."
She could hear the sorrow in his voice, read it in his mind. He
couldn't fake such sadness.

"They threw him into the ocean. I knew when he died."

General Ranier hugged her. She could feel his deep sorrow,
the anger in him beginning to stir. The outrage that he might
know the men responsible. "I'm sorry, Lily, he was a great man
and my friend."

"Don't worry about me, General. Arly sees to it that I'm perfectly safe. No one's going to bother me in my home," she assured him. "We've been together too long. They'll be afraid of
what we might say to one another. You're going to have to act
natural in front of them until we find proof."

"Not *we*, Lily, *me*. And I mean that, consider it an order. You
stay out of this. And if you know anything about those men and
their disappearance, you'd better tell me now."

Lily remained stubbornly silent.

General Ranier sighed. "I'm afraid poor Delia is going to
have a terrible headache after these next couple of dances. You
check in with me, Lily, every day. Call and speak with Delia
and let her know you're all right."

"I will, General." She kissed his cheek. "Thank you for just
being you. You have no idea how relieved I am."

Lily watched him stalk through the crowd before turning
back to survey the dancers. Lily began walking the perimeter of
the dance floor. A slow, leisurely circuit. Excitement was blossoming. Hope. Fear. So many emotions, intense and difficult to
control. Her pulse leapt, her heart raced.

Come to me, Lily. Ryland's voice brushed seductively in her
mind. She could hear his raw hunger. There in the midst of danger and intrigue she knew what he was thinking and it had nothing to do with generals and colonels and conspiracies.

He was here in the same room with her. Ryland Miller.
Somewhere in the shadows, a part of the throbbing music. A
part of her. She moved through the crowd, her body alive.
Needy. Seductive. Her breasts ached and her skin felt hot. Her
blood thickened and heated, pooling low to pulse in time to the
music.

Lily knew he was watching her, she could feel the weight of
his stare. Everything feminine in her rose up to answer his call,

reveled in his stare. She moved as only a lover could move, her body saying without words what her heart could not. Men stopped her briefly, murmuring invitations. She barely noticed, shaking her head, knowing he was watching her effect on other men as she moved with complete confidence through the crush of bodies. Knowing he watched her with hot, hungry eyes. For Lily, there was only her phantom lover, bold enough, arrogant enough, crazy enough to dare follow her here when he was in far more danger than she could ever be.

Lily knew she should leave, not give in to temptation. Ryland was in danger even coming near her. But the risk of discovery only added to her heightened awareness, her sizzling senses. Her body came alive. Her heart lifted and she found herself smiling. Her hips swayed, a sultry invitation as she wound in and out of the crowd on the edges of the dance floor. She was grateful she had dressed with such care earlier, sliding the shimmering dress over her scented skin, pretending it was for him. Ryland. Pretending she was meeting him on the dance floor.

Of course he had read her fantasy in her mind while she stood in front of the mirror showing him the dress lovingly caressing her breasts, hugging the curve of her hips. She had wanted him to crave her while she was gone. To think about her back so daringly bare all the way to the curve of her buttocks.

Lily didn't look to see where their enemies were. She trusted Ryland to know. She trusted his men to protect him, to watch the colonel closely and keep him away. Lily continued her slow pace around the room, waiting. The anticipation building. Heat curled low, a damp, rich invitation, her body calling to her lover.

She felt his breath first, on the nape of her neck. The heat of his body, close to hers. His hand slid, fingers splayed, around her waist, intimately, possessively, just under her breast so that she ached for his touch. He moved with her, a perfect union as he took her out onto the dance floor, whirling her into the mass of couples.

Lily looked up at him as their bodies came together, touched briefly, and parted. She looked up and he stole her breath. His black hair spilled around his head in a freefall of silky curls. His gray eyes glittered a molten silver. His body glided next to hers, barely touched, skin sliding against skin, his hand guiding her steps with complete mastery. Intricate steps, their bodies brushing intimately. It was exciting. Erotic. Making love on the dance floor just as she knew it would be.

Ryland's eyes held hers captive. She couldn't look away from him. Didn't want to look away from him. She wanted to be lost there for all time, in the heat of his hunger. The music moved through them, over them, surrounded them with fire and passion. As he whirled her close, holding her against him for several heartbeats, his hand caressed the side of her breast, finding creamy skin along the edges of the material of her gown.

Fire raced through her, flames licking over skin like tiny fiery tongues. Her nipples were taut so that each time she moved, her dress teased with the friction. He drew her close again, into the shelter of his arms, their bodies swaying in perfect accord to the music. Lily was grateful for the pulsing light that helped to hide the couples on the large dance floor. Her body molded itself to Ryland's, every step they rubbed against one another, her breasts against the heavy muscles of his chest, his hands skimming along the curve of her hip, caressing her bottom, the feel of his thick erection pressing against her with every step. A building of heat that smoldered and breathed with a life of its own.

She turned her head from his shoulder to look for the colonel, afraid they had been on the dance floor too long to escape detection, even in the dim light.

Don't think of another man, think only of me. The words brushed in her mind. His knuckles deliberately brushed over her nipples, his mouth touched her neck. They moved apart, swayed together, his hand sliding dangerously over her thigh, brushing along the apex of her legs. Her entire body clenched, her blood thickened.

The breath rushed out of her lungs, her heart stuttered. Every sane thought was gone, the other dancers were gone. Only Ryland remained real with his hard body and glittering eyes. He whirled her away from him again, brought her back, a captive between his legs, his thighs trapping her leg, his fierce arousal riding along the curve of her hip for a brief moment of anticipation, of total awareness.

He held her there while his body moved to the pounding beat of the music, his hips surging suggestively. Each movement sent lightning arcing through his bloodstream as his thick erection came into contact with her soft, yielding body. The passion of the music was a pounding in his head, in his body.

He had wanted to be different this time, to do all the little things a woman needed a man to do. The whispered laughter. The intimate talk. The shared outings. He wanted to court her the way Lily deserved. But his body went up in flames the moment he was with her. Not just flames but a firestorm burning out of control. Hot and bright and dangerous.

He had to hear her breath catching in her throat, see her eyes go sultry. She was so damned sexy, so hot his every restraint, his every control was gone around her. Dangerous for her, dangerous for anyone who tried to interfere.

The music was ending, the last notes dying away. He intended to let her go, to watch her circle the room, to be satisfied with the brief contact, but little jackhammers were ripping through his brain and he hurt so bad he was afraid he wouldn't be able to walk, getting them safely off the dance floor.

The next number was slow and dreamy, the lights lowering even more. With Lily in his arms, Ryland guided the way through the mass of moving bodies away from any watchers. The captain had his hands full. The woman in the flame-colored dress at the bar had taken to Ryland's suggestion quickly and easily. He knew his men were in the shadows, waiting for him to slip away. Expecting him to return Lily to the security of the house now that they had ensured her safety and allowed him his one dance. Ryland checked that eyes weren't following their progress as he moved Lily deeper into the shadows where he wanted her. Where he needed her.

SIXTEEN

◆

THE spiraling staircase was a massive structure. In scouting the hotel, Nicolas had discovered the hidden recesses in stairwell. Built in the thirties, the building had been renovated since, and inside the locked utility closet there was a small, narrow door that had been covered over with paper. It led to a tiny private room that had most likely been used for things illegal. Nicholas had shown him the hideaway in case of an emergency. Ryland was certain this was an emergency.

He took her beneath the stairs, turned a corner, and went down a small series of steps to the utility closet door. He had no problem getting past the heavy lock and moving her right through to the small, narrow room where so many others had secreted themselves over the years. He laughed softly and told her, "In the speakeasy days, they had peepholes in here. You can still see the cracks."

She didn't answer him. Couldn't answer him. She didn't know whether to slap his face for being so completely arrogant and certain of himself, or whether to fling herself at him and kiss him senseless.

They stared at one another, the heat flaring relentlessly between them. He made the decision for her. His body crowded hers deeper into the shadow of the stairwell, his arms tightening possessively. "Kiss me, Lily. I have to have your mouth."

She couldn't resist the ache in his voice, the lure of the forbidden. Lily tilted her head back, gasped when his lips fused with hers. Hot. Starving. She tasted passion. She tasted desire. His tongue stroked and cajoled, sweeping aside her every inhibition, her every fear, so that she answered him, fire for fire.

This man was hers. He belonged to her. Wanted her. Needed her. She could never resist the urgency of his need. He was devouring her, right there in the shadows, his hands cupping her buttocks to align her body more perfectly with his. From mere feet away came the murmur of voices, laughter, and the chink of ice in glasses. The music invaded through the cracks in the thin walls, so loud it nearly shook the floor, filling the tiny hidden room. Ryland lifted his head, his eyes dark with raw passion as he looked into her blue gaze. His body was painfully aroused and she was looking up at him, bemused.

He could see the outline of her nipples, dark, thrusting against the thin clingy material of her gown. The sight drew him, tempted him. He slid his hand up the side of the dress, pushing the material away from her ribs, inching it out of the way to expose one full breast.

The cool air on her heated skin only added to her acute sensitivity. She wanted him right there, wanted his hands on her, his body buried deep in hers. The addiction to him was beyond anything she had ever experienced or had conceived could be possible. She wanted to rip away his shirt and feast her eyes on his chest, run her hands over his muscles, feel his need of her growing in her hand, against her body. Lily moved deliberately, bringing up her hands, running her fingertips along her ample curves, tracing a path down her flat stomach, reveling in the way his hot gaze followed.

Ryland's body hardened even more. She looked lush and sexy, pressed against the wall, her lips swollen and dark from his kisses. She looked wanton, her elegant gown shimmering, her breasts teasing his heightened senses. His fingers followed the path hers had taken over her breasts, skimmed the soft flesh, lingered, stroked, and massaged.

He felt her body tremble in response. He breathed warm air over her already taut nipple, slowly bent his head to temptation.

She moaned when his mouth, hot and moist, closed over her breast. His tongue danced to the music, stabbed and caressed. He suckled strongly, wanting to devour her, brand her.

At that moment, more than anything else, he needed to bury his fingers deep inside of her. Needed to feel her wet response. Ryland pressed closer to her, trapping her body there in the darkness, his hand finding the hem of her dress, circling her ankle with his fingers. He slid his palm up her calf, lingering for a moment as he traced the scars with loving care. His hand caressed her knee, slid all the way up her bare thigh.

Lily cradled his head, drowning in sensation. This was sheer madness. She heard her soft muffled groan as he found the heat of her damp curls. "Ryland," she whispered into his dark hair. "I'm going to go up in flames."

"I want you to, Lily. Burn for me." His fingers encountered the tiny scrap of underwear. His teeth nipped the side of her breast. "I thought you weren't wearing underwear. I'm so disappointed."

The sexy little thong was no hindrance as he pushed his finger into her, testing the depth of her response to him. Her gasp excited him more. The muscles of her fiery sheath clamped tightly, velvet soft, so tempting his body shook with urgency to bury itself in her. She was so beautiful to him. So necessary to him. She had no idea what she meant to him.

Ryland closed his eyes and simply indulged his hunger for her, losing himself in the temptation of her body. He pressed his finger deep into her heat, his mouth hot and insistent on her breast. Her fingers tangled in his hair, holding him to her. The music was swirling around them, the sounds of feet on the stairs, the voices and laughter.

His mouth left her breast to travel up her throat to her chin. "Unzip me, Lily." He breathed the temptation. Whispered it. A sinfully wicked plea.

"Ryland . . ." It was a soft, breathless protest, even as her hands found the front of his trousers, her fingers sending tongues of fire racing up his hard shaft as she obeyed. "This is insanity. We should go home. . . ." she trailed off, her lungs starving for air. She wanted him so much, right there, just like that, wild and out of control and so hungry for her he couldn't possibly wait.

Ryland was rigid with need, hard and thick and pulsing with hunger. A craving. He caught her leg, wrapped it around his waist even as he forced her back tighter against the wall. "You're burning up for me, honey," he whispered, "don't say no. They won't find us here." He pushed her gown higher, bunching it around her waist. "Don't leave me like this. I've never needed anything more." Not wanting to take the chance she might deny him, Ryland brought his body against her moist heat. His hands found the tiny strip of red lace and ripped it away, leaving her fully exposed for him. "Want me back, Lily. Want me like this. Maybe it's the wrong place and the wrong time, but want me anyway."

Lily closed her eyes as she felt him, thick and hard, probing against her entrance. He was large, her body tight. It seemed an impossibility there in the tiny room with its peepholes and history. And there was danger. . . .

Ryland stayed perfectly still, waiting. Praying.

Her fingers curled in his hair. "I want you more than anything," she admitted, rubbing enticingly against him.

Slick with heat and moisture, she accepted him, inch by inch. He filled her until she was gasping, her breath coming in little pants of pleasure. She needed him too. Needed him buried deep inside her, a part of her, sharing the same body.

Ryland began to move, deliberately finding a hot, passionate rhythm that matched the sultry music pounding around them. Fast and slow, deep and hard, he never wanted it to end. She was so tight, her body made for his. The soft little sounds coming from her throat were driving him mad. Her nails bit into his back, her breath came in little gasps, and her eyes were cloudy with heat.

He lifted her, so that she was forced to curl both legs around him, to open herself more fully to his possession. He drove deeper, his hands biting into her waist. "Ride me, baby, come on, take all of me." He whispered the temptation, watching her face, the heated color, the pleasure he was giving her.

She moved, her muscles clenching, tightening, sliding up and down, over him, following the driving beat of the music as he had done. Lily forgot where she was. Who she was. There was only the pleasure coursing through her body, the fire washing over her as she threw back her head and indulged herself.

Dancing lights burst behind her eyes and she closed them, moving to the beat, riding his body, every muscle dazzled and alive. She could feel her body winding, tightening, clenching around his. Wanting him. Greedy for him. Demanding him.

Ryland murmured something she didn't catch, his hands tightening on her, biting deep as he thrust fiercely into her. Lily threw back her head, shuddering with pleasure as her body spiraled out of control, wave after wave shaking her. Her hair was a dark cloud around her, teasing her breasts as they jutted brazenly. She felt a scream of acute pleasure welling up and hastily buried her face against his shoulder. His heavy muscles muffled her cries as she allowed one leg to drop back to the floor, needing to hold herself up.

Her body was an inferno, velvet soft, yet gripping him tightly. The friction was nearly unbearable, so much pleasure it was nearly pain. He thrust deep one last time as the music crescendoed, as his body erupted, a hot volcano that nearly took his head off. His legs turned to rubber, his body turned to lead as if she had drained his very strength. He rested her back against the wall, his forehead pressed to hers, struggling to regain his ability to breathe.

They stayed that way, twined together, leaning against the wall for support, the only way to stay upright. Lily attempted to regain her ability to breathe, listening to the next song, a slow, moody number. One leg still curled possessively around his waist, their bodies intimately tight together. She was so aware of his every movement, his every breath, the hand stroking her calf.

Lily was astonished she didn't fall over when Ryland was finally able to move, kissing her neck and slowly straightening up. Her leg somehow managed to unwrap, her foot dropping to the floor, releasing him. He handed her back the little scrap of useless underwear.

Lily stared down at the torn lacy thong in shock then lifted her gaze to Ryland. A slow grin was spreading across his face. Self-satisfied. Male. She couldn't help the slow answering smile curving her mouth.

Ryland studied her. She looked thoroughly loved. She still leaned against the wall, her gown bunched around her waist, her breasts thrusting toward him. Her mouth was swollen from his kisses and he could see his seed trickling down her thigh. "You're undoubtedly the most beautiful woman I've ever seen."

Slightly shocked that she felt no embarrassment, Lily casually used the red thong to clean her leg. Ryland caught her hand, took the scrap of lace back, and slowly performed the task. His fingers seemed to linger and caress her sensitized flesh so that little aftershocks began all over again.

"You can't do that," she whispered. His mere touch was producing an ache that would never be satisfied.

"You wouldn't believe what I can do," he said with complete confidence, his fingers dancing inside her, teasing and provoking, urging her body to move against his stroking thumb.

She went over the edge so hard and fast the orgasm took her by surprise. Lily caught at his shoulder for support, her body trembling and aching. "You have to stop or I'm going to scream and bring everyone running."

He kissed her again and again, wishing for more time with her. "I want to spend hours just making love to you, Lily."

She looked around her at the shabby little room. "I can't believe we're in this smutty little room. Worse, I can't believe I want to stay in here with you."

Ryland leaned into her, found her mouth with his, a slow melting. Where they sizzled before, burning hot and fast, now they smoldered. "I love you, Lily Whitney. I really do love you." His hand curved around the nape of her neck, his thumb tipping up her chin so she had to meet the steel in his eyes.

"I know you love my body."

"Damn it, is it so hard to say it? I feel it every time you touch me. When you kiss me. Stop being so damned stubborn. I could use a little help here."

"Two damns," Lily said thoughtfully. She circled his neck with both arms, leaned her full, generous breasts into his chest. Her teeth nibbled on his neck, his jaw. "I guess I'll have to give this some thought if you're going to be so insistent."

He heard the soft teasing note in her voice and the hard knots in his belly began to relax. "I am going to be insistent, Lily. I was thinking we could go home and pick up this conversation in our bed."

"You're very sure of yourself, aren't you?" Her tongue danced in his ear, teased the corner of his mouth.

"Lily, you're playing with fire here." He pulled away from her. "I'm two seconds from taking you all over again and we really might get caught." One of them had to be strong. He tucked her breasts inside her dress, straightening her neck clasp. She didn't help him, but stood staring up at him with her enormous eyes drinking him in. Almost daring him. Ryland pulled her gown down resolutely, tugged until it fell around her gracefully.

Lily's hand brushed the front of him suggestively, dropped lower, rubbed and caressed, branded him hers before tucking him back inside his charcoal slacks.

His entire body clenched, shuddered, and went up in flames at the dancing intimacy of her touch. Lily might not have experience, but she had confidence and she knew he wanted her. "I'm not going to survive this, Lily." He was pleading for mercy.

She took pity on him. The role of seductress was one Lily was finding she loved but real life was intruding and she could see Ryland's rising tension. "I didn't tell you how handsome you look in a suit. Where did you get it on such short notice? And all the others? They must have been wearing suits."

"Arly. He's a very useful man."

Lily smiled. "Isn't he wonderful?"

"I don't know if I'd go that far, honey. When are you going to introduce me to Rosa? I'm getting kind of tired of ducking under your bed and hiding in the closet on the mornings she decides to bring you tea. Although that closet *is* bigger than the trailer I grew up in." He looked her over carefully, brushed her hair back over her shoulder. "After we get out of here, you need to fill me in on the captain and the general. You took quite a chance talking with him. It took the combined efforts of all of us to keep Higgens and the others away from the two of you."

"I think the captain owes you a big thank-you. That woman was going to take him home and show him a good time."

"It was in her mind to find a handsome serviceman husband," Ryland said. "She was dressed for seduction and he was obviously determined to seduce."

"Don't be glaring at me," Lily said, laughing. "I didn't want anything to do with that man."

Ryland ran his finger down her spine, all the way to the curve of her bottom. "He was touching you like he owned you."

"Like he *wanted* to own me." Lily reached for his hand. "He gave a thought or two to the money. That's what he wanted, not me. And it was just one of those fleeting thoughts. He was ordered to stick close to me and I'm willing to bet tomorrow morning he'll have a lot of explaining to do."

"He won't care," Ryland said with confidence. "He'll think she was worth it."

"How are we going to get you out of here?" Lily tried not to feel anxious. Ryland exuded tremendous confidence. "Have the other men gone? Is anyone watching Higgens?"

"They'll fall back, don't worry about them." Ryland tugged at her, drawing her through the tiny room toward the closet. "You're coming with me, Lily. I'm not leaving without you. The men will expect you to get clear with me. You risked your life for us, to get information to help us, we're not about to leave you here unprotected. They all know I'd never leave you here alone. That's not up for discussion, by the way, if you're thinking of arguing with me."

Lily rubbed her chin along his shoulder. "I'm tired and my leg is going to decide to give out on me after all that dancing. I've got so much to tell you." She didn't want him thinking it was his idea for her to leave. Of course she was going to leave immediately. Her bruises were the perfect excuse. Later she would tell Phillip Thornton her head had been throbbing and she had slipped out to get home and rest.

I can't hold them off any longer. Higgens is sending men in every direction looking for Lily. Take her out by the back stairs and I'll cover for you. The warning from Nicolas was so strong even Lily caught the urgency in his voice.

Ryland reacted instantly, catching Lily's hand, springing toward the closet door. He went through it first, dragging her up the stairs and around the corner until they were pressed against the wall under the spiral staircase. The crowd was close, breaking off into small groups seeking elusive privacy to talk business even as they watched the dancers. Ryland relied on his instincts, threading through the people, using the crowd as cover. He was in a dark suit and could merge with the shadows and blend, but Lily was in dazzling red, sexy and alluring, her dark cloud of hair spilling around her, so she drew the eye. If he gave up his coat his white shirt would be a neon sign.

Lily realized she was endangering Ryland. "Go without me, I'll catch up. John is waiting with the limo." She tried to untangle her fingers from his, but he shackled her wrist and yanked her to his side.

One strong arm curved around her waist. There was steel in him, she discovered. Another side to the passionate lover who could be so tender and loving. "Just do as I say and stay quiet. We aren't separating, Lily, so don't waste time arguing."

She glanced up at the intense concentration on his face. The silver eyes moved restlessly, alertly, searching through the throngs of people unerringly to find the stern-looking men working their way across the ballroom floor and along the walls and darker corners.

Ryland knew the soldiers were looking for Lily and her sexy red dress. He would have spotted her immediately. He urged her down the long hall, hugging the wall, shielding her smaller body with his larger one to minimize the risk of her being seen. They were looking for a woman, not for Ryland Miller. The cloakroom was beside the elevator. Ryland took the number from Lily and strolled up to the attendant, presenting the card. Lily's cloak was floor length and hooded, a long drape of black velvet. Gratefully he enfolded her in its warmth.

On your right. I'm blurring your image a bit.

Ryland drew Lily into his arms, pressing her back into the multitude of potted plants, an ardent lover, his back to their right, his entire body protecting her from prying eyes. He murmured softly, deliberately, amusement in his voice as if they were sharing some secret, intimate joke. All the while she felt the flow of energy growing around them until it was nearly crackling in the air. Together the two men urged the soldier dressed in the dark suit to look the other way, to catch a glimpse of a red gown and hurry after the woman as she rounded a corner.

Ryland immediately rushed Lily toward the stairs, a man so eager to be alone with his lover he was impatient to get her out of the crowd. There was a brief moment when they had no choice but to walk in the lighted hallway. He could only hope the cape was long enough to cover the red hem of her gown as Lily walked quickly.

"Take off your shoes," he ordered as they made the comparative safety of the stairwell. "I don't want your high heels to slow us down if we have to run."

Lily held his arm with one hand and removed the thin-strapped shoes with the other. "I happen to like these shoes," she said. "I don't want them lost."

"Just like a woman, worried about shoes at a time like this." Ryland rolled his eyes as he tugged on her hand. "They're going to be waiting for us on one of the floors below, Lily. They shouldn't be swarming the way they are."

They raced down two flights of stairs. "Why would they unless they knew you were here? Could they have spotted you or one of the men inside earlier?"

"I doubt it." They went down two more flights.

Lily was definitely limping now. She tried to let go of his hand, knowing she was holding him back. She knew from long experience, her muscles would begin to spasm and eventually she would be dragging her leg. "You're the one in danger, Ryland, not me. What are they going to do here to me in front of all these people? I'll go back to the ballroom and join a group. Have Arly send John in for me."

"Keep moving, Lily," Ryland snapped, his expression grim. "This isn't a democracy." His fingers shackled her wrist, pulled her down another flight of stairs.

"My leg, Ryland," she began.

Ryland's palm covered her mouth. She felt his sudden stillness. His arms were around her, holding her to him, moving her backward on the third-floor landing above the stairs. He peered down, his mouth pressed against her ear. "The stair light is gone below us. Someone's there waiting. I can feel them."

She couldn't feel anything but the terrible pain as her calf muscles knotted and her lungs burned from running down several flights of stairs. Her heart was beginning to pound. What could have tipped Colonel Higgens off to Ryland's presence in the building? Or was he really looking for her because she had spent too much time with General Ranier? *Maybe the general was so angry he inadvertently hinted at the truth to Higgens.*

The thought frightened her. Ranier would be in danger, maybe even Delia, his wife. If Higgens and Thornton had been willing to chance committing murder already four times, they weren't going to stop because their next victim was a general.

Ryland's lips moved, his voice so low she hardly caught the words. "It's Cowlings. His telepathic ability is almost nil, but he feels the surges of energy. We're going down the stairs. Stay close to the wall and keep the cloak around you."

She nodded to indicate she understood. Ryland's arms slipped off of her, taking most of the warmth with them. Lily shrank back against the railing as he began the descent into the dark region below them. He made no sound as he stalked down the stairs like the predator he was. Lily touched his back for reassurance. She could feel the ripple of his muscles as he crept down the stairs. She tried to emulate his silence, placing her feet carefully and doing her best to control her breathing. Even so it sounded overloud in the quiet of the stairwell.

A door opened briefly far above them and loud laughter spilled out. The smell of cigarette smoke drifted down. Ryland froze, remained unmoving, holding up his hand to indicate to her to freeze in place. They stayed motionless until the door slammed shut on the voices, leaving behind silence. His hand touched hers. Their fingers tangled and he squeezed hers in reassurance.

Lily tried to hold her breath during the descent to the second-story landing. The closer they got to the second floor, the harder her heart pounded, until she was afraid it would burst out of her chest. The surge of adrenaline caused her body to tremble violently. Ryland was as steady as a rock. She couldn't detect that his heart rate had risen at all and her thumb was rubbing nervously back and forth over the pulse in his wrist. Lily blinked. Ryland's wrist slid away from her.

Suddenly he was gone and she was alone, flattened against the wall on the fourth stair from the landing, trembling alone in the dark. There was no sound at all. Lily sought inside herself for a calming moment, forcing air through her lungs until she had slowed her heart and brought her breathing back under control. She waited, not giving in to the impulse to reach telepathically for Ryland. If Cowlings were anywhere close, he would feel the sudden surge of energy.

The urge to move was sudden and immediate. A whispering sounded in her head but she couldn't quite make out the words. Lily stayed still, hugging the wall, not trusting a connection that wasn't strong and intimate as the one she always had with Ryland. Nicolas was extremely strong and she knew him. She felt he would have managed to send her a clear message. She waited, wrapped in her velvet cloak. Tense. Afraid. Holding her ground.

It seemed an hour. Time slowed down. Nearly stopped. Lily hated the silence, when it was usually her refuge. There was a whisper of movement, felt more than heard. Cloth brushing against the wall very close to her. Lily tried to make herself smaller, held her breath, waiting. She stared directly toward the sound. Little by little she began to make out the stealthy shadow looming large, stalking her there in the dark.

Everything in her screamed to break and run, but she forced a stillness. Trusting him. Trusting Ryland. She could feel him close to her, Breathing with her. For her. Giving her the strength to wait for the threat to reach out to her.

Something heavy dropped from above, landed on the stalker's back, hooking the neck, jerking hard, dropping both bodies to the landing. She could hear the sickening thud of fist against flesh.

Go now! The voice was sharp and clear in Lily's head. Nicolas, not Ryland.

She hesitated one heartbeat then did as ordered, slipping past the two struggling, viciously fighting men. She started down the flight of stairs, glanced back. The two men were on their feet now. One shadow broke and ran toward her, leaping, taking flight, determined to get his hands on her.

Lily tried to run, pushing off with her bad leg. Her muscles seized. The leg gave out, and she found herself sitting down hard in the middle of the staircase. It was the only thing that saved her. The man would have hit her squarely in the back had she not fallen. As it was, he kicked her shoulder as his body overshot hers. Lily nearly tumbled down the stairs with the force of the impact. He landed several steps below her, spun around, and scrambled toward her. She could see his eyes, the sheen of triumph. His hands reached out, grabbed her ankle, and yanked.

Lily slid down the stairs even as Ryland loomed up, a dark solid menace. His kick caught Cowlings squarely in the head. The man fell backward away from Lily.

Ryland caught her, dragged her to him, his hands running over her body to check that she was uninjured. "Are you hurt? Did he hurt you?"

Her hand slid down his chest, came away sticky and wet. "Ryland?"

"It's nothing, Lily, he had a knife in his hand. It's a graze, nothing more. Can you walk?"

"I don't know. It's like that, sometimes I work fine and then it just gives out completely when the muscle's too stressed." She wanted to pull his shirt up to examine his chest, but he was dragging her up, his arm around her waist, urging her down the last flight of stairs to the entrance to the first floor.

Ryland pushed open the door, glanced around, and hurried her toward a side door. *Behind you.* The warning came as Cowlings rushed out of the stairwell. Ryland ducked into an alcove, pushing Lily away from him while swinging around to face Cowlings. The two men circled warily.

"I'm going to kill you, Miller," Cowlings snarled, wiping blood from his shattered nose. His face appeared much like pulp. Even his eyes were swelling.

"You're welcome to try," Ryland answered softly.

Lily concentrated on the picture on the wall to Ryland's right and it began to tremble violently. It suddenly jumped free and flew toward Russell Cowlings. It rocked and spun, dipping low, picking up speed as it rose sharply. Cowlings ducked and dodged, desperately trying to avoid the attacking picture.

Ryland lunged at him, feigning an attack, distracting him. Cowlings stumbled backward, turning his attention to his human opponent. The picture slammed down hard over the top of his head, breaking through canvas, glass, and frame and settling around his neck. Cowlings looked more stunned than hurt.

"Go, Lily." Ryland had no choice. If he left their enemy alive, Lily would be in danger, as would all of his men. He couldn't bear for her to be a witness.

She obeyed, limping heavily as she went. Her leg was throbbing so badly it was making her feel sick. Nearly useless, she was dragging herself toward the exit. The heavy drape along the alcove wall suddenly leapt to life; it reached out and whipped around her, wrapping her up in coils of material. The drape wound so tightly it threatened to cut off her air. Lily was unable to see anything or to fight the heavy folds. Her arms were locked to her sides.

Her leg gave out and she fell, trapped in the ever-tightening coils, suddenly in danger of suffocation. *Ryland!* Panic-stricken, she gasped his name in her mind.

She knew he was in a fight for his life. For all their lives. She was even ashamed that she had pleaded for his help, risking distracting him, but she couldn't help herself. Lily had never felt so panicked in all her life.

Be calm. That was Nicolas. It was amazing that she could hear him when she was screaming so loudly in her head.

She breath was shallow and she closed her eyes and began to use her brain. She had tremendous power, tremendous control. Years of practicing had honed her skills. Russell Cowlings was preoccupied with fighting and he was not nearly as strong as she was. Lily began to fight for control of the heavy drapes. The battle didn't last long. Cowlings had no stamina for a prolonged mental fight nor did he have the necessary skills built up to divide his attention.

Ryland went in low and mean, needing a quick finish. Nicolas was close but he was controlling security cameras and steering any late-nighters away from the alcove. Cowlings was a vicious fighter and quick. He had always been one of the best in hand-to-hand combat and was smart enough to keep out of reach, snapping a series of hard kicks to force Ryland to stay away from him.

Ryland fought down the urge to move too quickly, taking his time, blocking the kicks and pushing slowly inside. He was the stronger physically and once he got his hands on Cowlings it would be over. Ryland caught sight of the two-foot-high ash-tray just inside the alcove. The round cylinder was made of metal. Even as he kept up his slow pursuit of Cowlings, he concentrated on the cylinder, forcing the canister to tip over slowly, floating lightly to the thickly carpeted floor to keep from making noise.

Blocking several vicious kicks, he sent the cylinder rolling between Cowling's legs, causing him to stumble back. Instantly

Ryland exploded into action, driving in fast with the edge of his hand to Cowling's throat, crushing everything in it's path as it drove through. It sickened him, watching the man fall. Watching him struggle to breathe, an impossible task. Ryland tried to feel nothing. Tried to go dead inside.

He whirled around to find Lily's enormous eyes staring at him in horror. She scrambled out from under the heavy draperies, trying to crawl to Cowlings with the vague idea of helping him.

Get clear! Get clear! There are too many coming down and I can't hold them off.

Ryland caught her around her waist, lifted her bodily into his arms, and sprinted for the door. He burst into the night, running for the corner where he knew Arly waited in the car.

"I have to go with John. If the limousine is still parked and waiting for me, Higgens is going to know I didn't leave immediately," Lily protested.

Ryland didn't slow down, didn't glance at Nicolas as he emerged from another door and paced alongside of him. They separated at the car, diving from either side into the backseat. Ryland dumped Lily onto the floor.

"Go, Arly, go now." Ryland's voice was harsh. He told Lily, "Call John on the cell phone and tell him to get the hell out of there."

Lily glanced up at Ryland's grim face and obeyed him. John protested, wanted to know what was going on, but the urgency in her voice finally convinced him. He promised to leave for home immediately.

"Thanks for hanging back and covering us," Ryland said.

Nicolas shrugged. "Kaden took the children home. They were happy to play for a while. I wanted a little more excitement so I thought I'd just hang around." He leaned down to examine Lily's face. "Are you all right? Are you hurt?"

"Ryland is. Cowlings had a knife," she said.

Arly twisted his head around to stare. "What the hell happened?"

"Just drive," Ryland snapped. "It's a scratch, no more," he added in protest as Lily came up on her knees and Nicolas lifted his shirt to look him over.

"You're damned lucky, Captain," Nicolas said. "You should

have broken his neck when you had him the first time. You knew he had to be taken out. You gave him a shot at you deliberately."

Ryland didn't answer, staring out the window, his fixed gaze turbulent.

"She could have been killed, Rye. He was going after her to shake you up."

"Damn it, Nico, I know that. Don't you think I know that?" Ryland swung his head around to glare at Nicolas.

Nicolas shrugged his broad shoulders with studied casualness. "You should have killed him the first time you laid your hands on him back at the fence when we escaped."

Ryland leaned his head back against the seat and closed his eyes, bile rising. He fought it down, his fingers finding and tunneling in the thick silky strands of Lily's hair. He closed his fist and held her that way. Unknowing. Just needing her presence.

SEVENTEEN

◆

"DAMN it, Lily, I just killed a man. I liked him. I've been
to his parents' home. What the hell did you want me to
do?" Ryland was pacing back and forth, raw, pent-up emotion
boiling to the surface and spilling out, making his voice harsh.
"He was a good soldier. A good person. I don't know what the
hell happened to him." He was remembering Russell Cowlings
and the memories hurt.

He couldn't look at her, couldn't see the horror in her eyes
again. Resolutely he kept his back to her as he paced the length
of her bedroom and back again. Lily was still running her bath,
her velvet cloak thrown carelessly over the back of the stuffed
armchair. Her sexy red gown was in a heap on the floor. He
snatched it up and crushed the material in his hands. "You could
have been killed, Lily. He could have killed you. I let him go
the first time because I was worried what you might think.
Damn it." The words exploded out of him. "I'm good at what I
do. You can't just look at me with accusation and shake me up
so I can't function. Do you have any idea what would have happened if he had gotten away? I put all the men in danger to keep
from killing him in front of you." He hoped that was true. He
wished it were true. If it wasn't, it meant he had hesitated be-

cause Cowlings had been a friend. And that was a bad, bad thing. Either way he deserved the whip in Nicolas's voice.

Lily pinned her hair up and stepped into the hot bathwater, praying it would help unlock the muscles knotting in her leg. Her shoulder throbbed where Cowlings had made contact in his leap on the stairway and she knew she had a terrible bruise there. She hadn't bothered to check; tears were running down her face and she doubted she would even see her image in the mirror. She ached for Ryland. Felt his pain. Felt how sick he was and how angry at himself. He was yelling at her, but she knew his fierce rage was really directed at himself.

Steam rose around her as Lily forced her body into the hot water. She couldn't comfort him. She couldn't think of any way to take away his pain. He had reached out to her when her father had been murdered. He had been there when she found out she had been an experiment. She could only sit in a gigantic marble Jacuzzi filled with hot steamy water, crying and wondering why someone with her brain didn't have a clue what to do.

"Lily?" Ryland rested his hip against the bathroom doorjamb, her gown still crumpled in his hand. She hadn't looked at him once since they'd raced out of the hotel. Not one single time, as if she couldn't bear the sight of him. She couldn't have hurt him more if she'd plunged a knife in his gut. "You might as well just understand something right here and now. This is what I do, what I've been trained to do, damn it!"

She didn't look at him, staring straight ahead. Ryland stepped closer. He was going to have an ulcer before he ever got a commitment out of her. He could see the ugly black and purple bruise forming high up on the back of her shoulder. "Are you listening to me?" The harsh rage was gone from his voice. "I'm not letting you go because you saw me doing something that was necessary. You may as well know I won't. It's a stupid reason for you to give up on us." He brought the red material up to his face, rubbed it against his jaw. He wasn't going to lose her.

Ryland had no idea how it had happened or when it had happened, but she was so firmly entrenched in his heart, in his soul, he couldn't breathe without her. When she still didn't answer, just sat there with steam curling her hair and tears falling into the water, he sighed heavily, the anger draining out of him. "Don't cry, honey. I'm sorry I had to kill him." His voice was very low and controlled. "Please stop crying, you're tearing my heart out."

"Get a clue! I'm not crying because you had to kill him, Ryland. I'm sorry he's dead, but he was trying to kill us both. I'm crying for you. I have no idea how to help you." Embarrassed, she threw water on her face to cover the tears.

He was silent, studying her averted face. "This is all for me? You're crying for me?" That was what she did. Turned him inside out with a few sentences. What was he going to do with her? "Lily, don't do that. You don't need to cry for me." Where his stomach had been in hard knots, now there was a warm glow. He felt like she'd handed him a Christmas present. No one had shed tears for him in a long time.

Lily heard the note in his voice. Happiness. She felt it in the room in spite of the weight of the guilt he was feeling. That little note allowed her to breathe again.

She turned her head to look at him over her shoulder. Her long lashes were spiked. Beads of water ran down her soft skin, to the tips of her breasts. In spite of the bruises, she was an alluring sight sitting there. Her hair tumbled and curled in the steam. Water bubbled and brushed lovingly at her body. She took his breath away. Stole his heart. She *cried* for him.

"I can't think when you look like that, Lily. Why did you have to be so beautiful?" He didn't mean physical beauty, but he couldn't separate one from the other. He was sick at heart with what he'd done. He didn't think the blood of a friend could ever be washed from his hands but somehow her tears had managed to do it. Ryland stared at her, in the middle of what looked like a crystal palace, a princess he didn't deserve but was going to keep.

"I wish I was beautiful, Ryland. You make me feel beautiful." Her vivid blue gaze drifted moodily over his rugged features. "How could you think I would blame you for saving our lives? I feel what it cost you. I felt it when you did it."

"I saw your face. You wanted to save him." He blinked away the tears burning unexpectedly in his eyes. His throat felt raw with pain.

"I saw yours. I wanted to save him for you." She reached out her hand to him. Waited until he took her fingers and settled on the edge of the Jacuzzi tub. "We're connected somehow. And you're right. It doesn't matter if my father found a way to manipulate the attraction between us, I'm grateful you're in my life."

Ryland brought her hand to his mouth, nibbled on her fingers, resisting the urge to gather her close. She humbled him with her generosity. "Does your shoulder hurt?" He leaned forward to brush a kiss against the vicious bruise.

"I'm fine, Ryland. What about your ribs? Arly said he cleaned the scratch but you know knife wounds are notorious for infections." She sounded anxious, not at all his perfectly calm Lily.

He knelt beside the tub, reached beneath the bubbling water for her calf. He began a slow, deep massage, working her knotted muscles with infinite gentleness. "Don't worry, Arly scrubbed it with some kind of foul-smelling stuff he called bug juice. It burned like hell. Nothing could be alive, not even the tiniest germ."

"When I was a child, he swore by that stuff. I think he makes it up in the laboratory like the proverbial mad scientist. Every time I fell down, he swabbed it over my knees and turned my skin a very ugly shade of purple."

Ryland laughed. "That's the stuff, all right." He felt her wince beneath his massaging fingers and gentled his touch even more. "Tell me about Ranier. What do you think?"

"He was telling me the truth," Lily said. "I was so relieved. I've known him most of my life and I'm not certain I could have taken it if he had been involved in a plot against my father. Apparently, he received none of the messages my father sent him. Not his letters, or his emails, and not the phone calls. Interestingly enough, the general's aide is a brother to Hilton, the man Colonel Higgens sent to keep an eye on me." She reached under the water, gripped his wrist. "General Ranier was suddenly very worried, as if he were connecting dots to something. I think there's been a security leak for a while and he's suddenly putting two and two together."

"Maybe. If there's been a problem with a leak, they wouldn't advertise it. The investigation would be internal. No one would suspect Colonel Higgens. His record is impeccable.

I certainly preferred in the beginning to believe it was your father betraying us all. And General McEntire . . . it's still difficult to believe that he would be involved in selling out his country. It's a nightmare, Lily. This entire thing has been a nightmare."

"Do you think Cowlings was a plant? Someone Colonel Higgens placed in the program? I remember when I read his file, he scored low on most of the criteria for psychic ability. I thought he was allowed in because Dad wanted to see if the enhancement would work on someone with little or no natural talent. And it did."

Her voice had slipped back into her professional, completely interested tone. Ryland knew immediately the discussion had gone from personal to clinical. Instead of annoying him, it made him want to smile. "He might not have been telepathic, but he certainly was able to take command of an inanimate object. That was really great."

"Lily, you did destroy your father's original notes on the experiment, didn't you? He wouldn't want it repeated."

The cramps in her leg were slowly beginning to ease under his ministration and the hot water. Lily breathed a sigh of relief and sank deeper into the bubbles. "Dad thought the experiment failed," she pointed out.

"Only at first," he said calmly. His fingers itched to shake her. "He suspected someone had sabotaged it and he still felt strongly enough to tell you to get rid of his work. You have to honor that, Lily. You can keep the tapes of the exercises in case you need them for the other women when we track them down, but the rest of it, you have to destroy so this is never repeated."

"It was brilliant, Ryland." She sat forward, her blue gaze alive with interest. "What he did was totally brilliant from a purely scientific standpoint."

"I volunteered, Lily, the men and I, but you and the other little girls had no choice. What Peter Whitney did to you was totally wrong from a humanitarian standpoint." Ryland's strong fingers encircled her ankle, gave her a little shake. "Think how you felt, Lily, seeing those little girls. Seeing yourself. Think how those women feel now and what they must have gone through all these years. And my men, how they are going to have to guard themselves for the rest of their lives to keep from ending up in an institution. Yes, from the standpoint of a military operation, with the help you're giving us now, the experiment may have been a success. It was very cool, by the way, to be able to divide my energy and fight Russell Cowlings even while I was working with the other side of my brain. But the point is, we have to function as a group. Those without an anchor to draw the excess energy away from them are always going to have problems living a normal life."

"I know, I know. But Ryland . . ."

His grip tightened. "There are no buts, Lily. These men and the women deserved a normal life. They want families. They have to support those families. They don't have your money and this fancy house to help provide a sanctuary for them to live in. I can't believe you're even contemplating the idea to continue."

Lily gave a small sigh. "I'm not, Ryland. I'm really not. I can't help but find it interesting and rather brilliant." She ducked her head. "I can hardly bear the thought of giving up anything that was my father's. Especially his handwritten notes. They make me feel like he's still here with me."

His hand tangled in her hair. "I'm sorry, Lily. I know it hurts to lose a parent. You didn't have a mother and I didn't have a father. We're going to make interesting parents when we have children."

She laughed, dispelling the shadows in her eyes. "I wouldn't know the first thing about children."

Ryland leaned over the edge of the tub to kiss the top of her head. "That's all right, honey, you can always get books off the internet."

Lily glared at him. "Very funny. Those books were very informative."

"I'm not complaining." The smile faded from his face. "I'm sorry about Russell Cowlings, Lily. Nicolas was right, you know. I could have ended it immediately, when I first had my hands on him. I let him go. I kept thinking about his parents, about the way he was in training. And I kept thinking about how you might not forgive me for making a kill. I didn't want it to end that way. Instead, I put you in danger." He caressed her bruised shoulder lightly. "He would never have hurt you like this if I had just done my job."

"I'm glad it bothered you, Ryland. If it was easy for you, that's when I'd worry." Lily yawned, tried to cover it with her hand.

"Come on, honey," he responded immediately. "Let's go to bed. We can figure this all out in the morning. Is your leg feeling better?"

Lily nodded. "Much better, thanks." She shut off the Jacuzzi jets and stepped out, seating herself on the tiled bench to towel off.

Ryland took the towel out of her hands and performed the task with long slow strokes, rubbing away the small tempting beads of water. "I wish I could supply proof to General Ranier, but I don't have anything but conjecture at this point. That's not going to get me out of a court-martial."

Lily went very still, her eyes wide. "Maybe we do have proof, Ryland. That disk. It's still in my lab coat pocket. I hung the jacket on the peg by the door inside my office when I came back from the clinic. I didn't take any meds until I was home because I didn't trust anyone. I was hurting so bad I just came home. I wish I had remembered it at the time. How could I have forgotten something so important?"

"Maybe because someone hit you on the head and knocked you out?" he ventured.

Lily limped past him back into the bedroom, yanking open the doors to her closet. Ryland frowned as she whipped through shirts on hangers. "I've been meaning to talk to you about this closet. A family could live in it." He took the shirt she was trying to yank over her head out of her hands. "What are you doing?"

"Going to Donovans to get that tape." She pulled the shirt back to her.

"Lily, it's four o'clock in the morning. What are you thinking?"

"I'm thinking Colonel Higgens isn't an idiot and when he discovers Russell Cowling's body in that alcove after he obviously sent him to watch me, Higgens will arrange a little accident or kidnapping or just plain murder at my office. If I go now, I have a chance to get that disk and get out clean. He won't be expecting me to go there. He'll be looking for a way to penetrate the security of my house or use someone I love—

John, Arly, or Rosa—to get to me." She wiggled into the shirt, dragging it over her generous breasts. "This is my one chance to get the disk. He doesn't know about it."

"It's four o'clock in the morning! You don't think that might raise even a security guard's suspicions?"

She shrugged, selected a pair of slacks, and dragged them on. "I doubt it. I go there at all hours. They all think I'm a little bit crazy." She leaned over and kissed his mouth. "Don't look so worried. I know this is a calculated risk but it's worth it. Higgens doesn't know about the disk. They think the recorder with the disk in it in their possession is all there is. I don't even know if it's anything. It could be blank, but if it isn't, it might be the proof we need against Higgens. It would clear you and the others and General Ranier would have to listen."

"I don't like it, Lily."

"You'd like it less tomorrow, in the light of day when Higgens and Thornton have had a chance to regroup and plan. I know Thornton. He's drunk right now and sleeping it off at home. He's nowhere near Donovans. I'm telling you, Ryland, if we want that disk, this is our only chance to get it. Right now."

"Lily, you can hardly walk."

"Stop throwing up roadblocks when you know I'm right. There's no way I'm walking into that place a few hours from now. It's now or never." She lifted her chin. It took a tremendous amount of courage to decide to go and she didn't want to have to argue, afraid she might give in when she knew it was a necessity.

She could see the struggle on Ryland's face. He would have gone in a heartbeat, but Lily was at risk, not Ryland. She touched his arm. "You and a couple of the others can stand by to act if I need help. Cowlings was the only one we knew of who could detect telepathic communication and he's dead. If it's necessary we can use that and also turn the guards the other way so I can get out. We have to act fast, right now."

Ryland swore softly but nodded his head, knowing she was right. The disk was too important to let go. If it held any information at all, even Peter Whitney's suspicions, it was worth the risk. They would have to chance getting out from under Higgens's military guards positioned around the estate and it was growing lighter. It could be done, but it was trickier. Even

Lily couldn't simply waltz outside. The guards would tip Higgens off immediately.

"I'll let Arly know we'll need the use of the vehicles he has stashed off the property." Ryland capitulated completely. "I'll round up the team."

"I'm just going to run in and come right back out. You and the others can stay here and if I need help, I'll let you know." She pulled on her watch. "Arly put a mini communicator in my watch. He can monitor me too."

Ryland called Arly to alert him, as Lily searched for a jacket. "We aren't going to wait here, honey, we have to stay close to you to be of any use." He spoke into the phone in a low voice, hung up, and turned back to her. "Don't give me any argument on this or you aren't going anywhere."

She rolled her eyes. "I just love it when you get all macho on me. You don't have to worry, Ryland. I'm afraid. I don't want you hurt, but I rather like knowing you're close by. I'm not taking any chances."

They hurried to beat the rising of the sun, going through the tunnels and once more using their combined strength to direct the guards' attention elsewhere. It was easier as the guards were much sleepier. Nicolas and Kaden jogged to the garage behind the groundsman's cabin to get out two cars. Arly drove Lily the distance to Donovans with the second car close behind, stopping a few blocks from the chain-link fence surrounding the property.

Arly stopped at the gate, looked bored as the guard shone a flashlight throughout the car and carefully checked Lily's ID. "New driver, Dr. Whitney?" he asked.

She shrugged. "My security man. Thornton and Colonel Higgens are concerned for my safety." She sounded bored, slightly irritated. "I figured it wouldn't hurt to placate them."

The guard nodded and stepped away from the car. Arly took the hot little Porsche smoothly into the parking lot and followed her directions to the block of buildings where her office was located. "I should have considered that changing drivers might make the guards suspicious with everything that's been going on around here. It's always been John driving the limousine or just me driving the Jag alone." Lily sighed. "If I say get out of here, Arly, don't argue, just go. If they get me, I don't want them to get you."

"I will, don't worry about me. You just get in and get out fast." Arly looked at her anxiously. "I mean it, Lily, straight to your office and back."

She nodded. "I promise." Her heart was in her throat. She was definitely not heroine material. At the first sign of trouble she planned to run like a rabbit. Lily glanced down at her leg. She was still limping and the leg was reacting badly. It was her own fault, dancing several dances without resting it in between. Making wild love. Running down stairs. She had forgotten to do everything necessary to keep her leg from giving out and now she was paying the price.

Lily waved at the guards, easily passing through security. She often preferred working at night just to avoid the sounds of people and the emotional turmoil and energy that always surrounded them. Now, as she heard her own footsteps echoing in the empty hall, she was fixated on the many cameras tracking her progress.

She could feel panic beginning in the pit of her stomach. A thousand butterfly wings taking flight at once. Her stomach started doing somersaults in time to the frantic beating of her heart. Even her mouth went dry as she stepped into the empty elevator and rode it down to the lower regions where her office was located.

Only the dim lights in the tracks along the center of the hall lit the interior. Spooky shadows she had never noticed before were everywhere, moving as she moved, as if following her. It seemed impossibly quiet. Lily was tempted to talk to herself for added courage.

She unlocked the door to her private office and went inside, closing it behind her. She was certain a camera must have been planted in her office, so she tried to be casual, donning her white jacket as she always did and going straight to her desk as if she had forgotten something important.

Lily began rifling through the drawers. She unlocked the lower drawers, dropping the key into the pocket of her jacket and palming the tape as she did so. It was very small, able to fit in the microrecorder. She put her hands on her hips as if frustrated, sliding the disk into the pocket of her slacks. With feigned irritation, Lily closed all the drawers, did a once-over of her desktop, dropped the key into her purse, and hung her jacket up.

No matter how many times anyone viewed the tape, she was certain they would never spot the disk or realize it even existed. With a huge sigh of relief, she jerked open the door to her office.

Hard hands struck her solidly in the chest, driving her backward so that she landed on the floor, blinking up in surprise and alarm. A stocky man who looked very much like Capt. Ken Hilton from the fundraiser stalked across the office while Colonel Higgens quietly closed the door. She knew she was looking at General Ranier's aide.

Higgens stared down at her with his cold flat gaze. "Well, well, you certainly are much more brazen than I ever gave you credit for being." He strolled across the floor, all the more menacing for his lack of anger.

Lily stared up at him, not attempting to rise, still fighting for air. She rubbed her palm over her face, then clasped her fingers together in her lap, feeling for the small catch on her watch. Pressing the button, she alerted Arly to trouble and prayed he would leave.

"You left the fundraiser early."

Lily shrugged. "I hardly think leaving early warrants your friend shoving me to the floor."

"Did you know a man was killed on the first floor of the hotel tonight?" Higgens circled around her, his shoes brushing her slacks.

"No, Colonel, I had no idea. I'm hoping there's a reason you're attempting to intimidate me, because I'm about to call the security guards in here."

Captain Hilton slapped the back of her head.

Lily glanced down at his shoes. She had seen them somewhere before. She remembered the strange inch-long scratch zigzagging along the inside near the seam. She looked up at Higgens. "I take it you're threatening me in some way."

"Don't play dumb with me. You're not dumb. You have your father's records, all of them, don't you?" Higgens continued to circle her.

Lily rubbed at her sore leg, not looking at him. "If I had the records I would have given them to Phillip, Colonel. The code my father used on the computer here and at home in his office meant absolutely nothing. Everything I read in his reports, you already had access to. The things I put together, guesses, conjecture, I passed on to General McEntire. I also typed them up and sent both you and Philip a copy. Beyond that, I have no knowledge of how my father managed to enhance psychic ability in the men."

"I don't believe you. Dr. Whitney. I think you have a very good idea how he did it and you're going to write it all up for me. The entire process."

Lily did look at him then, her eyes wide and accusing. "Do you think your friend here is going to beat me in the head and knock it out of me? If you believed I knew the process, you wouldn't touch me. You couldn't afford to."

Colonel Higgens reached down, grabbed a handful of her hair, and dragged her up. Lily fought to get her bad leg under her. Tears swam in her eyes, but she refused to cry out. She kept staring at the shoes. At the scratch. Higgens thrust her away from him so that she stumbled back against her desk.

Lily caught at the edge to steady herself. There was no way she could run even if they took their eyes off of her for a moment. Her leg was too weak. She leaned her hip on the desk to ease her weight off her bad leg. "Are you selling the information to the highest bidder, Colonel? Is that what you do? Sell out your country?"

Hilton reached out casually and slapped her. Lily swore and went straight for his throat, chopping viciously with the edge of her hand. It was so unexpected, he didn't have time to block, but fell back choking under the blow. Lily followed up with a knee to the groin, dropping him to the floor and kicking his head hard, using the outside edge of her strong leg.

At once her weak leg collapsed under her, spilling her back on the floor, right beside the writhing man. Lily rolled over and drove her fist into his solar plexus, robbing him of air. She pulled back her fist again, angry enough to go for his throat a second time, but Colonel Higgens caught her under both arms and dragged her away from the fallen man.

"Get up, Hilton," he said in disgust. "Get off the floor before

I hit you myself. She's got a bum leg and she still kicked your ass."

Hilton rolled over and managed to push up to his knees, groaning the entire time.

Lily didn't struggle, allowing Higgens to help her to the desk where she sat on the edge. Her leg throbbed, already cramping viciously, but she looked at the two men without expression.

Hilton turned his head, still on his hands and knees, to glare at Lily. "I'm going to kill you with my bare hands."

Her gaze dropped to his hands, drawn by a force far more powerful than her will. She recognized his hands. Recognized his wrist. His watch. There had only been the briefest of moments, but she had seen what her father saw. Hands dragging him across the deck of a ship. A scratched shoe.

Raw energy massed in the room. Surges so powerful the lights flickered. The lamp on her desk exploded, shattering glass into fragments. Books flew off the shelves, heavy tomes hurtling through the air like missiles, pummeling Hilton. Pens and pencils, the letter opener, every sharp object in the room suddenly had one target in mind, covering the distance with blinding speed and lodging in Hilton's skin.

He went down screaming. Colonel Higgens casually drew his side arm and shot the desk inches from Lily. Shocked, she diverted her attention and the objects in the room fell harmlessly to the floor. Lily and Higgens stared at one another. He was pointing the gun right at her head.

"So, Dr. Whitney, your father obviously enhanced you too."

Lily's eyebrow arched. "He was interested in psychic enhancement and what it could do because I had natural ability. He saw what I could do and wanted to see if it could be developed to a much greater extent in others."

Hilton staggered to his feet, shuddering as he tried to pull the various objects out of his skin. Fortunately for him he was wearing a jacket that helped to keep most of the pen and pencil wounds shallow.

"Just in case you're wondering where the two hairpins that were sitting on the desk went, you'll find them in your bloodstream, winging their way to your heart," she said helpfully.

Hilton roared at her. "I'm going to cut you up into little

pieces and feed you to the sharks," he snarled. He looked nearly as afraid as he did angry.

"Really? You'd better make certain you hold on to the knife while you're doing it, otherwise you're the one that will be cut into little pieces and fed to the sharks." As she spoke, her voice conversational, without rancor, she concentrated on the gun in Colonel Higgens's hand.

The hand began to tremble, the gun wavered, tried to swing around and point in Hilton's direction. She watched Hilton's eyes widen in alarm.

"Stop it, Dr. Whitney," Higgens demanded. "I need your brain, but not the rest of you. If you don't want me to shoot your leg, you'd better behave."

Lily looked away from the gun. "That was me behaving, Colonel. I wanted him dead. I should have driven the shards of glass right through his skull." She smiled at him. "Don't worry, I'm tired. Unfortunately, the drawback to a natural talent is it doesn't last that long. That's why my father wanted to enhance the psychics, to make them stronger with more endurance."

"So you did discuss this with him."

"Of course we discussed it. We discussed it for years." She tilted her head. "Did you have my father killed or did Ryland Miller?"

"Why would I want your father dead?" Higgens demanded. "I needed the process. He was being stubborn."

"You didn't offer him the right things. Where is Miller?" Her voice was as cold as ice, her blue gaze direct.

Be careful, honey. Don't go too far. He's a smart man. Ryland's voice brushed at the walls of her mind, but he sounded far away.

Lily tossed the cloud of dark hair over her shoulder. *Not that smart. He had my father killed and he's using the same moron to come after me.*

Damn it, Lily, don't push him too hard, it's dangerous. Ryland was adamant.

"You want Miller?" Higgens asked.

Hilton, finally managing to straighten, tossed the last of the pens to the floor and took a step toward Lily. He stopped abruptly when Higgens held up his hand in a silent order, but he never took his vengeful gaze from her face.

Lily ignored him. "If Miller killed my father, then, yes, I want him. You track him down and kill him. Show me his body and I'll give you the process. Otherwise, go ahead and kill me. You'll never figure it out on your own."

There was a small silence as the colonel thought it over. "You're a bloodthirsty woman, aren't you? I would never have guessed. You're always as cool as ice."

"He killed my father," she pointed out. "Do you know where Miller is?"

"Not yet, but he can't just disappear. I have men looking for him. We'll get him. What did Ranier say?"

"General Ranier? What does he have to do with anything?"

"You spent a great deal of time with him," Colonel Higgens said, his eyes narrowed into tiny slits.

Lily felt an instant chill down her spine. She could feel the waves of malice pouring off of Higgens. The intent of violence. She forced a casual shrug, knowing she held the general's life in her hands. "He was concerned about me. Delia wanted me to go stay with them after my father's disappearance. She hasn't been well and the general wanted me to consider the idea for her benefit as well as my own."

"Did he mention Miller?"

"I did." Lily took a chance. "I was hoping Miller had contacted him but the general didn't know anything at all that was helpful. I dropped the entire conversation because I didn't want him to become suspicious. We talked about Delia after that."

"I think for your safety, Dr. Whitney, you're going to have to be placed in protective custody. I think Miller is a real threat to you."

"My house is safe enough."

"Nobody's safe from Miller. He's a damned ghost. A chameleon. He could be in the same room with us in plain sight and we wouldn't know it. It's what he was trained for. No, you're much safer with us." The colonel nodded at Hilton.

Hilton caught Lily's hands and yanked them out in front of her, snapping handcuffs tightly around her wrists. On the pretense of checking to see if they were on solidly he jerked her wrists back and forth maliciously.

"That's enough, Hilton. Let's get out of here."

Lily slid off the desk, testing her bad leg. She could limp, dragging her leg along, but it would never hold up if she had to run. With a sigh of resignation, she fell into line behind Hilton. Somewhere outside, the GhostWalkers were waiting. She hoped they were all the colonel said they were. Chameleons. Lying in wait to ambush her kidnappers.

EIGHTEEN

◆

LILY wasn't in the least surprised at the lack of security guards. Phillip Thornton had to be in on whatever Colonel Higgens was up to and he must have insisted Higgens have full cooperation. The guards had been pulled to another part of the laboratories. She kept her head down, concentrating on the mechanism locking the handcuffs. She had never been good with locks. Even after studying how they worked, she rarely succeeded in opening them. It took finite concentration, a focused energy with pinpoint precision and skill. Lily was angry with herself for not taking more care to acquire the skill.

We're in place, Lily. Use your leg. Slow them down. We don't want the colonel to think you're capable of running. Ryland sounded very confident.

Lily frowned. *I'm not capable of running. And don't get yourself caught. I can get out of this.*

You're such a little liar. You need me to rescue you.

The taunting amusement in his voice warmed her. It was only then she realized she was shivering with fear. Lily tossed her hair and rolled her eyes in case by some miracle Ryland could see her, but she slowed her pace, dragging her bad leg a little more.

Colonel Higgens put a hand on her shoulder. "I'll have

Hilton bring the car around so you don't have to walk so far."
Now that he thought she believed Miller had disposed of her father, he could afford to be civil.

"He looks like the captain I danced with at the benefit," Lily ventured, to keep him distracted.

"They're brothers. Neither is very bright, but they come in handy." The colonel put his hand on his gun as they entered the elevator. He had little control of the guards on the ground area and any of them might spot the handcuffs. "I'll shoot anyone who tries to stop us," he warned. "Think of this as a national security mission. You have a chance to save lives, Dr. Whitney. You choose."

He paused to snatch two lab coats from a small room close to the elevators, tossing one to Hilton. "You look a little worse for the wear—put that on and cover up the blood." The other jacket he arranged over Lily's wrists to hide the cuffs. "We're going to walk out all together, very close to one another. Hilton, you'll go get the car and bring it up to us."

He's sending his henchman to get the car. This man killed my father.

The warmth suddenly surrounding her was strong. She realized immediately the other men were tapped into the telepathic wave of energy, listening, waiting and ready to strike on her behalf. It made her feel a part of something. When had she gone from being so alone and devastated to belonging?

Does anyone actually use the word "henchman"? Ryland asked.

There was a collective murmur of negatives, a few laughs and snorts of derision.

I'm sorry, honey. The verdict is no one uses that antiquated word.

Antiquated? Her breath nearly stopped in her lungs when she spotted two security guards coming toward them near the end of the long corridor. *Should I have used "bad guy"? Would that be more modern?* The overload of adrenaline was making her shaky, almost high, but it numbed the pain in her leg, allowing her to function properly.

A few more minutes, Lily, Ryland encouraged her. *Your heart is beating too fast. Slow it down.*

Another voice broke in. *It's the anticipation of seeing us again. She likes me.* Gator drawled the words in his Cajun accent.

Lily had to keep from laughing in spite of the dangerous situation. She didn't dare look at Higgens, afraid her expression would give her away. The men were outrageous in their efforts to be reassuring.

I do, Gator. I thought you were so cute when I first saw you. The guards nodded to Higgens as they hurried past.

Changing of the shift. Everyone was tired. Higgens wasn't quite so stupid after all. The guards would not want to see anything unusual. They just wanted to go home to their families and rest.

You don't need to be looking at Gator anymore, Ryland decided. *Not if you're thinking he's cute. What the hell is cute anyway?*

Not you, Gator pointed out.

In spite of the banter, Lily sensed the edge of grim tension building in their voices. The double doors leading out into the complex were looming. She kept her head down and walked slowly, dragging her leg.

Hilton pushed open the doors and waved her through. Lily didn't look at him. He was dead. He just didn't know it yet. She kept walking until Higgens tugged on her arm, bringing her abruptly to a halt. Hilton trotted off. "That was smart to stay quiet with the guards. You wouldn't want blood on your hands."

Lily lifted her head to look him directly in the eye. "Don't let the fact that I'm a woman fool you, Colonel. I don't mind violence under the right circumstances. Someone is responsible for killing my father and I'm going to find them."

He smiled at her. His eyes were flat. "I hope you do, Dr. Whitney."

The car pulled up beside them. Higgens reached out to open the door for her. Lily half turned as if to slide onto the passenger seat. Instead she snapped out a front kick, putting her weight behind it. The kick took Higgens precisely in the solar plexus, driving the air from his lungs so that he collapsed like a deflated balloon. As he went down, Kaden loomed up behind him, finishing her work with a vicious chop to his neck. Colonel Higgens dropped to the asphalt like stone.

Kaden didn't hesitate, shoving Lily into the car and crowding in after her. "Go, go." *Phase one completed. We have recovery. Repeat, we have recovery.*

"They'll stop us at the gate," Lily pointed out. "Kaden, get these cuffs off me. I can't stand them." She was phase one. The retrieved object. The idea irritated her but not as much as the metal cuffs on her wrists.

"We're in possession of the gate at the moment, Lily," he replied gently. "Just a few more minutes. As soon as I know we're clear."

"Did Arly get out?" She was looking at the driver in an effort to identify him. He wore the white lab coat Hilton had been wearing.

Jonas glanced at her in the mirror and winked. "Arly's waiting outside the gates with the Porsche. Sweet little number, that car. I'd like to drive it sometime." He sounded very hopeful. He pulled the car right up to the gate. The uniformed man simply opened the door and slid in on the other side of Lily so she was surrounded.

Ryland framed her face in his hands and kissed her hard. "Damn it, Lily, I'm going to find a padded room and lock you up in it where I know you're safe," he said, then turned to watch their back trail. Lily could see the gun in his hand.

Behind them, the laboratories rocked with several loud explosions. She turned to look out the back window. Smoke billowed into the sky. "Who did that?"

"Kyle, of course. He does like to blow things up."

"There are a lot of innocent people working there," she pointed out.

Jonas drew the car up beside the Porsche. Arly was out of the car and pacing back and forth. They were four blocks from the laboratories and could hear the sirens blaring in alarm. Ryland dragged Lily out of the backseat and put her in the Porsche, taking the keys from Arly before the man could protest.

"What are we doing?" Lily asked.

"Getting you away from that place fast," Ryland replied.

"I didn't even get to hug Arly," she said. "He must have been so worried."

"*He* was worried?" Ryland changed gears with more

strength than finesse. "You took ten years off my life. You'll have to hug Arly later. Right now I want you as far away from Donovans as fast as I can get you away. As far as I'm concerned the place can burn to the ground." A muscle jerked along his set jaw. "They could have killed you, Lily."

She leaned her head back against the seat as he maneuvered his way in and out of the light traffic. "I know. I was really afraid. But I got the disk and Higgens never had a clue." She closed her eyes. "Hilton was the man who threw my father overboard."

Ryland glanced at her, worried. "I know, honey. I'm sorry. Are you hurt? Did they hurt you?" He wanted to stop the car and examine every inch of her.

Lily shook her head wearily without opening her eyes. "Not really. But I was really, really afraid. He was going to kill me after he got the process out of me."

Ryland frowned. "You don't know the process, do you?"

"Not exactly. I see where my father was going and it wouldn't be hard, knowing him as well as I do, to figure most of it out. It's all in his laptop in the laboratory at the house. Everything is there. I would have made something up for Higgens." She was exhausted, wanting desperately to crawl into her bed. She held up her manacled wrists. "Can you get these off of me?"

She sounded so close to tears his heart turned over. "As soon as we get to the garage in the woods, honey. Hang in there a little longer."

Lily looked down at her hands. "I read about this kind of thing in those books, you know. In real life, it isn't nearly as exciting as reading about it."

Ryland put his hand over hers, his thumb stroking small caresses over her wrist. The cuffs were too tight, cutting into her skin. "I could do a lot with a bondage scene," he said, forcing speculation into his voice, hoping to make her laugh. If she cried, it was going to rip his heart out. "I think silk ties would do better than metal cuffs." His thumb traced the bluish circles forming on her wrist. "This would never happen with me. You have to be more discerning, Lily, when you go around experimenting with bondage." He wiggled his eyebrows. "I'd make a great master."

She nearly choked. "Master? I see. I'd be your slave."

He grinned at her wickedly. "That's one way to look at it. But tying you to the bed and taking my time exploring your body sounds good to me. I wouldn't mind taking a few hours to just give you pleasure."

Her blue gaze collided with his. Her entire body flushed at the idea. "Thank you for taking my mind off of the handcuffs, they really hurt. And they make me feel trapped. I almost feel like I can't breathe with them on."

"We're right here, honey, just a couple more minutes," he promised as he eased the Porsche into the garage and closed the garage door, plunging them into darkness. He reached for her hands. "I don't have my tool kit, so I have to concentrate. It may take a little bit of time."

"I don't care, just get them off of me." She wasn't going to cry now that she was safe and almost home.

It took a few minutes, Ryland working at the skill with precision until she felt the cuffs loosen and drop off. He handed them to her as he scooped her up. "I'm going to carry you, honey."

"I'm too heavy." She was just grateful to have the cuffs off.

Ryland made a rude noise and pulled her from the small car.

"Don't we have to wait for the others so they can get the guards around the house to look the other way?" She was tired. She wanted to sleep forever.

"We can do it ourselves. One at a time. I'll let you know when we have to combine our energy." Ryland scooped her up and carried her from the building into the thick stand of woods.

The morning sun was filtering rays of light through the dense canopy above them. Branches and leaves swayed and danced to the mild wind. Lily looked around her in wonder. She had forgotten beautiful things could exist. Birds were calling back and forth to one another in spite of the chatter and scolding of squirrels.

Lily settled her head against Ryland's shoulder, circling his neck with her arms. "I kind of like this part of the bondage thing. It feels like you're my slave instead of the other way around."

He bent his head to scrape his teeth back and forth playfully along her neck, his tongue swirling to ease the tiny nips.

Lily laughed softly. "I think it's true about sex being on the minds of men every three seconds. You are thinking about sex instead of guards, aren't you?"

"You say that as if it's a bad thing. Of course I am. All this talk is stirring me up. How the hell do you manage to smell so damn good all the time?"

Lily felt the change in him, going from banter to business. He didn't stiffen, but there was power moving through his body, raw and deadly. He nodded toward their left. Lily felt the interruption in the natural flow of nature around them. A foreign presence was in the forest.

She closed her eyes, gave herself up to the common path, touching on the wave, feeding it, allowing Ryland to assume command. He did the directing, suggesting a walk in the other direction. The subtle flow of power persisted until the guard sauntered away, giving them free passage to the tunnel entrance.

Once inside, Ryland moved fast, knowing his way, taking her straight through the maze of passageways to the nearest corridor to her suite of rooms. Sunlight was pouring through the windows. He closed the drapes even before he laid her on the bed.

Lily stared up at his face. "I don't have the energy to find a recorder." She pulled the small disk from her slacks pocket and handed it to him. "Arly will have one somewhere. I just want to lie here and look at you."

He put the precious disk on the nightstand and knelt beside the bed to remove her shoes. "I want to look at your leg. Does it hurt?"

"I'm so tired, Ryland," she admitted, "I can't think about it."

Ryland tossed her shoes aside and dragged her slacks down, tossing them aside. "I forgot you weren't wearing underwear. For God's sake, Lily, no wonder I think about sex all the time. You go from scaring me to seducing me."

A small, reluctant smile tugged at the corners of her mouth. "How am I seducing you? I'm just lying here." The idea would have had merit if she hadn't been so completely exhausted. There was something about the way he looked at her that always managed to heat her blood.

Ryland examined her calf carefully, massaging the cramped

muscles. She lay quietly under his ministrations, her eyes closed, wearing only her shirt. The material was hiked up, showing her navel and the underside of one breast. Ryland slid his hand possessively up her thigh.

Lily opened her eyes a tiny slit. "I don't know what you think you're going to be doing, but I want to sleep for a month."

"I'm inspecting the damage," he said. And he was. There was the beginnings of a bruise on her thigh.

"It's on my backside and my chest," she murmured sleepily. "I hurt everywhere, Ryland. Thank you for taking the cuffs off, I know it wasn't easy."

He gently took possession of her hands, turning them this way and that, frowning down at the dark matching bracelets of bruises. "How did you get the bruise on your leg?" There was rage building in the pit of his stomach, but he fought to keep it under control, fought to keep his voice gentle.

"I don't know. I got in a fight. Hilton slapped me and I lost my mind for a minute." She turned on her side, snuggling closer to her pillow. "I went after him."

"He slapped you? What else did he do?" Ryland pushed the material of her top up her back. Her buttocks had two bluish smudges. He was beginning to wish he could kill a man twice.

"Don't worry, I got him back," she answered. There was satisfaction in her voice. "I would have beat the holy hell out of him if Higgens hadn't interfered. I probably got the bruise on my thigh when he shot at my desk. Wood splinters went everywhere. I was so angry I wasn't feeling much in the way of pain."

"He shot the desk right next to your leg?" Ryland rubbed his hand over his face. "Damn it, Lily."

She didn't open her eyes but she smiled. Rather smugly. "You say that a lot."

"Don't sound so pleased. I'm getting gray hair. You got in a fistfight with this man? I would have thought the daughter of a billionaire would be more sophisticated than that."

"I'm too modern to let some caveman beat me," she defended.

His fingers were massaging her scalp, searching for damage. "And he hit you in the chest? Let me see."

"I'm not letting you see my chest." Her laughter was muffled. "Go away and let me sleep. That's a lame excuse to look at my breasts."

"I don't need a lame excuse to look at your breasts," he pointed out. "I want to see the damage." He simply caught the hem of the shirt and tugged until she gave in and lifted her body enough to allow him to pull it off.

"I really am tired, Ryland. Take the disk to Arly and see if it's worth all the trouble we went to. Give me an hour to sleep and we can go to General Ranier and see if he'll help us." Her voice was dropping lower and lower until Ryland was certain she would just drift off.

He drew the sheet over her body and lay next to her until he was certain she was asleep. Ryland lifted Lily's limp hand and examined her bruised wrist in the light from the morning sun. "Damn it." He said the words softly as he bent his head to kiss the purple circles, trying to find a way to heal her. He held her hand to his chest, over his heart as if somehow the way his heart beat for her would remove the marks.

He was so completely immersed in his desire to heal Lily's bruises, so focused on her, he didn't hear or feel any disturbance. There was no sound but something made him look up and he found himself staring at an older woman. She was framed in the doorway, a mixture of shock and fear on her face.

Very slowly and gently Ryland placed Lily's hands on the sheet and sat up. "You must be Rosa," he said in his most charming tone. "I'm Ryland Miller. Lily and I are . . ." He sought hastily for a word. Any word. He didn't want to say "lovers" but "friends" seemed ridiculous when he was sitting on Lily's bed and she was naked beneath the sheet. The woman was making him feel like a teenager who'd sneaked into his girlfriend's room. He had absolutely no idea what he would do if she ran screaming through the house.

"Yes, I'm Rosa." She glared at him. "Why hasn't Arly told me about you? He must know you're in the house. No one can be in the house without his knowledge."

"Well, ma'am." The woman had pinned him with her steely eye and Ryland—whom full-grown men could not make afraid—squirmed. "It's complicated."

"It doesn't look very complicated to me." Rosa swept into the room, clucking her disapproval as she approached the bed.

She spotted the dark purple circling Lily's wrists and shrieked in horror. Rosa actually smacked her own chest.

Ryland was stunned into silence. The woman took up the entire room with her presence, intimidating him as no one had ever done. He couldn't tell if she were going to faint, or scream, or grab something and strike him over the head.

"What happened to my baby?" Rosa's gaze fell on the discarded handcuffs and her eyes went wide with shock. There was a sudden hushed silence.

Ryland felt color creeping up his neck. His shirt suddenly felt too tight and beads of sweat began forming on his skin.

Rosa stooped to pick up the offending manacles and dangled them in front of his face. She broke off into a torrent of Spanish. The tirade lasted so long she ran out of breath. It was the only thing that saved him. He had the feeling she had used up every curse she knew and some she'd just plain made up.

"Now, ma'am. Don't go getting the wrong idea," he said. "I didn't put those cuffs on her. Someone else did that."

"There is another man in here?" Rosa's head whipped around and she stalked to the closet, yanking open the door. "This is one of those ménage romances? You teach my little girl this?" She inspected every corner of the closet. "Tell him to get out here and face me!"

"Ma'am . . ." Ryland was torn between laughter at what she was thinking and desperation at the idea that she might try to toss him out. "Rosa, it isn't that at all. Lily was attacked tonight by an enemy. They tried to kidnap her."

Rosa screeched, her voice hitting high C and rattling the windows. She actually threw the handcuffs at him so he was forced to duck. Ryland leapt from the bed and tried to stop her. "Don't, for God's sake, woman, you're going to wake the dead. Stop it, will you?"

On the bed, Lily stirred, lifted her head slightly, and turned over to regard Rosa with sleepy eyes. "Did Ryland frighten you?"

"Me?" Ryland worked his finger around his shirt collar. "How can you say that? She thinks I've been playing some bondage game with you."

Lily's eyelashes fluttered, drifted down. "Well, you wanted

to play a bondage game with me, didn't you?" There was amusement in the soft sleepy notes of her voice.

"Lily, I was making you laugh, cheering you up." He was beginning to sweat under Rosa's disapproving gaze.

Someone snorted loudly in derision. Ryland whirled around to find Kaden and Nicolas standing in the doorway with Arly right behind them. Several other men were pressed behind him, trying to see in, drawn by Rosa's screams. With the door wide open, the soundproofing had done no good at all. Ryland threw his hands in the air in defeat and sat down heavily once again on the edge of Lily's bed. "Lily, wake up. This is your crazy household and you can deal with it."

Lily's soft laughter played over his skin like the touch of her fingers. "My knight's armor appears to have chinks in it. Rosa's harmless, a sweetheart, just be nice." She rolled over and the sheet dipped dangerously, exposing tempting creamy flesh.

Rosa gasped in outrage. Ryland caught the sheet and dragged it to Lily's chin. "Don't move. The neighbors have arrived."

Lily's lashes lifted and she gaped at the crowd gathering in her room. "Good Lord. What happened to the privacy acts? I'm certain I'm entitled."

"Not if you're screaming," Kaden pointed out.

She clutched the sheet to her. "I wasn't screaming," she denied adamantly. "That was Rosa! All of you go away. I want to sleep."

"I don't think you had sleeping in mind," Kaden ventured. "I distinctly heard you say Ryland was interested in bondage. Are you planning on putting cuffs on him, because I want to stay around for that."

"You were watching my movies," Arly accused.

"What movies?" Gator chimed in. "Are you holding out on us? You have some good bondage flicks and you're not sharing?"

"You're all obsessed with bondage," Lily felt compelled to point out.

"Lily!" Rosa's voice silenced the room instantly. "Who are these people and what is going on in my house? I demand an answer immediately."

Lily looked around for a robe. Ryland found one for her and, using the sheet for a screen, helped her into it so she could sit up. "I'm sorry, Rosa. I should have told you. My father was involved in something at Donovans. An experiment to enhance psychic talent." She stared at Rosa, willing her not to fall apart.

Rosa went pale beneath her smooth olive skin and searched for a chair. Arly helped her to sit down. Rosa's gaze never left Lily's face. "He did this evil thing after all we went through before?"

Lily nodded. "Things began to go wrong. Someone wanted his notes. They wanted the process for themselves to sell on the market to foreign governments and terrorist organizations. Even in the private sector, enhancement could be used for profit. In order to do that, they had to convince Dad the experiment was a failure. They did that by murdering the men one by one and making it appear to be the results of side effects."

Rosa crossed herself, kissed her thumb. "This is not right, Miss Lily."

"I know, Rosa," Lily said softly, wanting to comfort her. "Dad became suspicious that the deaths were due to sabotage not side effects and he asked me to look things over. He didn't tell me anything, obviously hoping I would see something without prejudice. Unfortunately once I was brought into the project, these people thought I could provide them with the process for enhancing. So they murdered Dad and threw his body into the ocean."

"Madre Mia!" Rosa stifled a cry of alarm and reached out for Arly's hand, holding it tightly. "You are certain, Lily? They've killed him?"

"I'm sorry, Rosa, yes, he's dead. I knew it from the time of his disappearance. These same people tried to use your fear to get into this house and search for Dad's work. They weren't able to do so, thanks to Arly, but they've continued to try."

Rosa rocked herself back and forth. "This is wrong, Lily. So wrong. He promised he would never do such a thing again. Now he's dead. Why would he do this thing?"

"These men are men he worked on. I helped them escape from Donovans and brought them here. One of the men is recovering from a brain injury."

Rosa was shaking her head furiously in protest. Lily continued doggedly. "I'm teaching them the exercises that worked for me and helped me function in the outside world. They have nowhere else to go, Rosa. They're wanted men, hunted, and if we turn them over, they'll be killed."

Rosa shook her head hard, not looking at Lily.

"They're like me, Rosa. Like me. Where else can they go? They need a home. You and John and Arly and me, we're all they have. Do you really want me to send them away to be killed?"

A sob escaped Rosa's throat. Arly hunkered down beside her chair and wrapped his arm around her shoulders, whispering something softly to her. She leaned her head against Arly's shoulder, all the while shaking it in denial but it was half-hearted.

"Rosa, I'm in love with Ryland." Lily admitted it in a low tone, but so clearly in the silence of the room, it was impossible not to hear.

Rosa looked up, her attention captured.

Lily tangled her fingers with Ryland's. "I do love him and I want to spend the rest of my life with him. This is your home. It will always be your home. You're my mother and no daughter could love you more than I love you. If you truly don't want Ryland and these men here, we will leave. All of us. I'll go with them."

"Lily." Rosa's eyes swam with tears. "Do not talk of leaving. This is your home."

"It is your home too. I want it to be their home for as long as they need it. I can help them. I know I can. We have a disk, something my father recorded and hid. I'm hoping there's incriminating evidence on it. If so, I'll make copies and give General Ranier one of them. If necessary I can go above him. If it clears their names, all to the good; if it doesn't, we'll keep working to find evidence."

"They have to come after you now, Lily. Colonel Higgens knows he tipped his hand. If he can't reacquire you, he'll try to kill you," Ryland said grimly.

"I know that. He'll find a way to search the house. It won't be easy and he'll never find the tunnels or the men." She looked at Kaden and Nicolas. "You'll have to really guard Jeff. He won't be able to move fast. Who's with him now?"

"Ian and Tucker. They won't let anyone bother Jeff," Kaden assured her with absolute confidence.

"Good. My escape is just going to make Colonel Higgens all the madder. He'll definitely come here with a warrant of some kind. He doesn't like anyone thwarting his plans." She leaned into Ryland. "You were right about him."

"I want to hear the disk," Arly said.

Ryland tossed the tiny disk to the security man. "You have anything that will play that?"

Arly caught the disk and stood up straight, digging through his pockets until he came up with a miniature voice-activated recorder. "Absolutely. I took it with me thinking it might come in handy if we were stopped." He popped the disk into the recorder after removing the blank one.

There was a small silence then a voice jumped out at them. "Take him to the clinic. Pump him full of that shit. Zap his brain a few times with electricity and it will look like he had a stroke. I want him dead by tomorrow." The sound of Colonel Higgens's voice was harsh. "And when Miller takes his sleeping pill tonight, take him to the clinic and fry his brain. I've had all I can take of his insubordination. Get the job done this time, Winston. I want Hollister dead and Miller a vegetable. If that doesn't convince Whitney his experiment was a failure, kill the son of a bitch. Tell Ken I want Miller taken care of tonight."

"Miller doesn't sleep much. We can't go near him if he's awake."

Higgens swore. "Ken can't field Whitney's calls forever. Sooner or later Whitney will get through to Ranier. I can arrange something for Ranier, maybe a fire. It has to look accidental. You can't just kill a general and his wife and not have an investigation. Faulty wiring would do it. First things first. Arrange for Hollister to have a breakdown so we can cause a little brain damage and get rid of that bastard Miller."

There was utter silence in the room. Ryland let out his breath slowly and looked at Lily. "I'd say that would be enough to convince Ranier. Arly, can you make copies for us?"

"No problem. I can make several and we'll keep the original in Lily's little safe room." Arly winked at her.

Lily reached for the phone and called the general's home. After a brief conversation she looked at the others in frustration. "The maid said they were out for the day and would return tomorrow morning. She wouldn't say where they went. At least he's taking precautions."

"Why don't you all get some rest? You were up all night and it's nearly noon now. If we can't talk to Ranier, we may as well take a break." Ryland wanted Lily to sleep. The bruises on her body were becoming more apparent with each passing hour.

"I can cook a meal for everyone," Rosa offered, throwing her support fully behind them in the one way she knew. "And I'm a nurse. Let me see this man who is ill."

"Rosa"—Lily slid deeper beneath the sheet—"make them do those exercises. I'm too tired to see that they do them."

"I thought we were taking the day off," Gator protested. "Kicking back, watching the old bondage films."

"You must never take a day off from the exercises," Rosa scolded. "It's important to do them every day." She started herding the men from Lily's bedroom, but suddenly turned back and marched stiffly to the bed. Glaring at Ryland she snatched up the handcuffs and took them with her.

Arly, falling into step beside her, leaned down and whispered wickedly in her ear. It earned him a slap on the arm but Rosa could be heard giggling as she closed the door behind them.

"Did you see that?" Ryland demanded. "She took the handcuffs."

Lily wiggled out of the robe and let it fall to the floor. "So you wouldn't think about using them on me."

"I wasn't thinking about using them." Ryland shoved a hand through his dark hair, tousling the curls more than usual. "Why does everyone think I'd use metal cuffs? I'd use silk." He leaned over Lily, pressed a kiss between her breasts. "I wouldn't mind tying you up but I'd use silk."

Her laughter was smothered by the pillow when she buried her face in it. "Poor baby, no one will believe you. Rosa thinks you're kinky."

"Well, I am," he admitted. "But just with you. And she took the cuffs and went giggling out of the room with that bondage freak Arly. Now that's scary stuff."

Lily summoned enough strength to smack him with the pillow. "That's disgusting. Don't even think about the two of them doing anything together. Rosa is like my mother and Arly . . . well . . . he's Arly." She looked at Ryland. shook her head. "No way. It isn't possible. They would never . . ." She trailed off again and shuddered.

Ryland laughed at her. "Yes they would. He looks at her with that look in his eye. Men know these things." He dropped his clothes on the floor and slid beneath the sheet, wrapping his body around hers protectively.

"I don't want to know so don't let me in on it if you find out Arly and Rosa are seeing one another. Do you think General Ranier and Delia are really okay?"

"I think Ranier is a wily tiger and Higgens grabbed the wrong tail. He's gone somewhere to stash his wife. That's what I'd do, and he'll come back prepared to fight a battle. He won't stop until he's dead or he's won." He circled her body with his arm, cupping her breast in his palm possessively. "I didn't much like having all those men in here knowing you were wearing nothing but a sheet. We're going to have some serious talks about underwear."

Lily laughed and turned over to face him. Her gaze drifted lovingly over his face. "You're the most beautiful man I've ever seen. When you're around, I can't see anyone else." Her fingertips traced the contours of his face. Found the rough-edged lines, the small scars, his stubborn jaw. All the while she looked at him with love.

"I'll have to make certain I'm always around, won't I?" he said.

"I think that would be a good idea," Lily agreed.

NINETEEN

◆

RYLAND came awake just after nightfall. He lay listening
to Lily's soft breathing. She lay close to him, her body
pressed tightly against his, fitting up against him like a glove.
When he shifted, the texture of her skin, rose petal soft, slid
over his rougher skin, reminding him always of the beauty of a
woman.

He had checked on the men several times throughout the
day. Most slept but Nicolas was always awake, always on the
watch. He simply grinned or saluted or nodded, but rarely
spoke. Ryland stretched lazily, trusting to Arly's alarm systems,
but not to the easy way everyone seemed to treat Lily's bedroom.

He slipped from the bed and locked the door, ensuring complete privacy. Naked, he padded to the window and slowly slid
the heavy drape to one side so the moonlight would spill across
the bed and illuminate Lily's skin. He found it astonishing that
she didn't recognize her own beauty. She took his breath away
as she lay there sleeping, her dark hair tumbling like so much
silk on the pillows.

It was exciting to stand there in the shadows and watch her
as she slept. To be able to pull the sheet from her body and simply enjoy the lush sight. To devour her with hungry eyes. The

cool air hit her body and she moved, sprawling out in the bed, one hand flung across his pillow as if reaching for him. His body hardened into a painful ache. Every cell needed her. His heart pounded when he looked at her. Lily. Where had she come from? How had he managed to find her? Elusive Lily. Sometimes he felt as if she were water he held in the palm of his hand, tantalizing a thirsty man, only to slip away just when he went to take a drink.

He wanted her. All of her, not just her body, but her heart and soul and her brilliant mind. His jaw hardened. Few things escaped him when he hunted. Lily was too important to him to let her slip away.

Lily turned her head toward him unerringly, as if sensing danger in the darkness. "Ryland? Is everything all right?"

"It's just perfect, Lily," he answered.

"What are you doing?"

"Looking at what's mine." He waited a heartbeat. "Thinking about all the ways I want to make love to you."

"Well, then." There was soft amusement in her voice, soft invitation. "Is all that thinking getting me anywhere?"

His hand cupped his body, slid over the hard thickness, testifying to his response, to his indulgence in fantasies. "I think so."

"Come here where I can see." Lily laughed softly, joyously in invitation. "I've always thought indulging your every fantasy would be fun. What is it you want right this minute?"

Ryland thought about it. "More than anything, I want to take away every bruise on your body. I want to get rid of every sore spot and replace it with feeling good. I want you to forget nightmares and sadness and think only of me, even if it's only for a few minutes. I want you happy and I want to be the man who makes you happy."

Lily felt a curious melting sensation in the region of her heart. Her body turned instantly to liquid heat. It wasn't at all what Lily expected him to say. Ryland was a wild man when it came to sex and he was standing over her with a predatory look on his face and raw hunger in his eyes. His body was hot and hard and demanding urgent relief. How was it possible to resist him when he could say things like that so sincerely?

"Come here, then, Ryland," she called softly.

He walked to the side of the bed, watched her turn on her side, reach for his body with caressing fingertips. She stroked his thighs and he let her, wanting to make her happy, knowing instinctively she wanted to explore his body in the same way he needed to explore hers. Her palm was hot on his thigh, her fingernails raking his skin lightly. Then her hand cupped his sac, squeezed lightly and teased so that he gasped with pleasure, shifting his stance to move closer.

"Lily," he protested, but it was a plea for mercy.

"No, just let me. I want to memorize you. Your shape. I love the way I can make you feel." The moonlight was spilling across his body. She liked watching her fingers on him, shaping him, dancing over him, teasing and making the breath slam out of his lungs. He could make her lose her mind so easily. With his hands. His mouth. With his body. She wanted to know she could do the same. That they had equal power between them.

Ryland could see it mattered to her. His body was as hard as a rock and her lingering caresses just might kill him, but he figured he'd die happy. "Someday, when the others aren't around, I'll share this with you, the way you make me feel. You'll feel it too," he said. The words came out between his teeth. He was watching her face emerge from the shadows, slowly inching toward him. She was beautiful, every classic line, her small patrician nose, her full, generous mouth. Her long feathery eyelashes. And her eyes. She looked up at him and he felt himself falling forward into her eyes.

Her mouth was hot and tight and wet, sliding over him, her tongue doing some kind of dance that had his brain exploding right out of his skull. His hands fisted in her hair, thumbs caressing the silken strands. He allowed his head to fall back and he closed his eyes, giving himself up completely to her, to the pleasure she brought him.

Her hands were everywhere, shaping his firm buttocks, exploring his hips, sliding along the columns of his thighs. She traced his ribs, his flat belly, urged his hips to a slow, leisurely rhythm all the while the flames of sensuality licked over his body.

When he knew another moment would take away all control, he gently, reluctantly, moved away from her. It was a struggle to get his breathing back, to find a way to force his leaden legs to move. Ryland made his way to the end of the bed and knelt there, looking down at her.

"Lily, I want this night for you. I want you to *feel* how much I love you. When I'm touching you and kissing you, when I make love to you, I want you to always know it isn't just about sex. There's so much more between us. I don't have pretty words to wrap it up in. All I can do is show you."

"You have beautiful words, Ryland," she protested. His fingers were massaging her calf muscles, taking her breath, robbing her of speech. It was always like that with him when he touched her. And he was right. She could feel his love. It flowed through his fingertips when he caressed her scars and each sore muscle. It was in his lips as they touched each bruise. In his tongue as it swirled over the discolored marks in a lazy sweet healing. The way he loved her brought tears to her eyes.

Ryland made his way up her legs, found her tight black curls, and delved there for treasure. Lily nearly came off the bed. He simply caught her hips and dragged her closer, indulging his taste for her. Making his claim. He wanted her to know there was no one else in the world for her. Or for him.

Lily cried out as wave after wave of ecstasy rocked her. Ryland's hands pinned her hips, leaving her open and vulnerable to him. He took his time, worshiping her body, heightening her pleasure in every possible way he knew. And his knowledge was considerable. She gasped for mercy, pleaded with him to take her, begged for his possession. All the while her body responded to his every touch.

He took his time, a leisurely exploration, every shadow, every hollow, committing to memory her every response. He found the bruises and the sore spots. He found every sensitive spot. She was frantic, trying to pull him to her, whispering to him there in the dark of the night.

Ryland settled his body over hers. Felt her softness, her skin nearly melting under his. Her hips cradled his lovingly. Her entrance was hot and damp with welcome. He pushed into her velvet folds, just the thick head so that she bathed him with flames. "Tell me, Lily. I need you to say it out loud."

Her gaze moved over his face. "Say what? I think you already are hearing me. I want you deep inside me where you belong."

"We fit together. We were made for each other." He pushed inside her deeper, her tight channel grasping, resisting, only to soften and welcome. The sensation ripped him up inside. "Do you feel that, Lily? Do you think it's ever been this way with anyone else? Do you think it ever could be?" He thrust a little deeper. His breath slammed out of his lungs. His fingers curled possessively around her hips, held her still while he took her slowly. His way. Thoroughly.

"I love you, Ryland, I'm not looking for another man. Tell me. Say it. What is it that you're looking for from me?"

Her eyes were too blue. Saw too much. Ryland could see the intelligence there. She was everything he was not. Rich. Smart. Sophisticated. She had more education than he would see in his lifetime. He tightened his hold on her and plunged in deep and hard. Long strokes designed to drive them both out of their minds. Take them from the reality of the world and into another of heat and fire and passion where nothing else mattered and she was wholly his.

There in the bed, in the light of the moon, he was a part of her. Would always be a part of her. He took himself to the limits of his control, riding her hard and deep, was rewarded with her breathless cries, her hands clinging to his, her body wildly meeting his, matching every rhythm he set without hesitation. She followed his lead with complete trust, without inhibition, giving herself fully to him.

Lily heard her own voice crying out, heard a sound in his throat as the flames engulfed them, as the world exploded around them leaving behind colors and lights and so much pleasure she could only lie there gasping for breath and staring up at his face. His beloved face. She loved every rugged edge, every scar, the blue shadow he could never quite get rid of. Wave after wave of pleasure shook her, an explosion of shocks, leaving her locked with him, sated, happy. Belonging.

She wrapped her arms around him tightly as if she could keep him there, in the same skin with her, the same body while their hearts pounded frantically and each tiny movement by one or the other sent a shock wave tumbling through both of them.

Ryland propped himself up on his elbows to take some of his weight, but refused to give her back her body. He feathered kisses up and down her face. Lingered over her mouth. "I love everything about you."

"I noticed." Her fingers tunneled in his hair. Curls. Ryland was all rough edges but he had shiny blue-black curls on his head. She loved it.

"I want to settle a few things, Lily."

Her eyes widened. A slow grin curved her mouth. "This sounds suspiciously like those 'we have to talk' moments in the movies."

"We do and be serious."

"I can't possibly think, let alone talk!" she protested. "I don't have a thought process anymore. You short-circuited my brain."

"Lily, you still haven't made a commitment to me. I want you to marry me. To have children with me. Do you feel the same way?"

There was a moment of silence while she stared up at him. He felt the response in her body, the slight movement to try to get free. "That's not fair, of course I want those things with you, I just don't know if it's possible. I have to find out what's in that room, Ryland. There's so much I still don't know. I have to search for those women. I made a promise to my father and I intend to keep it."

Ryland's hands tightened on her shoulders, gave her a little shake. "I need to know it wouldn't matter to you, Lily. Tell me it wouldn't. We can keep that damn room and read every file, watch every video, find those women together and make certain their lives are good. Tell me nothing we find will ever tear us apart." He framed her face in his hands, his body blanketing hers. "If you can say that to me, and mean it, then I say keep the room. We may need his expertise. Who knows, our children may be the real thing. But if you can't, Lily, if you can't look me in the eye and mean it, I swear I'll destroy everything myself."

Lily's vivid blue gaze drifted over his face, studying the intensity of his expression, the steel in his glinting eyes. A slow smile curved her mouth. She leaned into him, kissed his nose, his mouth, each eye. "Do you know how very silly that threat is? If I wanted to keep the room intact, I'd simply lie to you."

He shook his head. "Lying isn't part of your makeup. You

either want me for all time and it matters to you the way it does to me, or you don't. I want that commitment from you. All of it, Lily. What's in that room won't matter if you love me the same way I love you. I don't want less. I don't mind signing some prenuptial agreement dealing with your damned money and I don't mind not understanding what you do half the time. But I want to know, not guess, *know* that you love me and want me in the same way I do you."

She stiffened, her heart suddenly racing. "You're talking about leaving me. That's what you're saying, isn't it?"

"Lily, I'm saying I'm willing to take on your promises to your father. I'm willing to live here with you if that's what you need to be happy. I'm willing to make Arly and Rosa and John my family. All I'm asking in return is the same thing from you. Take on me and my family. Those men out there who have nowhere to go without help. Feel about them the same way I do. Lily, make a commitment. Is that so damned hard?"

He saw it in her eyes first. Deep down, where it counted. His heart nearly exploded right out of his chest. His mouth found hers and took the words from her, swallowed them so they could find their way to his soul. Lily. His Lily for all time.

She laughed and kissed him back, locked her legs around his waist to hold him deep inside her.

Ryland lifted his head alertly. Swore. "We've got company coming." He rolled off of her quickly.

Lily clutched the sheet up to her chin. "What do you mean?"

"I mean the children aren't in their beds sleeping." The door to the room burst open and several of the men strolled in.

"What in the world is going on? Don't you people have something to do besides harass me in my own bedroom? You happen to be interrupting a marriage proposal here." Lily tried outrage, hoping they would all get the hint.

Kaden shrugged carelessly. "Everyone knows you're going to marry him. He always was a little slow getting around to the actual doing."

"I asked her a dozen times," Ryland protested. "She was the one hesitating."

Lily glared at Ryland. "Why didn't you lock the door?"

"I did lock the door," he said. "That doesn't slow any of them down. Our children are masters at breaking and entering."

"Great. And did no one teach them the fine art of knocking?" She switched her glare to the men and treacherous Arly, hoping to wither them on the spot.

Several threw their hands up as if for protection, grinning like apes as they did so.

"Ian's got a bad feeling," Kaden announced when the laughter had died down. "He thinks something's going down with General Ranier right now."

Ryland sobered at once and handed the phone to Lily. "Call him. Gear up. We'll head over there now. We can check it out and see if there's been a disturbance."

"No one is answering at all, Ryland," Lily said with a small frown. "Someone is always there. Day or night there's staff. It isn't normal and that worries me."

"I just have a very bad feeling," Ian agreed. "We might be too late if we wait any longer."

"That's good enough for me, Ian," Ryland said as he shrugged into his gear without the least bit of modesty. "Get moving, Lily, I'm not leaving you here. I don't trust Higgens. Arly can keep Rosa and John safe but no way would he be able to stop the colonel from getting you."

Lily rolled her eyes. "He's only saying that to look macho in front of all of you. He knew I'd come whether he okayed it or not so he issued the big command. And, Mr. Big Shot, I happen to be ready. And a little privacy would help." She caught up the sheet, wrapped herself in it, and started toward the closet.

"Night gear, Lily, that means black." Ryland stuffed a tight one-piece black spandex suit into her hand. "This will work fine. I found it in that house you call a closet. And wear tennis shoes—you do own a pair, don't you?"

"At least ten pairs, sarcastic one. I'm not certain I can fit my body into this thing," she said but hurried into her bathroom to clean up quickly and try to squeeze into the pantsuit. "I'll look like a sausage."

"I'll help," Gator offered.

"I do appreciate your offer," Lily said, "and I may take you up on it."

"I'll shoot you first," Ryland warned Gator.

"He's so touchy, Lily," Gator said.

Lily came around the corner making a face at Ryland. "He's

a big baby, is what he is," she told Gator and fell into line beside Ryland as they hurried toward the tunnel. She leaned close to him. "There's no possible way to wear underwear in this outfit."

He covered her mouth and sent a steely glare toward his men. Not one of them had the audacity to make a comment but they all smirked at him.

IAN rolled under the hedge and scooted close to Ryland. "I don't like the feel of this place at all, Captain. Someone's in there and if it's the general, he's not alone."

I count four in the house and two guards on the north side. It was Nicolas checking in.

I've got two in the house and one guard on the balcony on the east side. This was Kaden giving his report.

Sniper on roof. One on roof across the street, Jonas added. *That is two snipers, two separate buildings.*

Ryland assessed the situation. *We need to be in the house. Any evidence that the general is inside?*

Man down in kitchen near the table. I can't see him well enough to know if he's staff or an aide. Best guess, the general's in the house and he has unwelcome company, Kaden offered.

Then we have no choice. Nico, clear the rooftops. Kaden, Kyle, and Jonas, take out the guards. If you don't know whose side they're on, make it soft. Otherwise make it clean and no guns. Absolute silence. Signal when you're clear and we have a go.

Lily hunched in the corner of the car, making herself as small as possible. She was a block away from the action. She knew Ryland had left one of the men close. She suspected it was Tucker and he had a way of making anyone feel absolutely secure. She couldn't see him, but he was out there making the night safe again. Arly sat in the front seat, betraying his own anxiety by tapping his hand on the steering wheel.

"You shouldn't be here, Arly," she said nervously. "I can't believe you came with us. John and Rosa . . ."

"Are safe. Rosa would have my head if anything ever happened to you. She told me to see to it personally that you returned safely. Well," he hedged, "you and your young man."

"Someone set guards around the general's house. Ryland's men are clearing them out now," Lily reported. She leaned over the seat. "Arly, how long have you and Rosa been an item?" She tried to sound very casual.

He looked at her sharply. "How long have you known?"

"Why did you want to keep it a secret?"

"I didn't want to keep it a secret. I've asked her to marry me a thousand times. She won't. It was always because she couldn't have children."

"Rosa's too old to have children, Arly, why would that matter?"

"That's what I told her yesterday. Not that I mind sneaking around—it adds a little spice. But I'm getting too old to be climbing in windows and creeping down hallways."

"Did she say yes?"

"I told her with the things we did together, she'd burn in hell if she didn't marry me. So she said yes."

"That must have been a charming proposal." Lily leaned over the seat to kiss him. "I'm glad, you need someone to keep you in line." She took a deep breath. "I'm really afraid this time. For Ryland. For the general. For all of them. And for us."

Arly squeezed her hand. "So am I. But I've seen some tough men who deal with some rough situations and I'd stack up your Ryland and his crew with them any day of the week."

All clear, Kaden reported.

All clear, Jonas echoed.

All clear, Kyle said.

Ryland held off waiting. If it were possible to clear the rooftops, Nicolas would do it. Ian was showing signs of extreme discomfort. That was a bad sign. Ian was much more sensitive to violent or murderous intent, the malicious waves of energy seeking him out, rushing for him almost to the exclusion of the others. Ryland could see the sweat beading on his skin.

It's a go. The rooftops are clear, Nicolas reported in the same soft tone he always used, giving nothing of his feelings away. *One soft, the other definitely hard.*

Ryland sighed. That made it much more difficult to choose. Higgens had brought soldiers with him, men simply following orders. Only one or two were in on his schemes. There was a higher risk in going into a situation knowing some of the men were innocent dupes. He made the decision.

We have four in the front of the house. If the general is home, that's where he'll be. Break into four sectors and make a sweep. Take out everything between you and the general. You must assume there are members of staff but treat them the same. Incapacitate and keep moving. Ryland was already making his way across the broad expanse of lawn, scooting on his belly, staying low in the open area.

Lily winced when she heard the order. She didn't want to distract them as they made their way into the house but she had a few questions to mull over. She posed them to Arly, needing to think things through. "It doesn't make sense that Higgens would have so many men willing to betray their country over this one project. He has to have a long history to be able to recruit and trust more than a couple of men."

Arly shrugged. "He's been in the service a long time, Lily. He's an officer, a person in power who might easily read the weaknesses in others."

"But Phillip Thornton and Donovans . . ." She trailed off, her mind racing. "We do have several contracts dealing with security issues but . . . Oh no. We could really be in trouble, Arly. Donovans has the defense contract dealing with satellite intelligence. If Higgens has access to that data in any capacity he would be able to sell the locations of U.S. satellites." Her fingers dug into Arly's arm. "He would have the information on our early warning systems or our ability to retaliate against a large-scale attack. Even the communications information would be available to him. Thornton doesn't have that kind of security clearance. There's only a few in the company with that kind of clearance."

"Is Colonel Higgens part of that?"

"Not to my knowledge." She tapped the edge of the seat. "This could be really bad, Arly. Surely Thornton's not that big a fool to sell national secrets." Lily wanted to pass the information to Ryland, but was afraid to distract him. The men were breaching the house, going in from four directions.

Ryland slipped over the porch railing, dropped silently onto the decking, and rolled away from the edge to give Ian room to follow. Dark shadows swarmed around the house, moving in from all directions, silent like the ghosts they called themselves. Blink and they were gone.

Ian moved into position at the door, making such short work of the lock it barely slowed them down. Ryland and Ian went inside nearly simultaneously, one going left, the other right, both at floor level and rolling into position to come up with weapons locked and ready. The entryway was clear. The house was dark, no lights on.

Somewhere outside a dog barked. Ryland felt the brief surge of energy and the animal subsided. He could hear the murmur of voices coming from the room opening to his right. He signaled to Ian and they positioned themselves to cover the entire layout of the room.

They've got a gun to Ranier's head. Do I have a go? I need a go right now. As always there was no tension in Nicolas's voice.

Do you have a clear shot? Ryland demanded.

Take out his aim, Nicolas responded.

You have a go. Ryland fed the energy already pouring into the room, using the power of their minds to twist the gun pointed at General Ranier away from him. When Nico fired the silenced shot, a bullet precisely between the eyes of the man holding Ranier hostage, there would be no chance of the gun going off and killing the general.

Higgens saw the hole blossoming in the middle of his man's forehead. Saw the man drop like a stone directly in front of the general. He whirled around, his gun in his fist, looking for a target. The only safety he had was the general. He pointed his weapon at him. The other two soldiers in the room gaped in shock, moved back to back for protection.

"I know you believe what Colonel Higgens told you," Ryland said softly to the two soldiers. "He's here to murder General Ranier and he's making you accomplices. Put down your weapons and back away. You're in an indefensible position." His voice rode the wave of energy, seemed to come from every direction. His men were feeding the two soldiers the uninterrupted flow of suggestion to obey.

The two men looked at one another almost helplessly and both laid their rifles on the floor and stepped back with their hands up. Immediately the flow of collective telepathy went to influence Colonel Higgens. He was expecting it and he was resistant, fighting for possession of his own actions.

"I'll kill him. Get up, General, we're getting out of here," Higgens stated. His eyes were wild as he looked around but couldn't see the men.

"I'm warning you one last time, Colonel. Nico has you in his sights. He never misses. You know his kill record. There is absolutely no way for you to shoot the general and he is not going to accompany you. Put down your weapon."

"Damn you, Miller, I should have killed you when I had the chance." Higgens snarled his hatred of the captain and turned and ran.

Round him up. Ryland hurried to the general while Ian searched the two soldiers. They were confused and cooperative, sitting on the floor with their backs to the wall and their fingers linked behind their heads.

Ryland helped the general to his feet. "I'm sorry we were late, sir. We didn't get the invitation immediately."

General Ranier staggered to a chair with Ryland's help. He touched his head and his hand came away sticky with blood. "That traitor pistol-whipped me." He sank heavily into the chair, his head down.

Ryland could see he looked old and tired, his face almost gray. *Call for the medics. Secure the house and get Lily in here.*

A grim-faced Nicolas shoved Colonel Higgens into the room. Nicolas marched him to a chair and thrust him into it. "The house is secure, Captain. We have three civilians down needing a medic. The man in the kitchen is dead. He's military."

"He was my bodyguard," Ranier said heavily. "A good man. I took Delia away and made certain she was safe then came back here so they would come after me. I had a feeling they would try and that she was in danger." He looked at Colonel Higgens. "You killed a good man tonight."

Higgens didn't say a word but his cold dead eyes never left Ryland.

"Sir, we've called the medics, they'll be here shortly. My men are seeing to your people. I'm Captain Ryland Miller." He saluted crisply.

"So you're the man all this fuss is about. Peter used to talk to me about enhancing psychic ability and I finally agreed to his crazy scheme, but I never thought it would really work." He sat back in his chair, rested his head against the leather. "If I'd believed him, I would have paid more attention to what was going on."

Ryland handed him a clean towel to press against his head. "My men and I are absent without leave, sir. We'd like to surrender ourselves into your custody."

"Well, now, Captain, I believe you were expressly given an order to do whatever was necessary to protect your men and our nation's secrets when you were given this assignment. To the best of your knowledge, is that what you've done?"

"Yes, sir, it is."

"Then I don't see any need for anyone to think you were away without leave; you were under orders. And as far as I can tell, your mission was a success."

"Thank you, sir. I do have one man injured." Ryland looked at Higgens. "You can put attempted murder down along with all the other charges to be brought against him."

Lily burst into the room, hurled herself straight at General Ranier. "Look at you! Look at this. Has anyone called an ambulance? Ryland, he should be lying down."

The general hugged her to him. "I'm fine, Lily, don't fuss. He just shook me up a little. I've been trying to put the pieces together ever since we talked."

"It has to be the defense contract. Higgens must have been selling secrets for some time," Lily said, dropping her voice. "This experiment was only a bonus for him. He was willing to sell the information, but he couldn't have had that many men in place so quickly unless he's been up and running for some time. Years, I'm guessing."

"He can't have been alone. He was never involved in the satellite defense program," General Ranier pointed out. "I thought the same thing, Lily. We've had our suspicions that information was being leaked, but Colonel Higgens never was a suspect. His record is impeccable."

"I have a disk my father recorded. He must have left the voice-activated recorder secreted somewhere he was certain the colonel would talk openly. Dad was very suspicious of the colonel. On the disk, you can clearly hear the colonel plotting your death and

Delia's using a fire in your home as the means of the "accident." Arly made copies and we have the original to be used for voice comparison."

General Ranier looked across the room at Colonel Higgens. "How long has this been going on?"

"I deny everything. They're making up the entire story in an attempt to cover up their own cowardice and guilt," the colonel replied. "I refuse to address this nonsense without my attorney present."

"I believe General McEntire is involved, sir," Lily said with sorrow, knowing she was crushing Ranier. "I'm sorry, I know he's your friend. But I think he's the ringleader and Higgens works for him. I think Hilton was planted in your office to keep an eye on you and either plant incriminating documents should there be need, or keep anything that was suspicious from reaching you. Such as my father's numerous messages." She looked at Higgens. "McEntire had nothing to do with the experiment. He didn't even know about it at first. You didn't really believe it would work. And then you saw them in action and you realized no one else knew the potential. There was real value and for the first time you were in on the ground floor. You didn't let your boss McEntire in on it at first, did you?"

Higgens stared at her with malevolence.

"You were the one who decided to sabotage the experiment so my father would think it was a failure and the project would be shut down. But he was so much smarter than you anticipated and he became suspicious of the brain bleeds. They didn't make sense when he wasn't using electrical pulses. He'd told Thornton of the danger, hadn't he? So you used it to kill the men."

"I'm lost, Lily," General Ranier admitted.

"I'll make certain you understand fully just how many men he murdered for monetary gain," Lily said. "You're going to spend the rest of your life in prison, Colonel, with your friend McEntire. None of that money you sold out your country for and murdered for is going to do you any good, so I hope that you enjoyed every penny while you had the chance to spend it."

"General McEntire?" Ranier echoed. "He started in the Air Force. As a young man he was assigned to the National Reconnaissance Office. Later he worked in building and operating spy satellites. He was influential in getting Donovans the defense contract."

"He's buddies with Thornton," Lily pointed out.

"They went to school together," General Ranier said sadly. "We all did."

"I'm so sorry, General," Lily said and put her arms around him.

TWENTY

"THE story broke this morning in the papers, the networks, and radio," Arly announced. He leaned over and kissed Rosa squarely on the mouth, grinning unashamedly as she smacked him with a rolled-up newspaper. "McEntire, Higgens, Phillip Thornton, and several others were charged with murder, espionage, and several other crimes."

"It took them long enough to complete the investigation," Jeff complained. He leaned heavily on his cane. "I thought I was going to die of old age before they finished it. What took so darned long?"

"General McEntire and Colonel Higgens were well-respected men with impeccable records," Kaden said. "The rot started years ago, back in school when they decided they were smarter than the rest of the world and thought it would be a great game to be spies. Both of them liked the excitement of it and felt that outwitting everyone around them was half the reward."

Ryland nodded his head. "Thornton talked so much they didn't know how to shut him up. He wanted some kind of a deal. Thornton was in it for the money. He agreed to help Higgens sabotage the psychic experiment because he hated Peter Whitney. Whitney was smarter and had more money and power than

Thornton. They'd butted heads a few times, and Thornton always came out looking like an ass. His image was everything to him. Once he started imagining slights, he couldn't wait to get rid of Whitney. He gloated about helping Higgens lure him out to the ocean where they could kill him. He told him he had important information to give him about Higgens and Peter was worried enough to go alone."

Arly winced. "Lily wasn't there to hear that, was she?"

Ryland shook his head. "No, she's been so busy, trying to keep Donovans on its feet and save jobs and the corporation's reputation, she hasn't had time for anything else."

"Oh yes, she has." Jeff nabbed a handful of potato chips. "Ever since General Ranier put her in charge of our operation, she's spent the majority of her time thinking up masochistic exercises to strengthen our brains. When she's not doing that she's into physical fitness. And then there's therapy. The woman is a slave driver."

"You're just mad because she invited your family to come and see you and your mother sided with her over your therapy," Ryland pointed out. "And she better not catch you eating those potato chips either. Aren't you on some kind of nutritional plan?"

Rosa gasped and slapped the chips out of Jeff s hand. "What do you think you're doing? You eat an apple."

Tucker winked at Jeff and floated a bag of chips right off the counter straight to where he was lounging in the doorway. Rosa pretended not to notice, consoling herself with the fact that "the boys," as she called them, were all becoming stronger and practicing the things Lily had told them were important.

"Where is Lily?" Arly asked. "I haven't seen her today. She didn't go to the laboratories this morning, did she?"

"On her wedding day?" Rosa was horrified. "She better not have."

Ryland stood for a moment in the brightness of the kitchen, absorbing the laughter and the camaraderie that Lily had somehow managed to provide for them all. She had generously shared her house with the men. Had given her time and knowledge to the men. They were all stronger for the things she had done and the home she'd provided for them. Even Jeff had progressed remarkably well.

Ryland's entire team was in good standing with their commander and the unit was functioning well on practice missions. General Ranier was taking an active part in their day-to-day operations. Things couldn't be running smoother . . . for them. Lily was bearing the burden of it all. Making up for her father's mistakes. Frantically trying to save jobs and lives. Working secretly and silently to find the young women whose lives had been tampered with so early in their existence. His Lily.

He knew where she would go on her wedding day. He sent Nicolas a faint smile and sauntered casually out when he was feeling anything but casual. He went unerringly to her father's office, grateful that he had asked Arly to include his prints in the security code to open the heavy door.

The room was empty but he knew she was underground. He felt her, was drawn to her. He always would be. He locked the door after him, always conscious of security, just as Lily was. The room represented her childhood. It also held untold secrets of psychic research. Lily often got up in the middle of the night to go downstairs and read more. A lifetime of successes and failures her father had carefully recorded.

In spite of the horror she felt at what he had done, Lily was fascinated by it. As was Ryland. Now that his unit was functioning successfully without the threat of death, he wanted to know how to grow stronger. He wanted to know just what he was really capable of doing, what his men were capable of doing. The hidden laboratory was a storehouse of knowledge. He couldn't fault Lily for wanting to tap into it.

Ryland made his way down the steep narrow stairs, each step taking him closer and closer to her. He felt her easily now, the deep sadness that always seemed a part of her. His Lily, willing to take on the sins of her father and set the world right again.

Lily was staring at the frozen image of a young girl on the video screen. He could see evidence of tears on her face when she looked up as he approached her. Her long lashes were spiky and wet, and just looking at her hurt him.

Lily smiled at him. "I knew you'd come to me. I was sitting here trying to decide if my father was a monster. And I knew you'd come."

Ryland took her hand, squeezed her fingers tightly. "He was

a man with a sad life until you came into it, Lily. Remember the father you knew, not the man he once was. You changed him, shaped his life. You made him into someone worthwhile and he did his best for humanity after that." He sat down next to her, this thigh wedged next to hers, his body protectively close.

"I loved him so much, Ryland. I admired him and his brilliance. I tried so hard to live up to his expectations of me."

He brought her hand up to his mouth, rubbed her knuckles back and forth in little caresses over his lips. "I know you did, Lily. He was very proud of you, too. There's nothing wrong with a daughter loving her father. He earned that."

"I was trying to think how I would feel if I were one of the others. If I'd been abandoned because I was flawed. Can you imagine, Ryland? I'm almost afraid to contact them, even knowing I can help them should they need it." She touched the face on the screen. "Look at her eyes. She looks so haunted." There was a wealth of compassion in her voice.

"We have to do one thing at a time," he reminded her gently. "The investigation is over, the story was in today's news. McEntire and Higgens have been selling secrets for years to foreign governments. Everyone is scrambling to do containment and to see how much actual damage was done. My men and I are completely in the clear and there's nothing in our records that could damage our careers. In fact, we were honored for saving General Ranier and breaking this thing wide open. My men are able to be out in the field for longer periods and, even better, they can go without their anchors for extended periods of time. Jeff is improving every day. You've given them hope and a home and a place of safety. You turned all of our lives around, Lily."

She laid her head on his shoulder. "It wasn't all me alone, Ryland. Things just fell into place." She stared at the image of the little girl. "I look at her and I wonder where she is, what her childhood was like. If she'll hate me when she sees me." She looked at him. "I have to find her. Somehow, someway, I have to find her." She was pleading for understanding.

Ryland instantly framed her face with his hands. "Of course you do, Lily. The private investigator is working. We have several files and the places to start that your father gave us. We'll find them all. Together."

"I knew you'd say that too." She leaned into him. Kissed him. Took possession of his mouth like a master. "You always know what to say, don't you?" She murmured the words against his throat, her tongue tracing little designs on his skin while her fingers began a strange little tapping dance over his suddenly bulging jeans.

"What are you doing? Lily! That's driving me crazy. Where the hell did you learn that little trick?" How could she have such an instant effect on him? She could make his body so hard and so hot with just a simple movement.

She laughed at him. "The book, of course. It is our wedding night. I thought a few special tricks might be in order."

"I've got to read this book."

Her fingers continued stroking and tapping and caressing until he thought he'd go out of his mind. All the while her tongue kept the same rhythm on his throat.

"I can't stand in front of all those people with a hard-on, Lily," he told her firmly.

"Why not? Everyone comes into my bedroom when I'm naked under my sheet," she pointed out. Already Ryland was working his magic, dispelling her sadness, making her world right again. Lily caught up the remote and snapped off the video. "You always manage to make me feel like we're partners."

He caught her chin. "We are partners. Life partners. Ghost-Walkers. There aren't too many of us in the world and we have to stick together."

"I guess we do."

"So are you all right now? You're still going to marry me this evening?"

Lily laughed. "Absolutely. I have a high IQ. I'm not about to let you get away."

"So do it again."

"Do what again?"

"The thing with your tongue and your fingers. Do it again."

"I can't do it now. It's for our wedding night. I told you, I wanted to surprise you with my special trick."

"Yeah, well, you gave me the hard-on, now you have to do something about it."

Keep reading for an excerpt from

TOXIC GAME

The latest book in the Ghostwalker series
by Christine Feehan

Available now from Jove

"HOT as hell!" Barry Font yelled, wiping the sweat from his face. He looked around him at the crew he was transporting straight into the hot zone. He hadn't meant the strip of land they were setting the helicopters down in. They all knew it was bad. The last rescue attempt had been ambushed. Three dead, two wounded, and the helicopter had barely made it out.

The temperature was at least ninety degrees with 99 percent humidity and gusting winds that took that heat and shoved it right down your throat—and this was at night. His skin felt wet and sticky all the time. He wanted to strip himself bare and lie under the helicopter's rotor blades just to get some relief.

They dropped down out of the mountains, the helicopters running low enough to make his gut tighten as they skimmed along the lowlands heading toward the forest. They were sitting ducks making that run, and this area was infamous for frequent ground-to-air fire. With the Milisi Separatis Sumatra terrorist cell active and firing at anything, every man in the choppers was at risk. Gunners grimly watched out their doors on either side, but that didn't make him feel any less like he had a target painted on his back. Strangely, it wasn't the run that was scaring the crap out of him. He felt like he was trapped in a cage surrounded by predators.

The Air Force pararescue team didn't seem affected by anything as mundane as the heat or terrorists. The crazy thing was, they were mostly officers. Doctors. *What the hell?* As a rule, Barry thought most officers were a joke. These men had seen combat and looked as tough as nails. He'd never flown them anywhere before and hadn't known what to expect.

His crew had taken men into all sorts of combat situations, but he'd never seen a team like the one he was bringing in. He didn't even know how to explain their difference. It wasn't like he could name one single thing about them that made them stand out in his mind. They just gave off a dangerous vibe. Being with them really did feel as if he were inside a tiger's cage, surrounded by the big cats. They were that still, that menacing, and yet they hadn't said or done anything to warrant his nerves or the shiver of dread creeping down his spine at the sight of them.

They sat stoically while the helicopter swayed and jerked, bumping like it was in the rockiest terrain. They moved with the craft as if seasoned veterans of helicopter travel. Sweat trickled down faces—well, all but one. He looked at the man sitting at the very end of the jump seat. Dr. Draden Freeman, a gifted surgeon, was a fucking model, not a tough-as-nails soldier about to be dropped into the hottest zone in Indonesia.

Freeman had dark brown hair that was thick and wavy. At six-two he was all muscle, without an ounce of fat. His eyes were a dark blue and held an intensity; when he flicked Barry a careless glance at his remark, Barry's gut reacted as if punched. The man had rugged good looks that had catapulted him into stardom in the modeling world. Ordinarily, Barry and the crew would have been making fun of him behind his back, but no one did—especially after one of those smoldering, scary glances. Not one single bead of sweat marred his good looks.

"Five minutes out." The call came from the front via his radio.

Barry held up five fingers and the five men in the helicopter barely reacted. The helicopter was coming in with guns ready, knowing they wouldn't have much time to retrieve the wounded U.S. Rangers, Kopassus or civilians. The gunners were in position and tension mounted.

Members of the WHO, the World Health Organization, had come at the request of the government to examine the remains of the dead at a small village, Lupa Suku, in a remote part of Sumatra. Every man, woman and child had died of what appeared to be a very fast-acting and deadly virus, possibly a dreaded hemorrhagic one. Before they could set up their equipment, the WHO members had been attacked by a small terrorist cell known to the government.

The Milisi Separatis Sumatra, or MSS as the government referred to them, had sprung up in the last few years. They were growing fast and were well funded. Their goal seemed to be similar to that of most other terrorist cells—to take down the government. They were now suspected of having chosen the small village of Lupa Suku to test a hemorrhagic virus, but where it came from and how they got it, no one knew, but they needed to find out fast.

The rain forest of Sumatra was rich in plants and wildlife, although over the years even that had been shrinking significantly. The trees were thick, the taller dipterocarp shooting up to the sky providing shade, vines climbing them and flowers wrapping around them. Mangrove roots pulled sediment from the river leaving large areas of peat swamps with rich nutrients at their edges promoting thicker growth. The village of Lupa Suku was surrounded by the forest and tucked in just far enough from the river to be a perfect target.

The government had sent in their special forces, the Kopassus, to rescue the single WHO representative still alive. The Kopassus were known worldwide as tough soldiers able to stack up against any army. They were well trained and very skilled. They'd been ambushed as they were trying to aid the wounded man. A small force of U.S. Rangers had been called to aid the Kopassus who were pinned down, some reportedly badly wounded. The Rangers were then attacked and pinned down as well.

It began to look as if Lupa Suku had been sacrificed in order to draw the Indonesian soldiers into fighting a guerrilla-style war on the terrorists' home turf. Whatever the rumor, there were wounded men needing aid and six of them were soldiers of the United States. Now, this team was going to try to bring those soldiers out of the hot zone—along with any Kopassus and the remaining single living representative of the WHO.

"Two minutes."

Barry held up two fingers and the team moved, readying themselves for a quick departure.

"Ten minutes is all you've got and then we have to get into the air," Barry reminded them. "If we can't hold our position, we'll come back around for you."

Freeman flicked him a quick glance. It was one of those looks that seemed to burn a hole right through him. Barry shivered, not liking those eyes on him. They were intelligent, focused—almost too focused. They didn't blink, and it felt like death looking at him.

The team leader, Dr. Joe Spagnola, gave him a quick look as well. It pretty much said, "You maggot, if you leave one of my men behind, don't ever go to sleep because I'll be coming for you." At least Barry interpreted the look that way.

JOE Spagnola ignored the way the helicopter crew was looking at his team. He didn't look at them or his own men, but instead, reached telepathically to his GhostWalker unit. GhostWalkers were enhanced psychically as well as physically. The first they'd signed on for; the last, not so much. Still, they were classified soldiers and they did their jobs, no matter how fucked-up that was.

Each branch of the service had one GhostWalker team consisting of ten members. The first team experimented on had a few major problems. Some needed anchors to drain away the psychic energy that adhered to them like magnets. Others had brain bleeds. Every subsequent team had fewer flaws until Whitney, the doctor performing the experiments, had rolled out his prize group, the Pararescue Team. They might have what Whitney considered fewer flaws, but they also had more genetic enhancements than any of them cared for.

He leaves us, we'll be finding him and his candy-ass crew when we get out of here. Joe's voice slid into their minds.

DRADEN'S gaze shifted, just for one moment to Barry Font and then over to his fellow teammate, Malichai Fortunes.

There's a hundred and fifty volcanoes in Indonesia, Malichai, their fact man, informed them all telepathically. *We*

*can shove his ass out of the helicopter right into one of them if
he tries leaving any of us behind.*

Draden let amusement slide into his eyes for a moment but
didn't let it show on his face. Malichai had been spouting all
kinds of facts about the rain forest and the wildlife at risk there.
That was his way in a dangerous situation, and all members of
the team just let him carry on.

The enhancements made them predators any way you looked
at it. Hunters. They were very good at their jobs. They looked
like soldiers. Doctors. Officers. But they were much more than
that and anyone in close confines with them felt that difference
sooner rather than later. All of them could smell the fear the
helicopter crew were giving off and that fear had nothing to do
with flying into a hot zone. No, Barry and the crew were used
to that sort of danger—they just didn't like their passengers.

Draden could give a rat's ass if he was liked or not. He had
a job to do. They were going into enemy territory to bring out
the wounded and make certain they stayed alive until they got
them back to the hospitals.

The helicopter set down with a jarring thump and Draden
was out fast, running with his fellow teammates in the dark
toward the southern tip of the tree line. Deliberately, they'd
chosen to fly in at three in the morning, when the enemy was
least likely to be at its sharpest. The sound of the rotors was
loud in the night, something that couldn't be helped. He knew
the noise would draw the enemy. That couldn't be helped either.
They just needed a few minutes.

The terrorist cell had set their trap with live bait. They
knew the terrain and had chosen it carefully. The MSS had
the advantage, especially when the Indonesian government
had wounded soldiers waiting for help. They knew the author-
ities would send their elite, and it was a chance to mow them
down.

Draden fanned out to his left while Gino Mazza went right,
both flanking the others as Joe went down on one knee and
flashed the tiny blue light in each direction three times. They
received a response from the west. Instantly, they were up and
running again toward the returned signal.

Thirty feet from the thickest brush, they spread out even
farther, running in absolute silence as only GhostWalkers could.

Joe, Malichai and Diego Campo dropped down, their weapons ready, while Draden and Gino continued forward. Draden slipped into the cover of the brush, a place he was at home.

He found their contact ten feet in, crouched down in the thick buttresses of a dipterocarp tree. "How many wounded?" Draden asked, his voice a thread of sound.

"Fifteen."

Draden gave a mental shake of his head. Fifteen was a lot of wounded. They had room in the three helicopters, but maybe not the time to get them all in. "Anyone besides you who can help get them to the choppers?"

"Two others."

That wasn't good either.

"Enemy?"

"No idea of their numbers. They seem to come and go. At least we think they're gone and the moment we move, they open fire."

Draden nodded. "Any of you sick?"

The Ranger shook his head. "The only one to go near the village was Dr. Henderson and he was in full hazmat gear. We stayed out of there. Henderson wants the village burned."

Draden turned and signaled the others in. They came like wraiths, sliding out of the night in complete silence. Draden gave him the number of wounded telepathically while Joe tapped his watch.

Move fast, gentlemen. We don't have time to triage here. Get them into the choppers.

Joe didn't sound alarmed, but Draden felt it nevertheless. They had about eight minutes, and getting to the wounded would eat up another minute or two.

The Ranger was already on his feet, so they followed him through the thick forest to a small dip in the terrain hidden by brush and the buttresses of wide tree trunks. The Kopassus looked grim, two dead, three of them badly wounded, but guns steady as rocks. One was still standing and ready to pack out his teammates, already gathering their weapons. The Rangers were in similar straits, one dead, the others in various states of badly wounded or just broken and bloody. Those with lighter injuries were gathering up their teammates to pack them out. The WHO doctor, clearly in bad shape, staggered as he stood. None of them looked as if they could walk more than a few steps.

The GhostWalkers were all business. Gino took the worst Ranger, slapping field dressings on the wounds to keep him from bleeding out while he ran with the man to the choppers. The Kopassus followed with one of his fellow team members. Joe took a Ranger and Diego a Kopassus. Malichai took the civilian. One of the Rangers staggered to his feet.

"I can walk out."

Draden nodded and waved him after the others. He moved from wounded man to wounded man, giving them water and seeing to the worst of their wounds, all the while listening for any changes in the sounds of the night that would indicate members of the MSS had returned at the sound of the helicopters.

Gino was back, hoisting another Ranger onto his back. The Kopassus soldier returned with him and took another of the wounded. The Indonesian didn't look in good shape, but he wasn't leaving anyone behind. They wanted to pack their dead with them as well, not leave them behind, but the dead had to go last. Joe, Diego and Malichai all had taken the next round of wounded and were gone, disappearing into the darkness, when Draden felt his first prickle of unease.

He crouched low and signaled to the remaining soldiers for absolute silence. The remaining men showed why they were considered elite. In spite of their wounds, they immediately went into survival mode, weapons ready, sliding deeper into the depression for cover. Draden moved away from them, toward the north. There were no sounds of insects. Not even the continual drone of cicadas or loud croaks of tree frogs. For a moment, the forest had gone unnaturally quiet, signaling something was moving into it that didn't belong.

He was part of the forest and could read every sign. He moved fast, slipping through brush without a whisper of sound. Sinking into the thick foliage, he waited. A man emerged from a small group of trees, heading stealthily toward the encampment of wounded. Draden saw another fifteen feet from him, and a third man the same distance out as the terrorists moved in unison toward the small group of soldiers.

Draden waited until the nearest terrorist had passed him and then rose up swiftly, catching him around the head, his hand muffling any sound as he plunged his knife into the base of the skull before lowering the man to the ground. The forest floor was thick with vegetation and cushioned the fall of the rifle. Draden was already melting into the dark, making his way across the expanse to the next man in line.

As the terrorist turned his head toward where the fallen man should have been, Draden was on him, repeating the kill, and slipping away. Behind him, more of the terrorists were emerging into the kill zone. They were filtering through the trees and shrubbery, making little sound, coming up toward the encampment where the remaining wounded waited to be transported.

Draden took the third man on their front line and then glanced down at his watch. He needed to buy Joe and the others an extra couple of minutes to pack out the last of the wounded. Then he'd have to double-time it back to the choppers so they could get out of there before the MSS had time to get real firepower set up.

He reached up, leapt, caught the branches of a durian tree and pulled himself up, waiting for the next line of soldiers to pass in front of him. Although he was aware of every second ticking by, he was patient. The moment the five men crept through the darkness, he dropped down, so he was between the MSS filtering through the forest. They were creeping stealthily toward the helicopters, trying to insert themselves between the choppers and the remaining wounded soldiers.

MSS coming at you, Draden warned his team. *I'll buy some time.*

Draden moved much faster, risking being seen by one of the terrorists behind him as he cut down first one and then a second in that line. Glancing at his watch, he ran toward a third, his knife stabbing deep into the base of the skull as he shot past. He held on to the hilt of the knife, so that as he ran, it spun his victim around before the blade came free. He threw a balanced throwing knife sideways into the neck of another as he sprinted out of the protection of the trees.

We're in. We're away, Joe reported. *Circling to bring you home.*

Coming in on the run.

The last of the helicopters had lifted from the ground, gunners providing cover for him, spraying the tree line to keep the terrorists from taking aim at Draden. Diego and Malichai used automatics to aid the gunners as Joe and Gino worked on the wounded. A rope was dropped down as the chopper circled back. Draden kept running as gunfire erupted from the cover of the forest. Bullets spat around him.

The chopper came slipping out of the sky toward him, coming in low, the rope flying like a slinky tail. Behind him, the forest went strangely silent. No gunfire. He didn't stop. He leapt for the rope, his gloved hands catching hold, the jerk so strong it nearly pulled his arms out of their sockets. Still, his enhanced strength allowed him to hang on while the chopper began to climb.

He was twenty feet up when he felt the sting in his thigh, and his heart stuttered with instant awareness. He glanced down to see a dart protruding from his muscle and knew why the terrorists' weapons had gone silent. They had a sniper, and he wasn't armed with a bullet. He was armed with a virus. If Draden went up into the helicopter, he was condemning everyone in it to the same death as those in the village. Without real conscious thought, he let go of the rope, dropping out of the sky and back to earth.

Virus injection. It was the best information he could give them, so they would know to leave him behind.

Malichai was staring down at him, their eyes meeting as he fell away. He saw Malichai practically dive from the helicopter, but Diego caught him, holding him back. Draden landed in a crouch, his enhanced DNA allowing his legs to act like springs to absorb the shock. He somersaulted forward and stood up, facing the forest, his arms spread wide. Let them shoot him if they wanted, but if they didn't, he was infecting the bastards. He began walking toward the edge of all those trees and brush.

Draden. What the hell happened? Joe's voice slipped into his mind. It was faded, as if the distance was already too far. He heard the helicopter circling back so Joe would be able to reach him. He pictured Joe holding a weapon on the crew. He could get that intense.

By the time he reached the trees, the MSS members had faded away, leaving him to die however the villagers had. He'd seen the reports the Indonesian government had shared with the WHO. It was one of the reasons his team had been in the region. Two team members were two of the leading scientists developing treatments, therapies and pharmaceuticals in the field of viruses.

Infected with the virus.

Draden had taken the time to finish both his doctorate and MD, to be an asset to others on his team. He'd dabbled in biochemistry but finished his undergrad degree, a BS in genetics. Stanford offered a dual MD and PhD program and he'd taken advantage of that. He'd gotten his MD as an infectious disease doctor and his PhD in microbiology and immunology. He found it ironic that he would be dying of a weaponized virus after all that work to earn his degrees. Determined to be of some use, he decided to record everything he could about his symptoms, along with any suppositions he might have before he put a bullet in his head. He'd leave final conclusions for them.

Tell Trap and Wyatt I'll leave behind a recording. Don't know if they can use whatever I find, but they should be able to remotely access my recorder without touching the device.

I'm sorry, man. Trap and Wyatt may have ideas.

Draden knew, just from the earlier reports, that their ideas would be too late. The virus acted too fast. He would be dead before Joe had time to make it back to the States.

I'll torch the village. He hoped he'd get that done fast so he could hunt the terrorists who were infecting people and then using them as bait to kill more. He wanted to kill as many of the bastards as possible before the virus took hold and left him too sick to go after them.

He could hear the chopper circling back around a second time. *Hope you didn't put a gun to their heads.* He injected humor he wasn't really feeling into his voice.

Maybe if we get you back we can find the treatment before it's too late, Malichai said.

Too fast acting. Can't chance infecting all of you. We all signed up for a one-way ticket when we joined the GhostWalkers. It's just my turn.

Fuck! Gino hissed.

I'll take out as many of the cell as I can before I go down, Draden said, meaning it. He was going to make sure as many of them were dead as possible. Not because they'd infected him, but because they'd infected an entire village to use as a trap. *Joe, someone has to find out where this is coming from.*

I will, Joe promised.

Get the wounded out of here, there's not much you can do for me. Some of those injuries were severe.

Damn it, Draden. That was Gino.

He didn't feel as bad as they did. He didn't have much of a future anyway. *Just pissed I wasted all that time going to school instead of partying.*

Yeah, cuz you're such a party animal, Malichai said with an attempt at sarcastic humor. His voice was tight. The feeling in his mind—sorrow.

Tell Nonny she's the best. He should have told the old woman that himself. Wyatt Fontenot's grandmother had taken the entire team into her home. She'd cared for them as she would her own. He hadn't had that kind of affection from anyone since his foster mother had died when he was so young. He hadn't known anyone else was capable of loving others the way the woman he called mother had until he met Nonny. He should have told her, and he hadn't, not once. He was surprised at the emotion welling up. Yeah, he should have told her. She'd mourn for him, and it shouldn't have shocked him that his teammates would as well, but it did.

We can pick you up, take you back and try one of the treatments. I know they're not sanctioned yet, but some have worked when a virus is detected early enough, Gino said.

We don't know anything about this one yet and we can't take the chance, you all know that, he objected, because he could infect every one of them and when they landed, every doctor and nurse waiting to help the wounded. He wasn't having that on his conscience.

You have anywhere from a few days to twenty.

Joe, don't make this worse. Get the hell out of here and make certain every single one of the wounded survives.

There was the briefest of hesitations, but Joe was the commanding officer for a reason. He had to make the tough decisions. *You have my word. Damn honor serving with you, Draden.*

The others murmured similar sentiments. He didn't reply. What was there to say? He had never considered himself a sentimental man. In fact, he tried not to feel much at all, but living in Louisiana with his GhostWalker Team, emotions had crept in whether he wanted them to or not. He'd learned at a very early age that it was better to push feelings aside and use logic for every decision. Emotions fucked things up in ways that could be very, very bad.

Still, there was Trap. The man was a genuine crazy-ass genius with Asperger's. Super-high IQ and wealthy as all hell. Didn't have a clue about social cues. Draden had been the one to clue him in as often as possible. Trap didn't let many people in and neither did Draden, but they'd been there for each other.

Tell Trap he's the best. He'll do fine. Tell him—He broke off, shocked that he was choking up. He loved the man like a brother. *Shit.*

I got it, Joe said.

Draden let the forest close around him as the sound of the helicopter faded into the distance. He wasn't worried about being alone. He was used to it. He'd been alone most of his life, even in the midst of a crowd. He could handle that, no problem. He began to move fast toward the village of the dead. It was very small, only a few families, many related to one another. He was a very fast runner, but that would spread the virus through his bloodstream much quicker. Still, it might not be a bad idea just to get it over with. He played with that idea as he jogged, his animal senses flaring out to uncover anyone that might have been left behind to keep an eye on him.

He pulled up the facts about the village and region they'd been briefed on. The village's name, Lupa Suku, meant Forgotten Tribe and he thought it very apt from everything he'd read about them. The village was so remote, it wasn't even considered a sub-district of Rambutan. He knew that driving southeast from Palembang the thirty-four and some miles to Rambutan, villages along the road were more and more scarce. Eventually, that road became nothing more than a muddy broad path lined on either side by trees and brush. A few cars and buses shared the road with bikes and animals until it disappeared.

So remote, Lupa Suku could only be reached by bike, boat or animals such as a domestic ox. It was impossible during the wet season to get any motorized vehicle through. Heavy items tended to get stuck in the thick mud, so it was necessary to move everything via water. Most used a small boat to access the village via the Banyuasin River.

According to the briefing given by the representative of the Indonesian government, primary trade consisted of fish and rice. There was a small copper mine that was kept a secret by the locals. The copper was mined by hand a little at a time as they had no modern machinery. The government had turned a blind eye, acting as though they knew nothing about that little mine or the fact that the villagers traded the copper to poachers who came to the area looking for exotic birds. Money meant little to the villagers, so they tended to barter for the things they needed.

Draden figured bartering was how the terrorists had introduced the virus. It was possible that the virus had occurred some other way, via bugs or animals, but he doubted it. The WHO had been trying to find a source, but the fact that the nearby terrorist cell had used the dead villagers for an ambush, killing nearly all the WHO doctors and their workers, tended to make him believe they were responsible.

The terrorist cell was organized for being fairly new. Their job was to topple the government and unlike others targeting police officers, they had chosen to undermine the people's confidence in their government by introducing a hot virus. Draden and his team believed the village was their first large test. There had to have been other smaller experiments.

Lupa Suku was the perfect village to test the virus on. The people preferred to do their trading via boat, didn't allow outsiders to come to their village without a good reason or an invitation. They were secretive, mostly, the government thought, because they had the copper mine and didn't want outsiders to know about it. They were very self-sufficient and lived in accord with the animals in the forest. Very peaceful, they used their weapons only for protection.

During the times of the year when the rain made it very difficult to travel, the tribe went weeks without being seen by others. Lupa Suku was located a quarter mile inland of the river and couldn't be seen by passersby traveling on the water, which, again, made them a perfect target. The village kept boats docked and a sentry to watch over the area and call out should there be trouble. A virus would go unseen by the sentry.

Draden moved through the forest with confidence. He knew at least one or two of the MSS would have been left behind to observe him and tell the others what he was up to. He intended to burn the village and then go hunting them. He would kill as many as possible, leaving one alive to follow back to the main MSS village.

Trap and Wyatt, like Draden, were very familiar with hemorrhagic viruses. All three had worked on combining antibodies to target specific strains of Ebola. The antibodies had successfully saved monkeys that had been infected within twenty-four hours, but as the disease progressed, the success rate had dwindled. They had been in discussions, long into the nights, on how to raise those chances for those who were in the more advanced stages of the diseases.

From his studies into most hot viruses, Draden knew he didn't have long before he would be feeling the effects. His death would be a horrible one. He had a gun, and he was going out that way for sure. He just had to make certain he didn't wait so long that his body was too ravaged by the disease to be able to make the rational decision to use a bullet. He'd seen the effects of hemorrhagic viruses on a human being and his mind shied away from his gruesome future.

Even so, he picked up the pace, winding his way along the narrow animal trails he found leading through the forest toward Lupa Suku. He knew he had to be cautious, traveling fast the way he was. There were other dangers in the forest besides the MSS.

There were only about five hundred Sumatran tigers left and one of them had chosen the area around the village as its territory. The people of the village considered it an honor and lived in harmony with the big cat. According to the reports Draden had read, the tiger had showed up when a palm mill threatened its former habitat and the peat swamp near Lupa Suku had lured the endangered animal to claim new territory. The village made an agreement with the local poachers to leave the tiger alone in exchange for trading their copper exclusively with them. Even with that agreement in place, traps were set for poachers looking for tigers or other rare animals. Draden couldn't afford to be caught in one of them.

Heavy vegetation surrounded Lupa Suku. Tall dipterocarp trees joined at the top to gather into a canopy. Climbing their trunks were woody, thick-stemmed lianas and dozens of species of epiphytes. Orchids and ferns also lived on the trunks and derived their nourishment from the air.

Flowers were everywhere, and the exotic plants and vines were surprisingly colorful. Several trees and brush held the colored flowers up and out. Cicada trees lined a path from the water to the inland village, more trees forming a barrier to the peat swamp, the flowers threatening to blossom at any moment.

Draden drank in his surroundings with both appreciation and sorrow. The beautiful path led to a village that should have been thriving. Instead, it was now a path to certain death. The stench was unbelievable. The WHO camp had been set up a distance away from Lupa Suku, but still within sight. He could see that members of the MSS had ransacked the camp after killing the workers and doctors. Some lay dead in their hazmat suits. He went right past their camp and entered the village.

It was eerily silent. A pit had been dug and the bodies had already been placed inside of it for cremation by the WHO. Even the fuel was sitting there in cans. It would burn hot and fast. Draden made a quick circuit of the village to make certain no bodies had been left behind before he doused all buildings with the accelerant and then the bodies in the pit. He lit the entire thing on fire and then backed away from the terrible heat.

He was fortunate that it wasn't raining, although the forest around Lupa Suku was saturated. He moved into deeper forest, away from the flames shooting into the air, going farther inland so that the sentries the MSS had left behind would have to actively search for him.

He covered his passing through the peat swamp, using trees to travel in rather than making his way across the wet ground. He found a nice place to wait—the branches of a hardwood tree. Around him were aromatic spice trees, but this one had a nice crotch where several branches met at the main trunk, providing him with a semicomfortable place to rest.

Draden remained very still and quiet so that all around him the insects and rodents in the forest once more became active. They made for good sentries. He drank water he'd retrieved from one of the fallen Rangers' packs while he studied the forest around him. Fig trees were abundant, mass-producing enough fruit twice a year to feed many of the forest's inhabitants, including the endangered helmeted hornbill. The forests were rich in valuable hardwood and he saw the evidence of that all around him. The tree he'd chosen was in the middle of a grove of exotic fruit trees that attracted a tremendous amount of wildlife.

Colorful birds were everywhere. He identified scarlet-rumped trogon and the red-naped trogon. Eventually, he spotted the Asian paradise flycatcher and a blue-throated bee-eater. He'd already seen the blue-eared kingfisher when he'd been closer to the river. He looked for the rarest of the birds, the helmeted hornbill, wanting a sign of good luck, but there were none to be seen. This was a place poachers often came to trap birds to sell in other countries as there were so many sought-after species. That, in turn, could mean there were traps set by the villagers.

Farther out from the fruit trees was a small grouping of *Cinnamomum burmanni* trees. This village had everything it needed, not only to survive, but to thrive. The cinnamon in the bark could be harvested and traded as well as used by the villagers.

Draden took his time studying the layout of the forest floor. Once the members of the MSS came, he would have to move fast, kill most and then track one back to their nest. He wanted to know where every trap might be, so he didn't get caught in one. After mapping out the forest floor in every direction as far as he could see, he marked the places he thought a trap most likely would be set.

He closed his eyes and studied the effects of the virus on his body. He could find none. His guess was, going off incubation for the Ebola and Marburg viruses, he had two to twenty days to find the home of the MSS terrorists and kill them. As far as he was concerned, that gave him plenty of time to get his job done.

He might have dozed off but when the insects stopped their continuous droning, his eyes were quartering the forest floor for his prey. Two men approached from the direction of the burning village. He could smell the smoke, but the glow of the flames had died down. If the fire had licked at the surrounding trees and brush, it hadn't spread far, at least it didn't appear as though it had, thanks to the level of saturation from the continuous rain. There was nothing he could do even if the flames had found the trees and brush. Lupa Suku had to be burned for the good of the country.

Both men studied the ground, searching for signs that Draden had come this way. They were Indonesian and appeared to be used to tracking in the forest. They didn't hesitate as they moved through the dense vegetation. They were quiet and appeared to listen to the warnings of the animals and insects. Neither spotted him sitting up in the tree. He watched them for a few minutes, getting a feel for them. They talked back and forth in hushed tones, pointing out a bruised leaf and a crushed frond of fern as evidence of his passing. Since he hadn't come from that direction, he knew he wasn't the one leaving behind the signs for them to follow. Idly, he wondered who had.

He let them nose around right under the tree he sat in. Neither looked up. Not once. Their eyes were trained on the ground as they cast back and forth for any kind of a track. One squatted suddenly and pointed to the ground where Draden was certain a trap had been placed for any poachers. The trap was uncovered, proving him right.

It was hot. Rain began to fall, a steady drizzle that hit the leaves of the canopy and filtered down to the forest floor. Light was streaking through the sky, turning the rain to an eerie silver. This was a far cry from his modeling days. He waited until the guerrillas pointed in the opposite direction of the village and started to walk that way.

Very calmly, he put a bullet through the head of one and the shoulder of the second. It was deliberate and fast, a quick one-two, squeezing the trigger as he switched aim. One crumpled to the ground while the second jerked sideways, nearly went down but forced himself to stumble behind the thick buttresses of a dipterocarp tree.

Draden remained absolutely still. The two bullets had been fired fast. The sound of the gunshots had been loud, reverberating through the forest and quieting the insects. It didn't take long for the cacophony to start up again. In short time, the frogs began to join in. Mice scurried through the leaves. Beetles and ants found the dead body and the pool of blood that coated the debris on the ground. The forest returned to normal that quickly, as if the violence had never been.

The man he'd wounded would need immediate care if he wanted to live. Infections were almost a foregone conclusion in the high humidity and vast array of insects of the rain forest. As a native, the wounded man would know that. He would have to make his way back to the nest, the home of the Milisi Separatis Sumatra.

Draden didn't move, staying as still as any predator with his gaze fixed on his prey. No muscle moved. He didn't take his eyes from the man. He could just make out a part of his thigh and boot. The MSS member was stoic, but the pain had to be excruciating. Draden had made certain the shoulder was shattered. He went for maximum pain. He'd also put the man's dominant arm out of commission.

The man held out for over an hour. He had to have been worried about blood loss at that point. Draden was. He didn't want the man to bleed out on him and die. It would be far easier to follow him back to the nest than to backtrack.